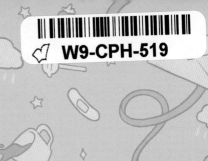

RAINBOW!

VOLUME I

tapas original

All rights reserved. Published by Graphix, an imprint of Scholastic Inc., *Publishers since 1920.* SCHOLASTIC, GRAPHIX, and associated logos are trademarks and/or registered trademarks of Scholastic Inc.

The publisher does not have any control over and does not assume any responsibility for author or third-party websites or their content.

This book is a work of fiction. Names, characters, places, and incidents are either the product of the author's imagination or are used fictitiously, and any resemblance to actual persons, living or dead, business establishments, events, or locales is entirely coincidental.

ISBN 978-1-339-01131-8 (hardcover)

ISBN 978-1-339-01123-3 (paperback)

10 9 8 7 6 5 4 3 2 1   24 25 26 27 28

First edition, March 2024
Printed in China 62

Michael Petranek, Editorial Director, Graphix Media

Book design by Salena Mahina

Art by Gloomy

Lettering & Compositing by Jesse Post

Photo ©: 5 ripped paper and throughout: Shutterstock.com

RAINBOW! VOLUME 1

BY SUNNY & GLOOMY

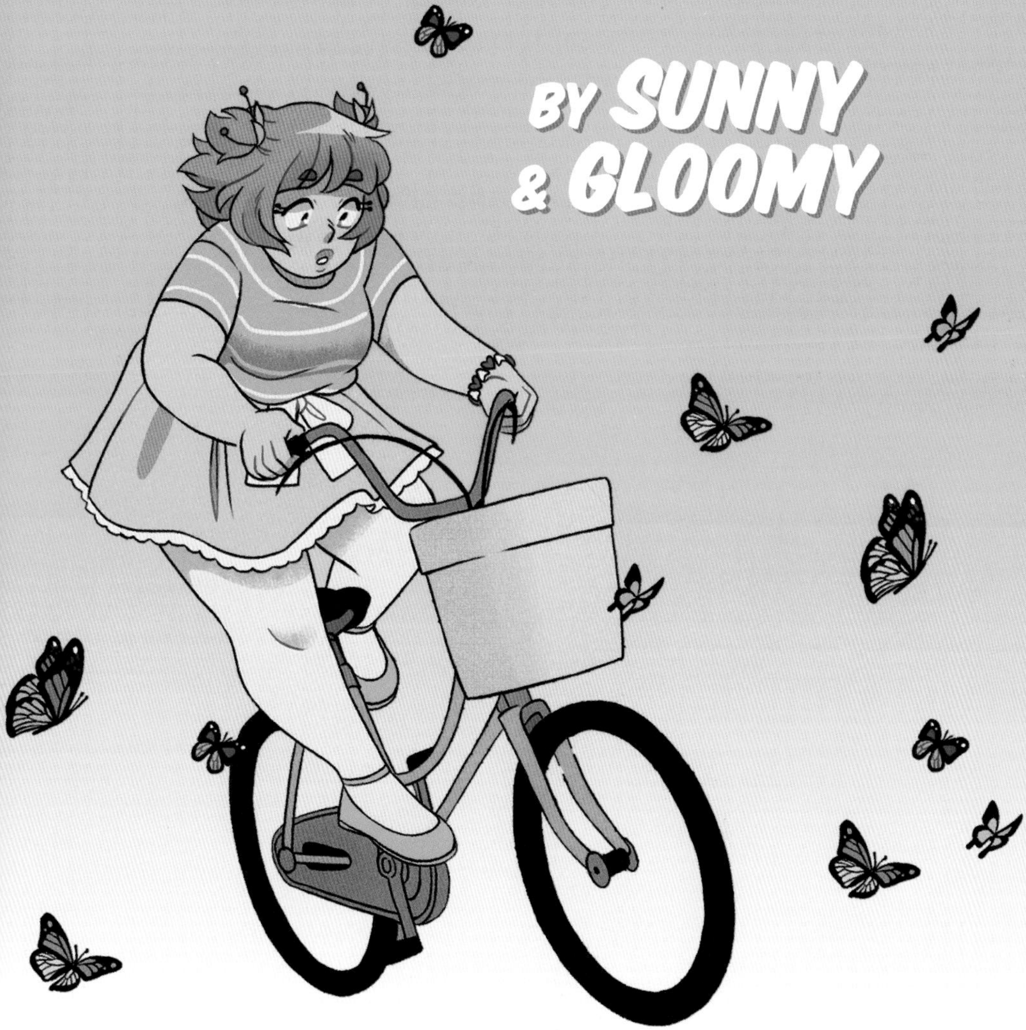

graphix
AN IMPRINT OF
SCHOLASTIC

To our younger selves, and all the kids like us.

Don't stop dreaming.

— Sunny & Gloomy

CHAPTER 1

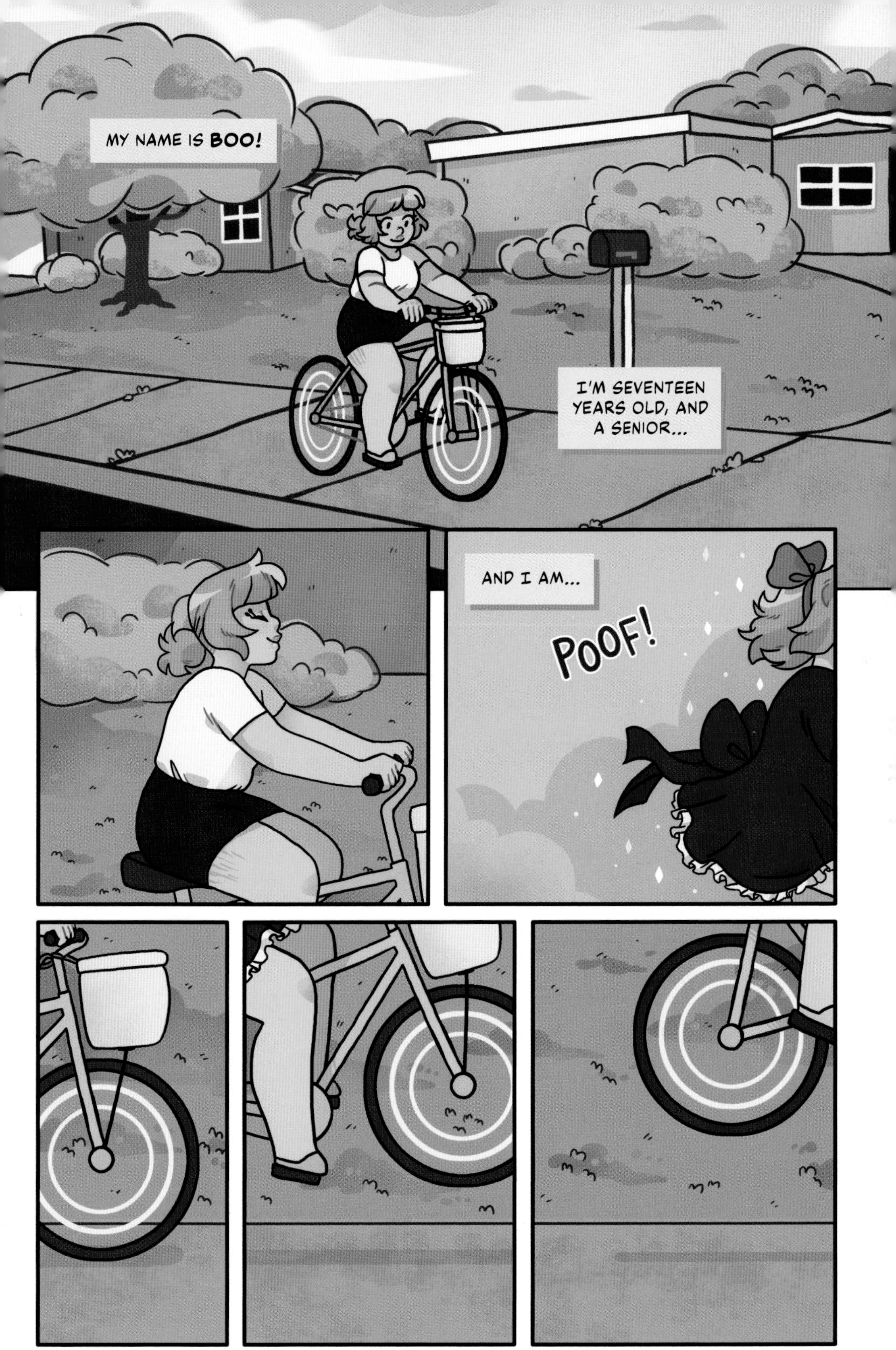
MY NAME IS BOO!
I'M SEVENTEEN YEARS OLD, AND A SENIOR...
AND I AM...
POOF!

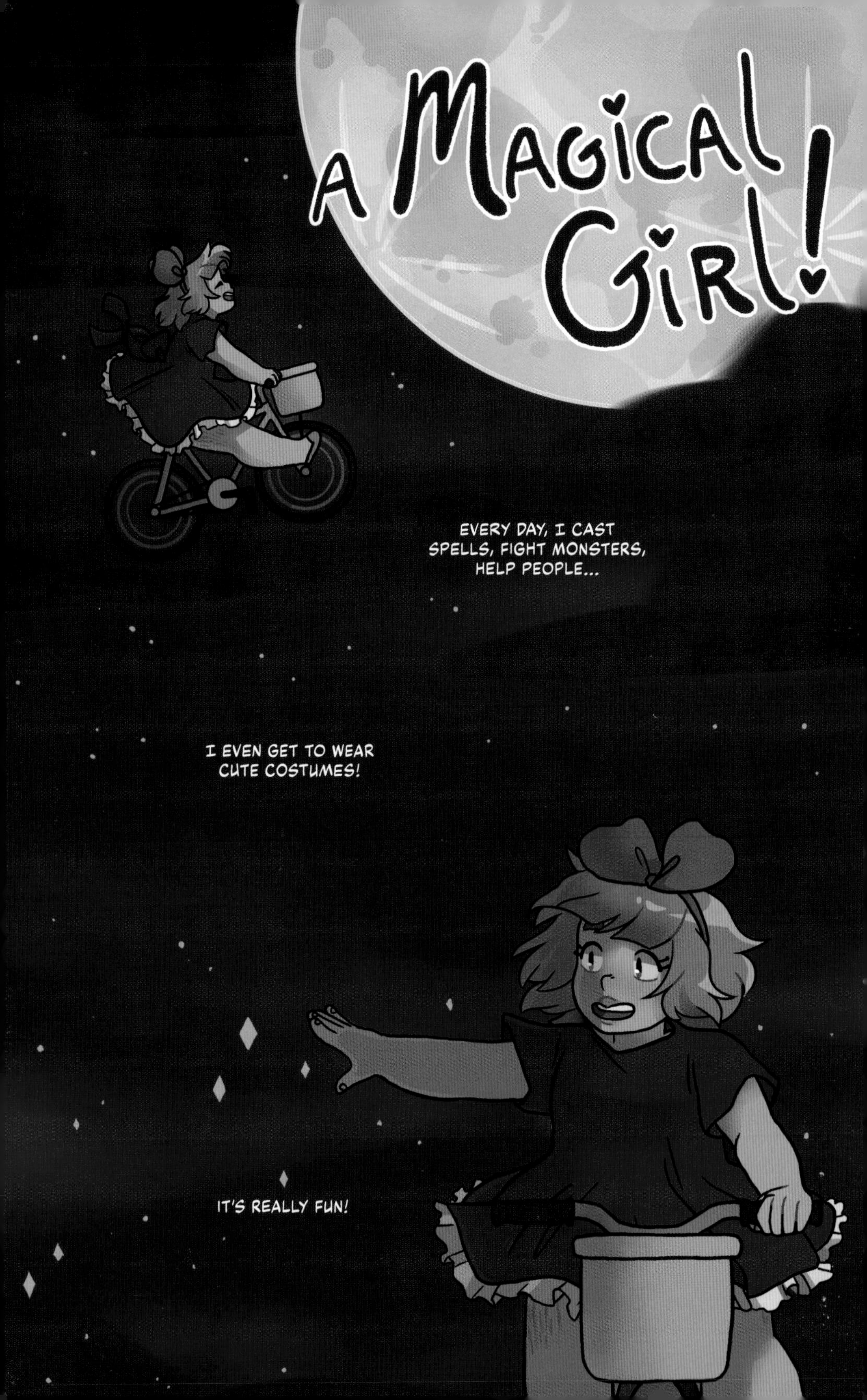
A MAGICAL GIRL!
EVERY DAY, I CAST SPELLS, FIGHT MONSTERS, HELP PEOPLE...
I EVEN GET TO WEAR CUTE COSTUMES!
IT'S REALLY FUN!

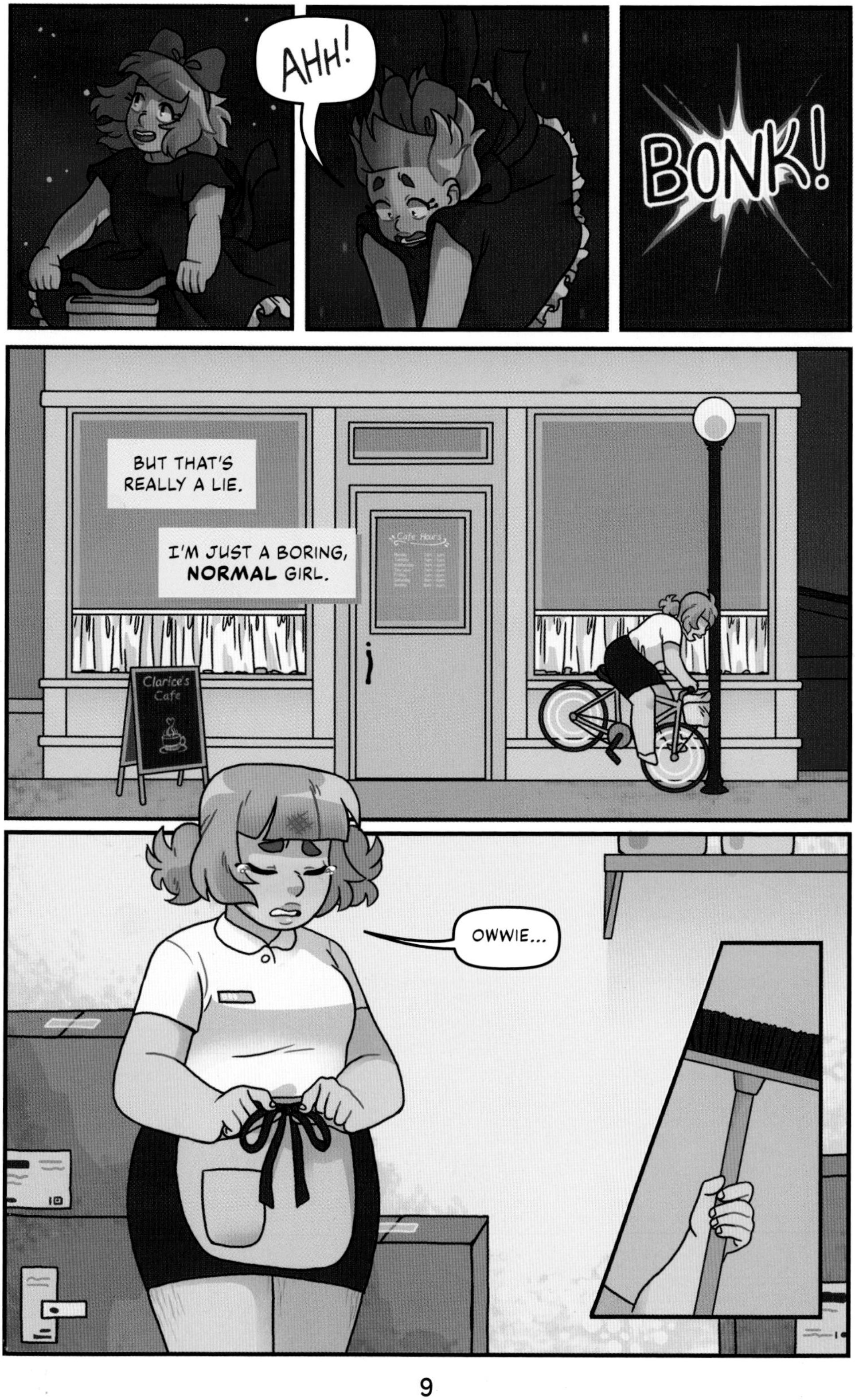

AHH!
BONK!
BUT THAT'S REALLY A LIE.
I'M JUST A BORING, **NORMAL** GIRL.
Clarice's Cafe
Cafe Hours
OWWIE...

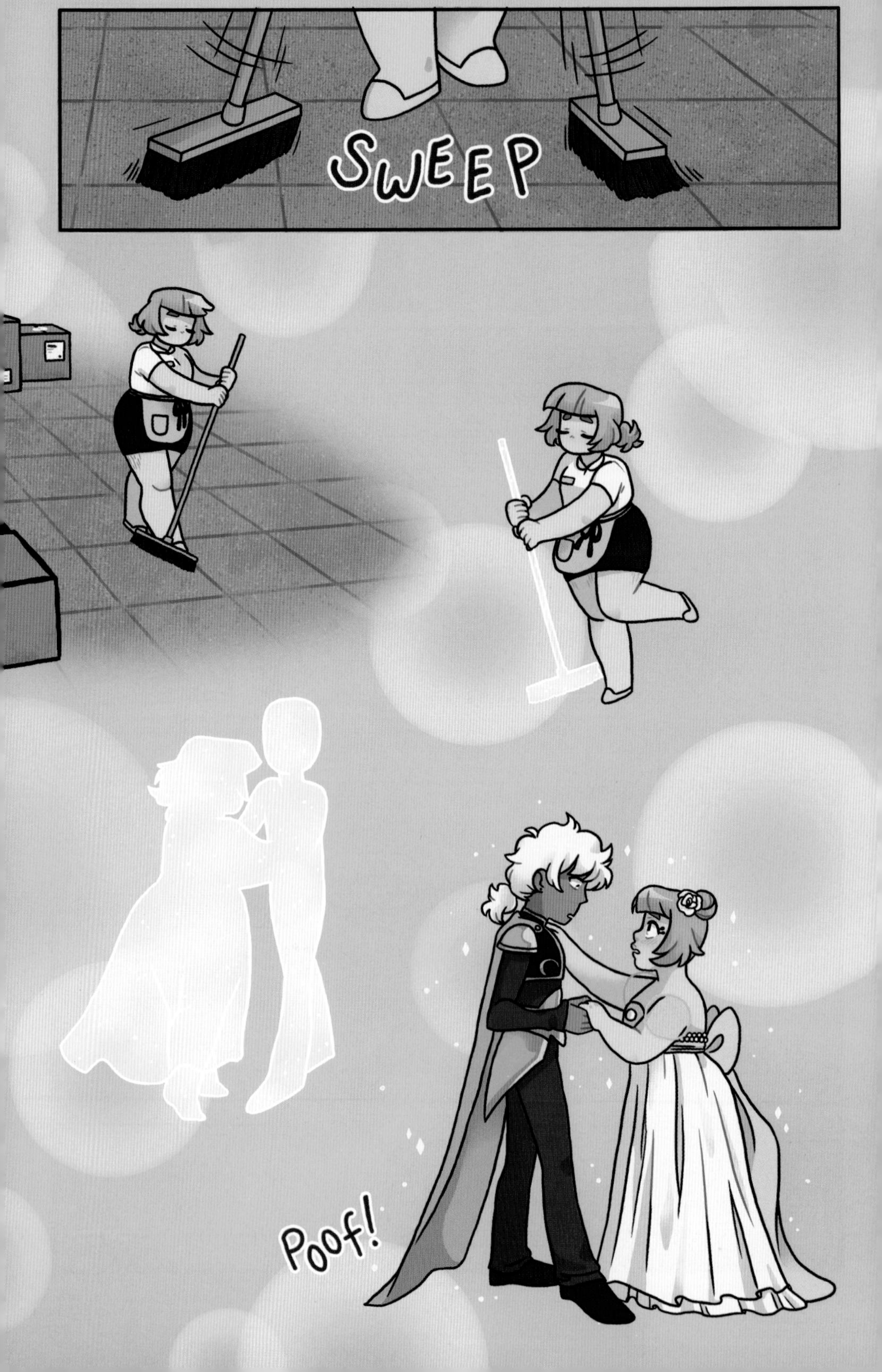
SWEEP
Poof!

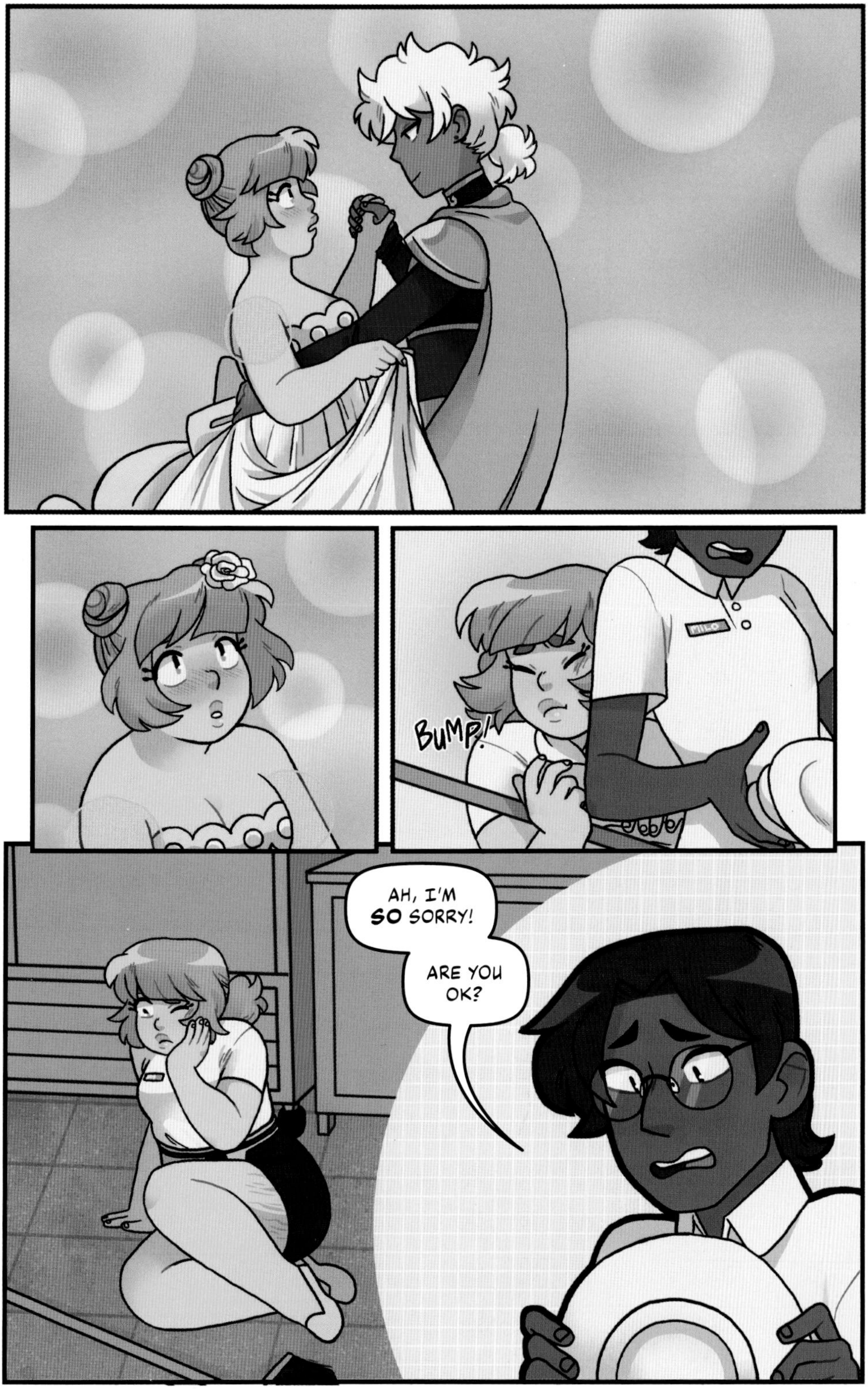
MILO
BUMP!
AH, I'M **SO** SORRY!
ARE YOU OK?

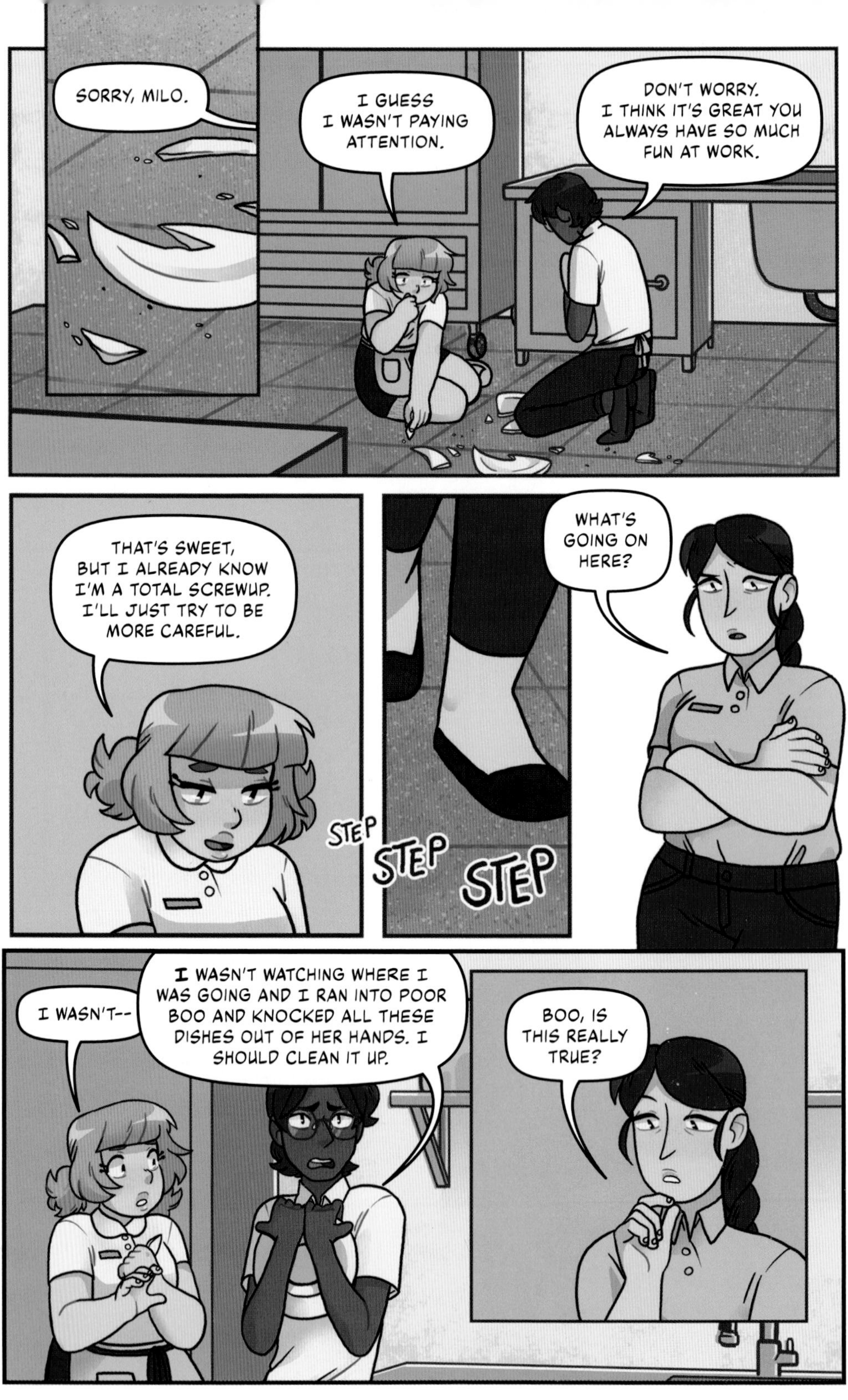
SORRY, MILO.
I GUESS I WASN'T PAYING ATTENTION.
DON'T WORRY. I THINK IT'S GREAT YOU ALWAYS HAVE SO MUCH FUN AT WORK.
THAT'S SWEET, BUT I ALREADY KNOW I'M A TOTAL SCREWUP. I'LL JUST TRY TO BE MORE CAREFUL.
STEP
STEP
STEP
WHAT'S GOING ON HERE?
I WASN'T--
I WASN'T WATCHING WHERE I WAS GOING AND I RAN INTO POOR BOO AND KNOCKED ALL THESE DISHES OUT OF HER HANDS. I SHOULD CLEAN IT UP.
BOO, IS THIS REALLY TRUE?

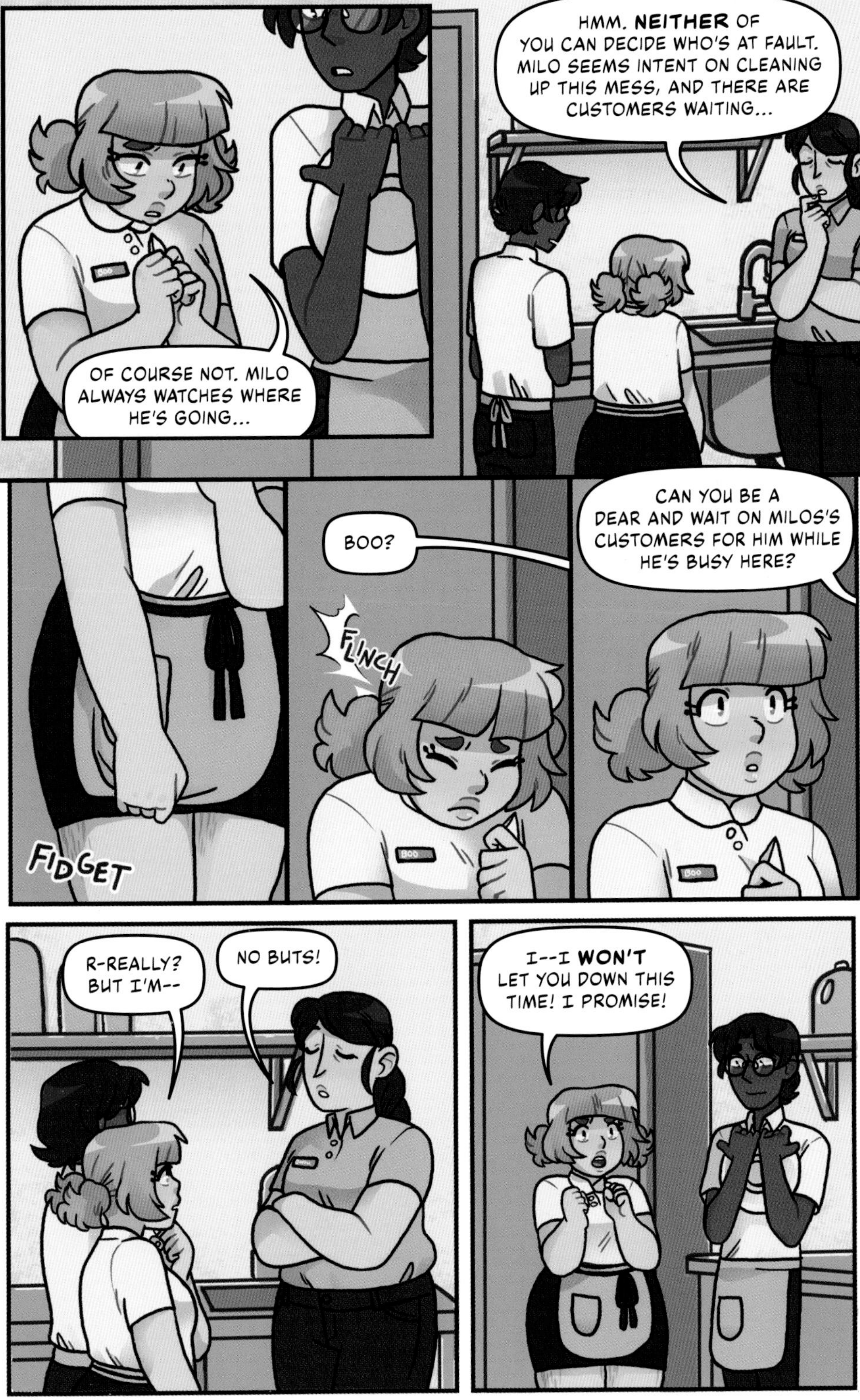
OF COURSE NOT. MILO ALWAYS WATCHES WHERE HE'S GOING...
HMM. **NEITHER** OF YOU CAN DECIDE WHO'S AT FAULT. MILO SEEMS INTENT ON CLEANING UP THIS MESS, AND THERE ARE CUSTOMERS WAITING...
FIDGET
BOO?
FLINCH
CAN YOU BE A DEAR AND WAIT ON MILOS'S CUSTOMERS FOR HIM WHILE HE'S BUSY HERE?
R-REALLY? BUT I'M--
NO BUTS!
I--I **WON'T** LET YOU DOWN THIS TIME! I PROMISE!

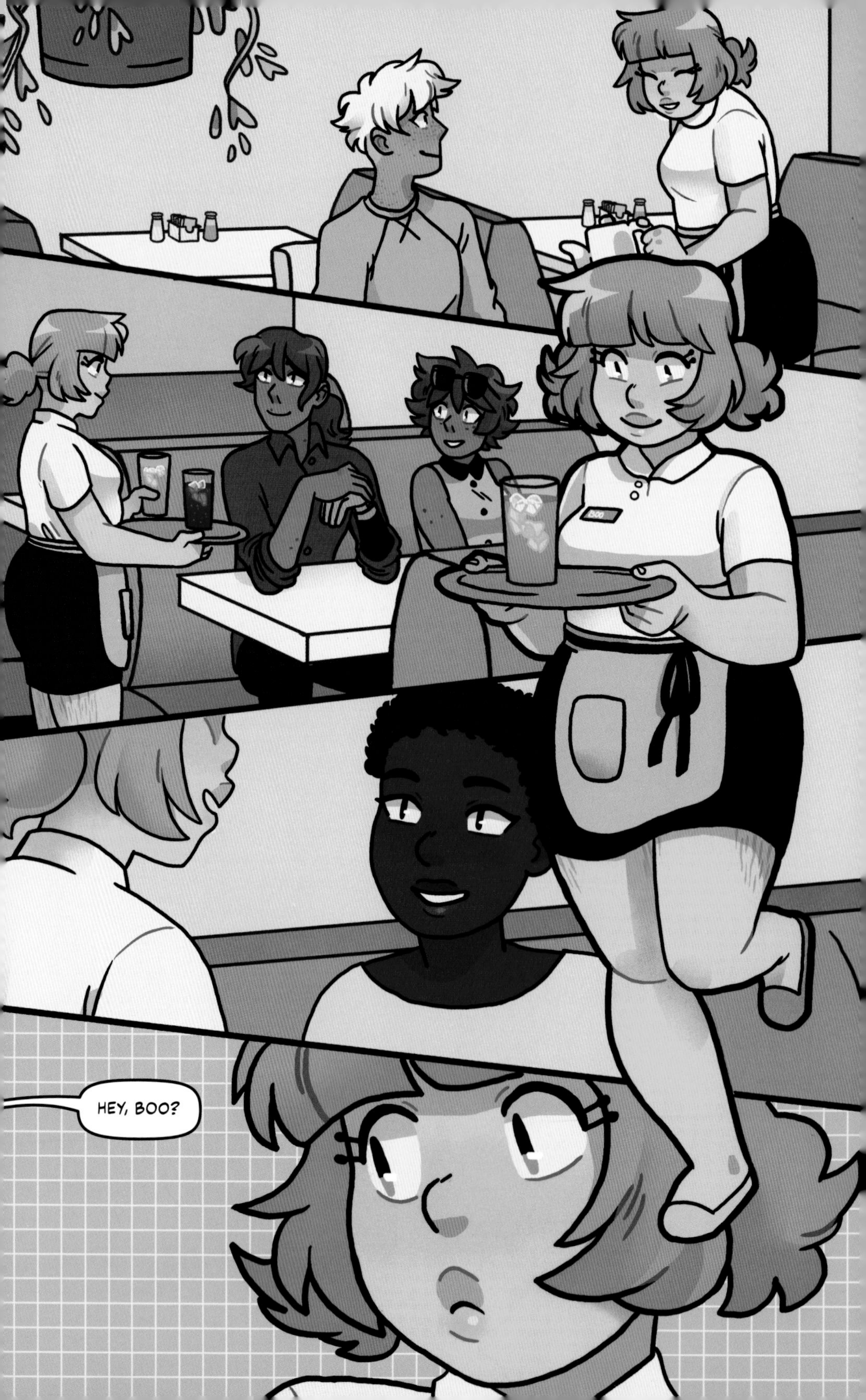
HEY, BOO?

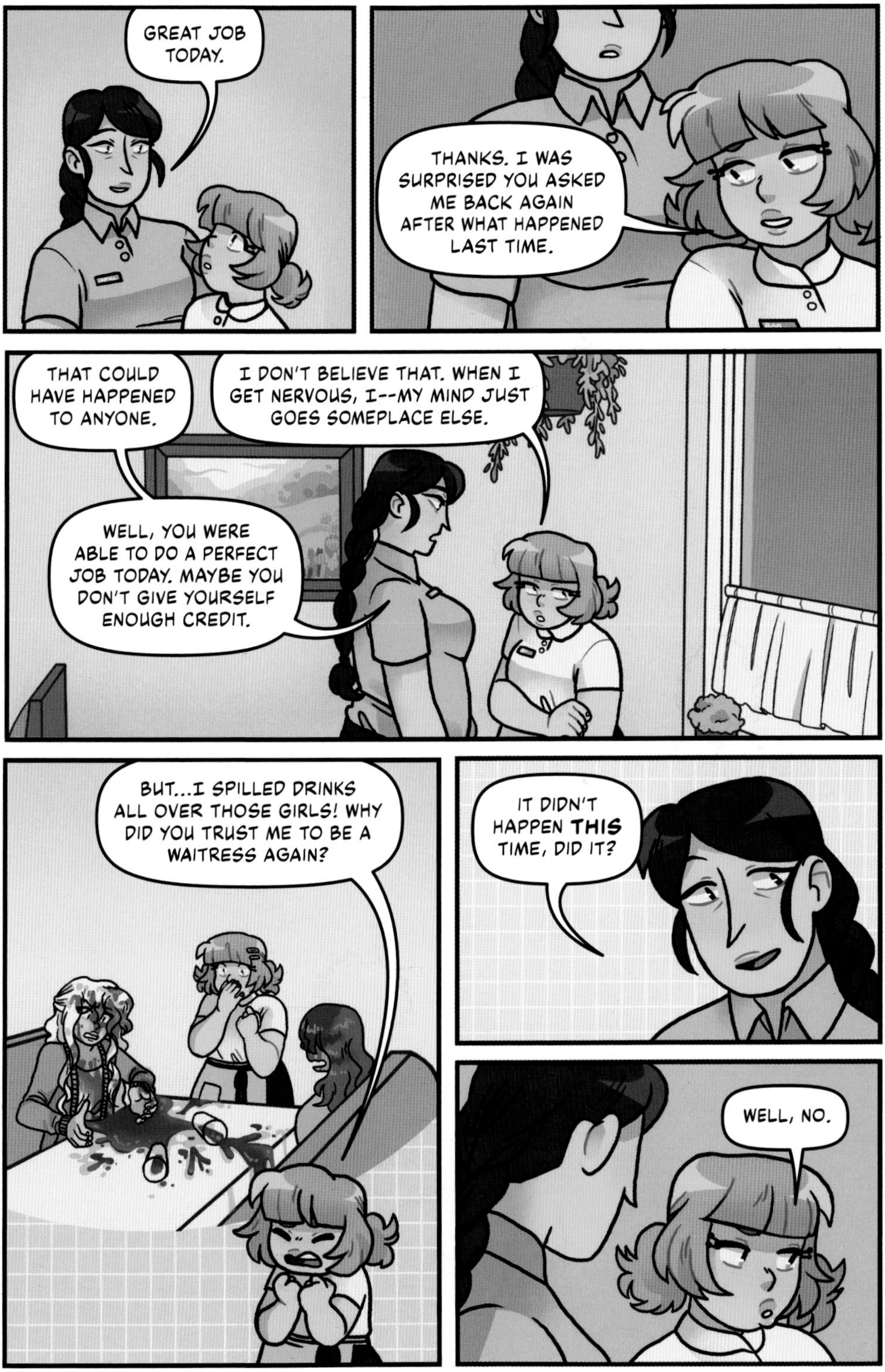
GREAT JOB TODAY.
THANKS. I WAS SURPRISED YOU ASKED ME BACK AGAIN AFTER WHAT HAPPENED LAST TIME.
THAT COULD HAVE HAPPENED TO ANYONE.
I DON'T BELIEVE THAT. WHEN I GET NERVOUS, I--MY MIND JUST GOES SOMEPLACE ELSE.
WELL, YOU WERE ABLE TO DO A PERFECT JOB TODAY. MAYBE YOU DON'T GIVE YOURSELF ENOUGH CREDIT.
BUT...I SPILLED DRINKS ALL OVER THOSE GIRLS! WHY DID YOU TRUST ME TO BE A WAITRESS AGAIN?
IT DIDN'T HAPPEN **THIS** TIME, DID IT?
WELL, NO.

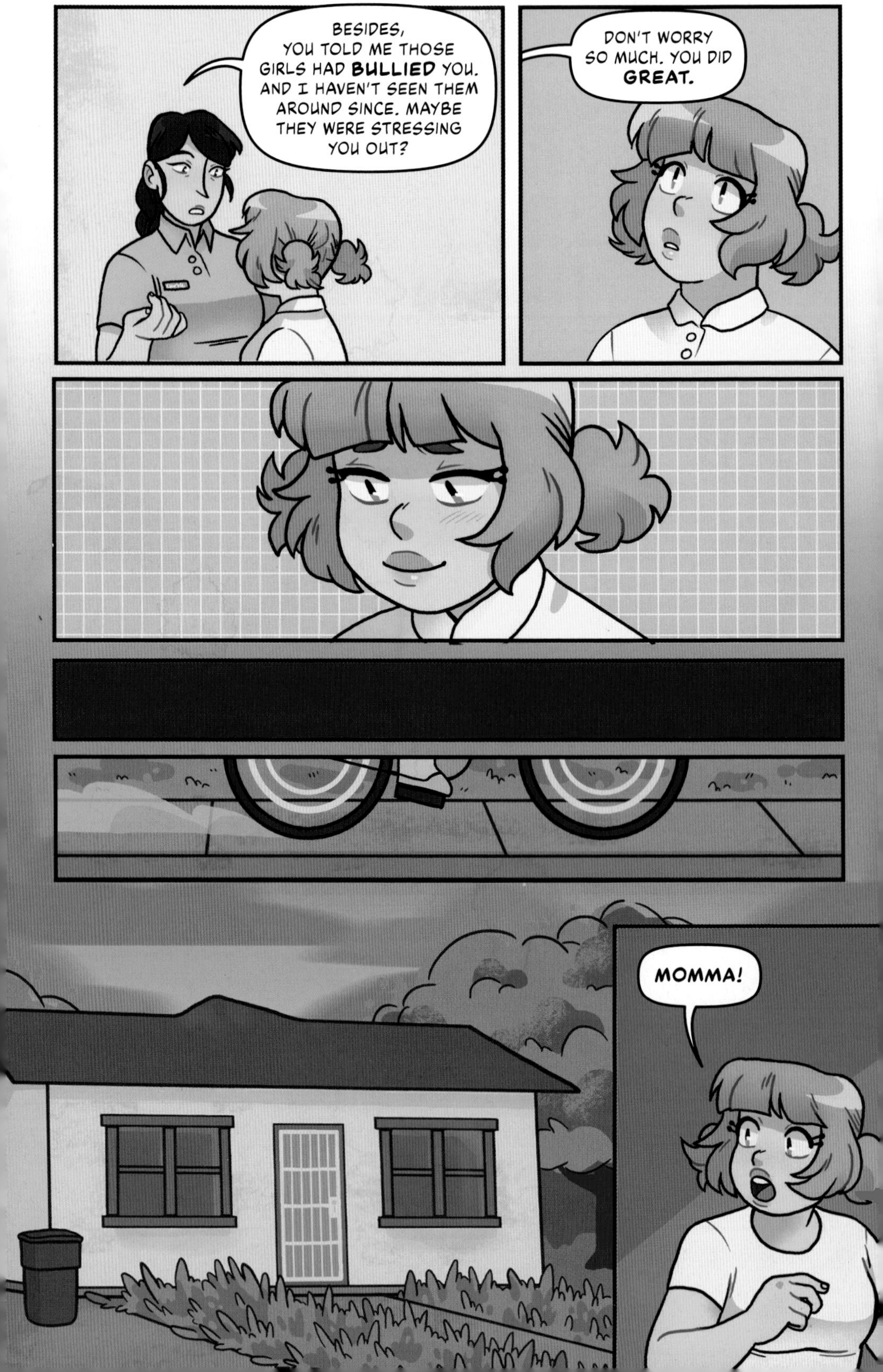
BESIDES, YOU TOLD ME THOSE GIRLS HAD **BULLIED** YOU. AND I HAVEN'T SEEN THEM AROUND SINCE. MAYBE THEY WERE STRESSING YOU OUT?
DON'T WORRY SO MUCH. YOU DID **GREAT.**
MOMMA!

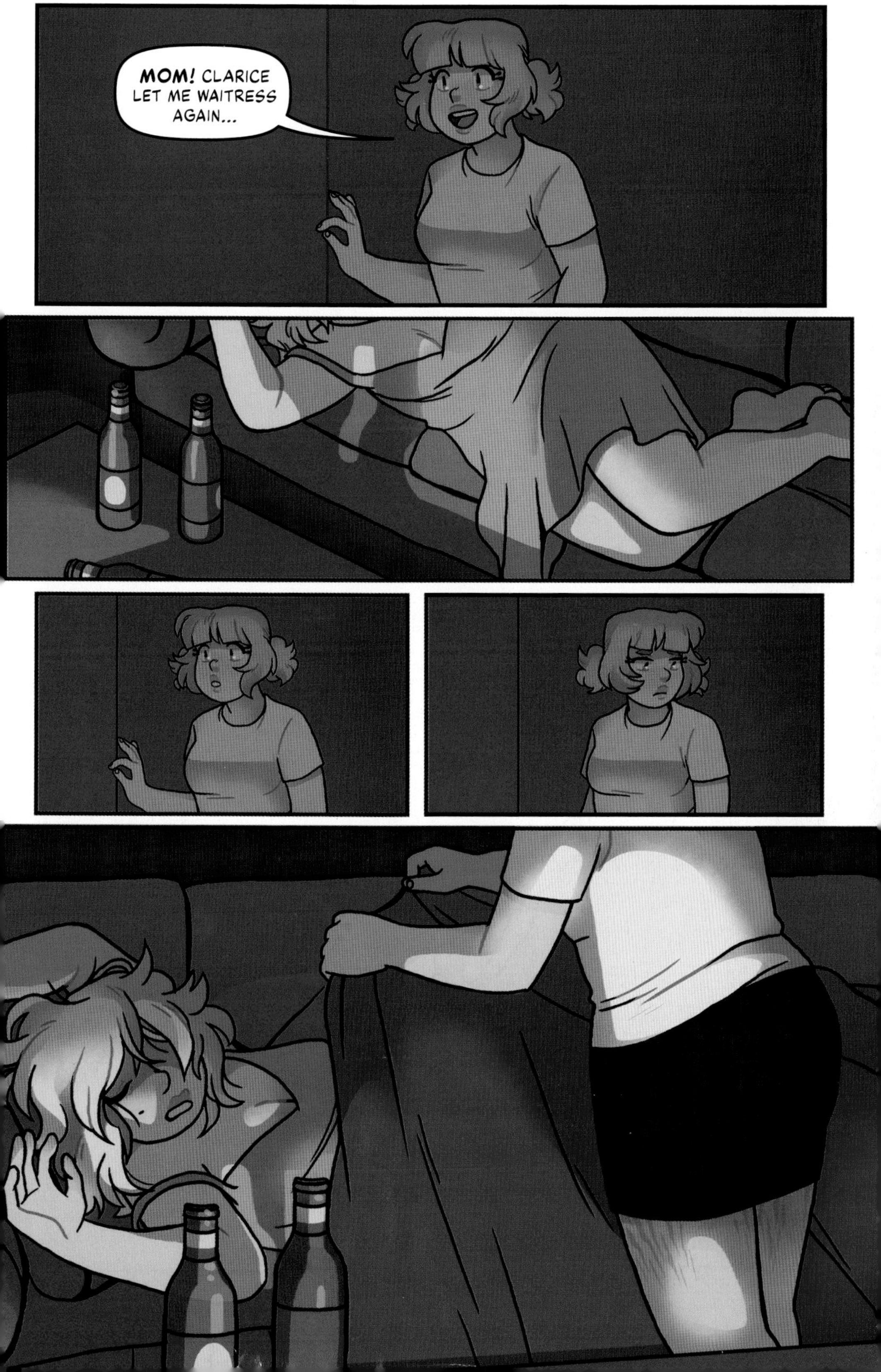
MOM! CLARICE LET ME WAITRESS AGAIN...

POP!

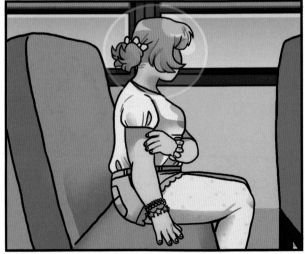

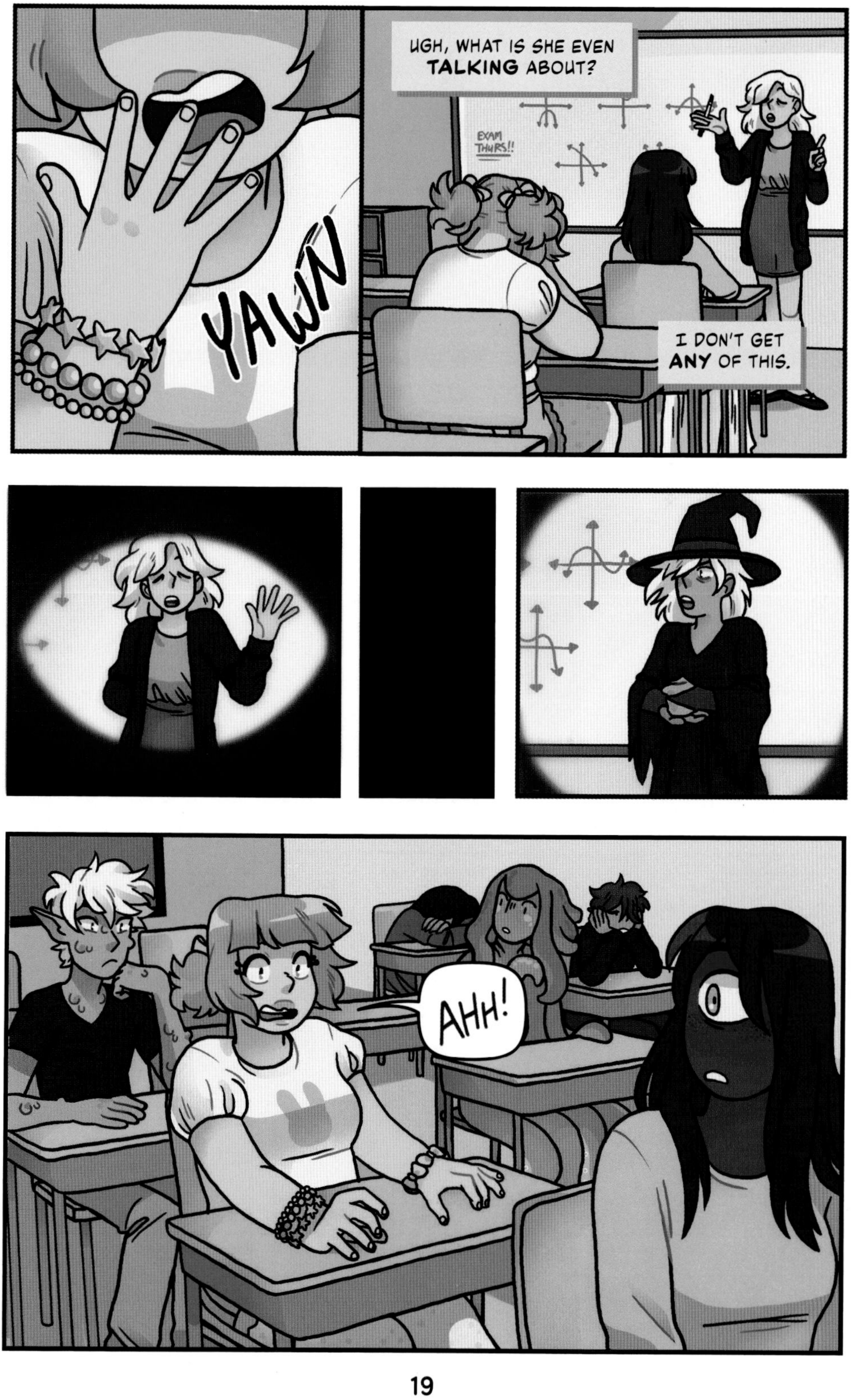
YAWN
UGH, WHAT IS SHE EVEN TALKING ABOUT?
EXAM THURS!!
I DON'T GET ANY OF THIS.
AHH!

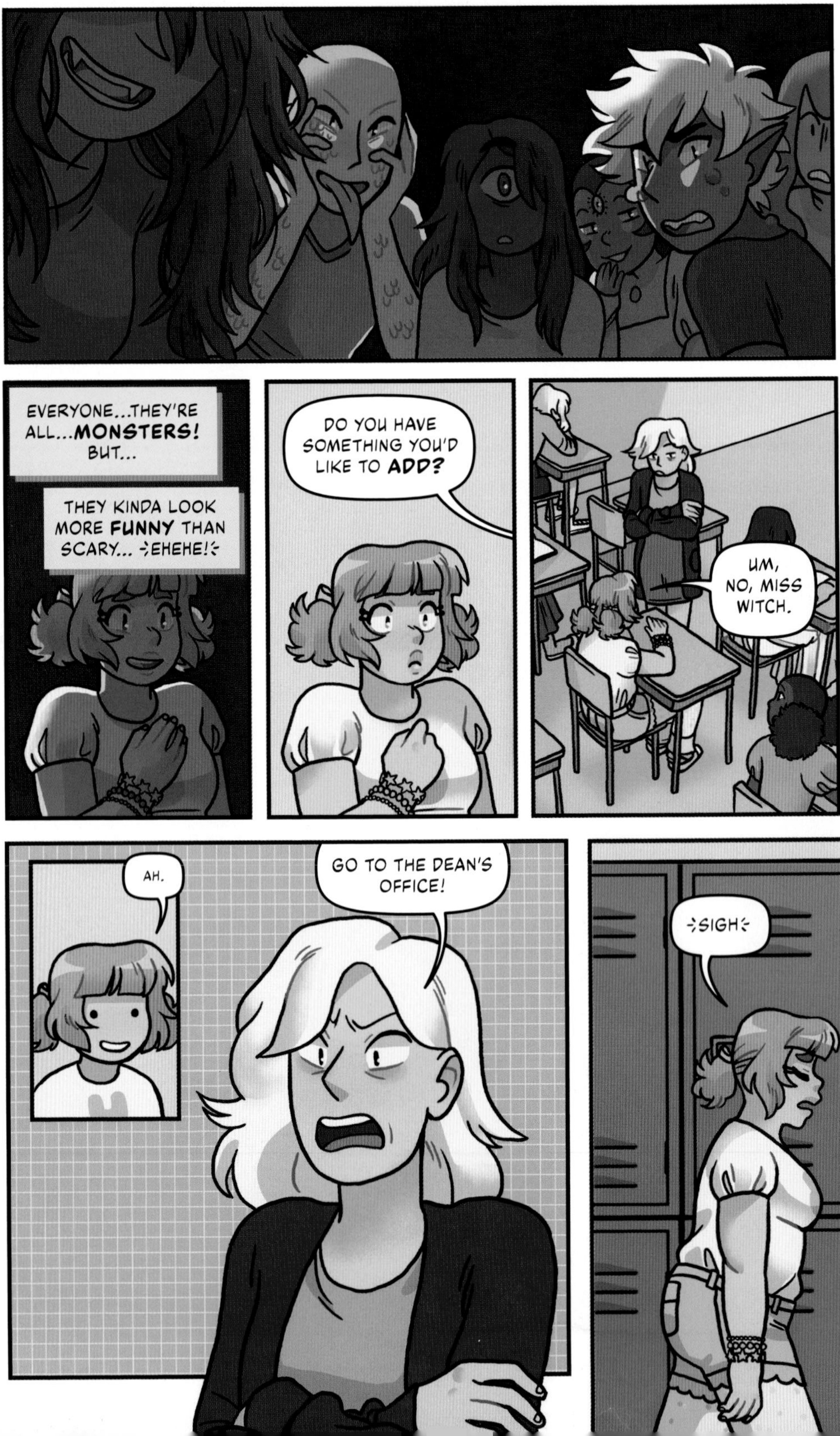
EVERYONE...THEY'RE ALL...**MONSTERS!** BUT...
THEY KINDA LOOK MORE **FUNNY** THAN SCARY... EHEHE!
DO YOU HAVE SOMETHING YOU'D LIKE TO **ADD?**
UM, NO, MISS WITCH.
AH.
GO TO THE DEAN'S OFFICE!
SIGH

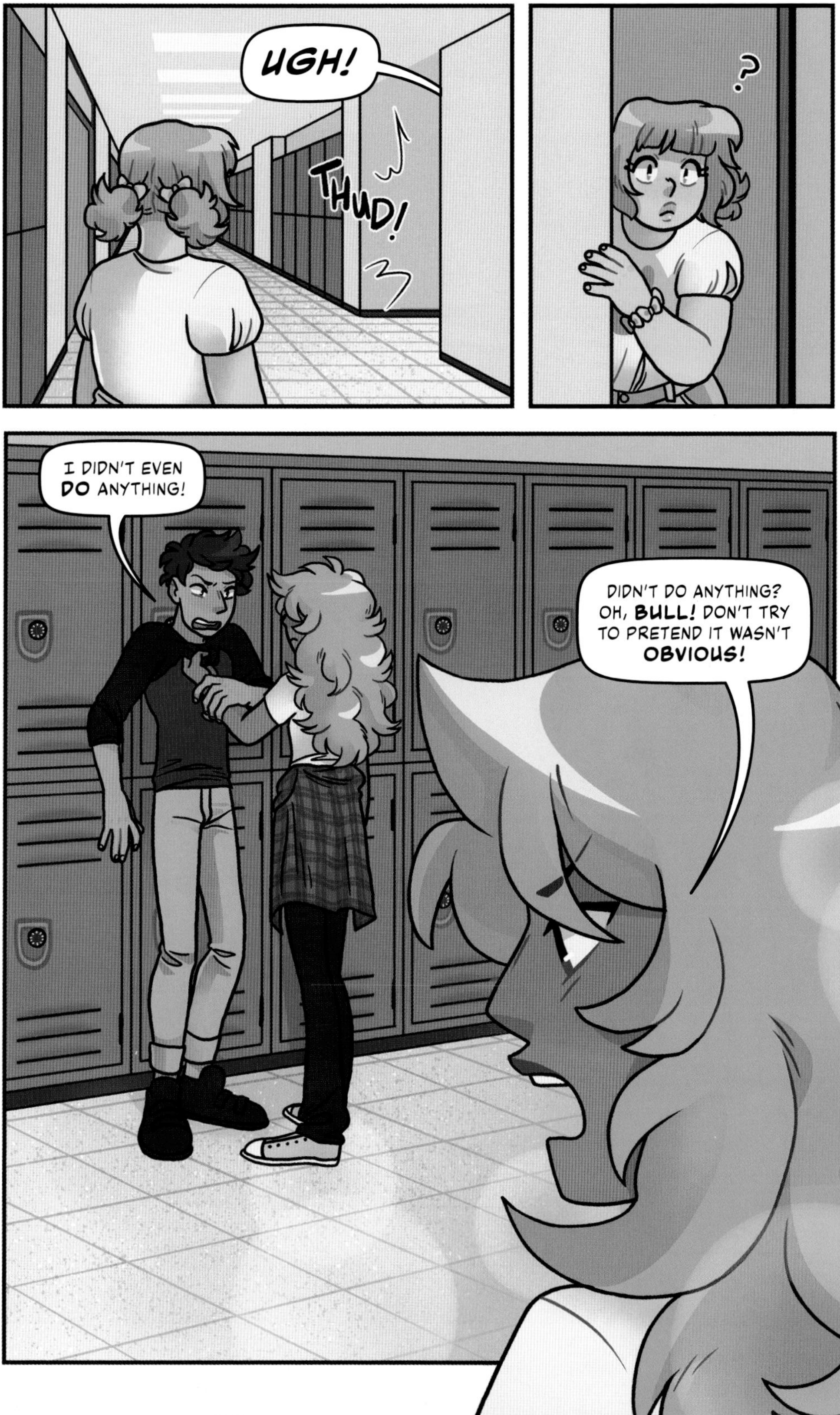

UGH!
THUD!
?
I DIDN'T EVEN DO ANYTHING!
DIDN'T DO ANYTHING? OH, BULL! DON'T TRY TO PRETEND IT WASN'T OBVIOUS!

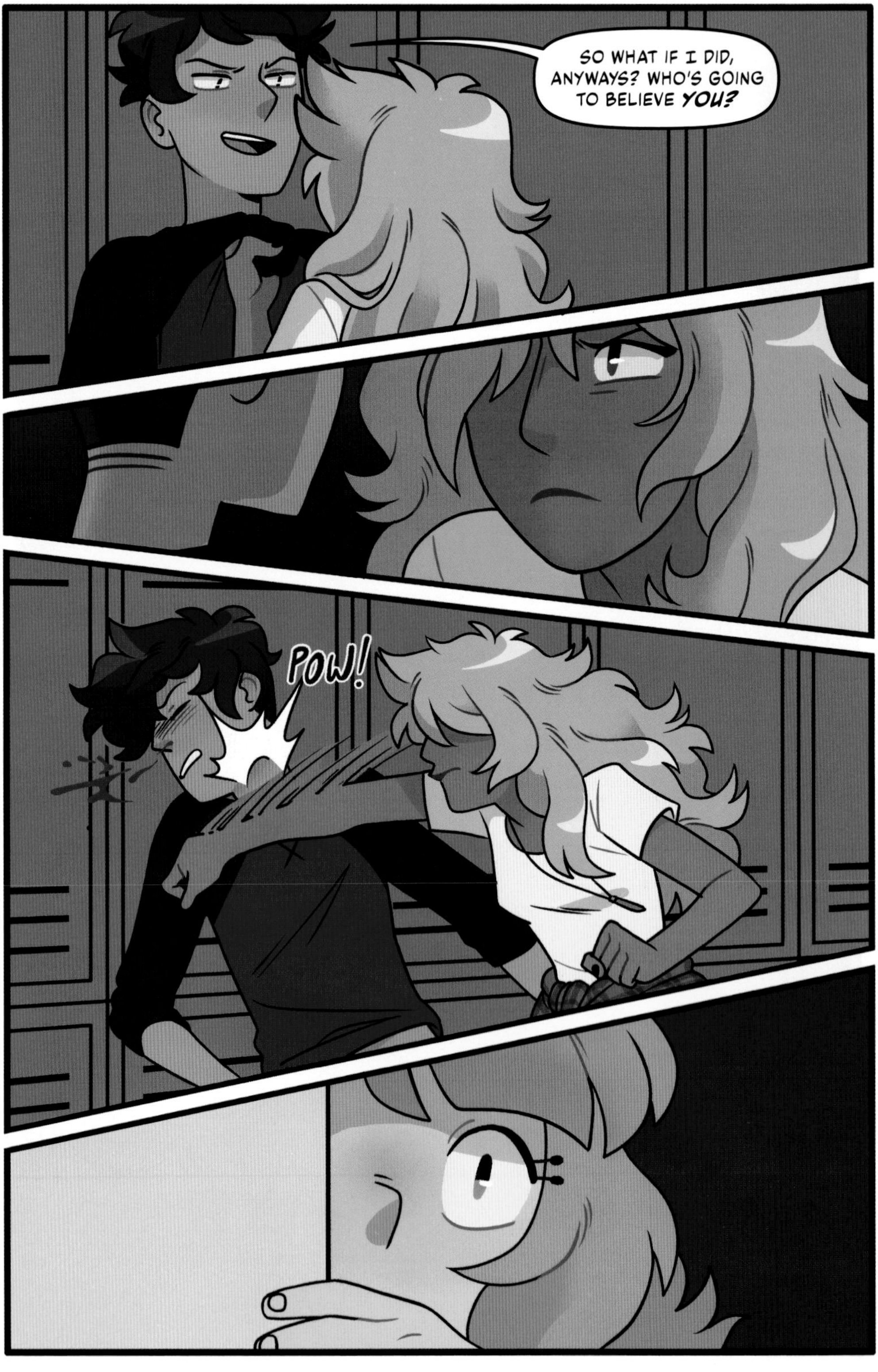
SO WHAT IF I DID, ANYWAYS? WHO'S GOING TO BELIEVE YOU?
POW!

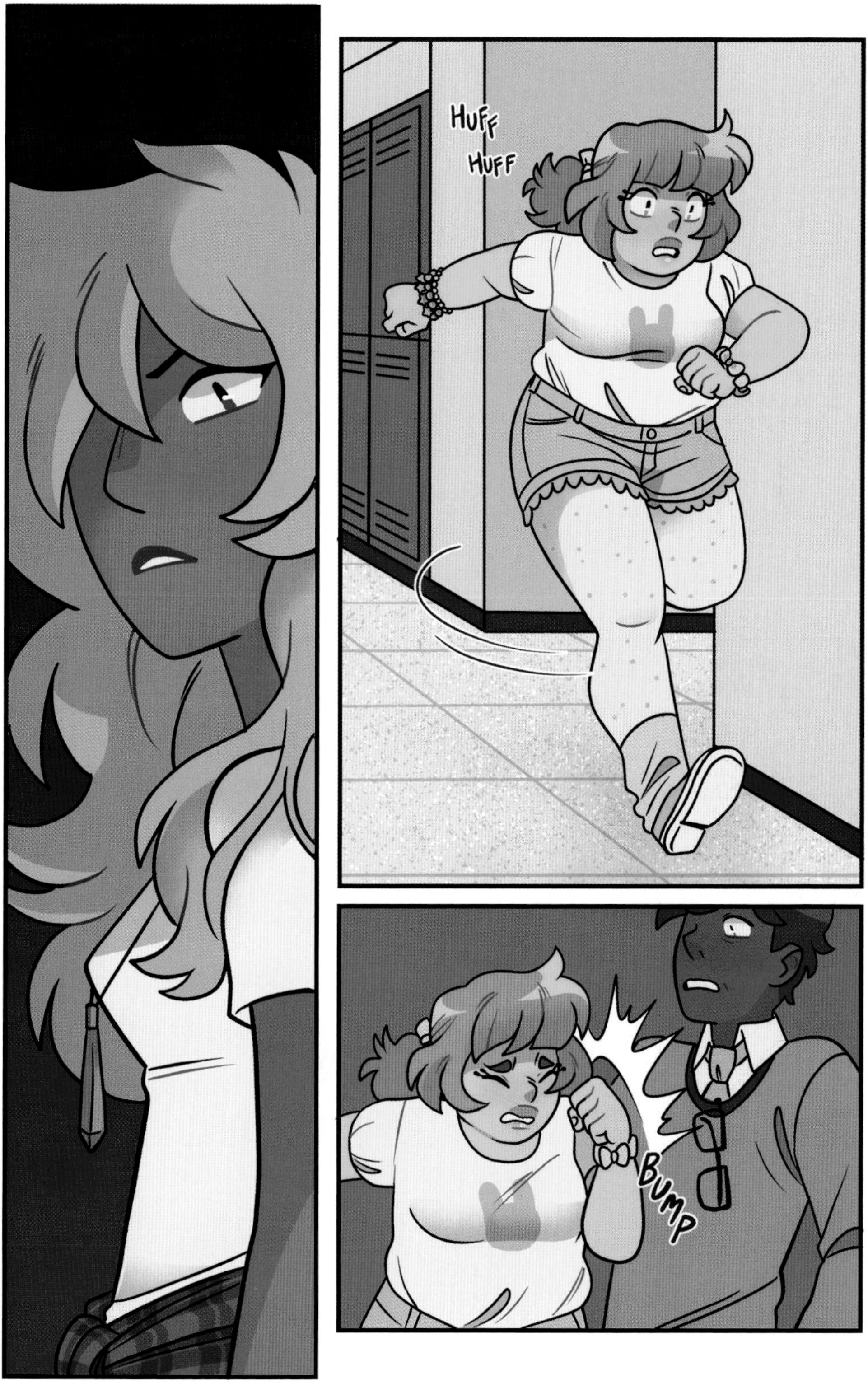
HUFF
HUFF
BUMP

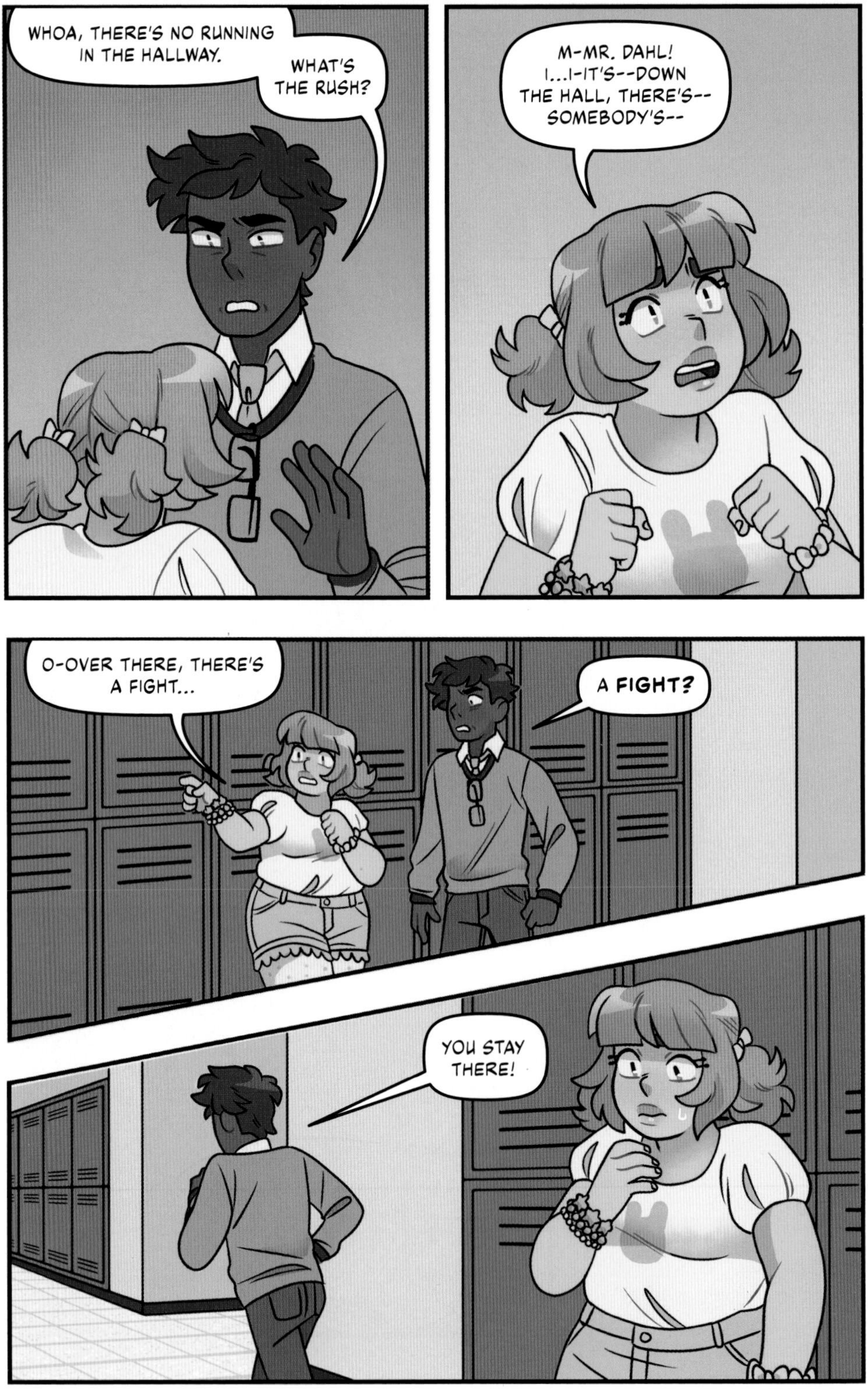
WHOA, THERE'S NO RUNNING IN THE HALLWAY.
WHAT'S THE RUSH?
M-MR. DAHL! I...I-IT'S--DOWN THE HALL, THERE'S--SOMEBODY'S--
O-OVER THERE, THERE'S A FIGHT...
A **FIGHT?**
YOU STAY THERE!

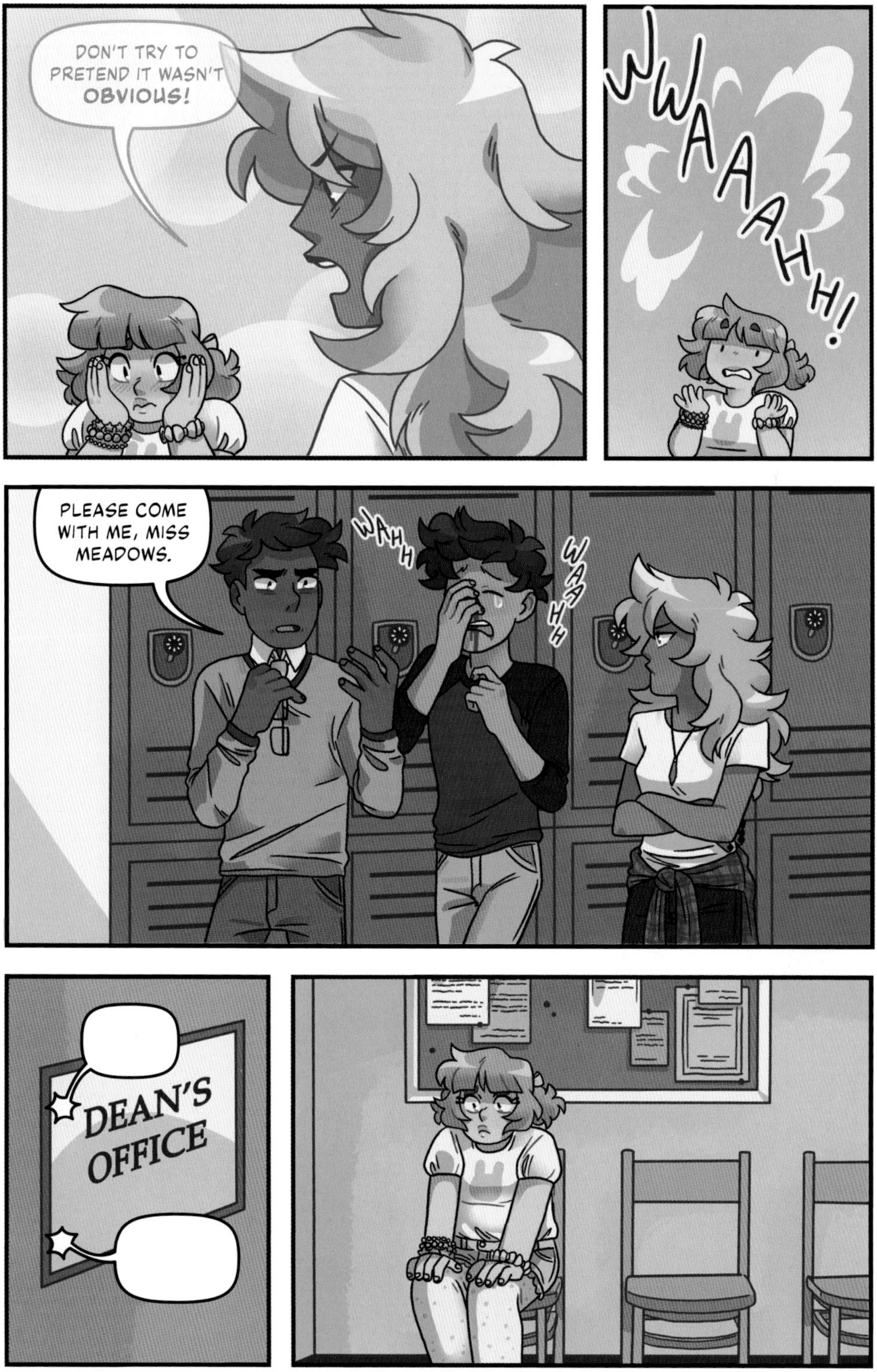
DON'T TRY TO PRETEND IT WASN'T OBVIOUS!
WWAAAAHH!
PLEASE COME WITH ME, MISS MEADOWS.
WAHH
WAAAHH
DEAN'S OFFICE

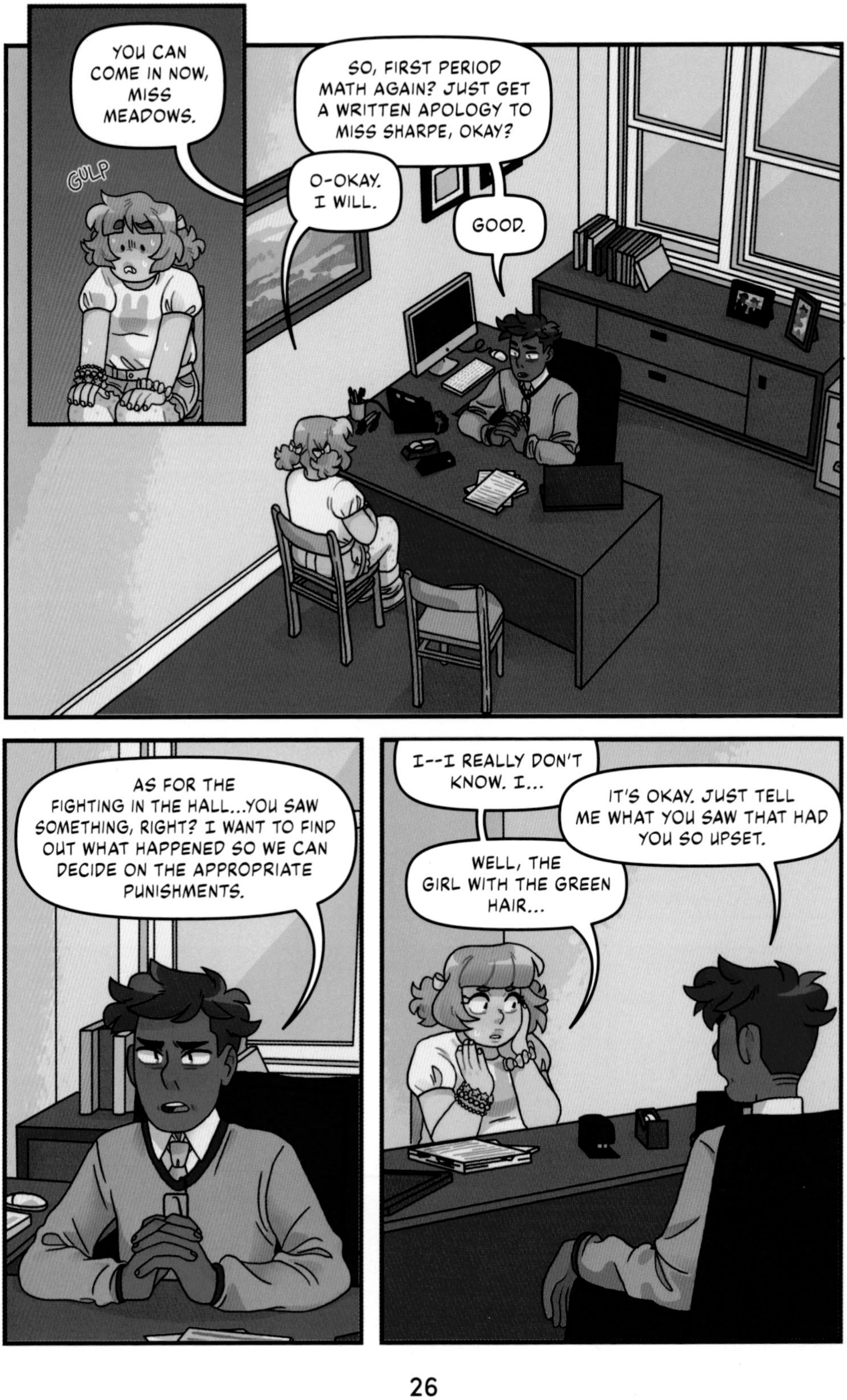
YOU CAN COME IN NOW, MISS MEADOWS.
GULP
SO, FIRST PERIOD MATH AGAIN? JUST GET A WRITTEN APOLOGY TO MISS SHARPE, OKAY?
O-OKAY. I WILL.
GOOD.
AS FOR THE FIGHTING IN THE HALL...YOU SAW SOMETHING, RIGHT? I WANT TO FIND OUT WHAT HAPPENED SO WE CAN DECIDE ON THE APPROPRIATE PUNISHMENTS.
I--I REALLY DON'T KNOW. I...
IT'S OKAY. JUST TELL ME WHAT YOU SAW THAT HAD YOU SO UPSET.
WELL, THE GIRL WITH THE GREEN HAIR...

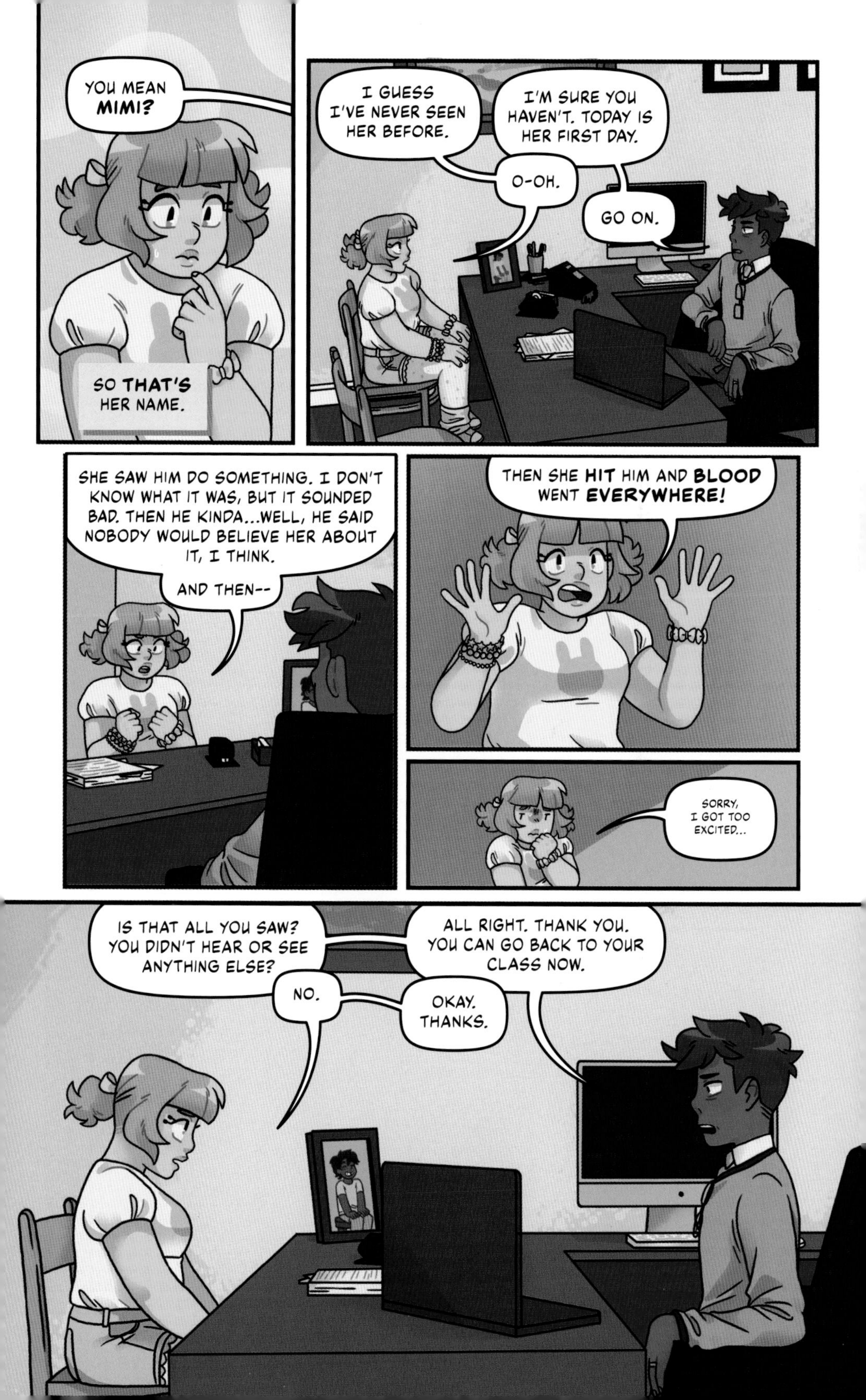
YOU MEAN MIMI?
SO THAT'S HER NAME.
I GUESS I'VE NEVER SEEN HER BEFORE.
I'M SURE YOU HAVEN'T. TODAY IS HER FIRST DAY.
O-OH.
GO ON.
SHE SAW HIM DO SOMETHING. I DON'T KNOW WHAT IT WAS, BUT IT SOUNDED BAD. THEN HE KINDA...WELL, HE SAID NOBODY WOULD BELIEVE HER ABOUT IT, I THINK.
AND THEN--
THEN SHE HIT HIM AND BLOOD WENT EVERYWHERE!
SORRY, I GOT TOO EXCITED...
IS THAT ALL YOU SAW? YOU DIDN'T HEAR OR SEE ANYTHING ELSE?
NO.
ALL RIGHT. THANK YOU. YOU CAN GO BACK TO YOUR CLASS NOW.
OKAY. THANKS.

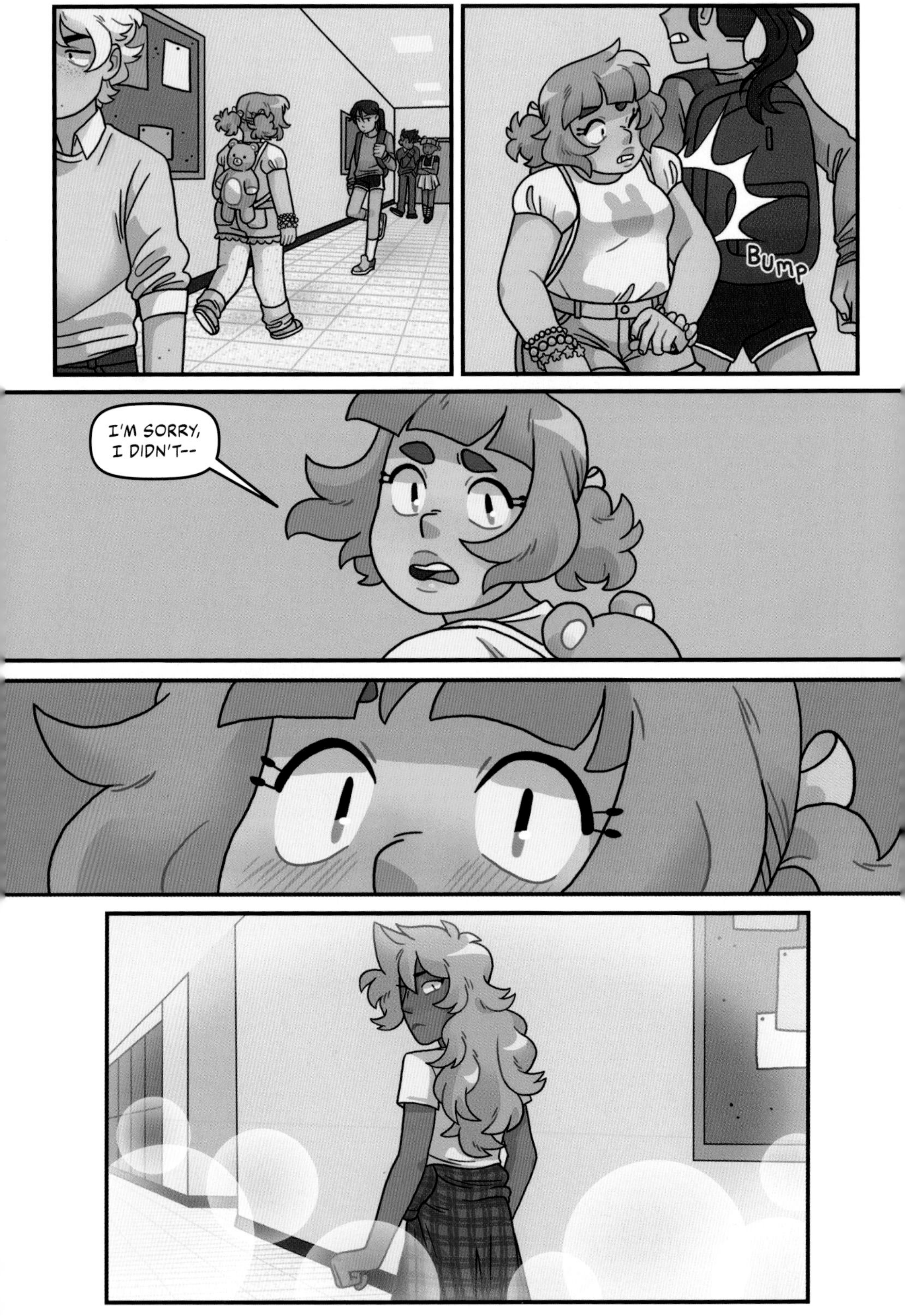
BUMP
I'M SORRY, I DIDN'T--

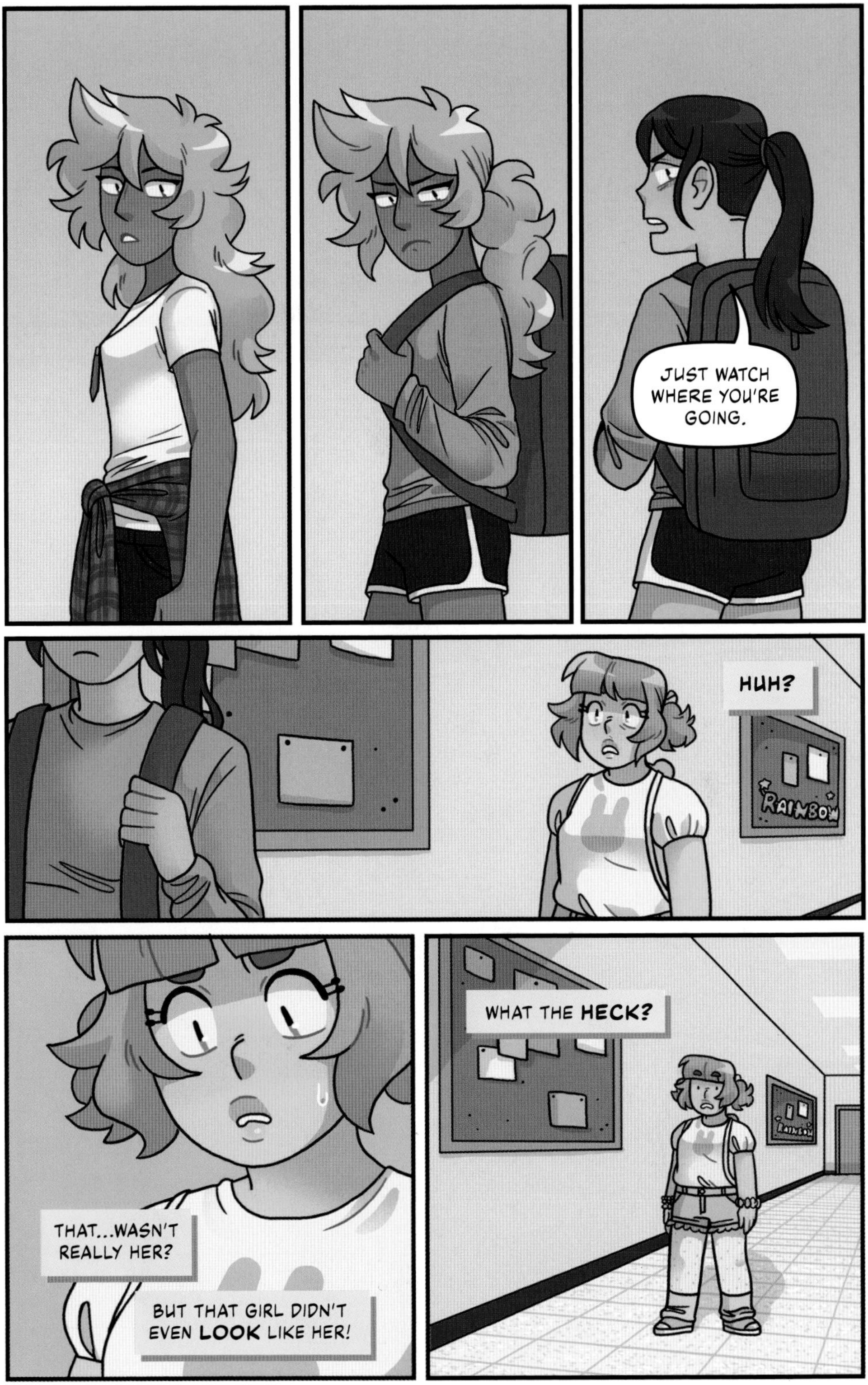
JUST WATCH WHERE YOU'RE GOING.
HUH?
RAINBOW
THAT...WASN'T REALLY HER?
BUT THAT GIRL DIDN'T EVEN LOOK LIKE HER!
WHAT THE HECK?

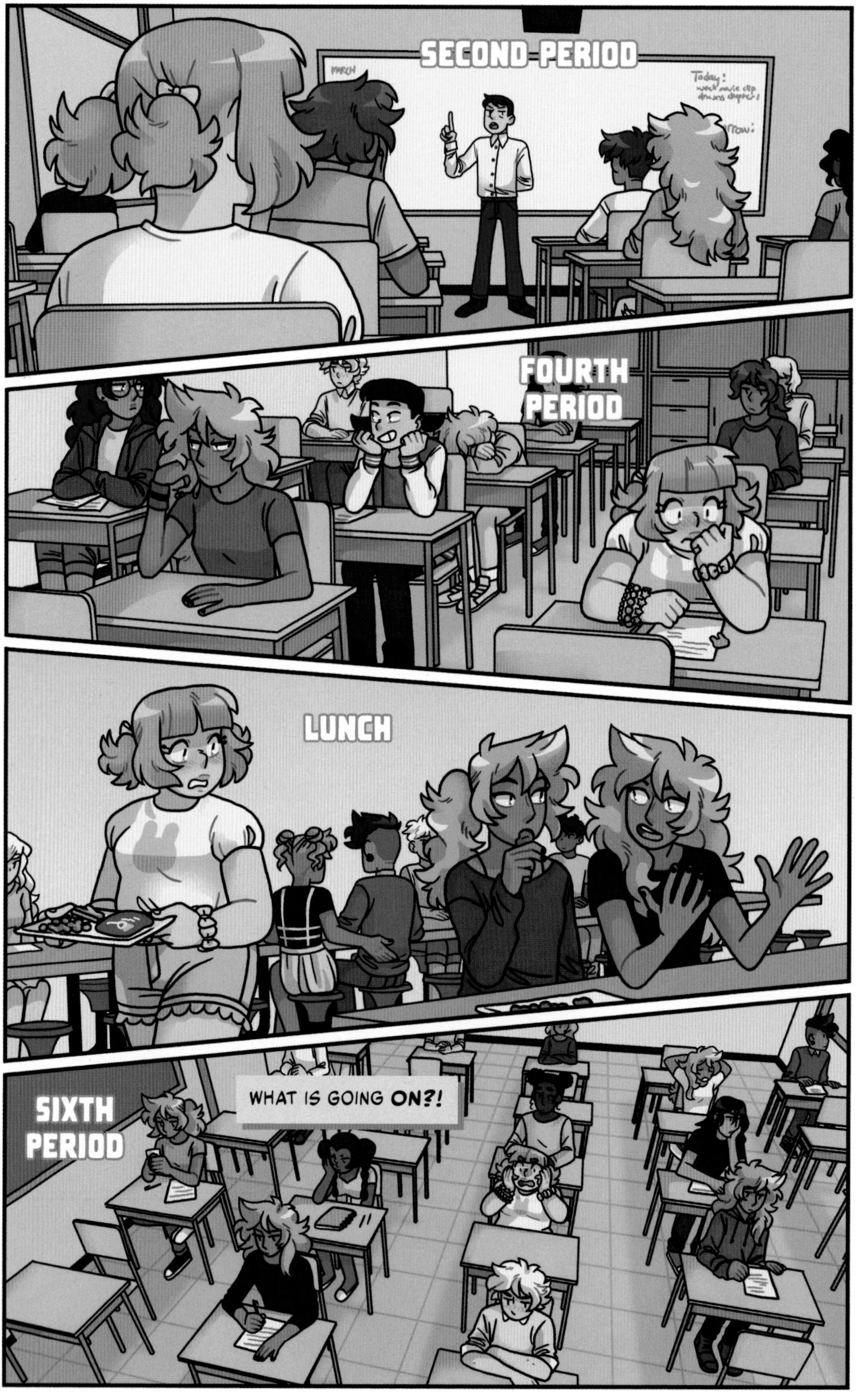
SECOND PERIOD
MARCH
Today:
FOURTH PERIOD
LUNCH
SIXTH PERIOD
WHAT IS GOING ON?!

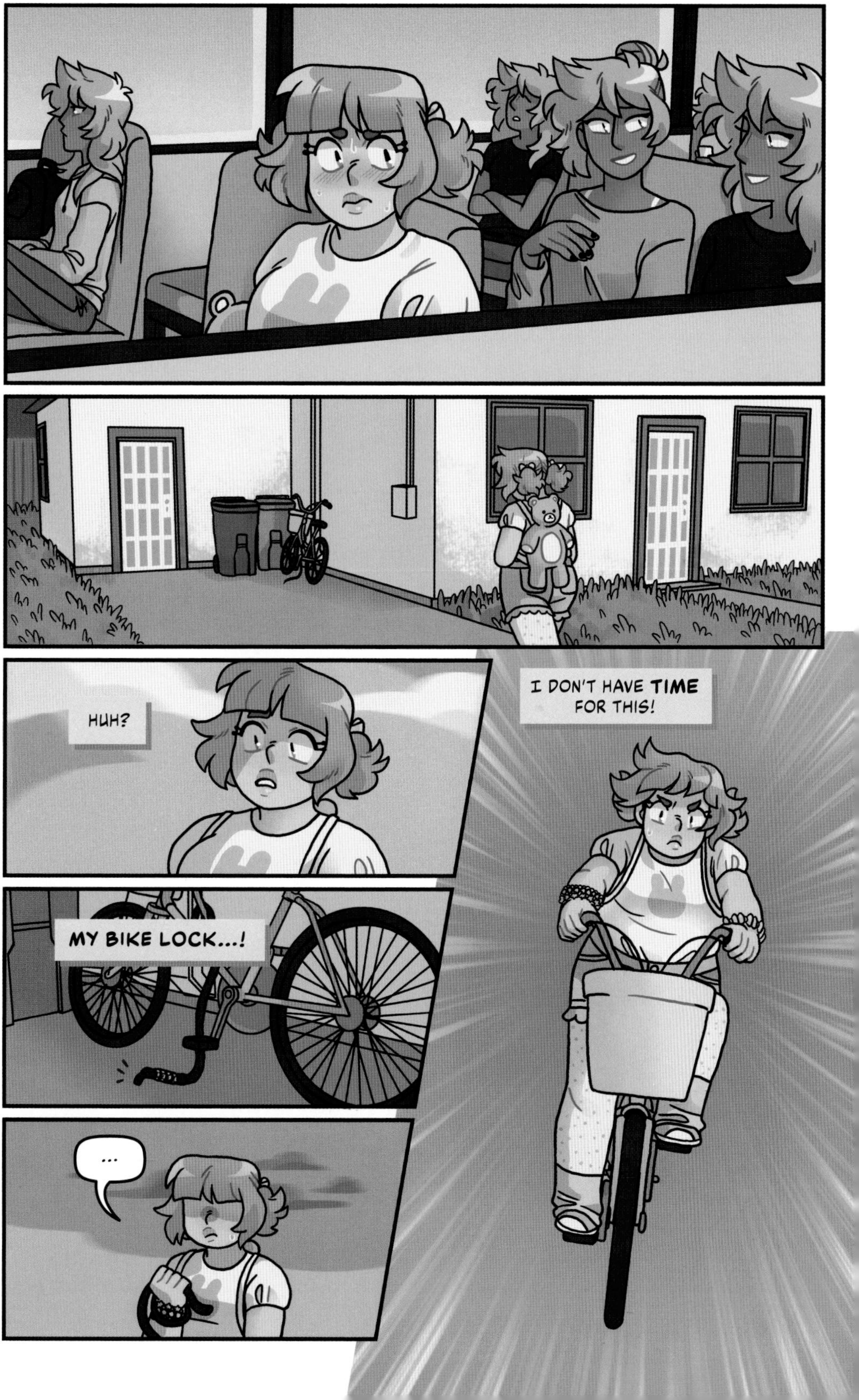
HUH?
MY BIKE LOCK...!
...
I DON'T HAVE TIME FOR THIS!

RRRUMBLE...

PLIP!

EEP!

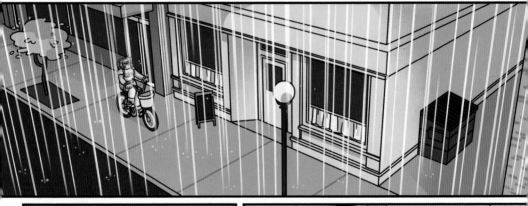

IT SHOULD BE OKAY THERE...HOPEFULLY.

HUFF HUFF

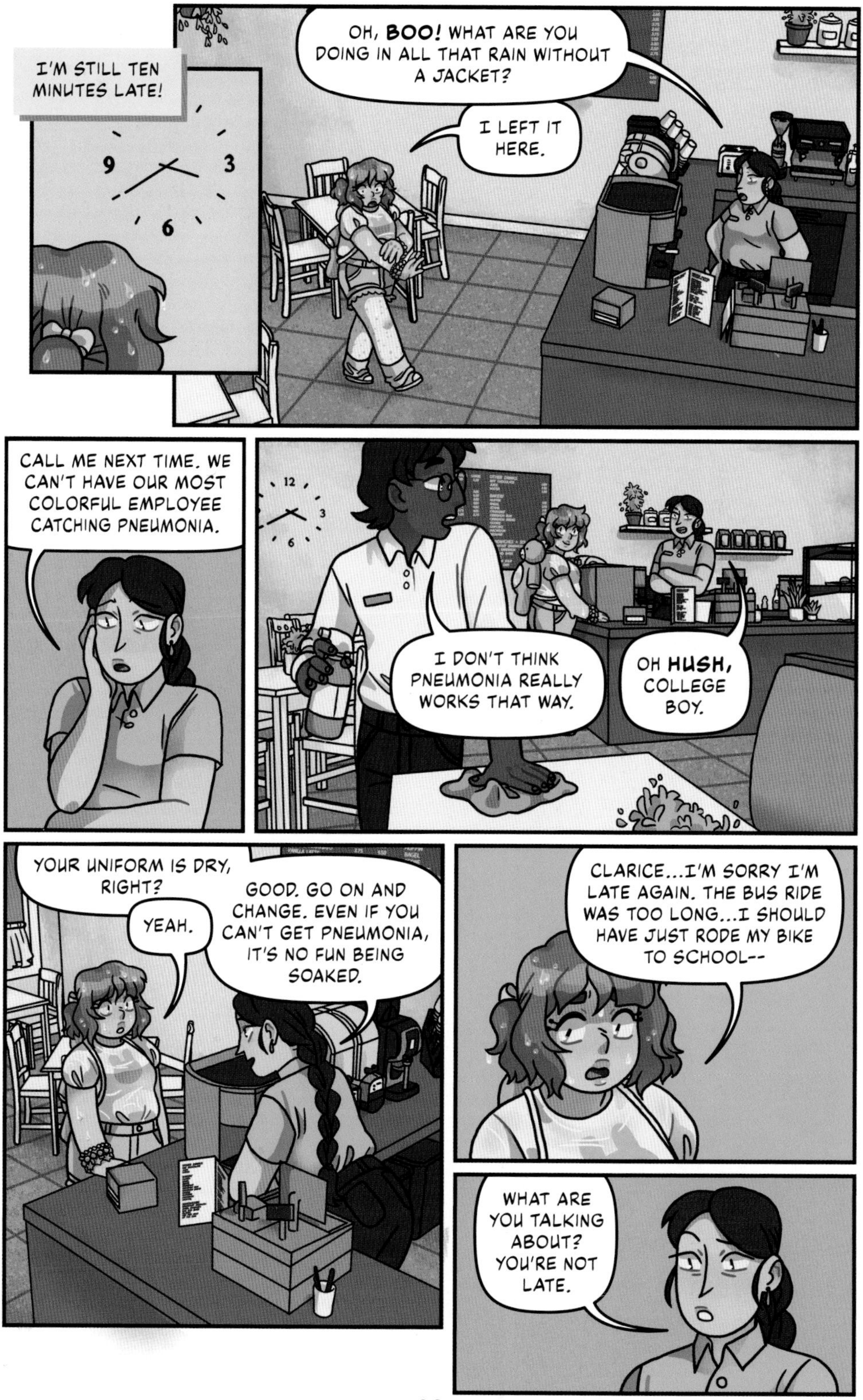

I'M STILL TEN MINUTES LATE!
OH, BOO! WHAT ARE YOU DOING IN ALL THAT RAIN WITHOUT A JACKET?
I LEFT IT HERE.
CALL ME NEXT TIME. WE CAN'T HAVE OUR MOST COLORFUL EMPLOYEE CATCHING PNEUMONIA.
I DON'T THINK PNEUMONIA REALLY WORKS THAT WAY.
OH HUSH, COLLEGE BOY.
YOUR UNIFORM IS DRY, RIGHT?
YEAH.
GOOD. GO ON AND CHANGE. EVEN IF YOU CAN'T GET PNEUMONIA, IT'S NO FUN BEING SOAKED.
CLARICE...I'M SORRY I'M LATE AGAIN. THE BUS RIDE WAS TOO LONG...I SHOULD HAVE JUST RODE MY BIKE TO SCHOOL--
WHAT ARE YOU TALKING ABOUT? YOU'RE NOT LATE.

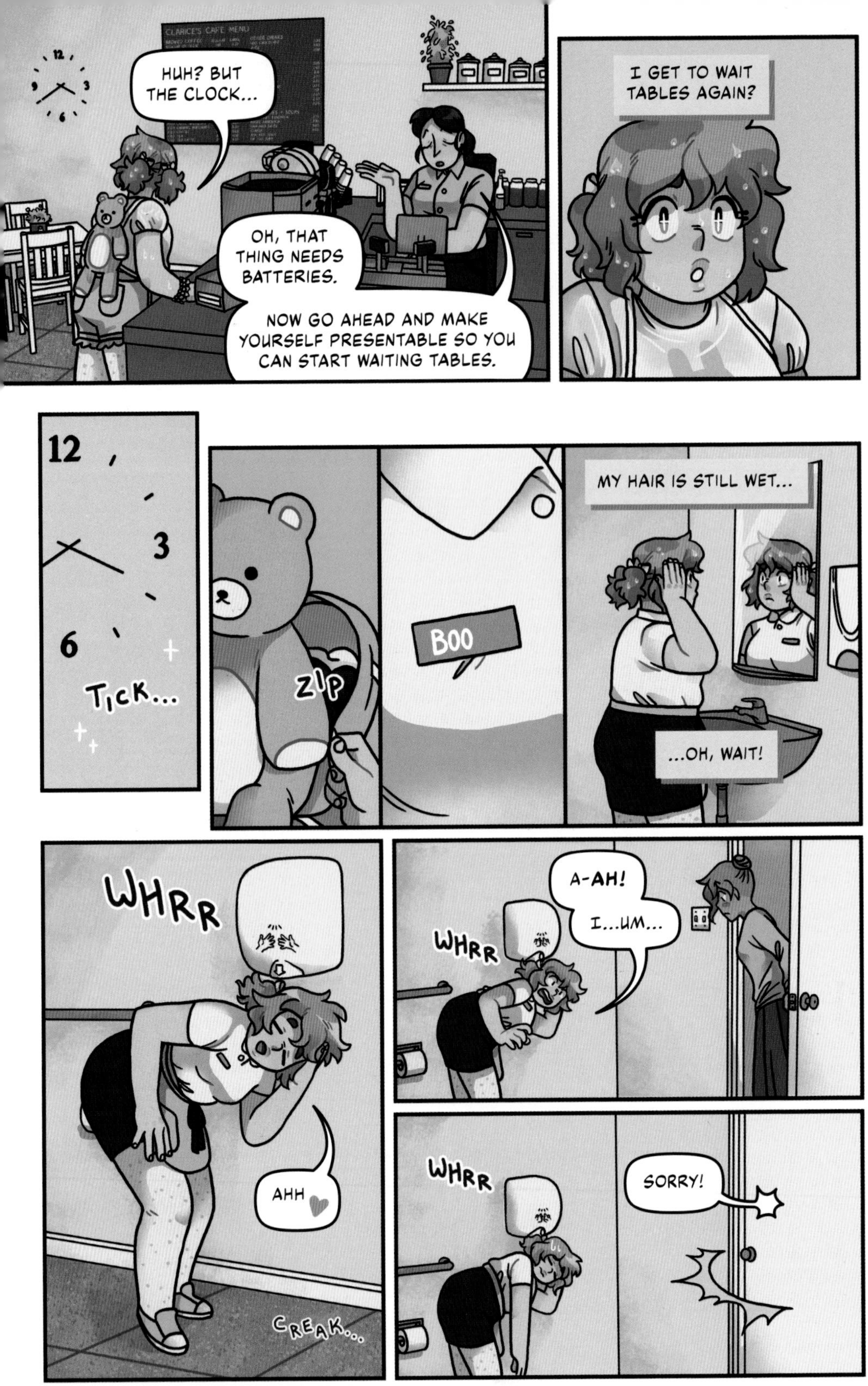

HUH? BUT THE CLOCK...
OH, THAT THING NEEDS BATTERIES.
NOW GO AHEAD AND MAKE YOURSELF PRESENTABLE SO YOU CAN START WAITING TABLES.
I GET TO WAIT TABLES AGAIN?
TICK...
ZIP
BOO
MY HAIR IS STILL WET...
...OH, WAIT!
WHRR
AHH
CREAK...
WHRR
A-AH!
I...UM...
WHRR
SORRY!

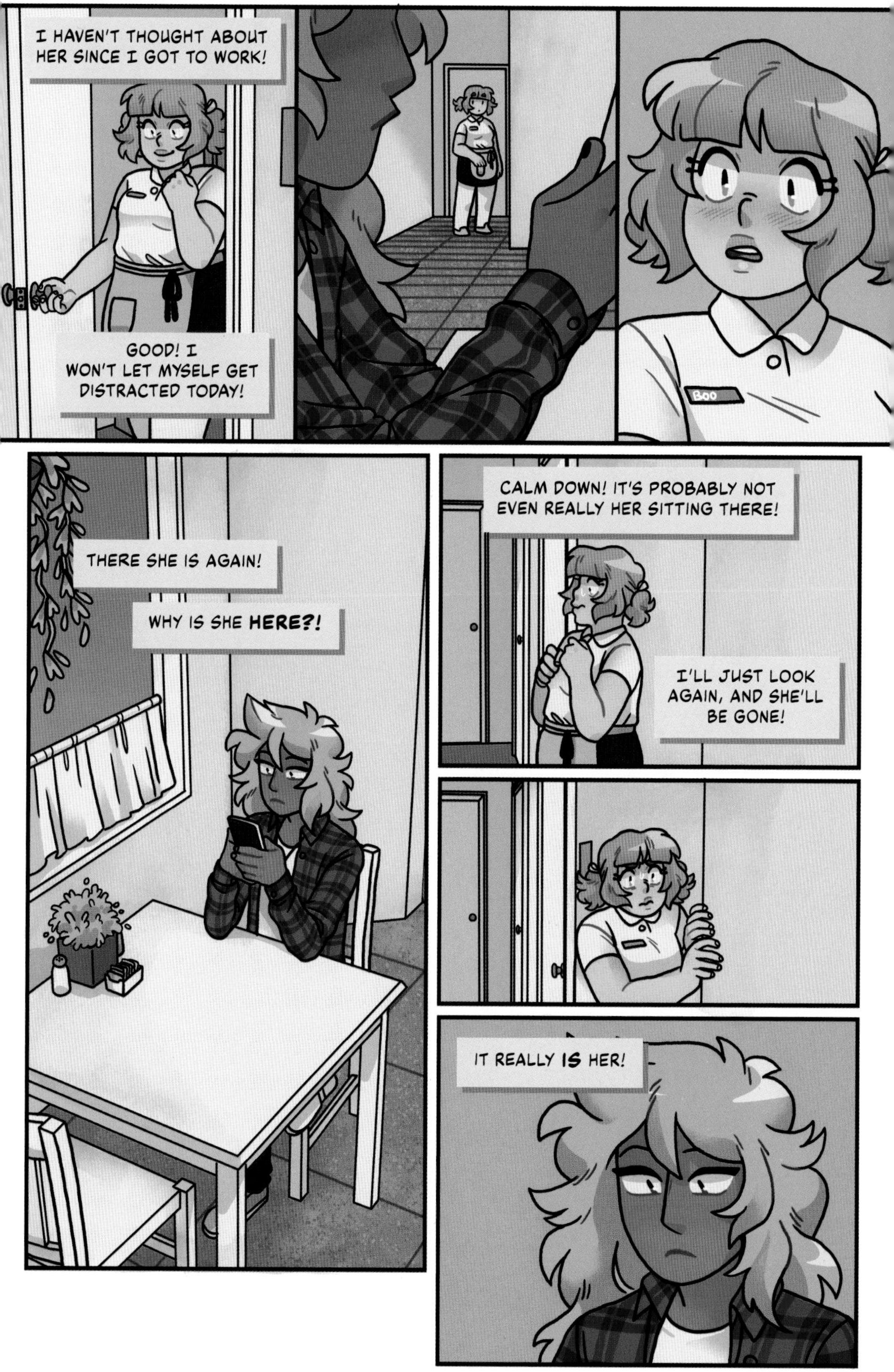
I HAVEN'T THOUGHT ABOUT HER SINCE I GOT TO WORK!
GOOD! I WON'T LET MYSELF GET DISTRACTED TODAY!
BOO
THERE SHE IS AGAIN!
WHY IS SHE **HERE?!**
CALM DOWN! IT'S PROBABLY NOT EVEN REALLY HER SITTING THERE!
I'LL JUST LOOK AGAIN, AND SHE'LL BE GONE!
IT REALLY **IS** HER!

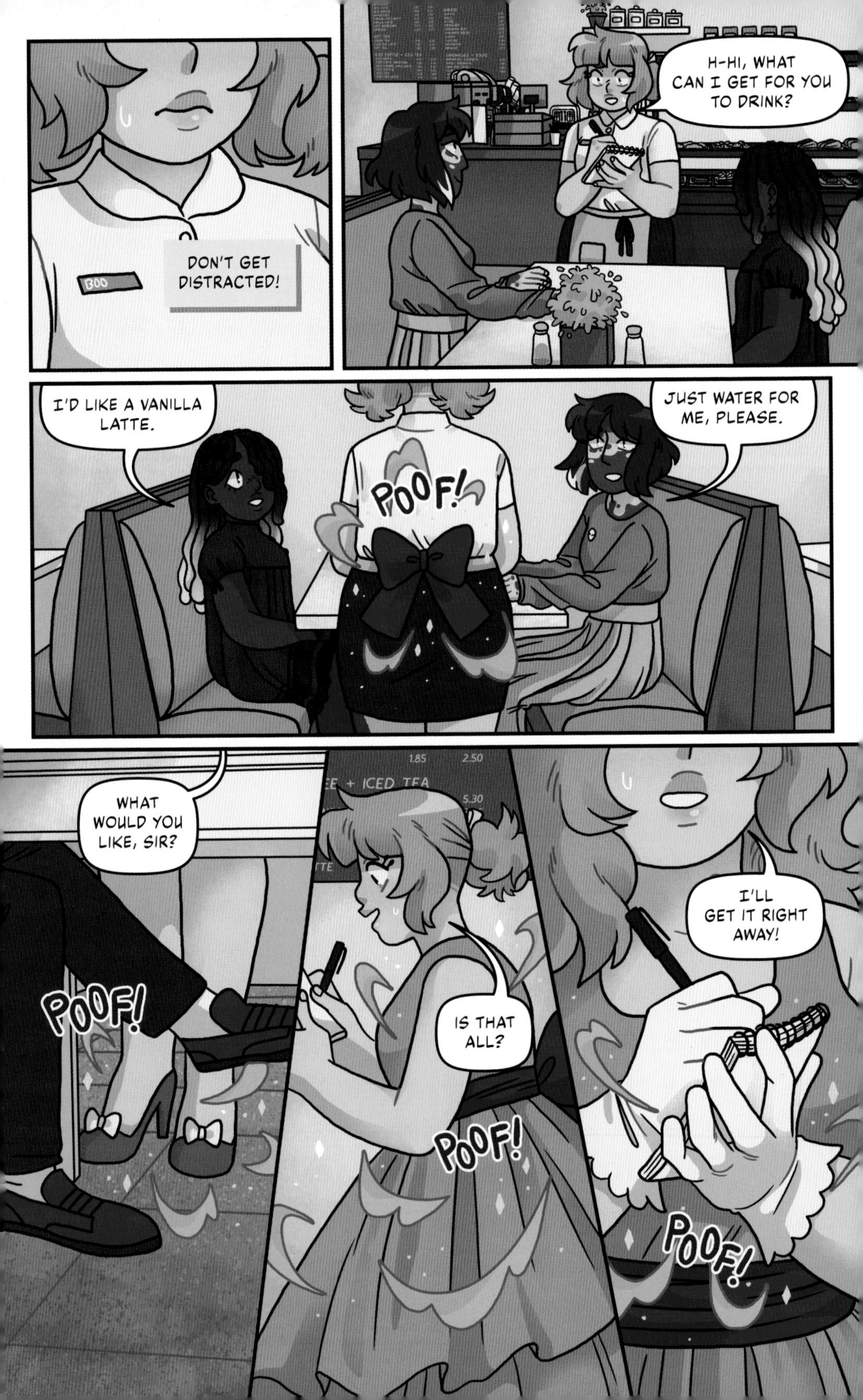
BOO
DON'T GET DISTRACTED!
H-HI, WHAT CAN I GET FOR YOU TO DRINK?
I'D LIKE A VANILLA LATTE.
JUST WATER FOR ME, PLEASE.
POOF!
WHAT WOULD YOU LIKE, SIR?
POOF!
IS THAT ALL?
POOF!
I'LL GET IT RIGHT AWAY!
POOF!

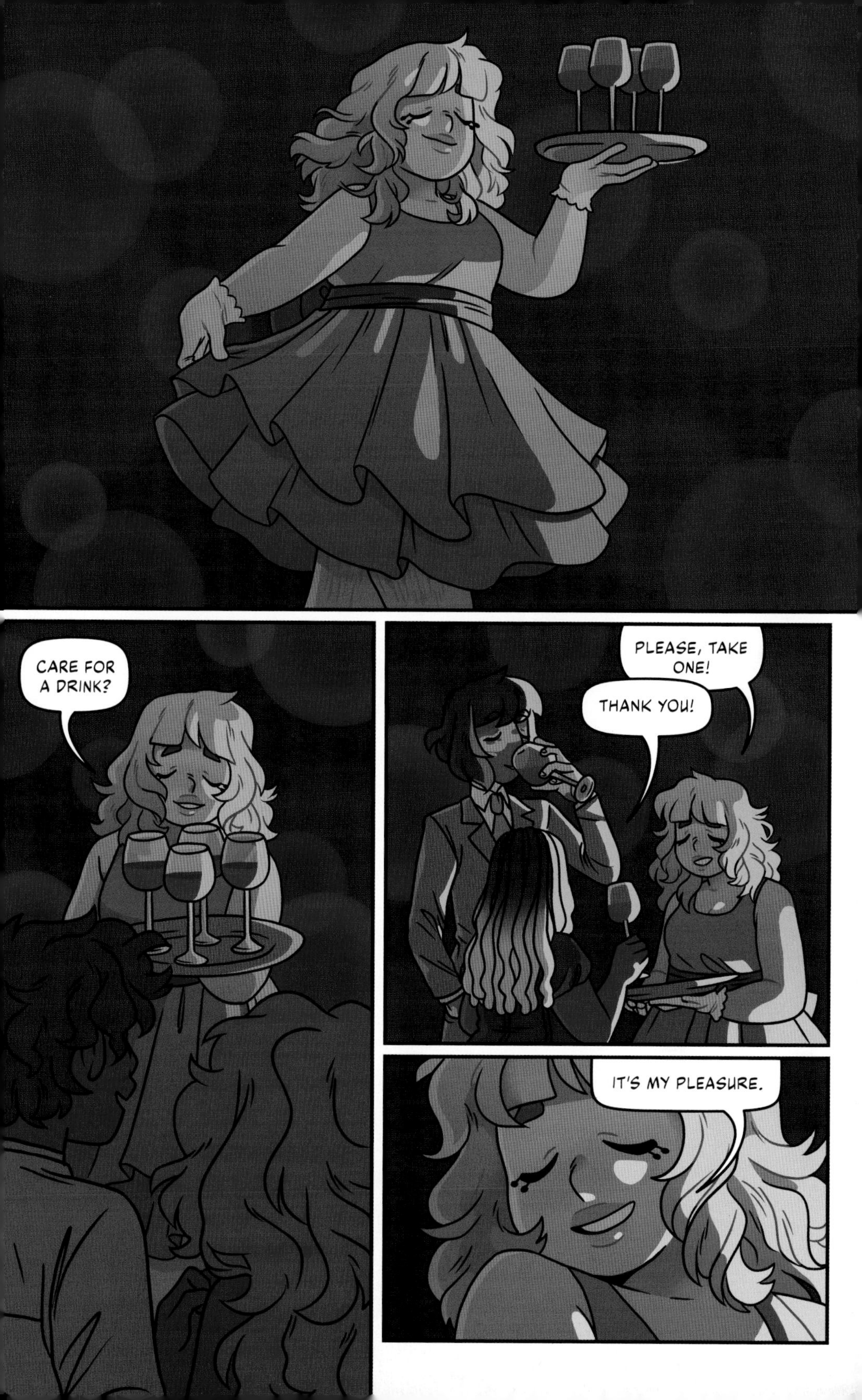
CARE FOR A DRINK?
PLEASE, TAKE ONE!
THANK YOU!
IT'S MY PLEASURE.

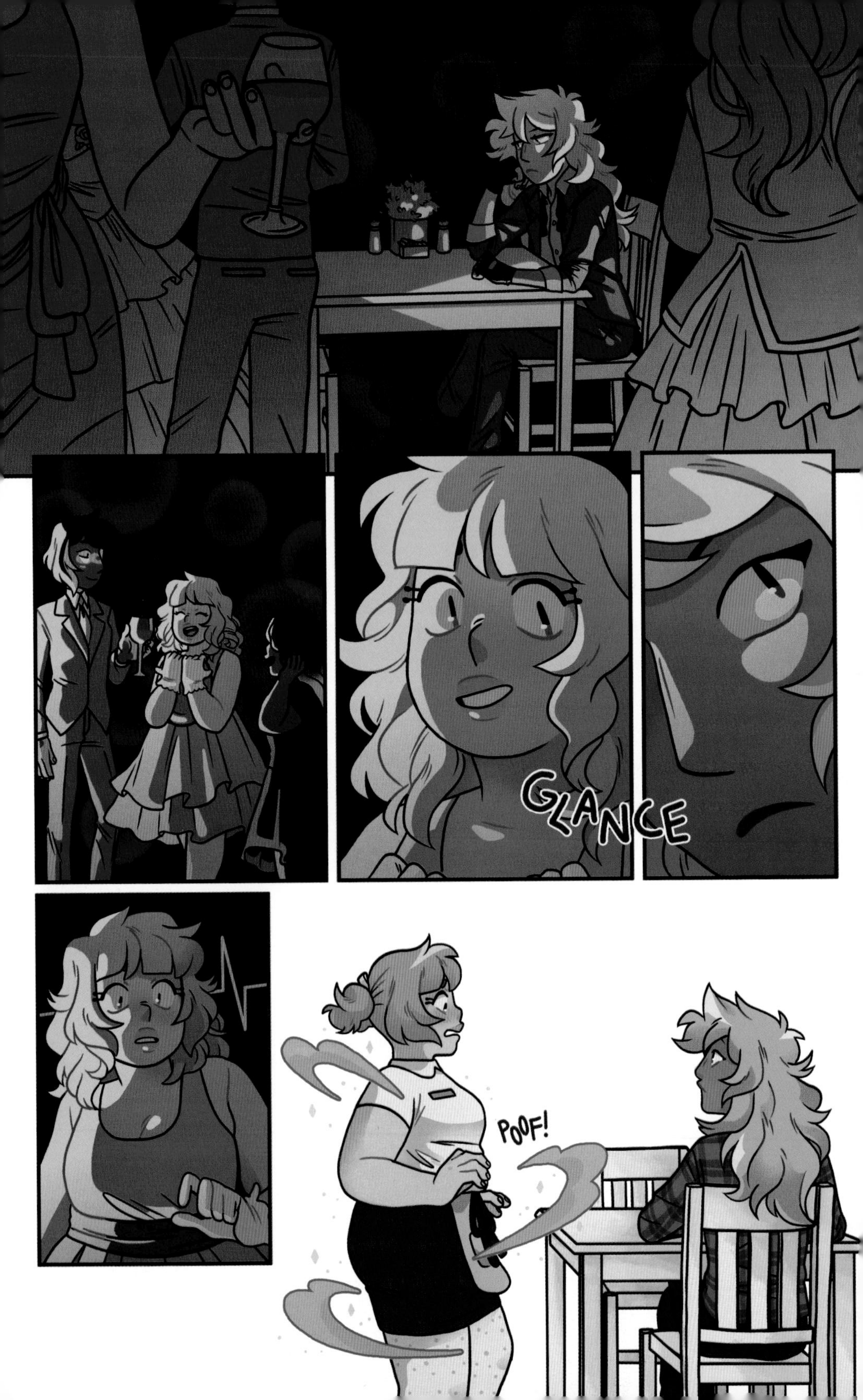
GLANCE
POOF!

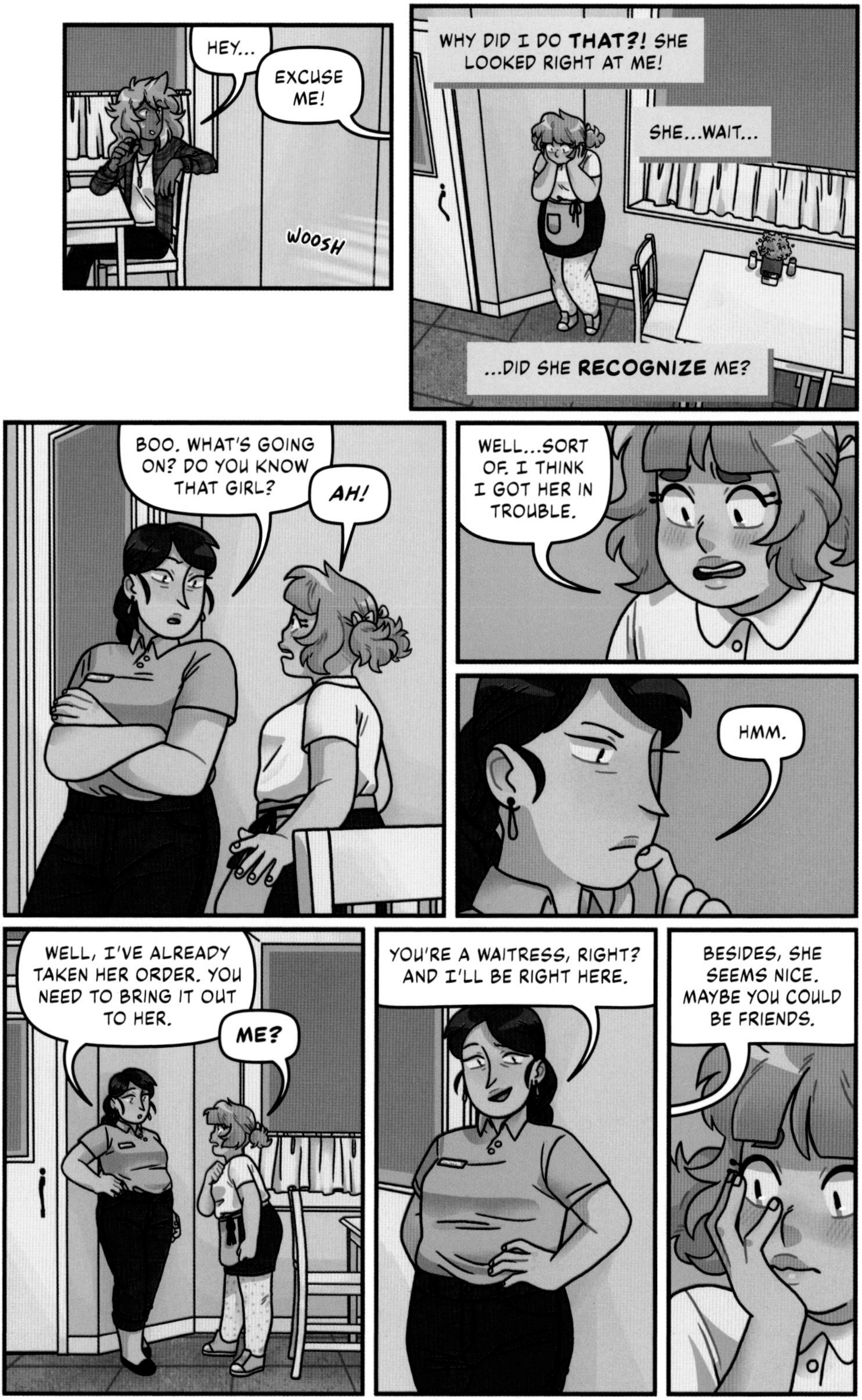

HEY...
EXCUSE ME!
WOOSH
WHY DID I DO **THAT?!** SHE LOOKED RIGHT AT ME!
SHE...WAIT...
...DID SHE **RECOGNIZE** ME?
BOO. WHAT'S GOING ON? DO YOU KNOW THAT GIRL?
AH!
WELL...SORT OF. I THINK I GOT HER IN TROUBLE.
HMM.
WELL, I'VE ALREADY TAKEN HER ORDER. YOU NEED TO BRING IT OUT TO HER.
ME?
YOU'RE A WAITRESS, RIGHT? AND I'LL BE RIGHT HERE.
BESIDES, SHE SEEMS NICE. MAYBE YOU COULD BE FRIENDS.

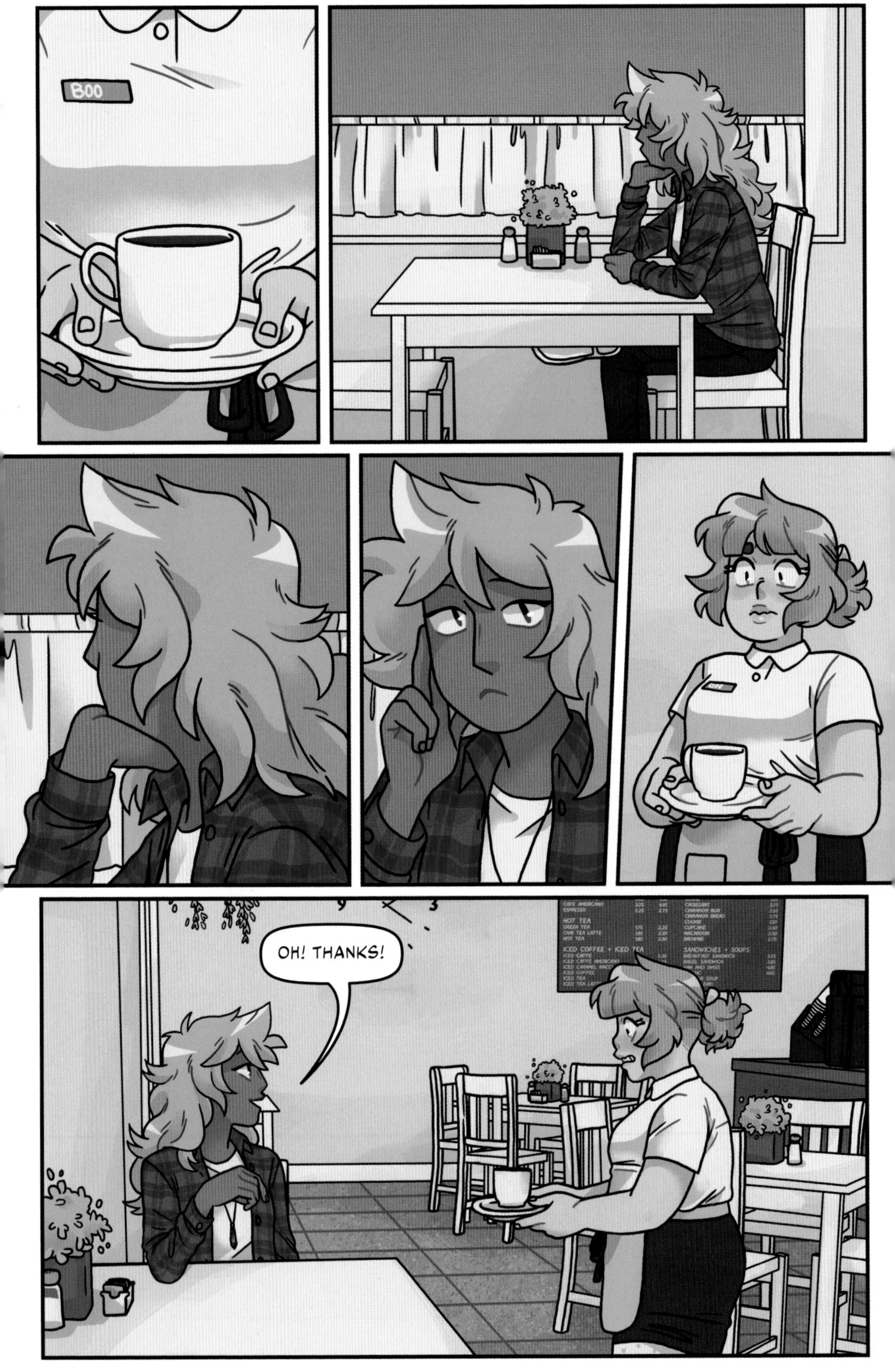
BOO
CAFE AMERICANO
ESPRESSO
CROISSANT
HOT TEA
GREEN TEA
CHAI TEA LATTE
HOT TEA
COOKIE
CUPCAKE
MACAROON
BROWNIE
ICED COFFEE + ICED TEA
ICED CAFFE
ICED CAFFE AMERICANO
ICED COFFEE
ICED TEA
SANDWICHES + SOUPS
BREAKFAST SANDWICH
BAGEL SANDWICH
HAM AND SWISS
OH! THANKS!

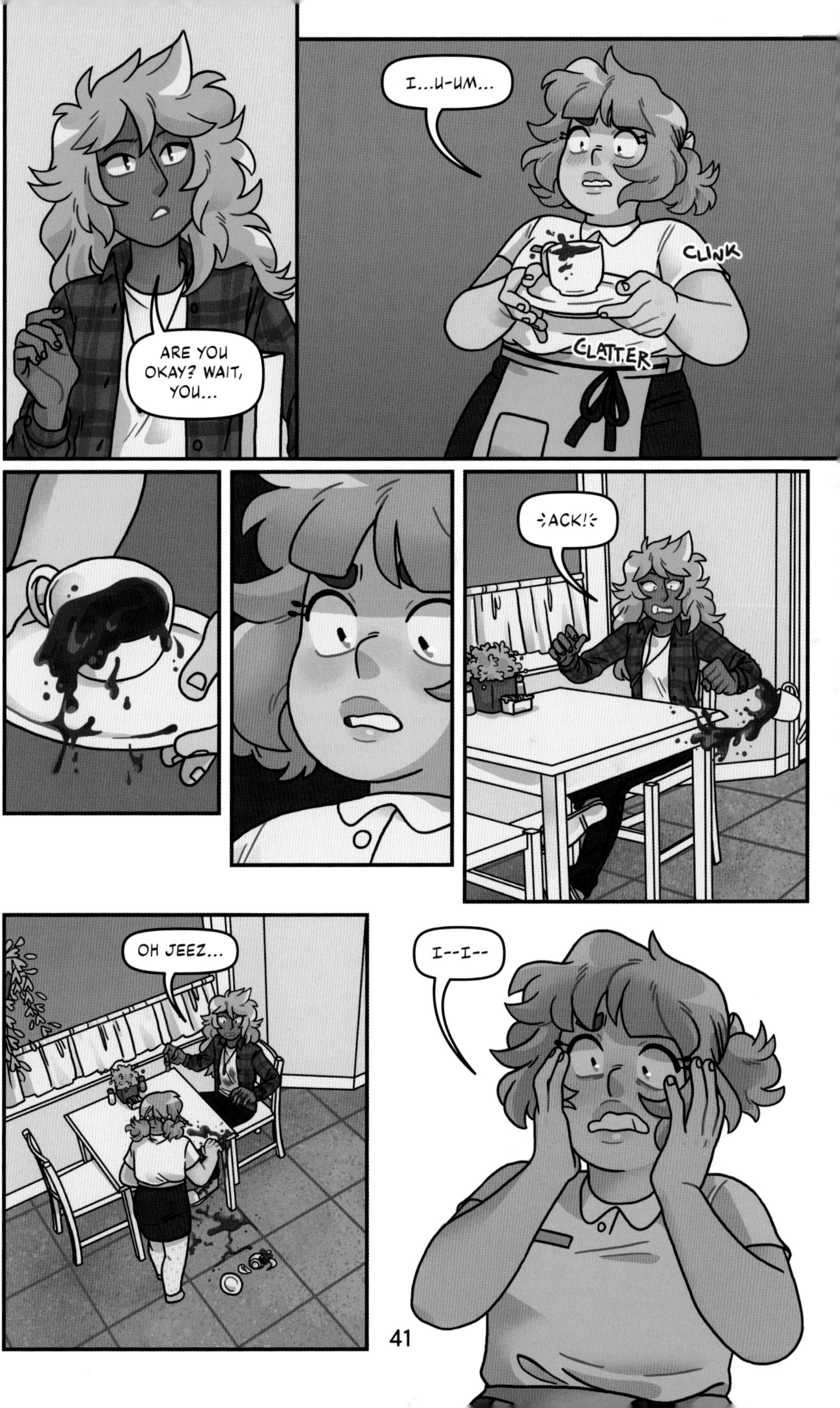
I...U-UM...
ARE YOU OKAY? WAIT, YOU...
CLINK
CLATTER
ACK!
OH JEEZ...
I--I--

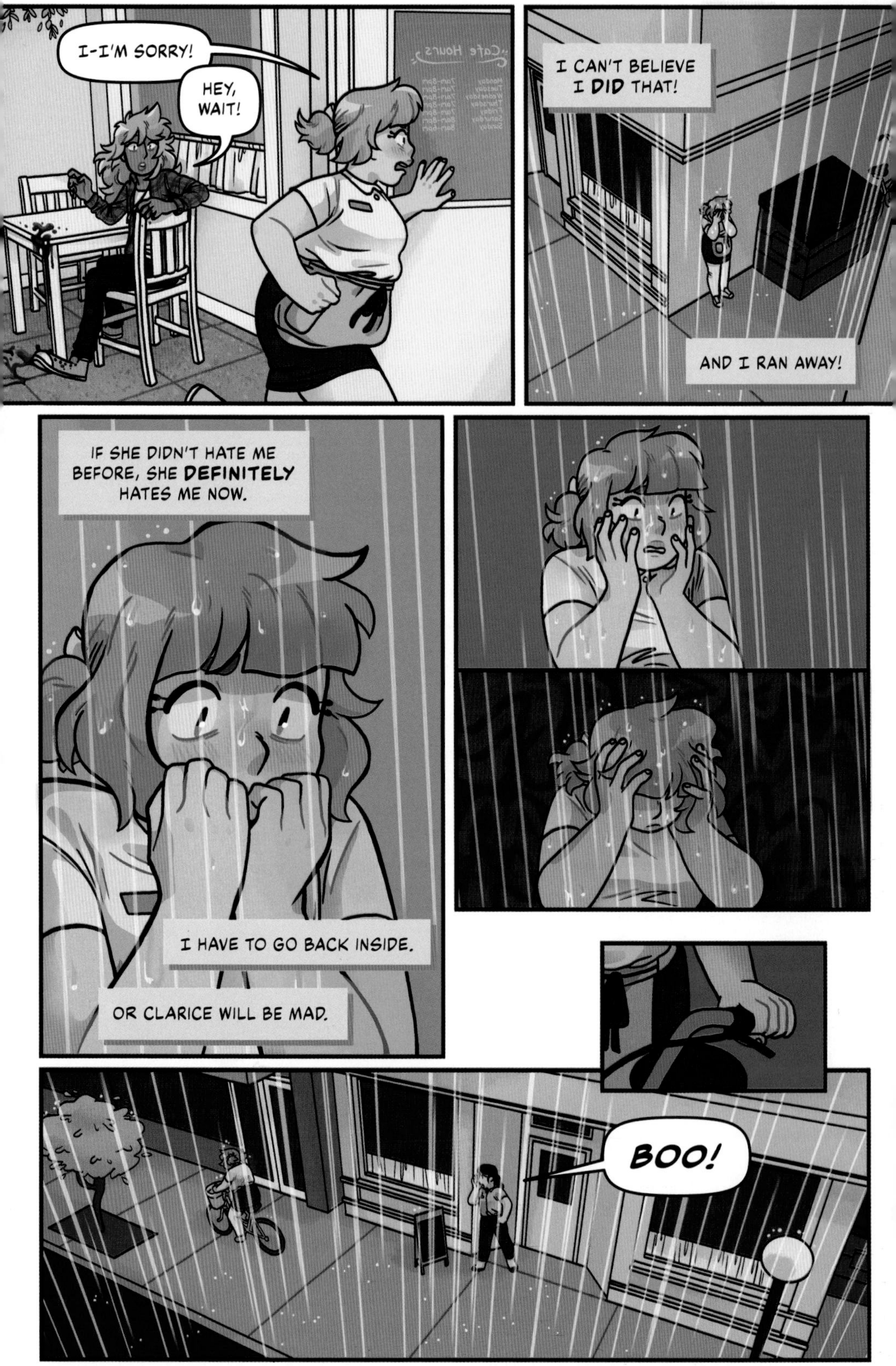
I-I'M SORRY!
HEY, WAIT!
I CAN'T BELIEVE I DID THAT!
AND I RAN AWAY!
IF SHE DIDN'T HATE ME BEFORE, SHE DEFINITELY HATES ME NOW.
I HAVE TO GO BACK INSIDE.
OR CLARICE WILL BE MAD.
BOO!

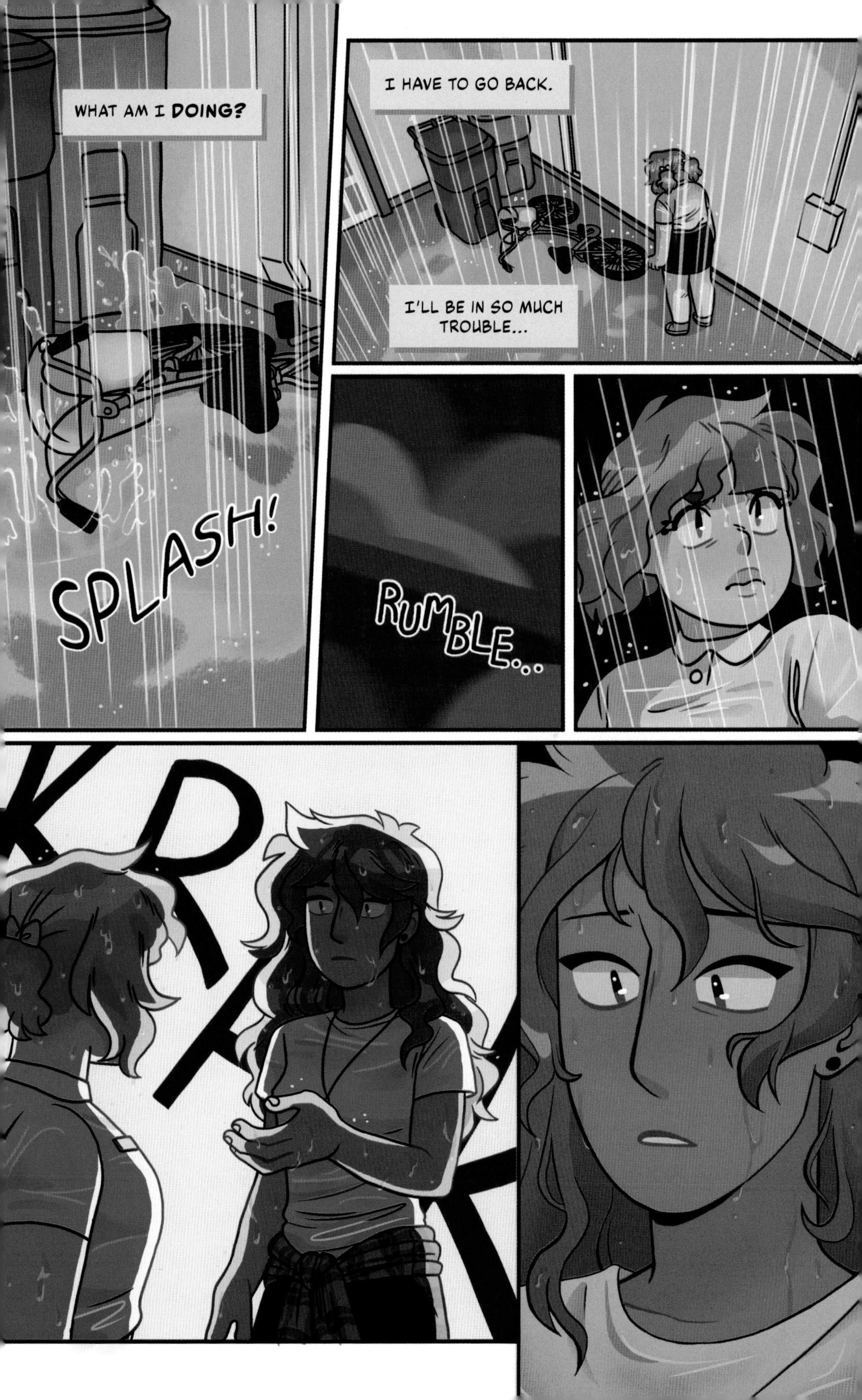
WHAT AM I DOING?
SPLASH!
I HAVE TO GO BACK.
I'LL BE IN SO MUCH TROUBLE...
RUMBLE...

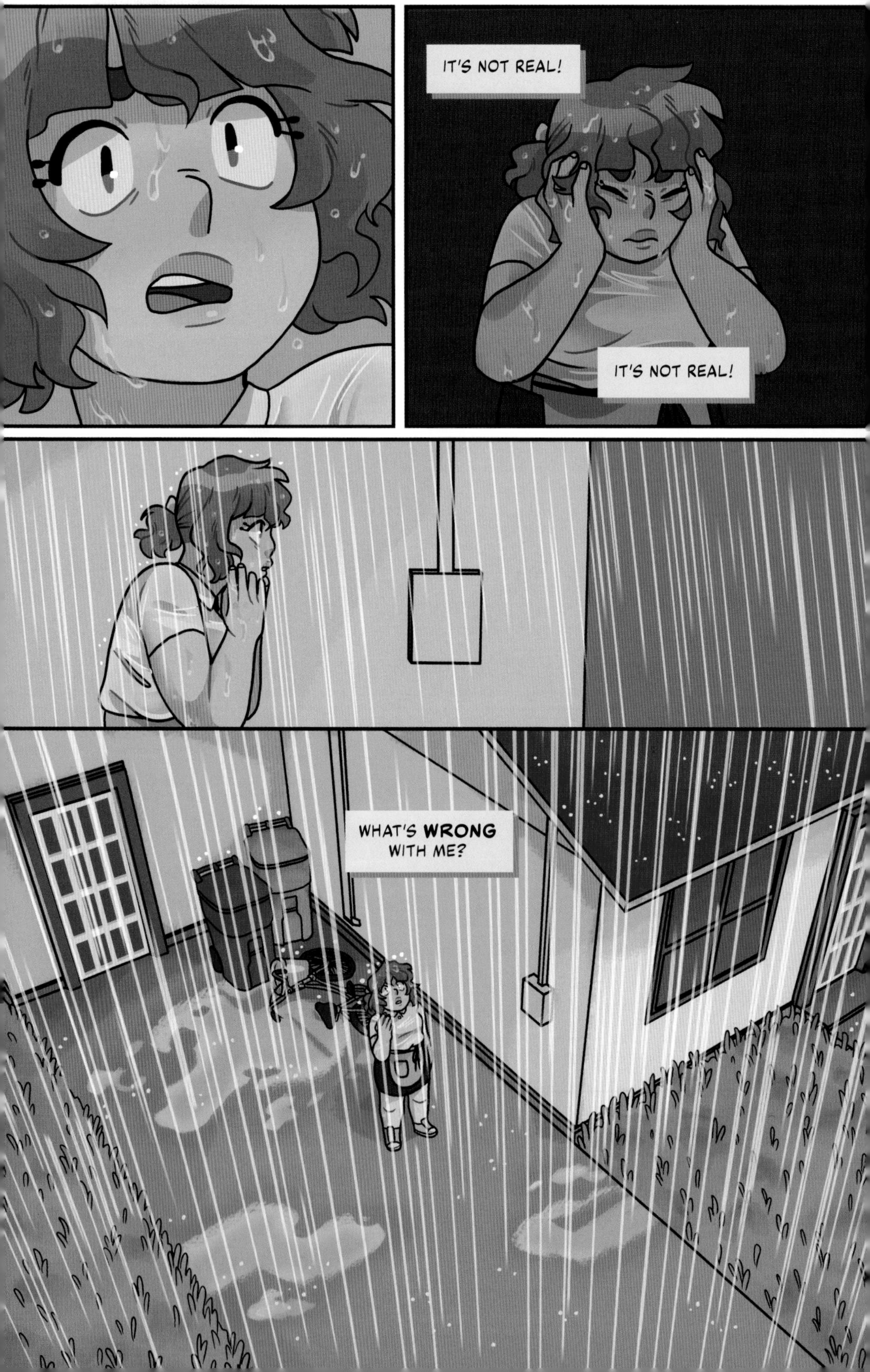
IT'S NOT REAL!
IT'S NOT REAL!
WHAT'S **WRONG** WITH ME?

CHAPTER 2

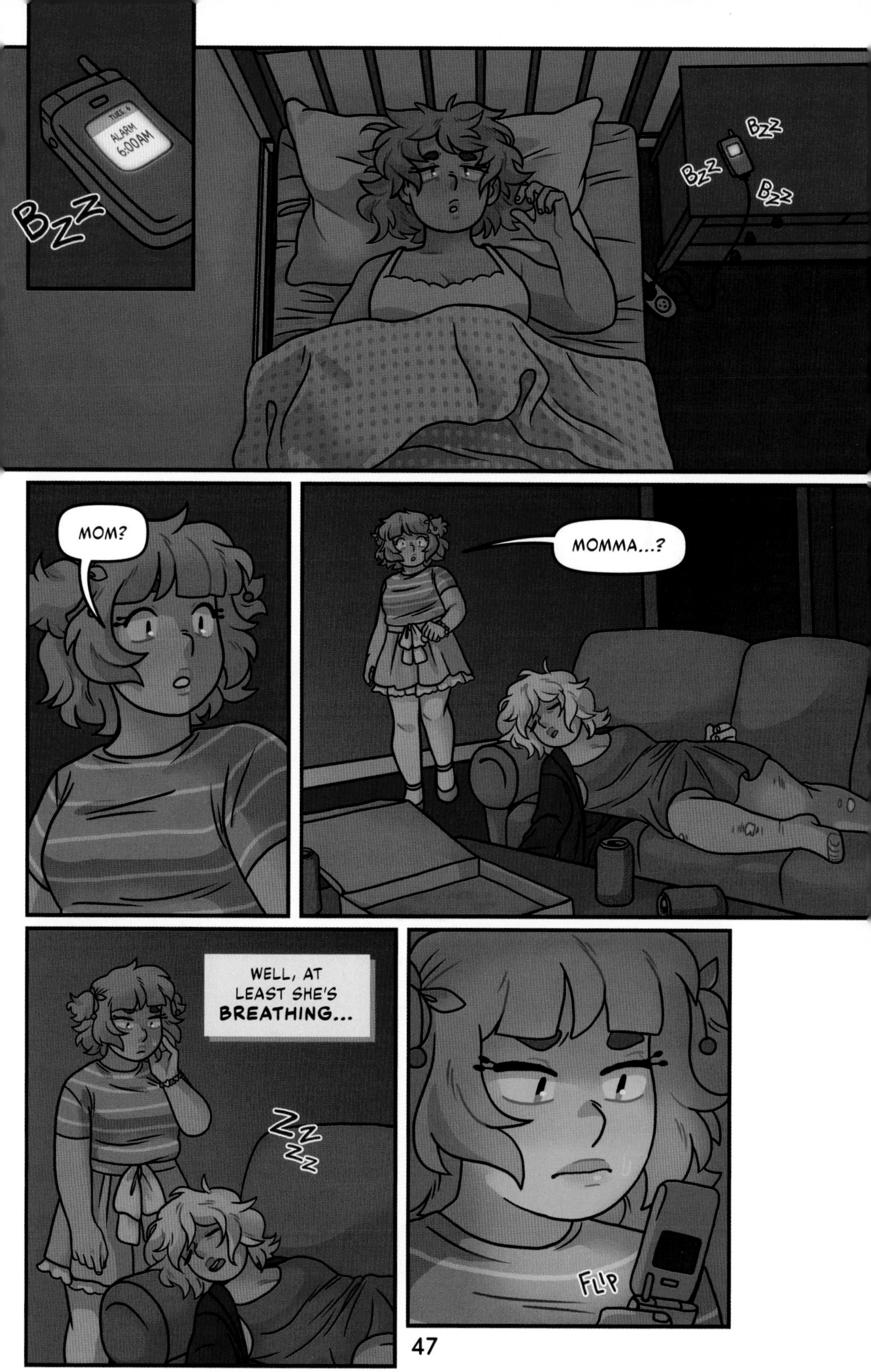
TUES. 5
ALARM
6:00AM
BZZ
BZZ
BZZ
BZZ
MOM?
MOMMA...?
WELL, AT LEAST SHE'S BREATHING...
ZZ
ZZ
FLIP

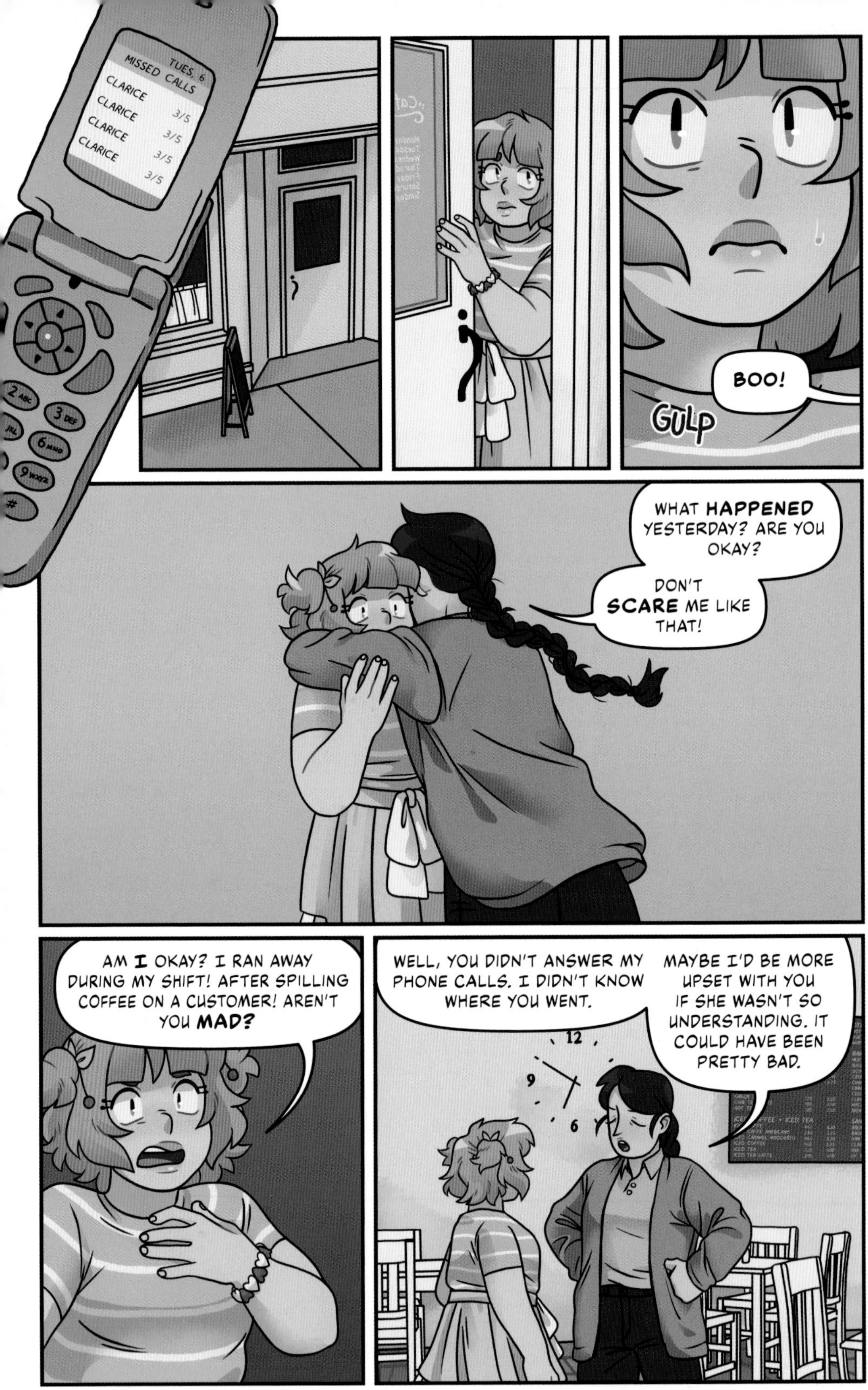
TUES, 6
MISSED CALLS
CLARICE 3/5
CLARICE 3/5
CLARICE 3/5
CLARICE 3/5
BOO!
GULP
WHAT HAPPENED YESTERDAY? ARE YOU OKAY?
DON'T SCARE ME LIKE THAT!
AM I OKAY? I RAN AWAY DURING MY SHIFT! AFTER SPILLING COFFEE ON A CUSTOMER! AREN'T YOU MAD?
WELL, YOU DIDN'T ANSWER MY PHONE CALLS. I DIDN'T KNOW WHERE YOU WENT.
MAYBE I'D BE MORE UPSET WITH YOU IF SHE WASN'T SO UNDERSTANDING. IT COULD HAVE BEEN PRETTY BAD.

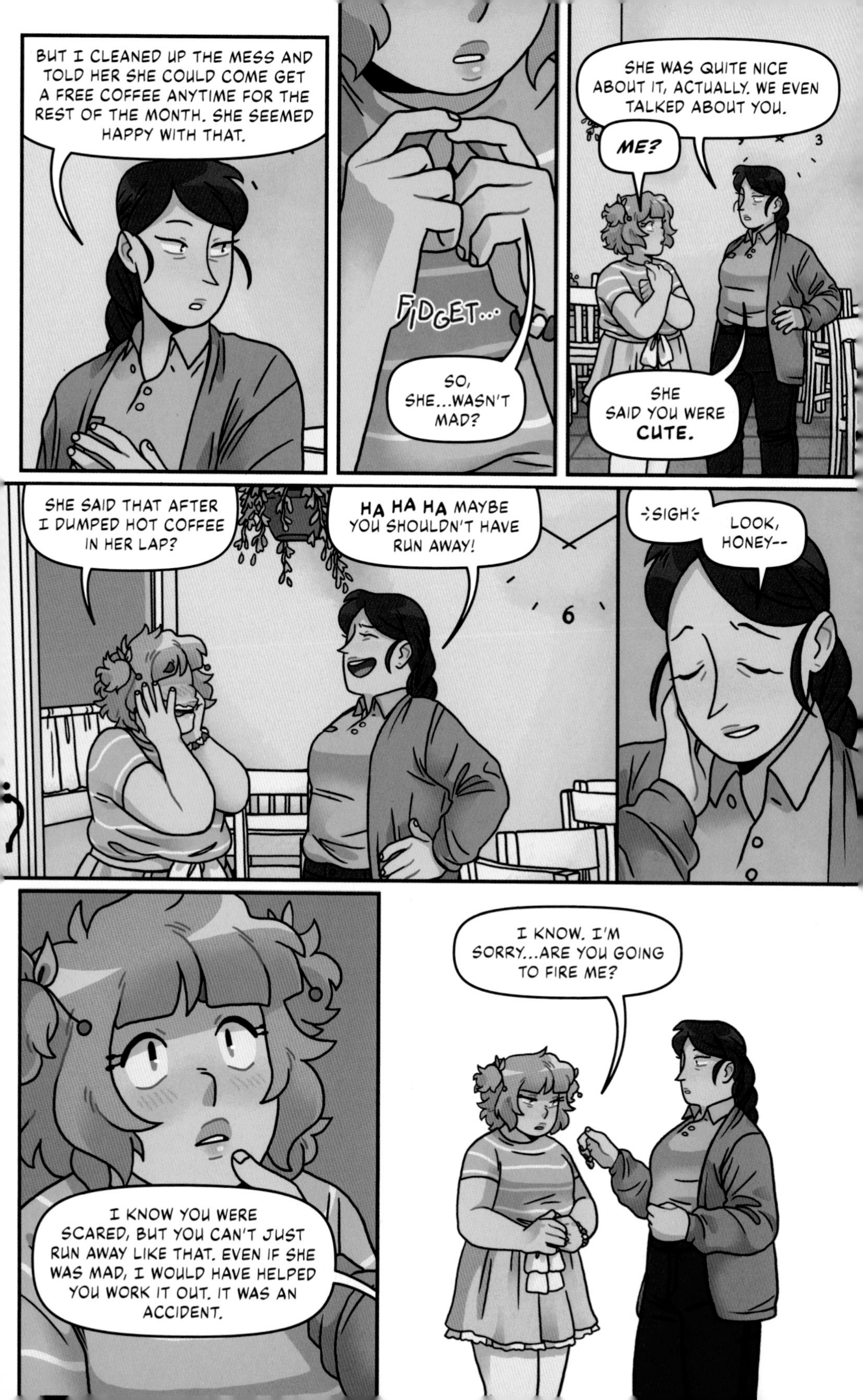
BUT I CLEANED UP THE MESS AND TOLD HER SHE COULD COME GET A FREE COFFEE ANYTIME FOR THE REST OF THE MONTH. SHE SEEMED HAPPY WITH THAT.
FIDGET...
SO, SHE...WASN'T MAD?
SHE WAS QUITE NICE ABOUT IT, ACTUALLY. WE EVEN TALKED ABOUT YOU.
ME?
SHE SAID YOU WERE CUTE.
SHE SAID THAT AFTER I DUMPED HOT COFFEE IN HER LAP?
HA HA HA MAYBE YOU SHOULDN'T HAVE RUN AWAY!
SIGH
LOOK, HONEY--
I KNOW YOU WERE SCARED, BUT YOU CAN'T JUST RUN AWAY LIKE THAT. EVEN IF SHE WAS MAD, I WOULD HAVE HELPED YOU WORK IT OUT. IT WAS AN ACCIDENT.
I KNOW. I'M SORRY...ARE YOU GOING TO FIRE ME?

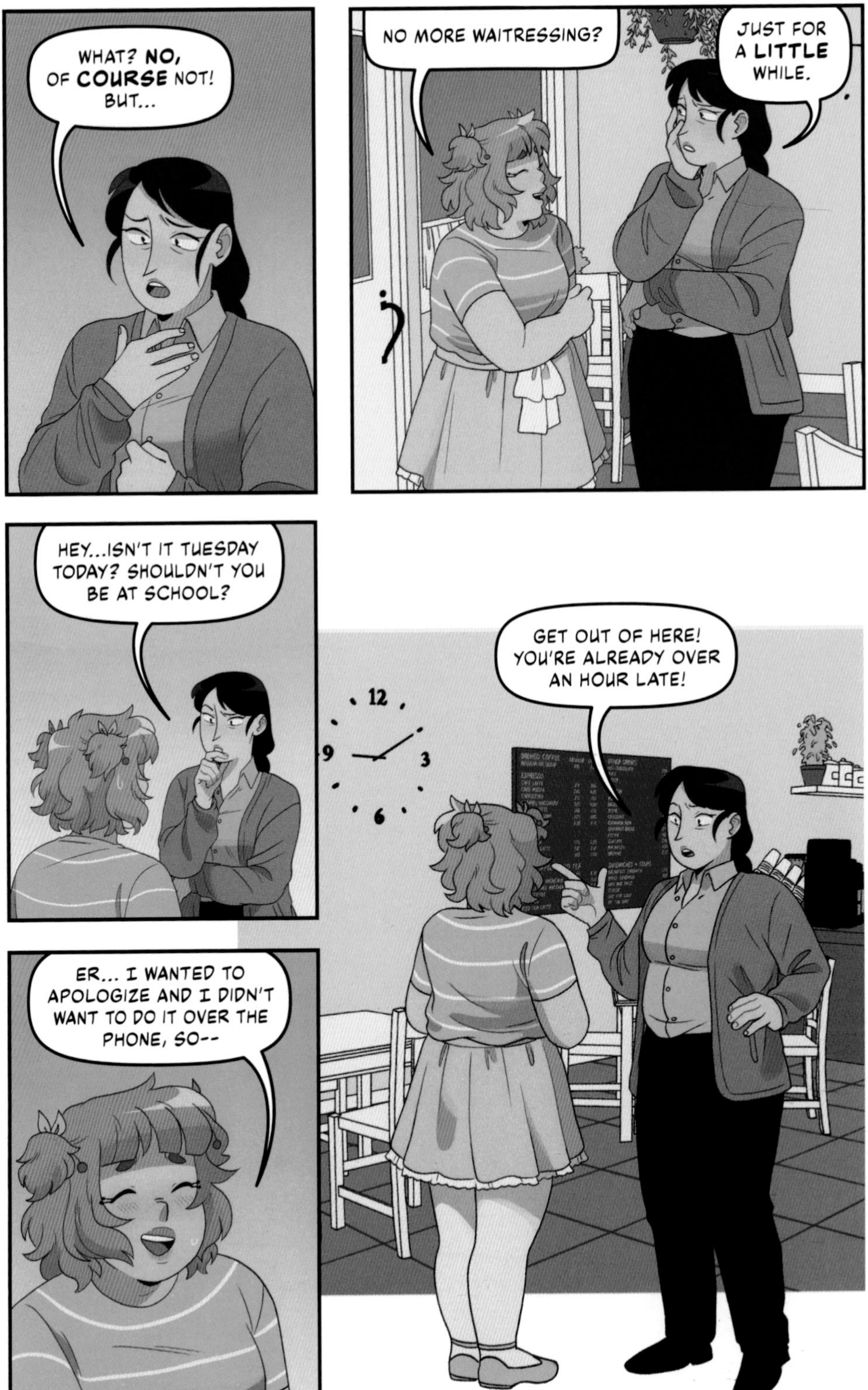
WHAT? NO, OF COURSE NOT! BUT...
NO MORE WAITRESSING?
JUST FOR A LITTLE WHILE.
HEY...ISN'T IT TUESDAY TODAY? SHOULDN'T YOU BE AT SCHOOL?
ER... I WANTED TO APOLOGIZE AND I DIDN'T WANT TO DO IT OVER THE PHONE, SO--
GET OUT OF HERE! YOU'RE ALREADY OVER AN HOUR LATE!

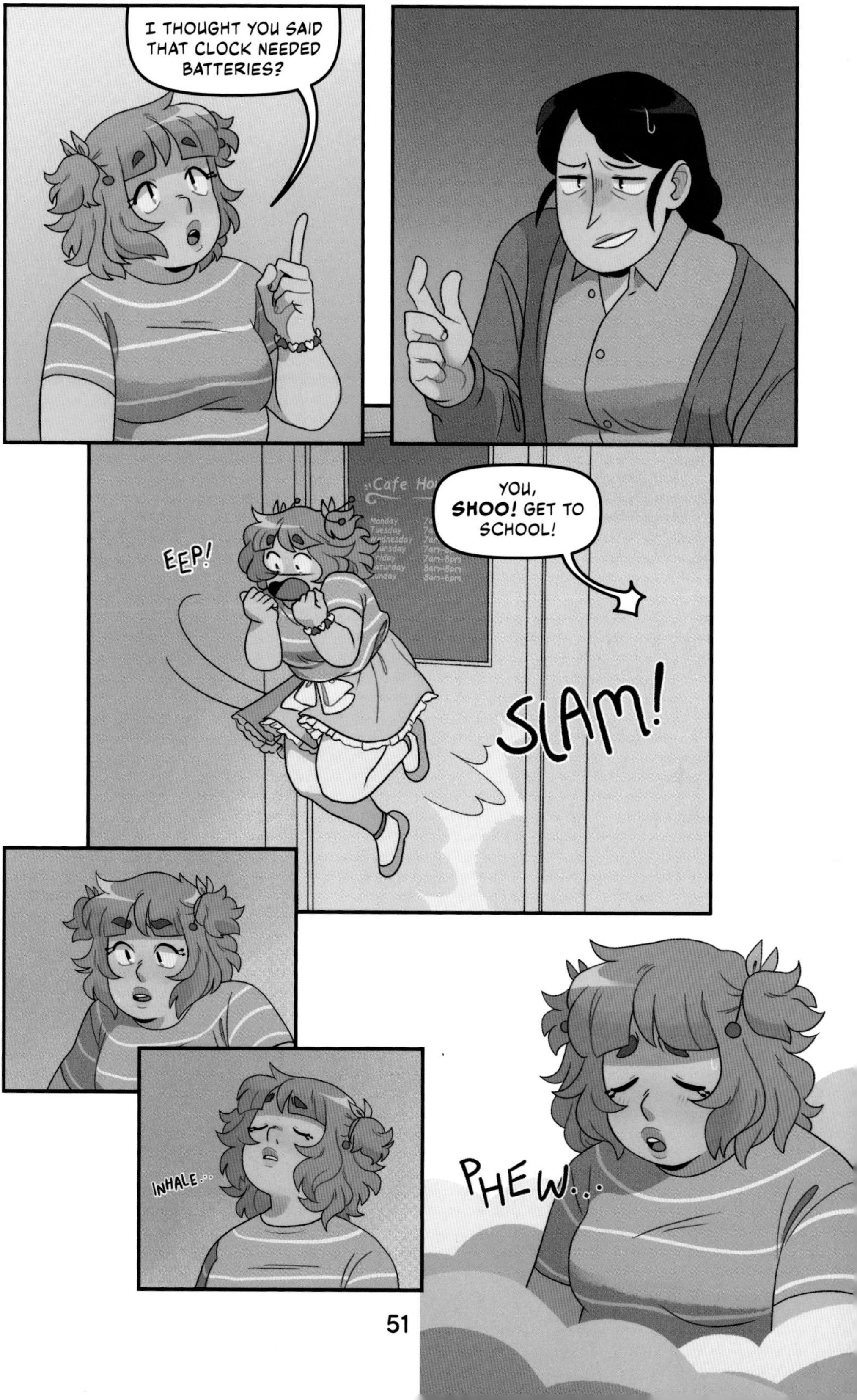
I THOUGHT YOU SAID THAT CLOCK NEEDED BATTERIES?
YOU, SHOO! GET TO SCHOOL!
EEP!
SLAM!
INHALE...
PHEW...

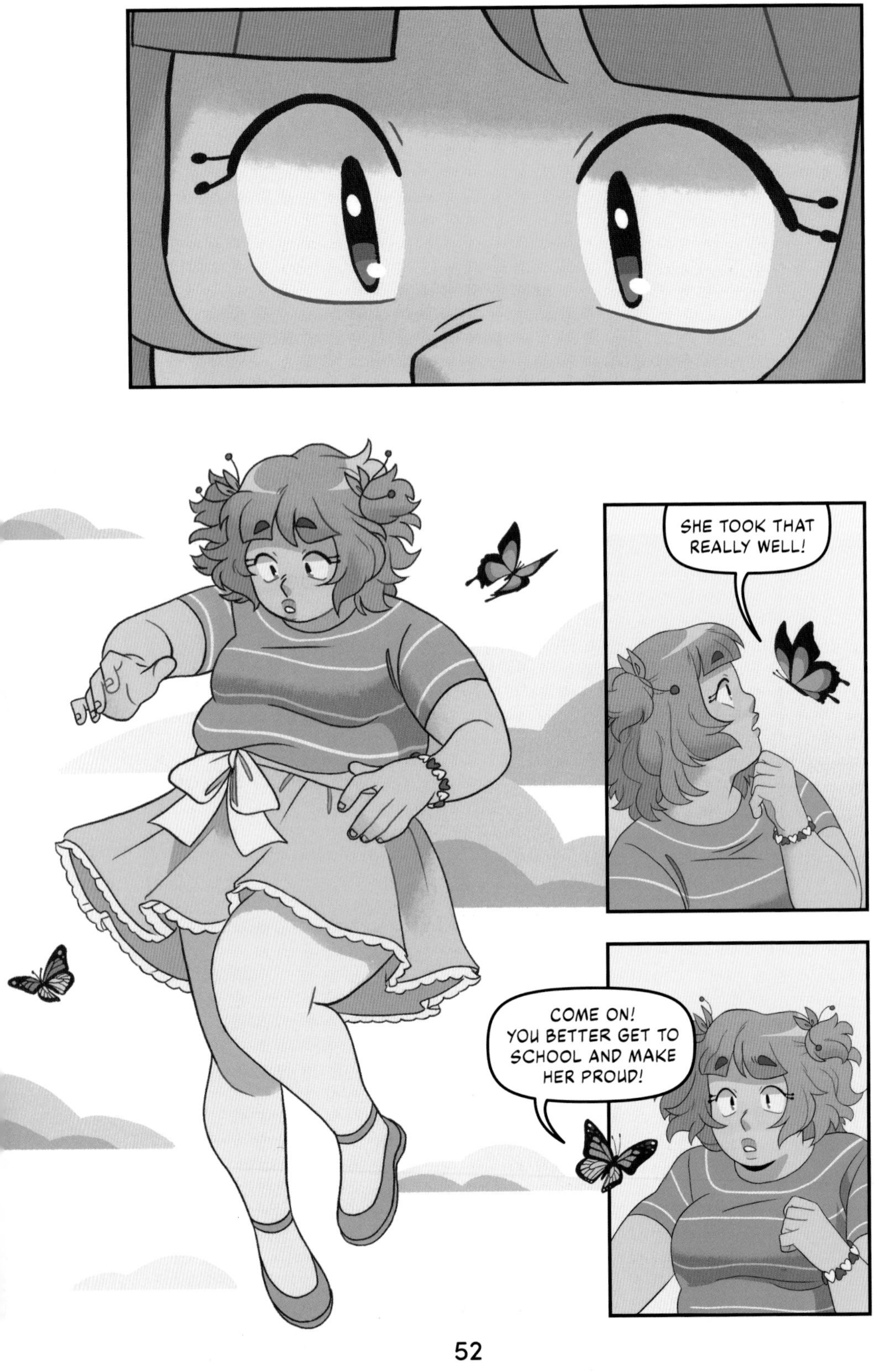
SHE TOOK THAT REALLY WELL!
COME ON! YOU BETTER GET TO SCHOOL AND MAKE HER PROUD!

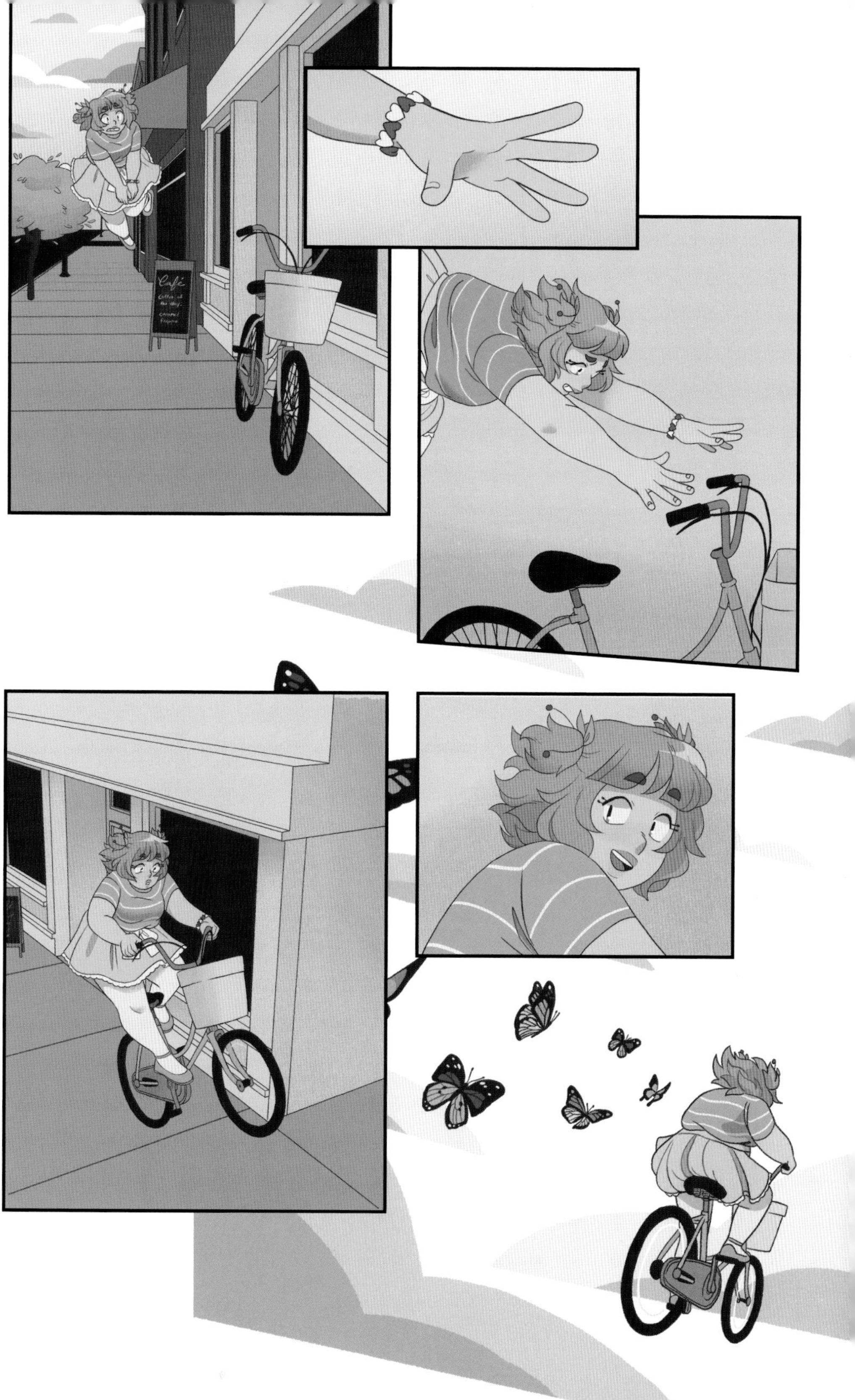
Café

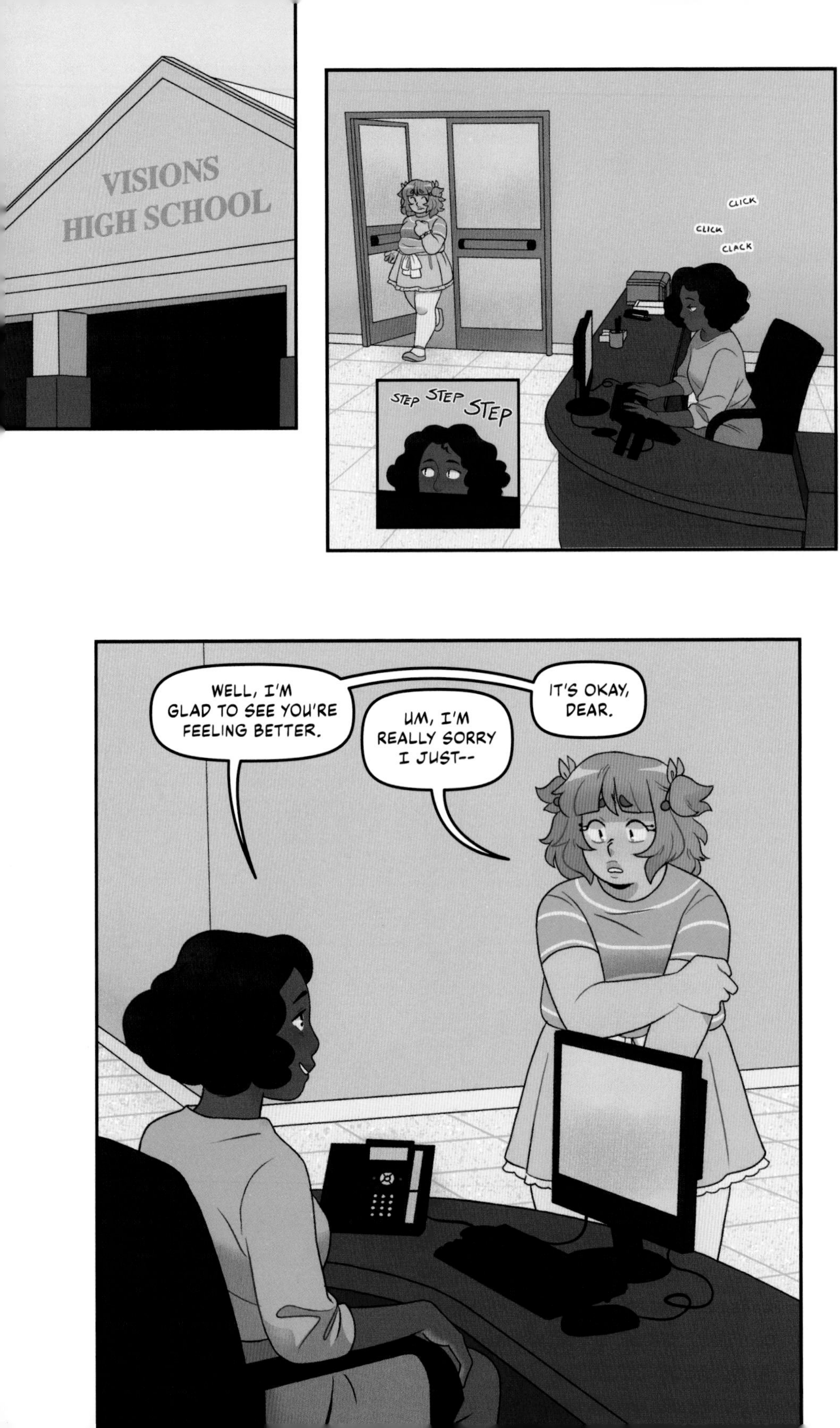
VISIONS HIGH SCHOOL
CLICK
CLICK
CLACK
STEP STEP STEP
UM, I'M REALLY SORRY I JUST--
IT'S OKAY, DEAR.
WELL, I'M GLAD TO SEE YOU'RE FEELING BETTER.

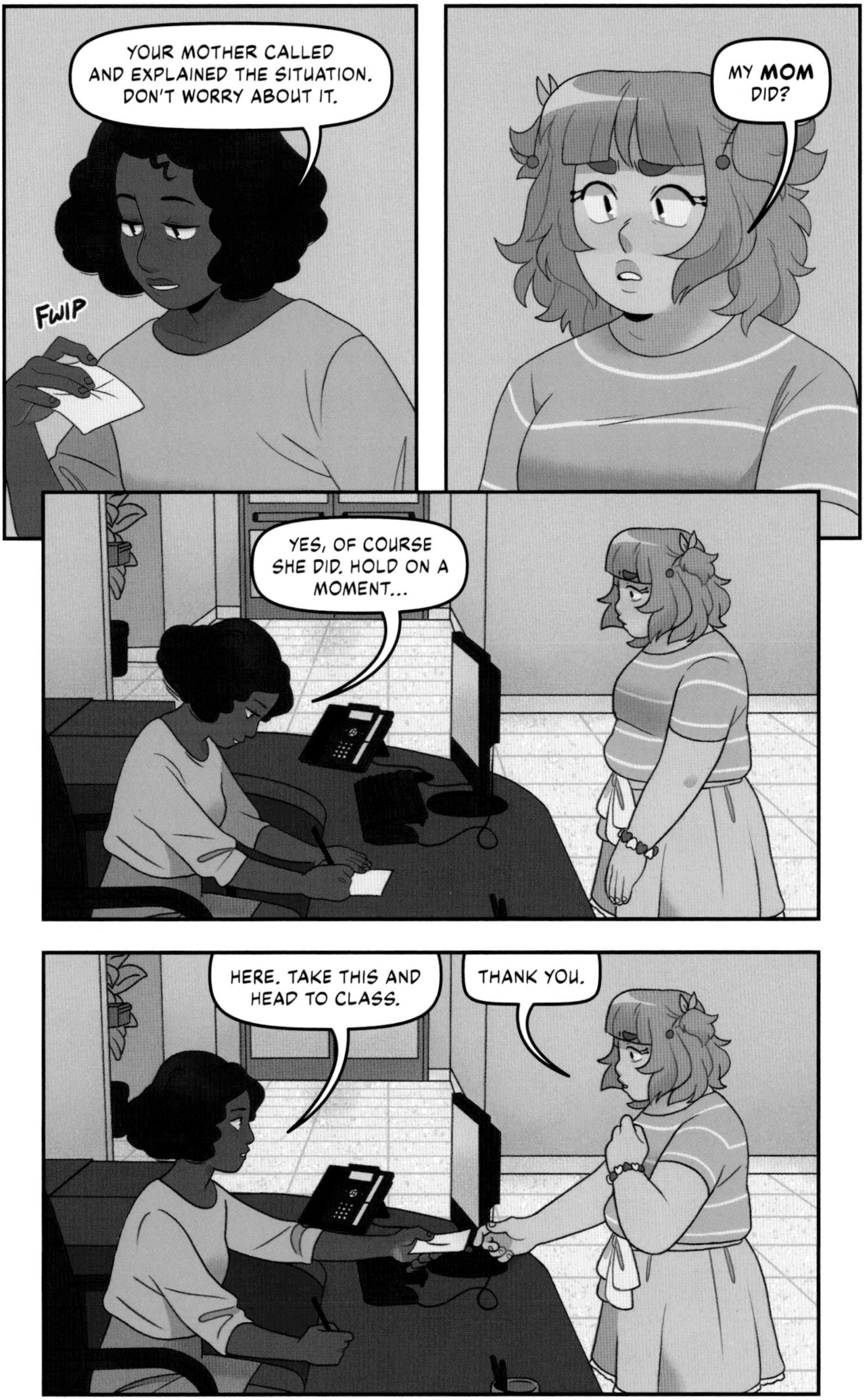
YOUR MOTHER CALLED AND EXPLAINED THE SITUATION. DON'T WORRY ABOUT IT.
FWIP
MY **MOM** DID?
YES, OF COURSE SHE DID. HOLD ON A MOMENT...
HERE. TAKE THIS AND HEAD TO CLASS.
THANK YOU.

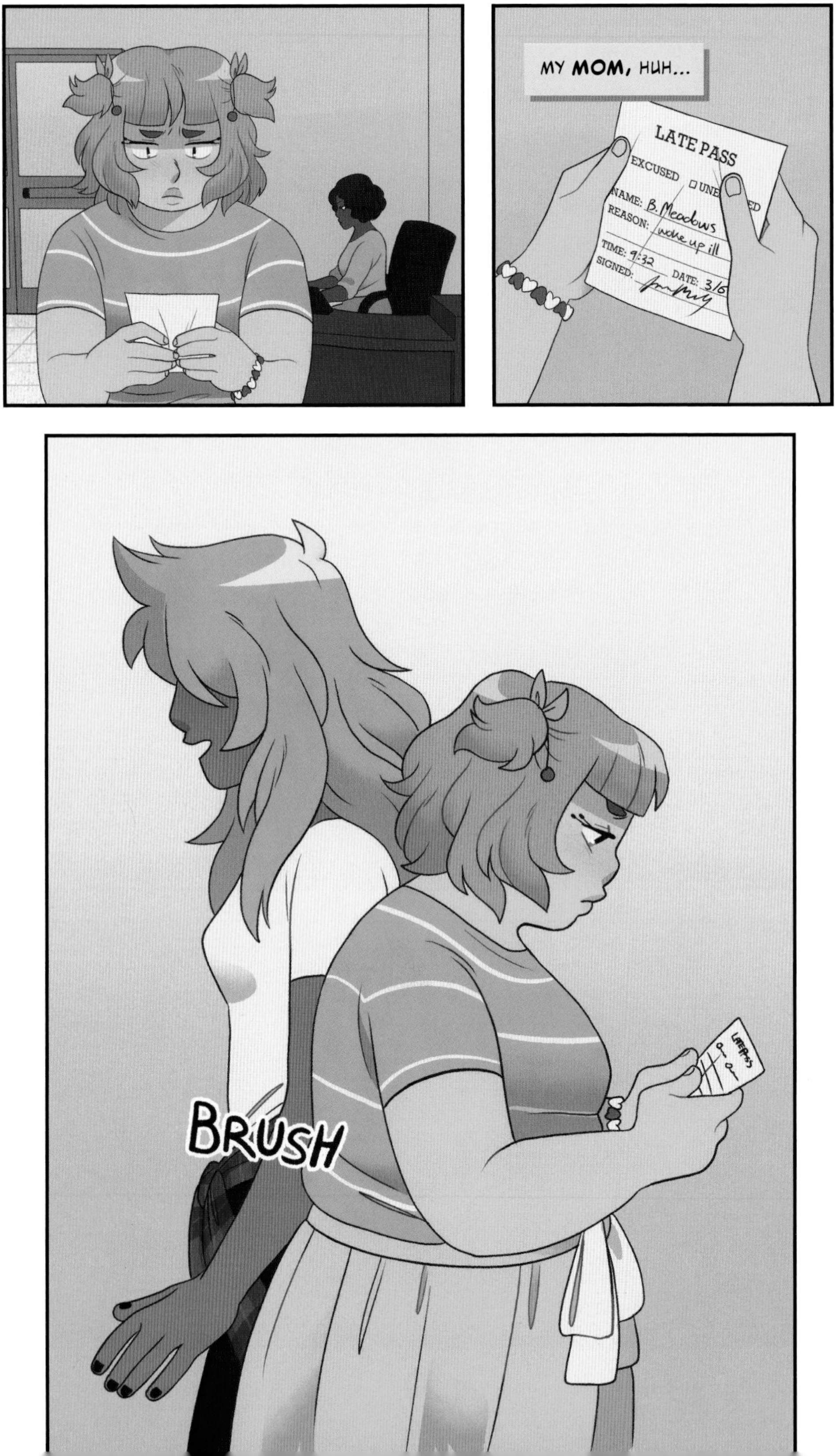
MY **MOM**, HUH...
LATE PASS
EXCUSED
NAME: B. Meadows
REASON: woke up ill
TIME: 9:32
SIGNED:
DATE: 3/6
BRUSH

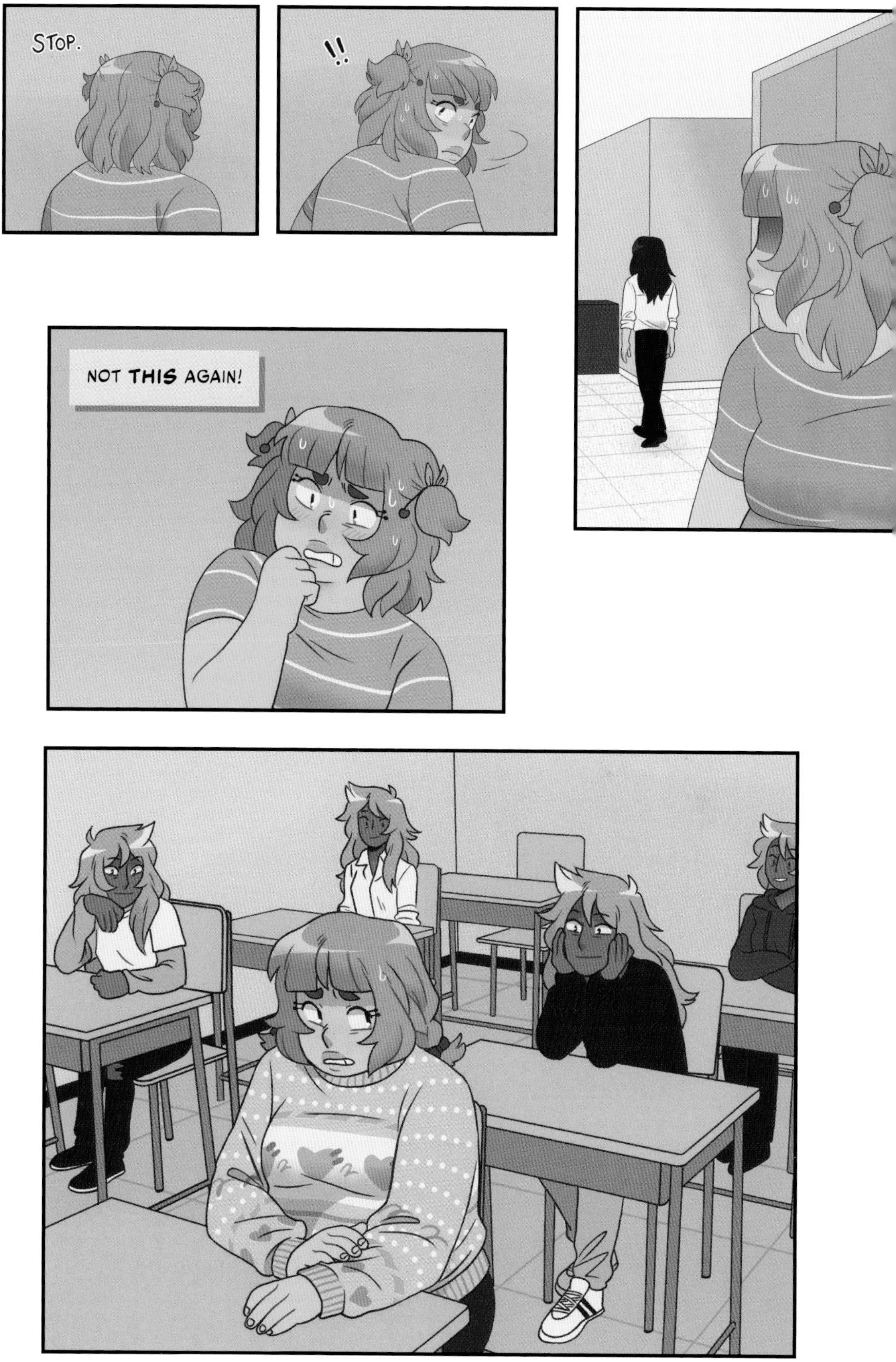
STOP.
!!
NOT THIS AGAIN!

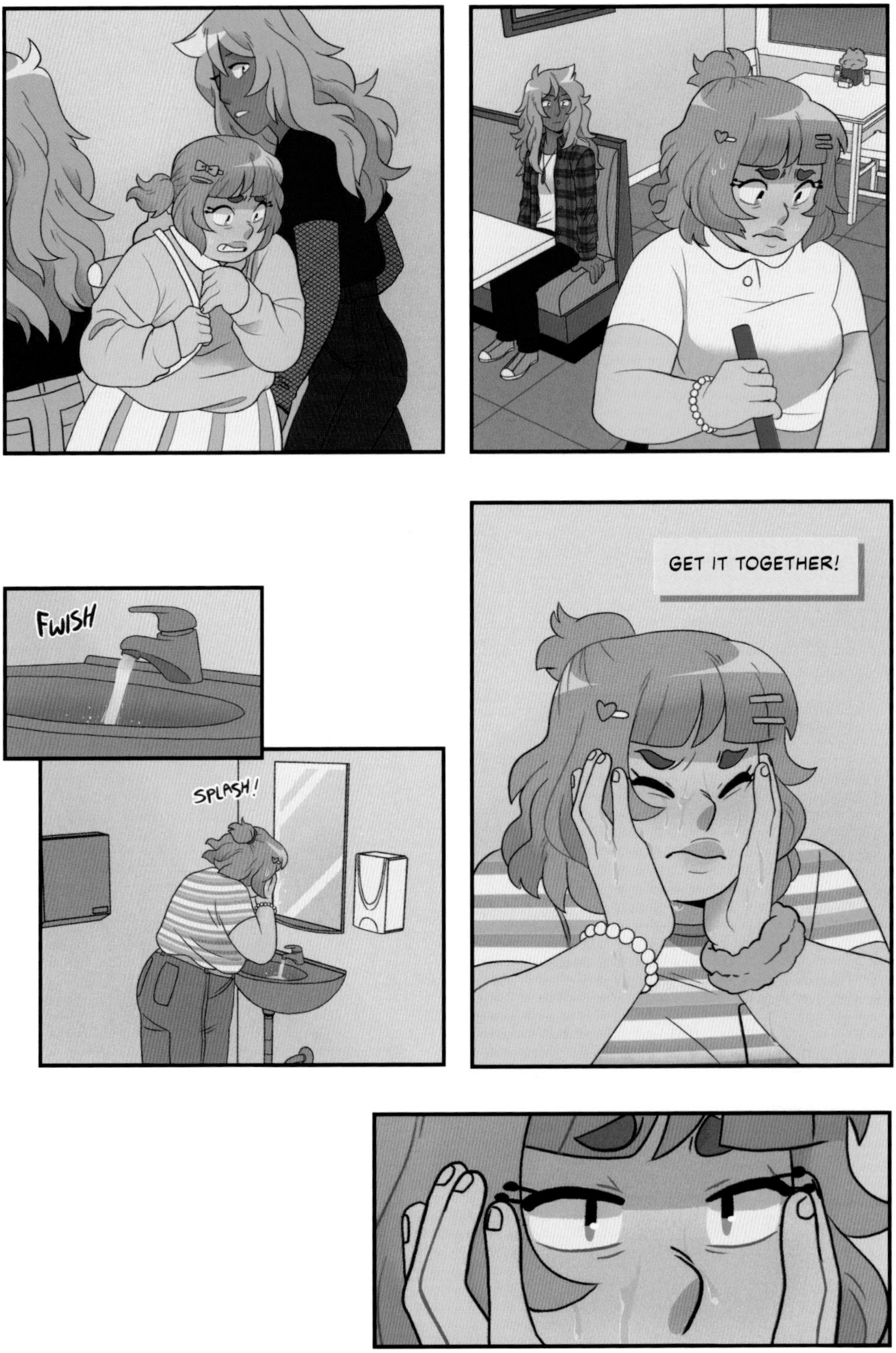
FWISH
SPLASH!
GET IT TOGETHER!

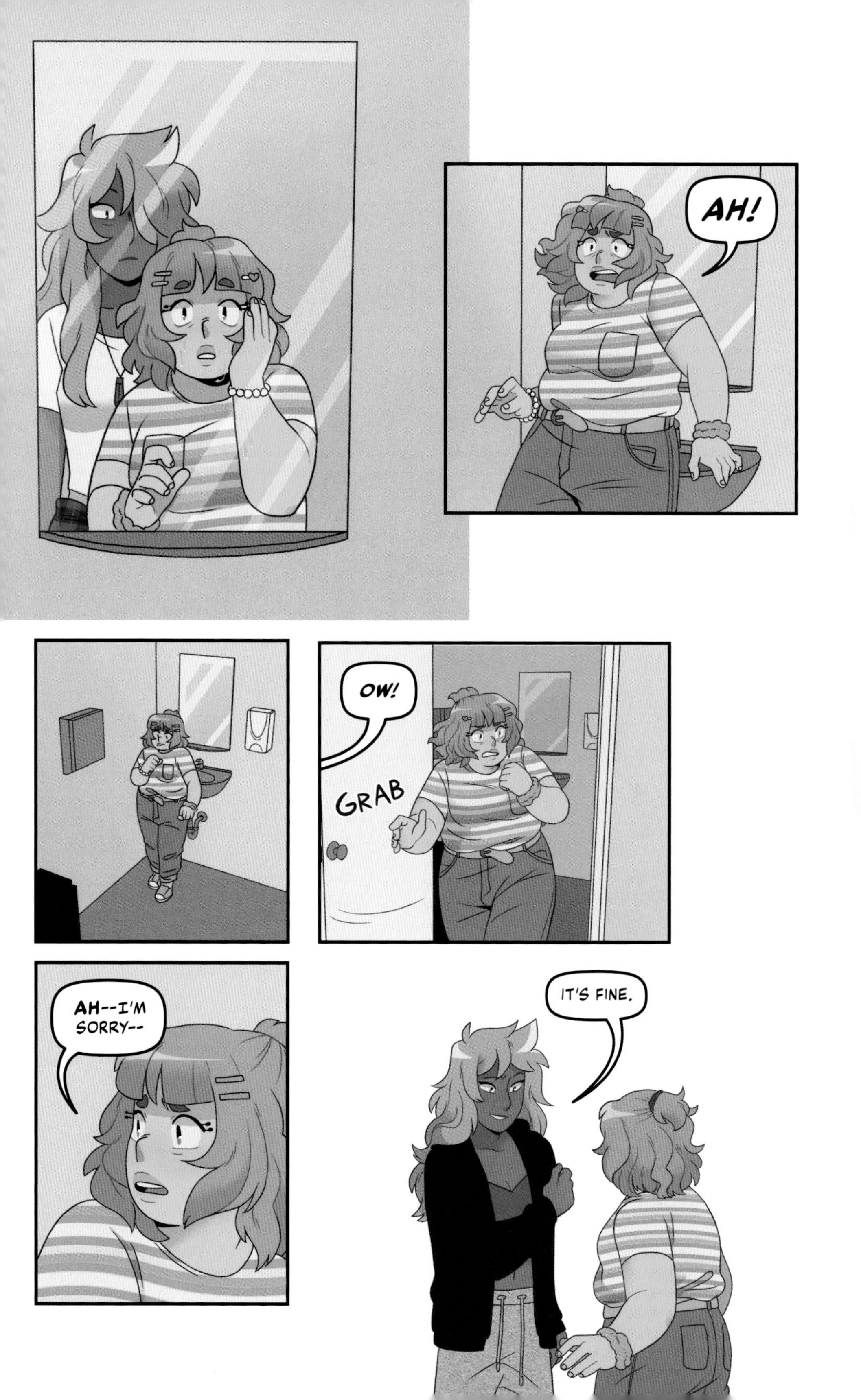
AH!
OW!
GRAB
AH--I'M SORRY--
IT'S FINE.

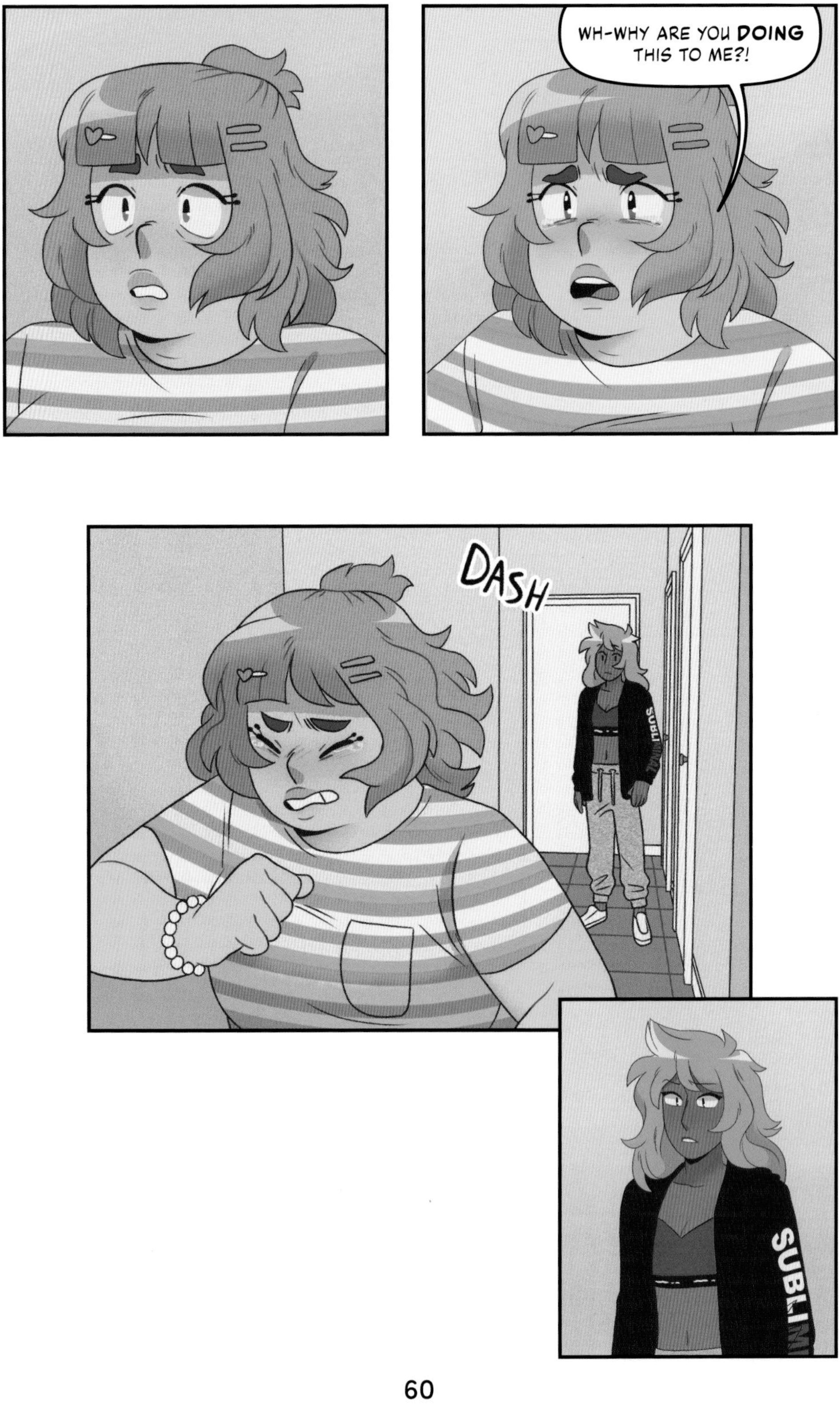
WH-WHY ARE YOU **DOING** THIS TO ME?!
DASH

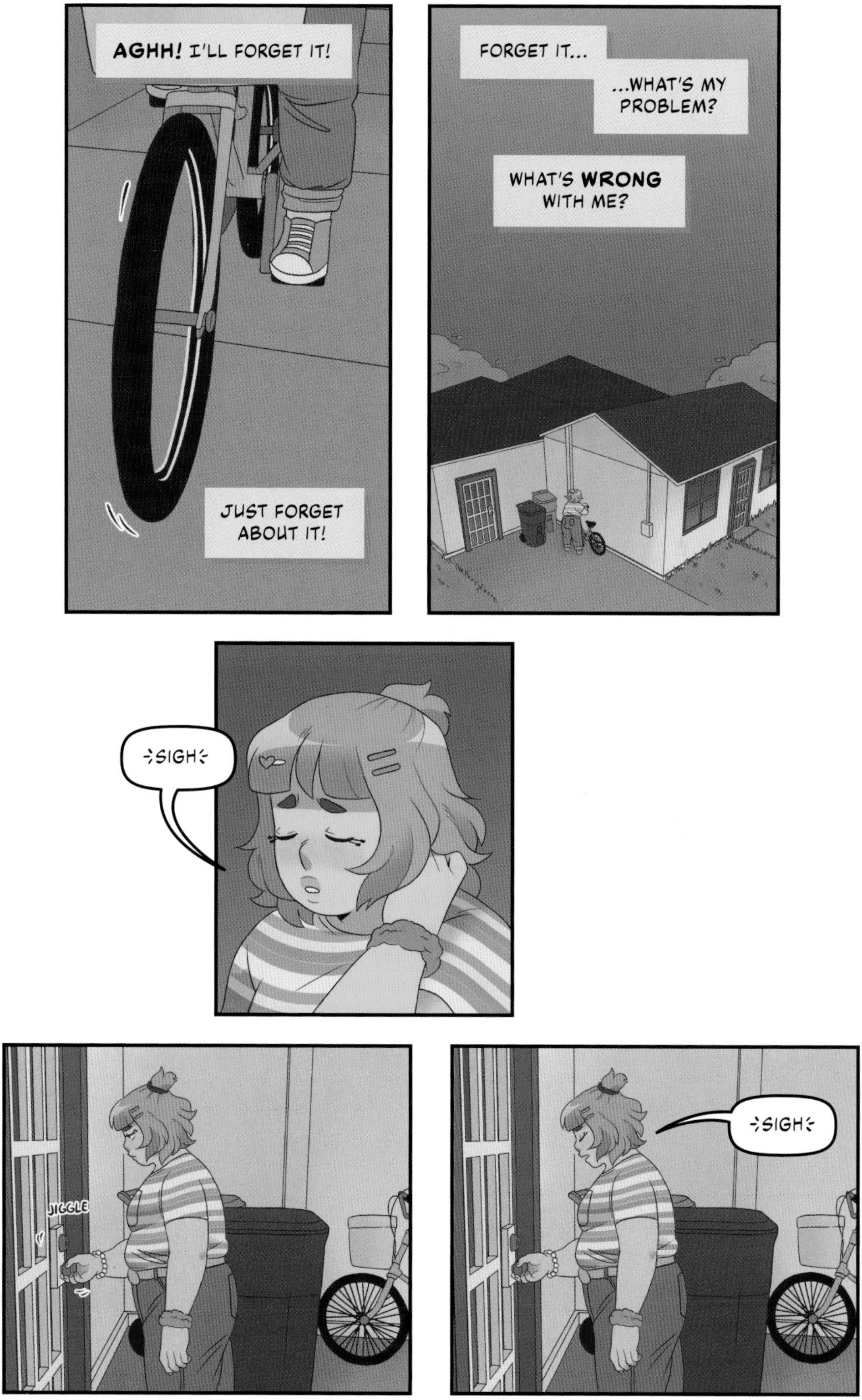
AGHH! I'LL FORGET IT!
JUST FORGET ABOUT IT!
FORGET IT...
...WHAT'S MY PROBLEM?
WHAT'S WRONG WITH ME?
SIGH
JIGGLE
SIGH

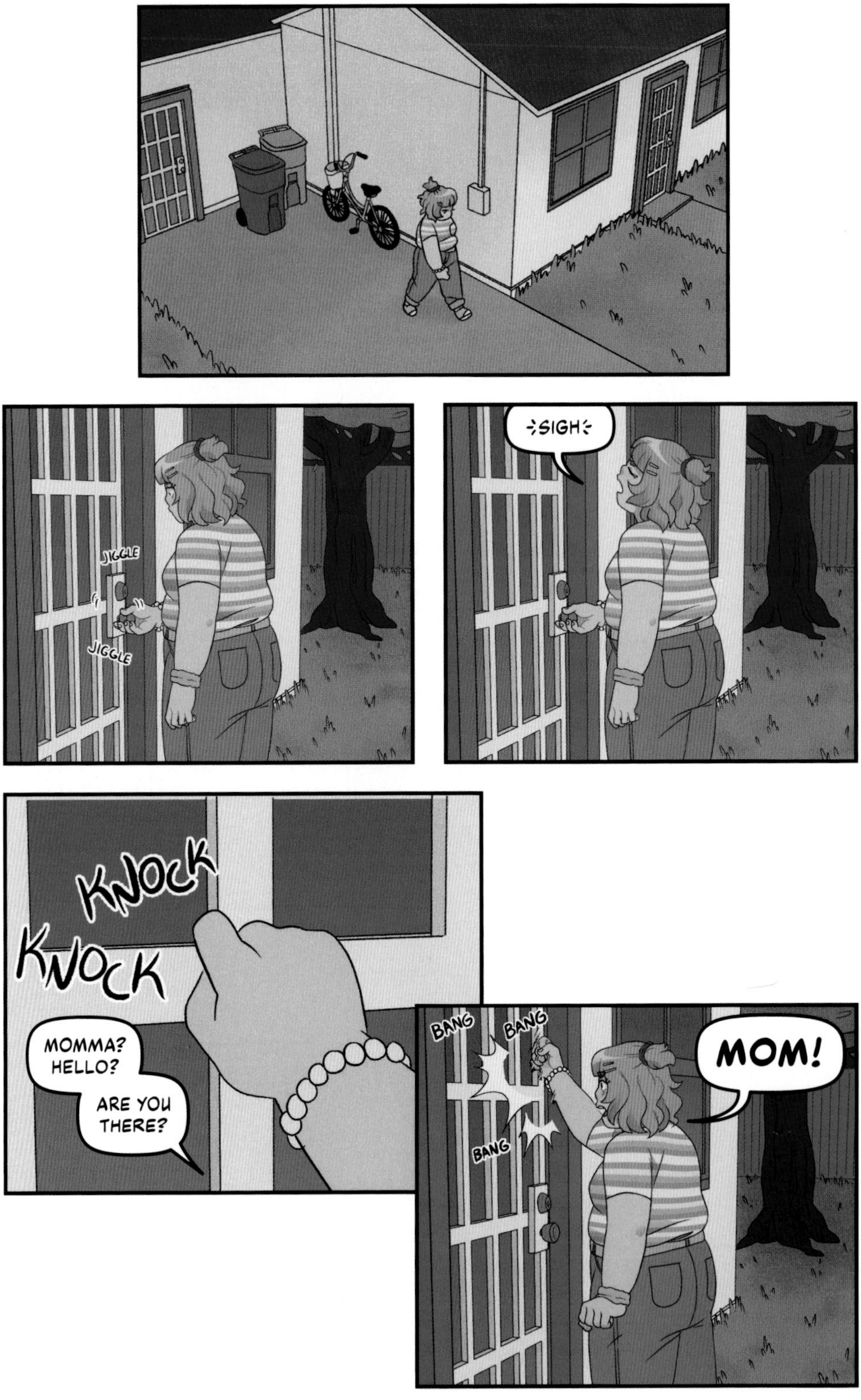

JIGGLE
JIGGLE
SIGH
KNOCK
KNOCK
MOMMA? HELLO?
ARE YOU THERE?
BANG
BANG
BANG
MOM!

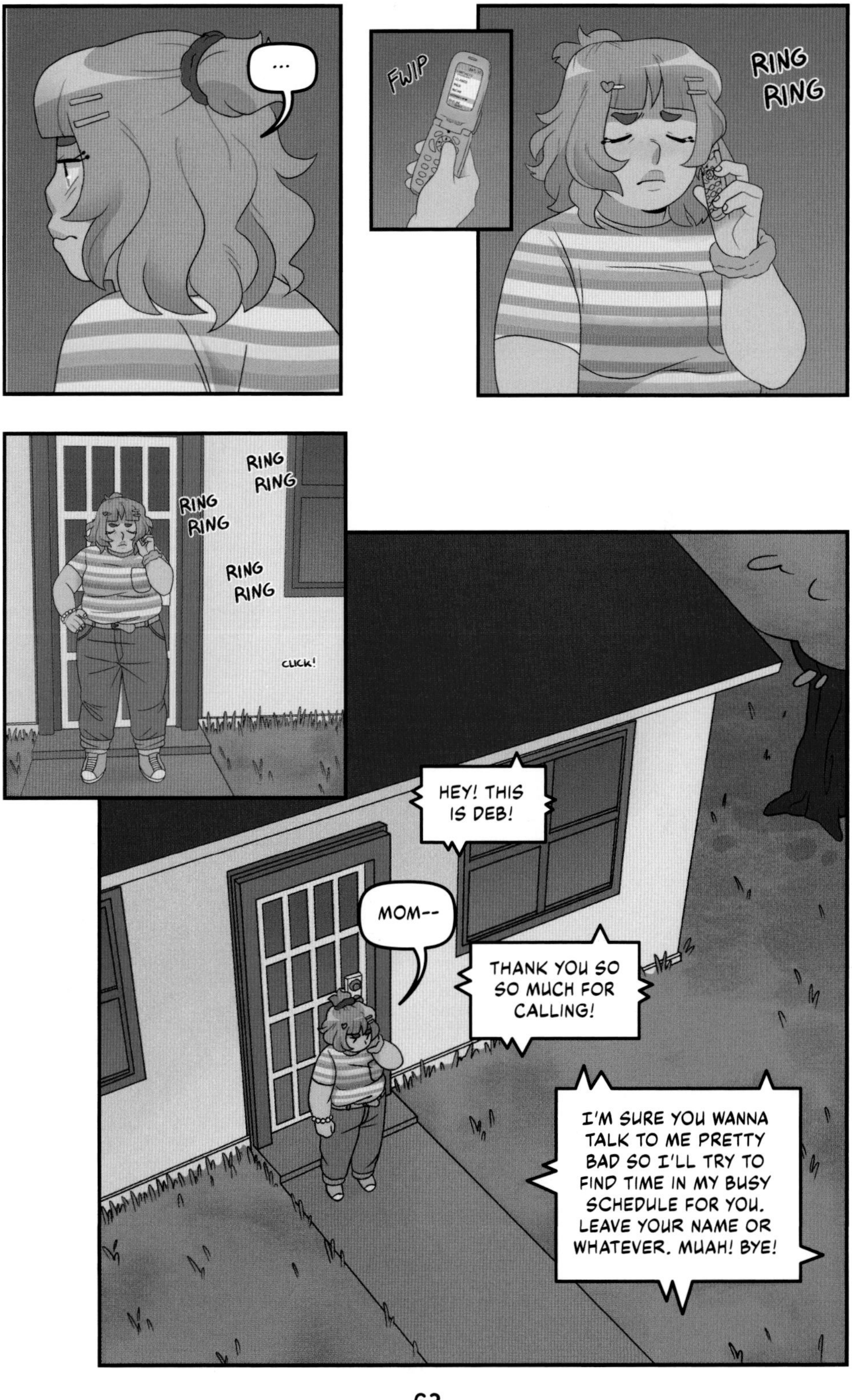
...
FWIP
RING RING
RING RING
RING RING
RING RING
CLICK!
HEY! THIS IS DEB!
MOM--
THANK YOU SO SO MUCH FOR CALLING!
I'M SURE YOU WANNA TALK TO ME PRETTY BAD SO I'LL TRY TO FIND TIME IN MY BUSY SCHEDULE FOR YOU. LEAVE YOUR NAME OR WHATEVER. MUAH! BYE!

MOM...

~ BREATHES ~

HEY, MOM. YOU KNOW YOU AREN'T SUPPOSED TO LOCK THE DOOR. YOU LOST THE OLD KEY, REMEMBER? I DON'T HAVE ONE. ARE YOU AROUND?

YOU'RE **HOME,** AREN'T YOU?

JUST CALL ME WHEN YOU GET THIS. I'M GONNA CLIMB IN THROUGH THE WINDOW AGAIN. OKAY. BYE.

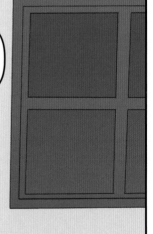

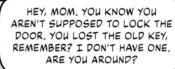

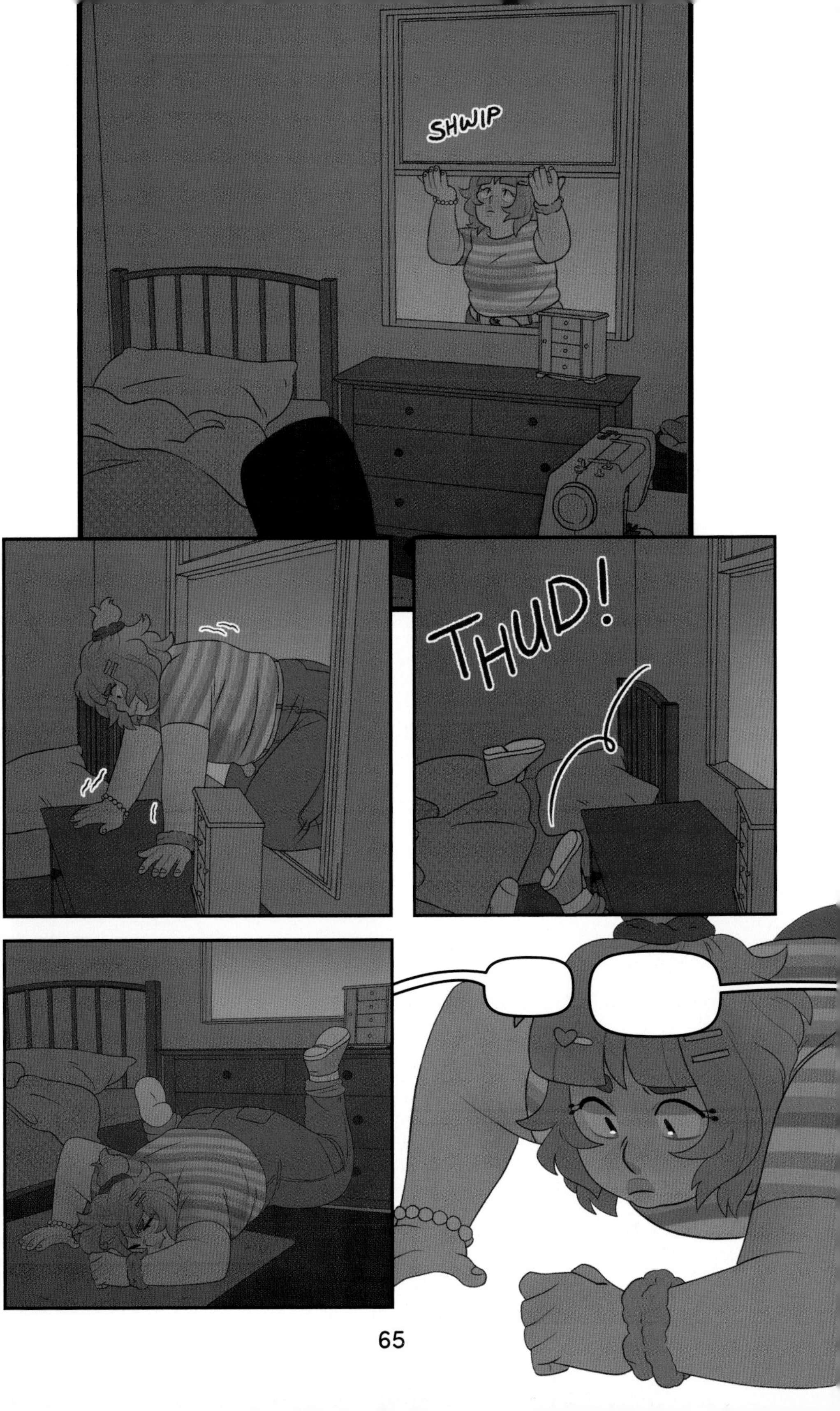
SHWIP
THUD!

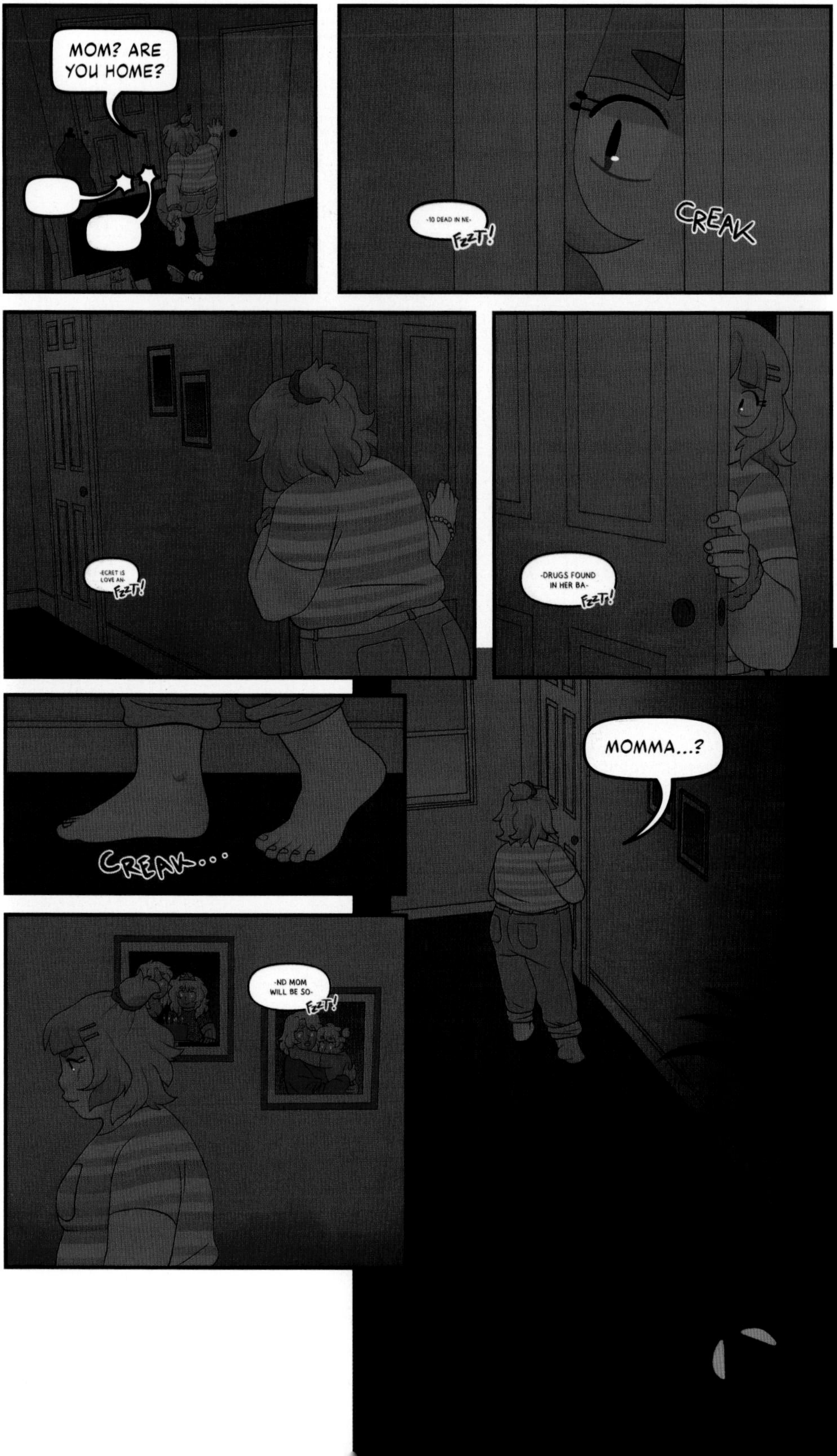

MOM? ARE YOU HOME?
-10 DEAD IN NE-
FZZT!
CREAK
-ECRET IS LOVE AN-
FZZT!
-DRUGS FOUND IN HER BA-
FZZT!
CREAK...
MOMMA...?
-ND MOM WILL BE SO-
FZZT!

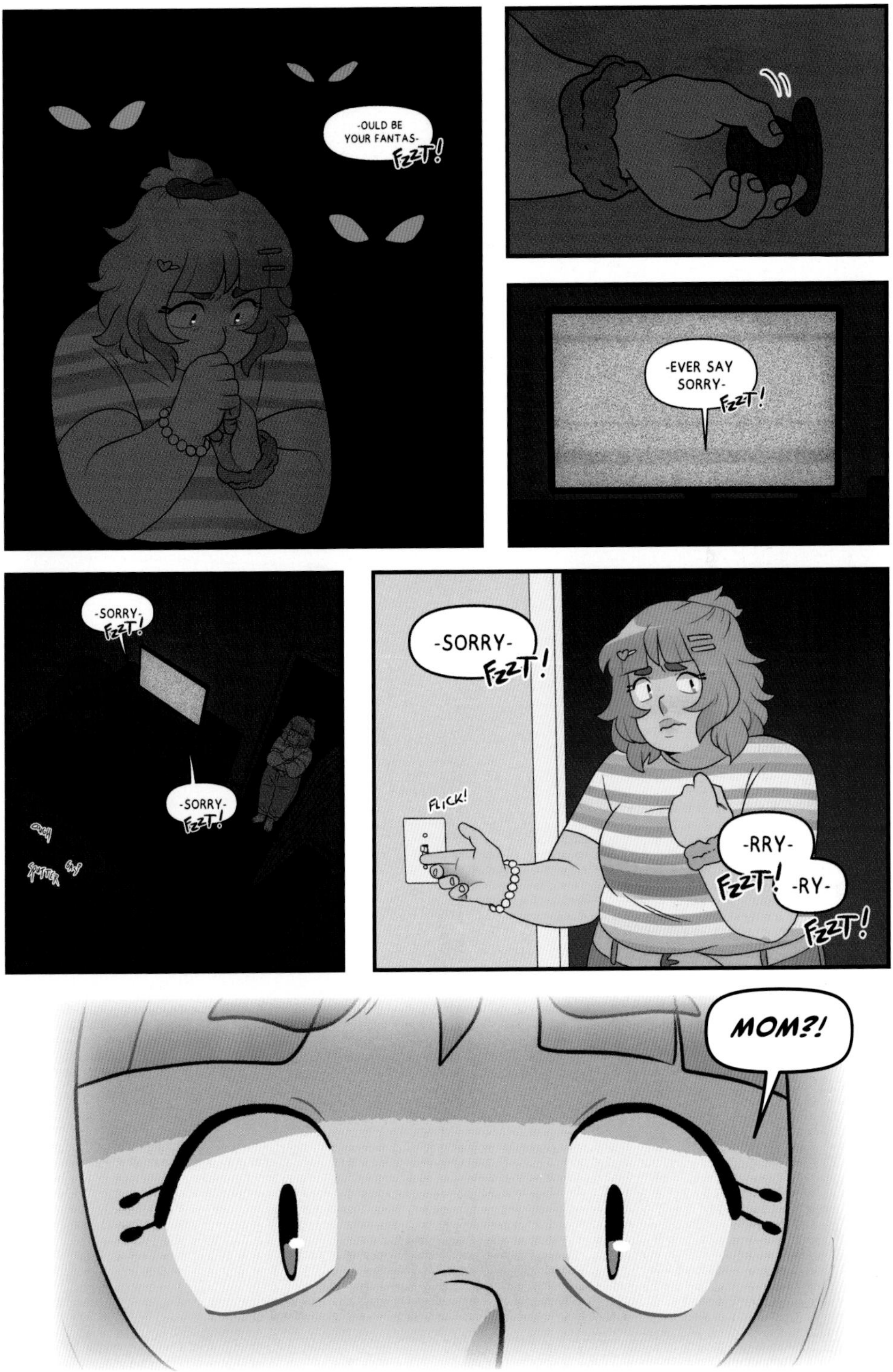

-OULD BE YOUR FANTAS-
FZZT!
-EVER SAY SORRY-
FZZT!
-SORRY-
FZZT!
-SORRY-
FZZT!
COUGH
SPUTTER
GASP
-SORRY-
FZZT!
FLICK!
-RRY-
FZZT!
-RY-
FZZT!
MOM?!

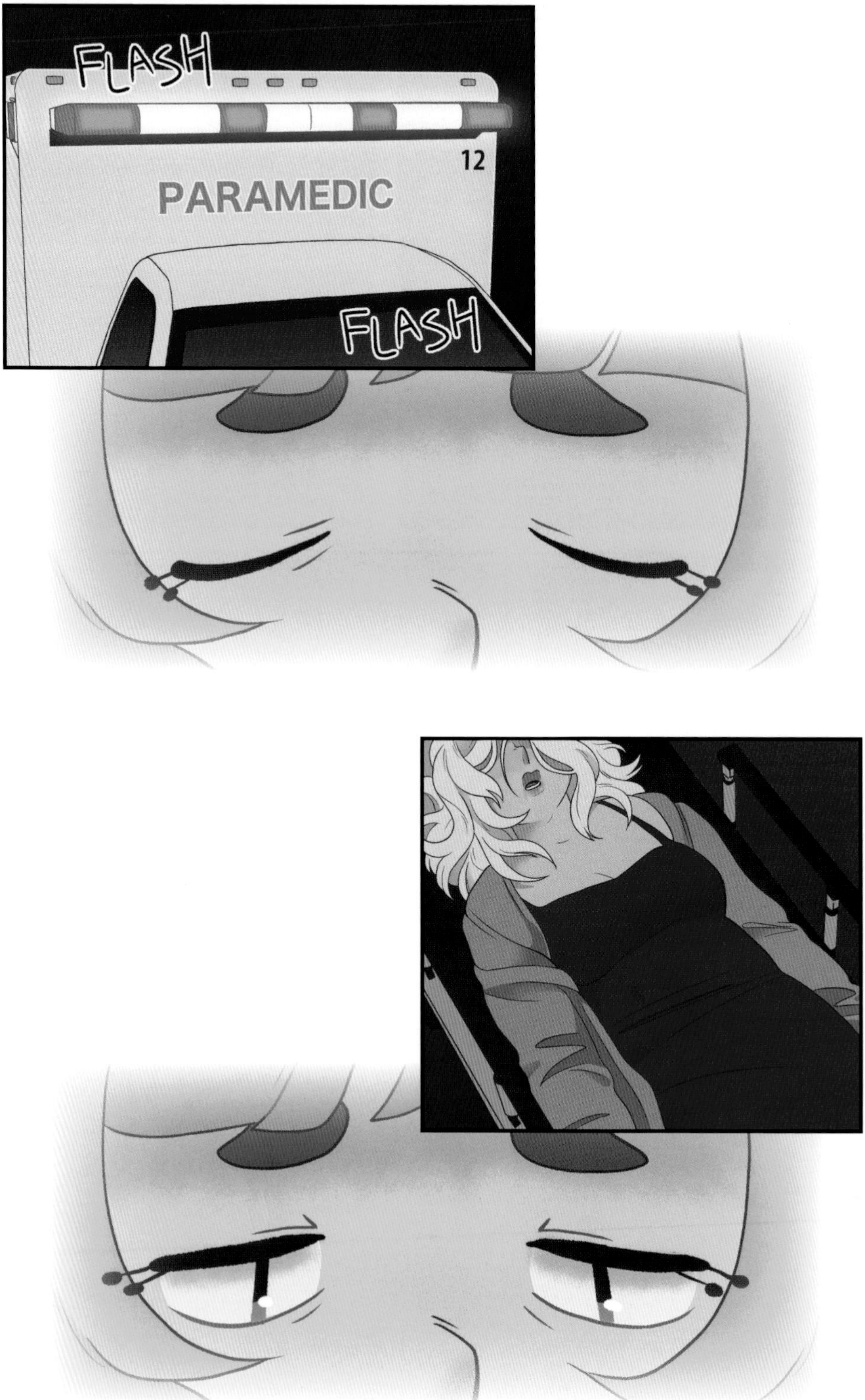
FLASH
12
PARAMEDIC
FLASH

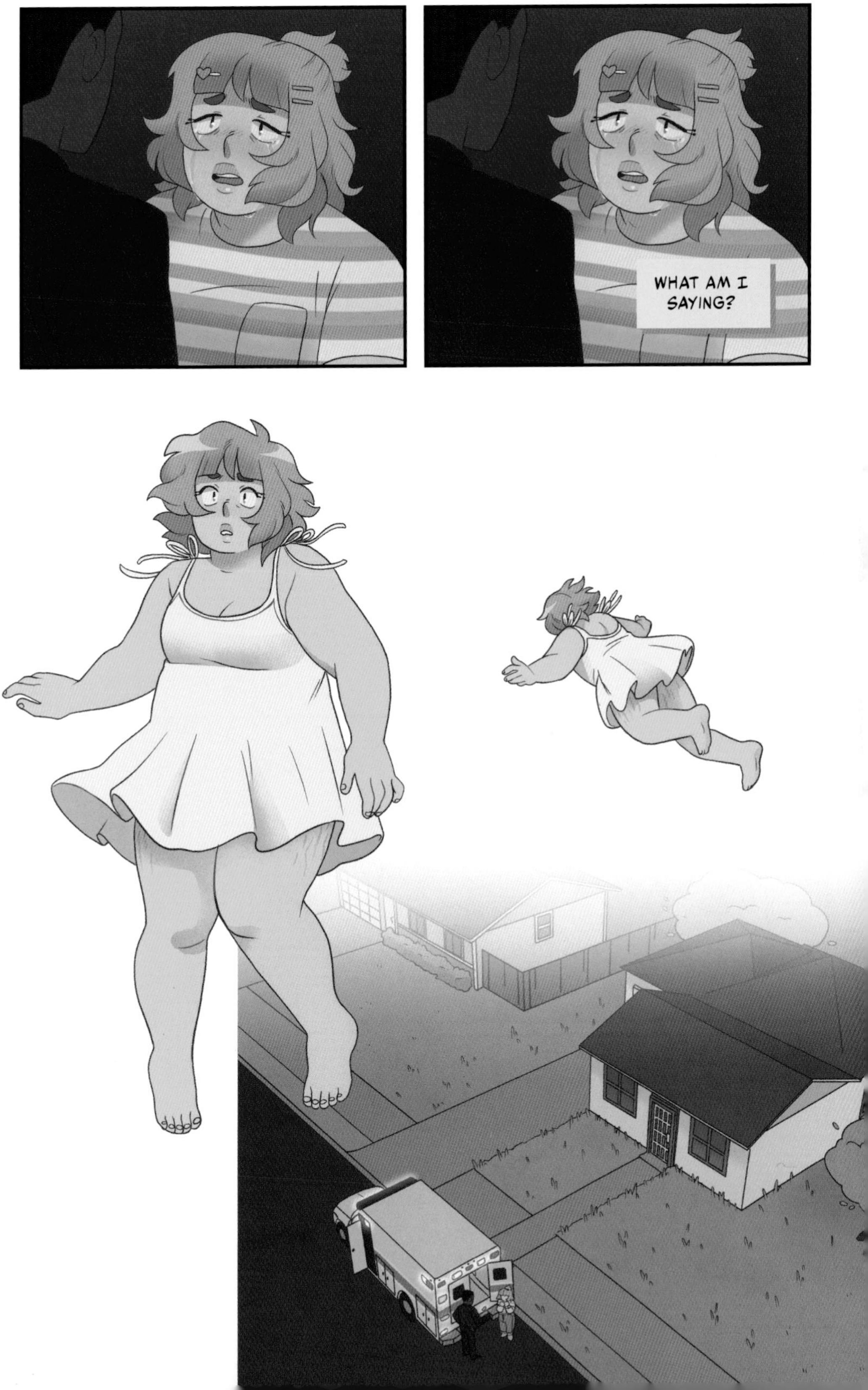
WHAT AM I SAYING?

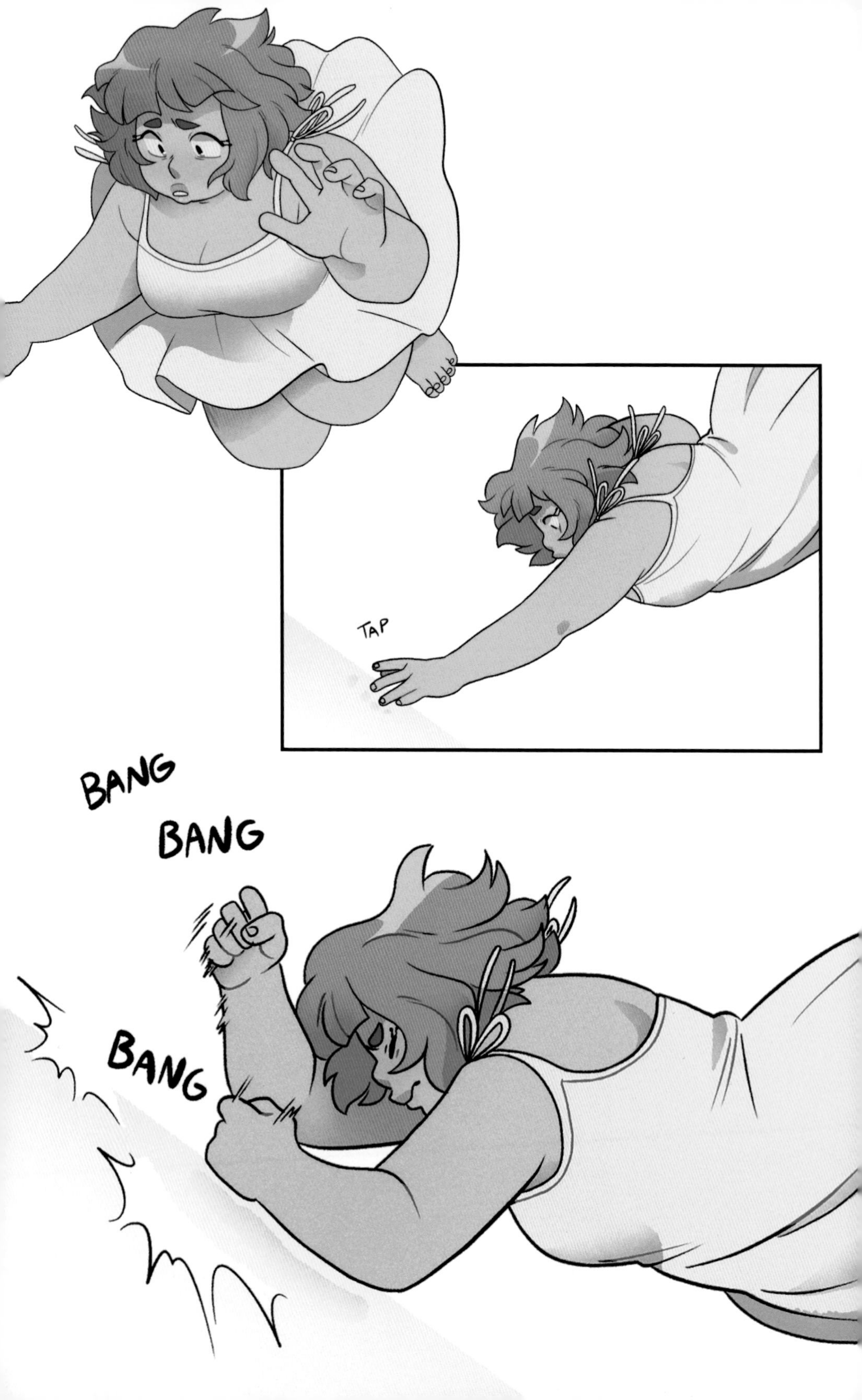
TAP
BANG
BANG
BANG

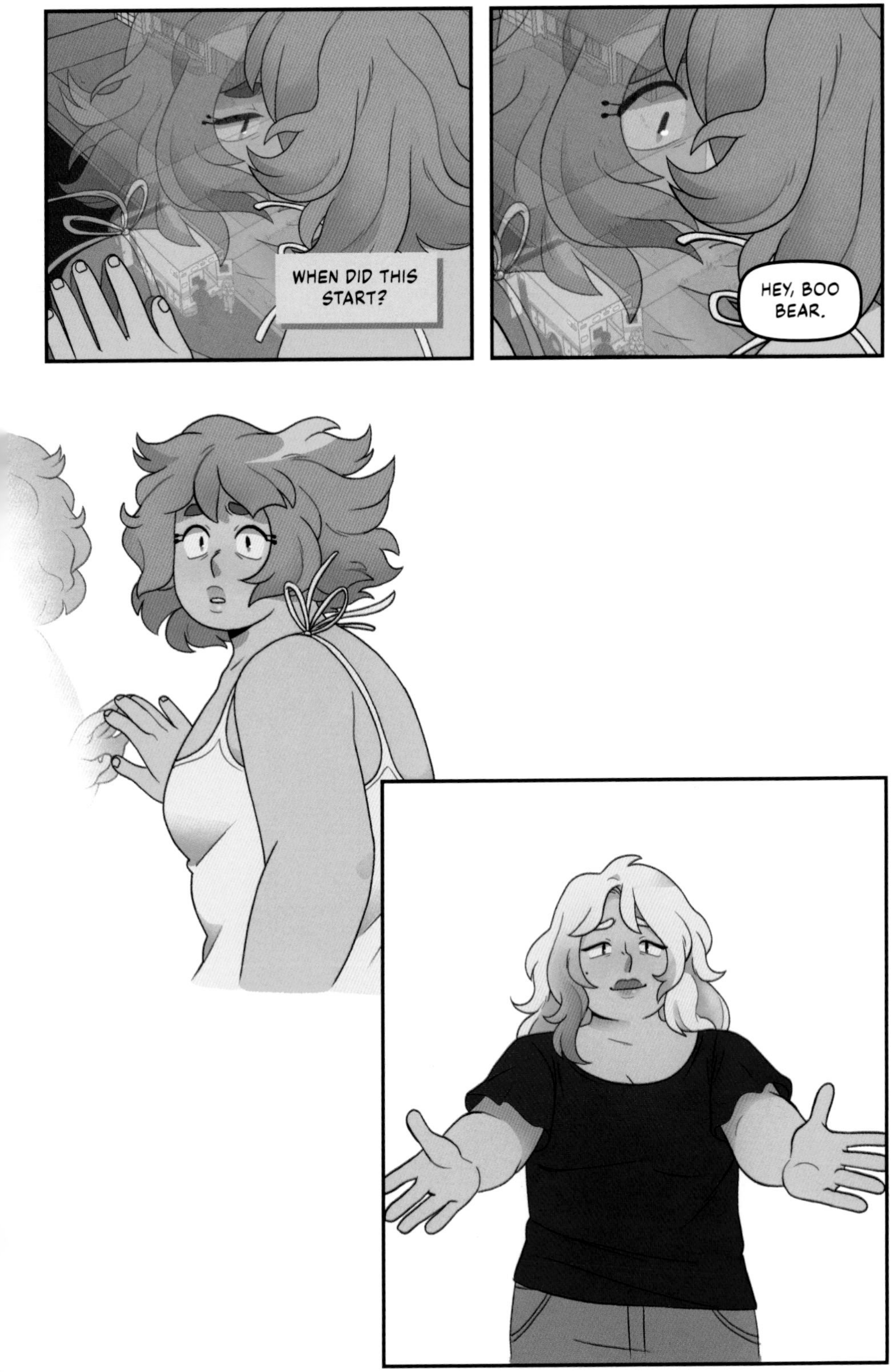
WHEN DID THIS START?
HEY, BOO BEAR.

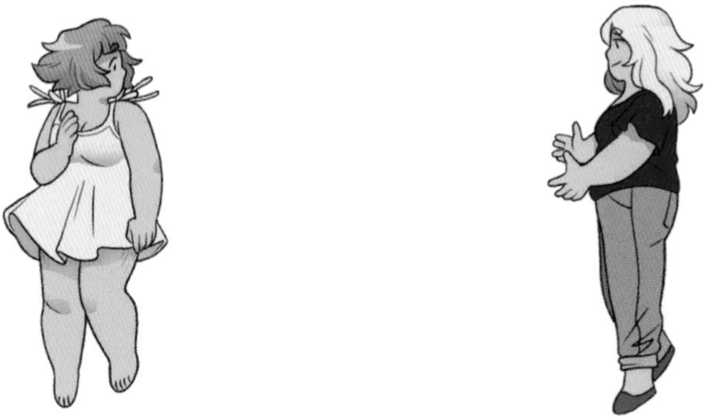

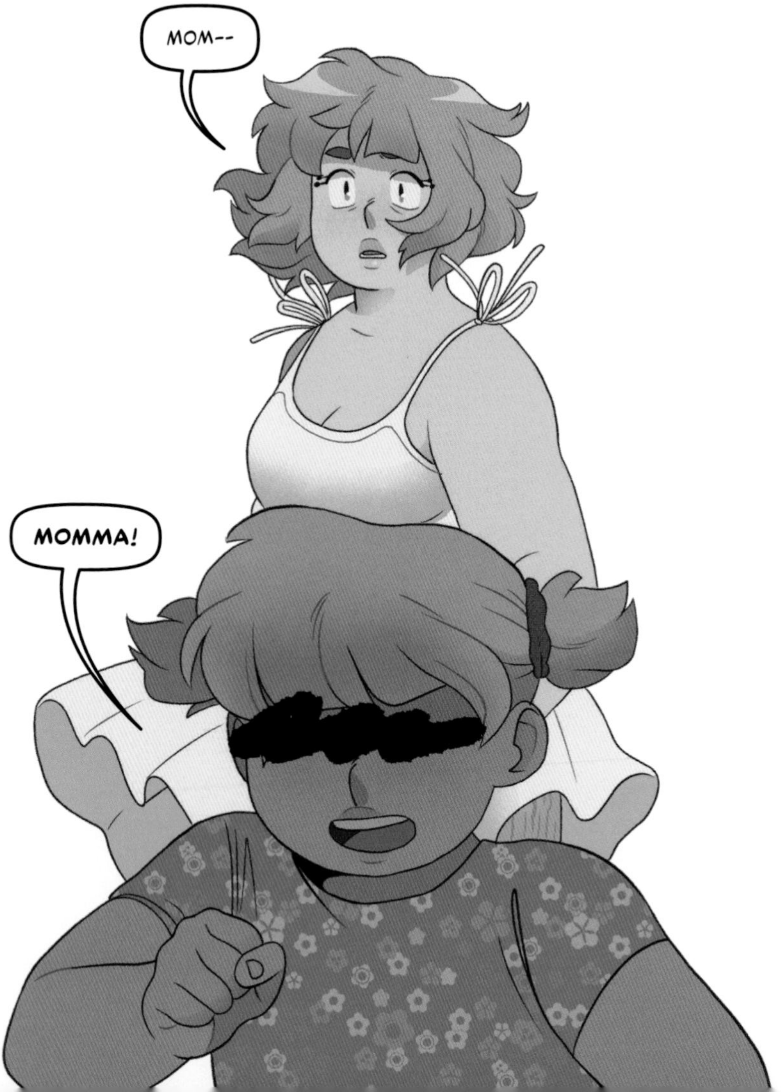
MOM--
MOMMA!

I WANT MY HAIR LIKE THIS!

MAYBE WHEN YOU'RE OLDER.

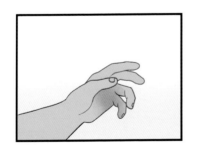

FWISH...

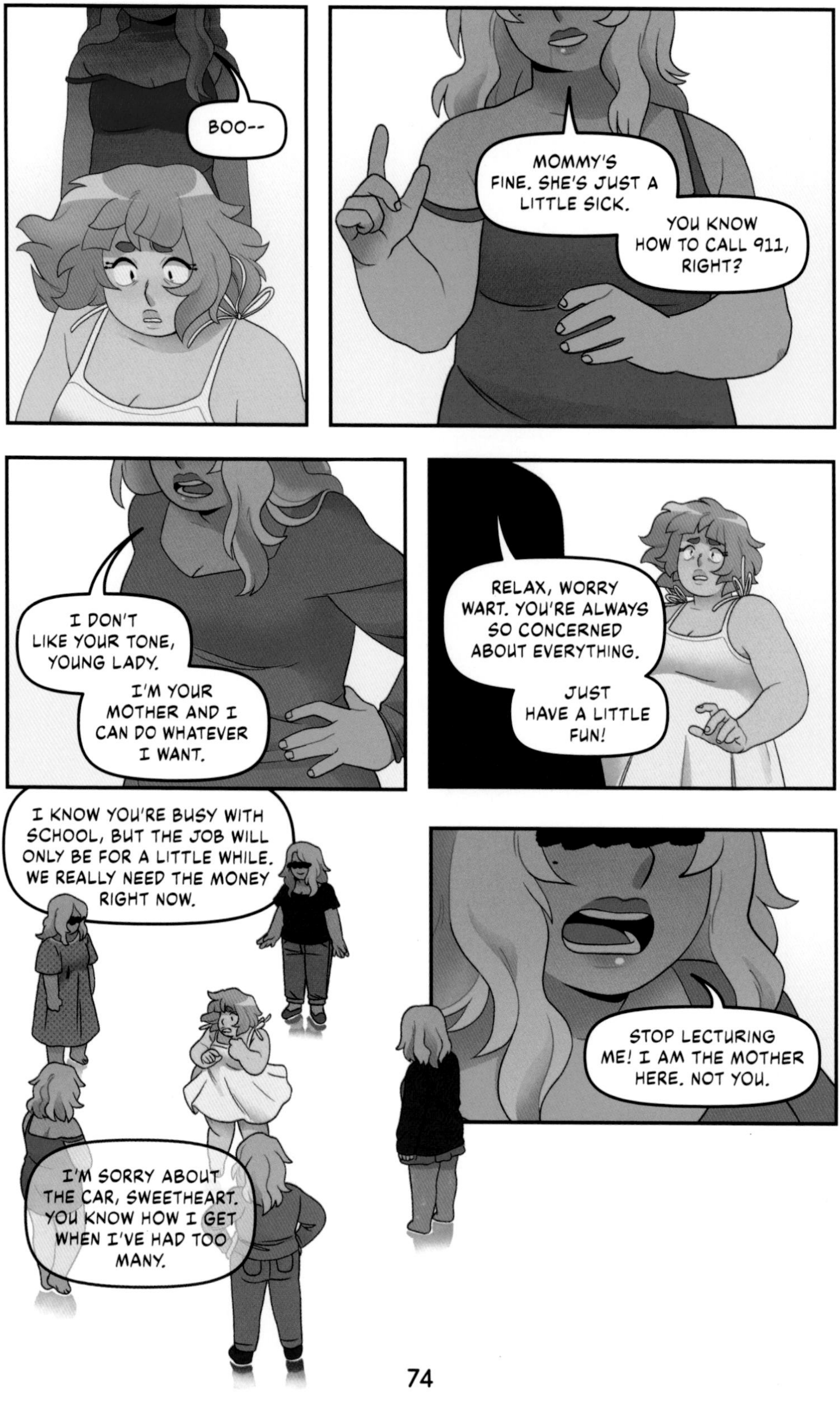
BOO--
MOMMY'S FINE. SHE'S JUST A LITTLE SICK.
YOU KNOW HOW TO CALL 911, RIGHT?
I DON'T LIKE YOUR TONE, YOUNG LADY.
I'M YOUR MOTHER AND I CAN DO WHATEVER I WANT.
RELAX, WORRY WART. YOU'RE ALWAYS SO CONCERNED ABOUT EVERYTHING.
JUST HAVE A LITTLE FUN!
I KNOW YOU'RE BUSY WITH SCHOOL, BUT THE JOB WILL ONLY BE FOR A LITTLE WHILE. WE REALLY NEED THE MONEY RIGHT NOW.
I'M SORRY ABOUT THE CAR, SWEETHEART. YOU KNOW HOW I GET WHEN I'VE HAD TOO MANY.
STOP LECTURING ME! I AM THE MOTHER HERE. NOT YOU.

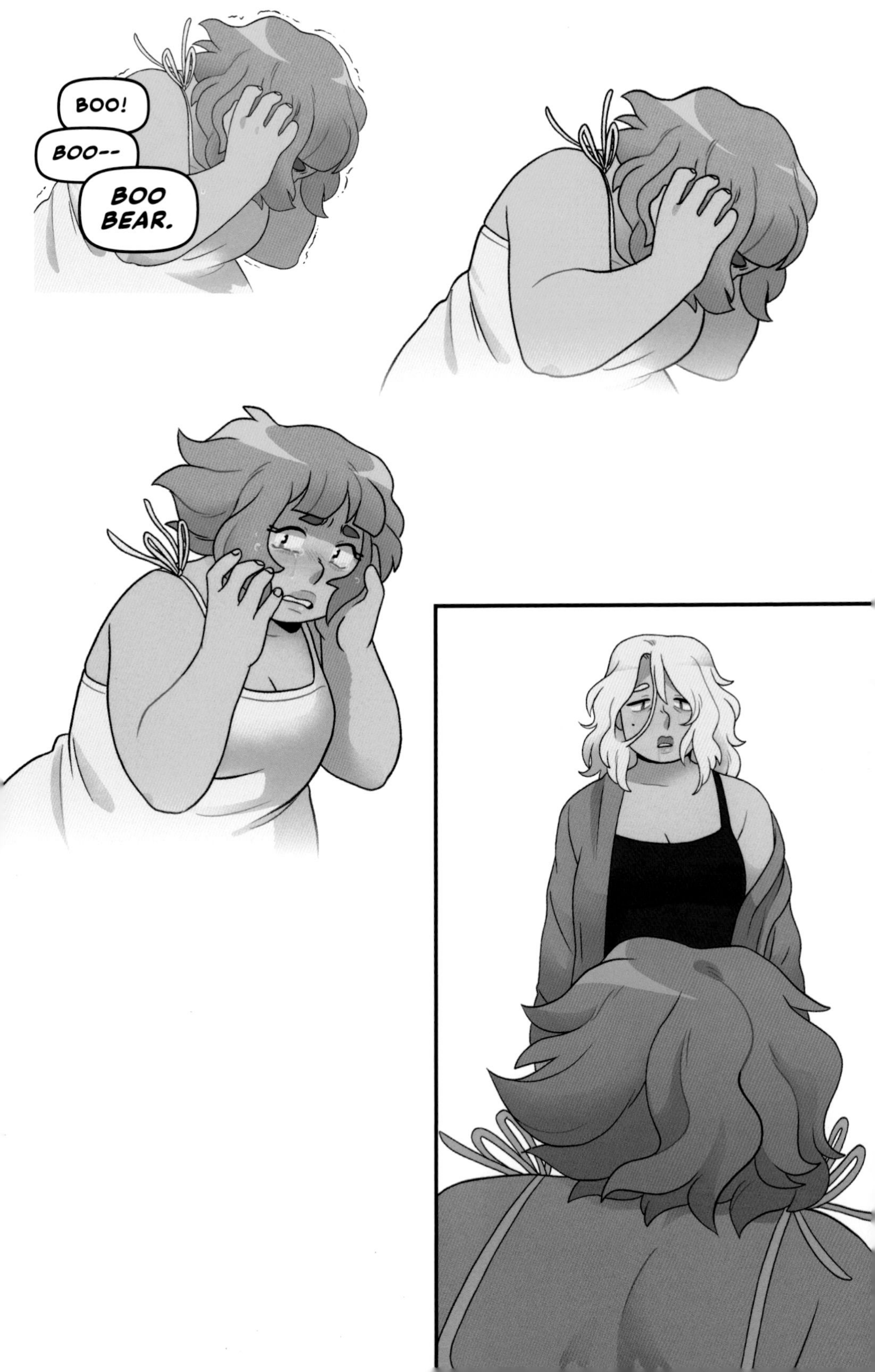
BOO!
BOO--
BOO BEAR.

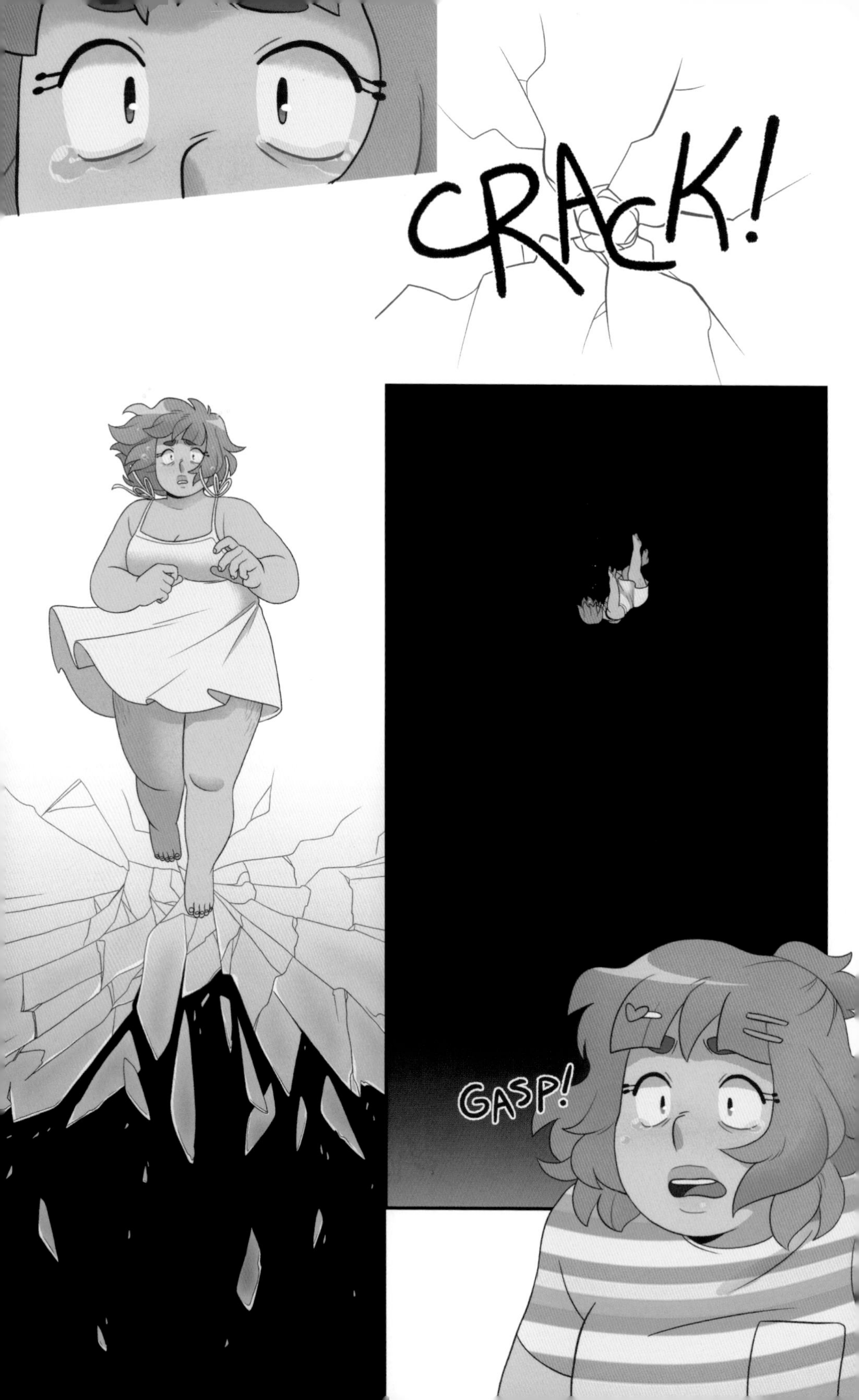
CRACK!
GASP!

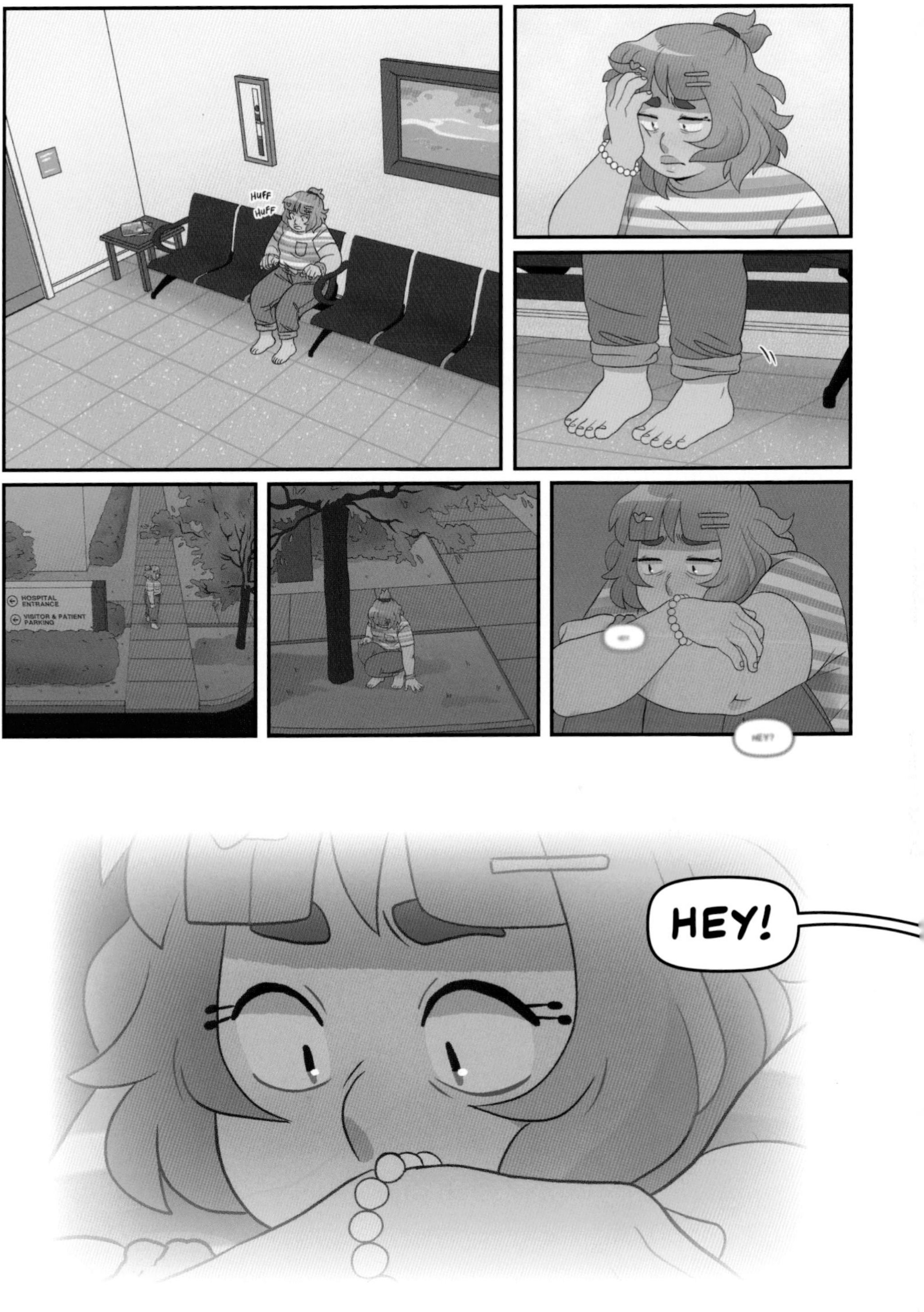
HUFF
HUFF
HOSPITAL ENTRANCE
VISITOR & PATIENT PARKING
HEY?
HEY!

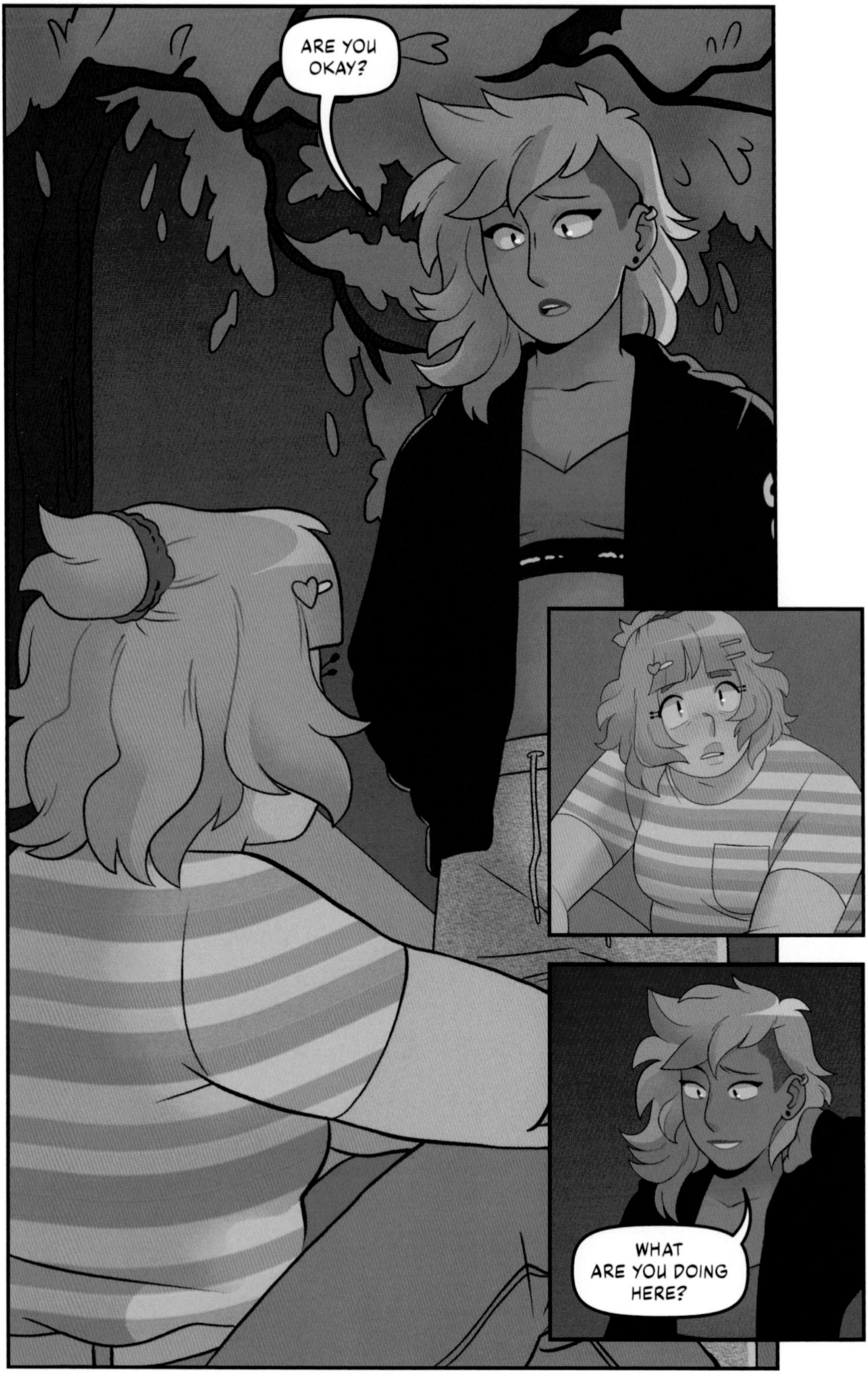
ARE YOU OKAY?
WHAT ARE YOU DOING HERE?

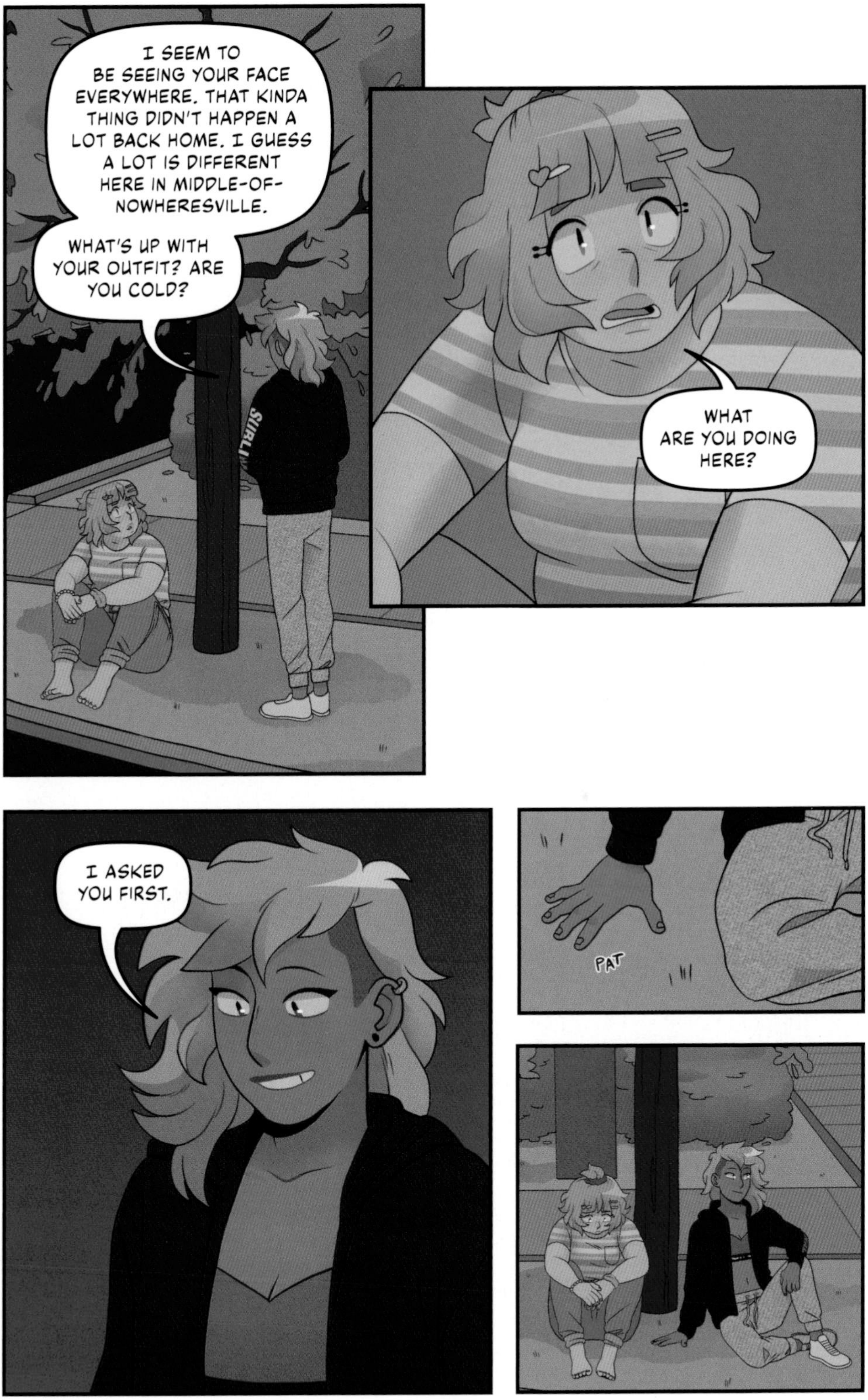
I SEEM TO BE SEEING YOUR FACE EVERYWHERE. THAT KINDA THING DIDN'T HAPPEN A LOT BACK HOME. I GUESS A LOT IS DIFFERENT HERE IN MIDDLE-OF-NOWHERESVILLE.
WHAT'S UP WITH YOUR OUTFIT? ARE YOU COLD?
WHAT ARE YOU DOING HERE?
I ASKED YOU FIRST.
PAT

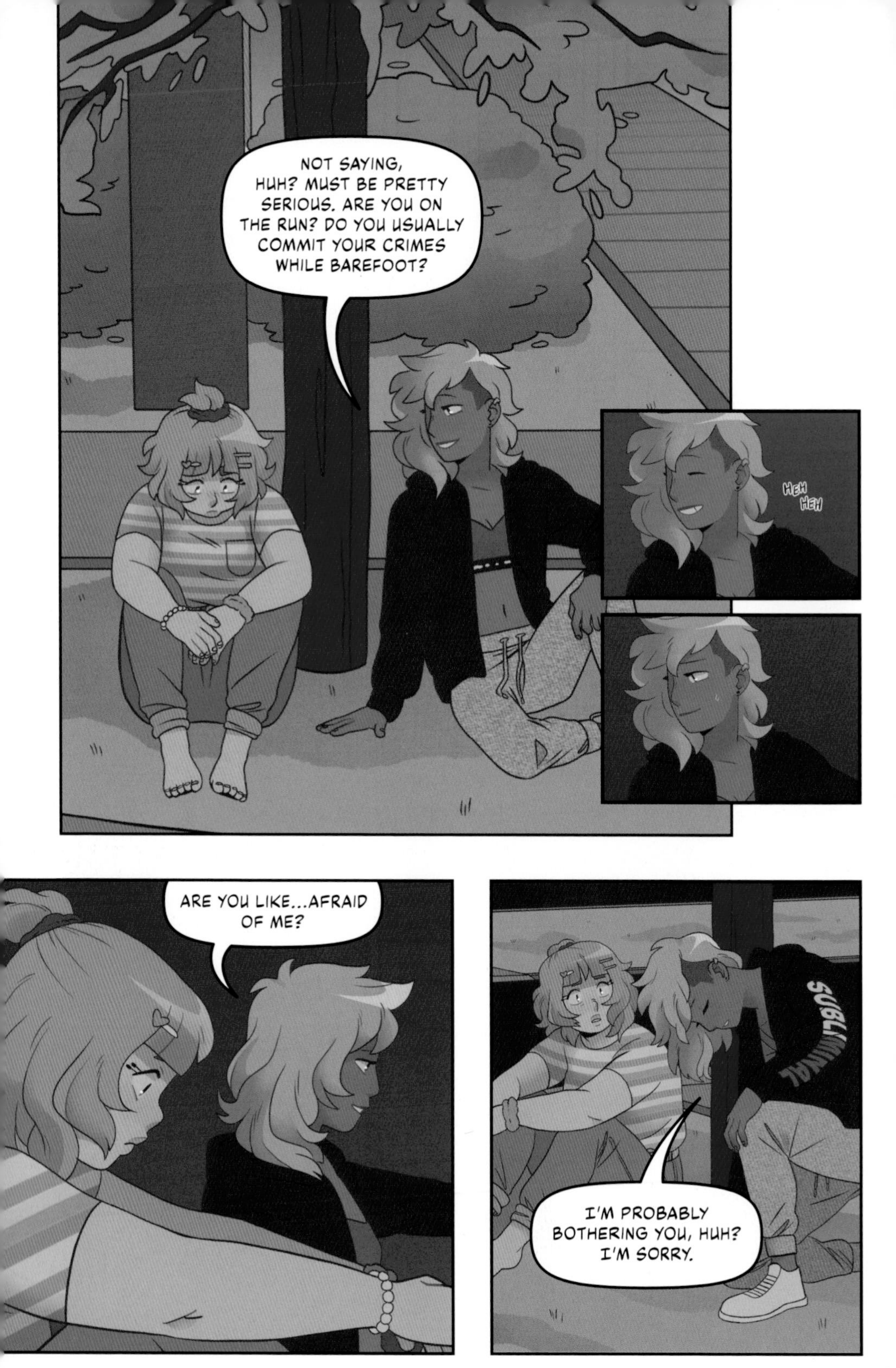
NOT SAYING, HUH? MUST BE PRETTY SERIOUS. ARE YOU ON THE RUN? DO YOU USUALLY COMMIT YOUR CRIMES WHILE BAREFOOT?
HEH HEH
ARE YOU LIKE...AFRAID OF ME?
SUBLIMINAL
I'M PROBABLY BOTHERING YOU, HUH? I'M SORRY.

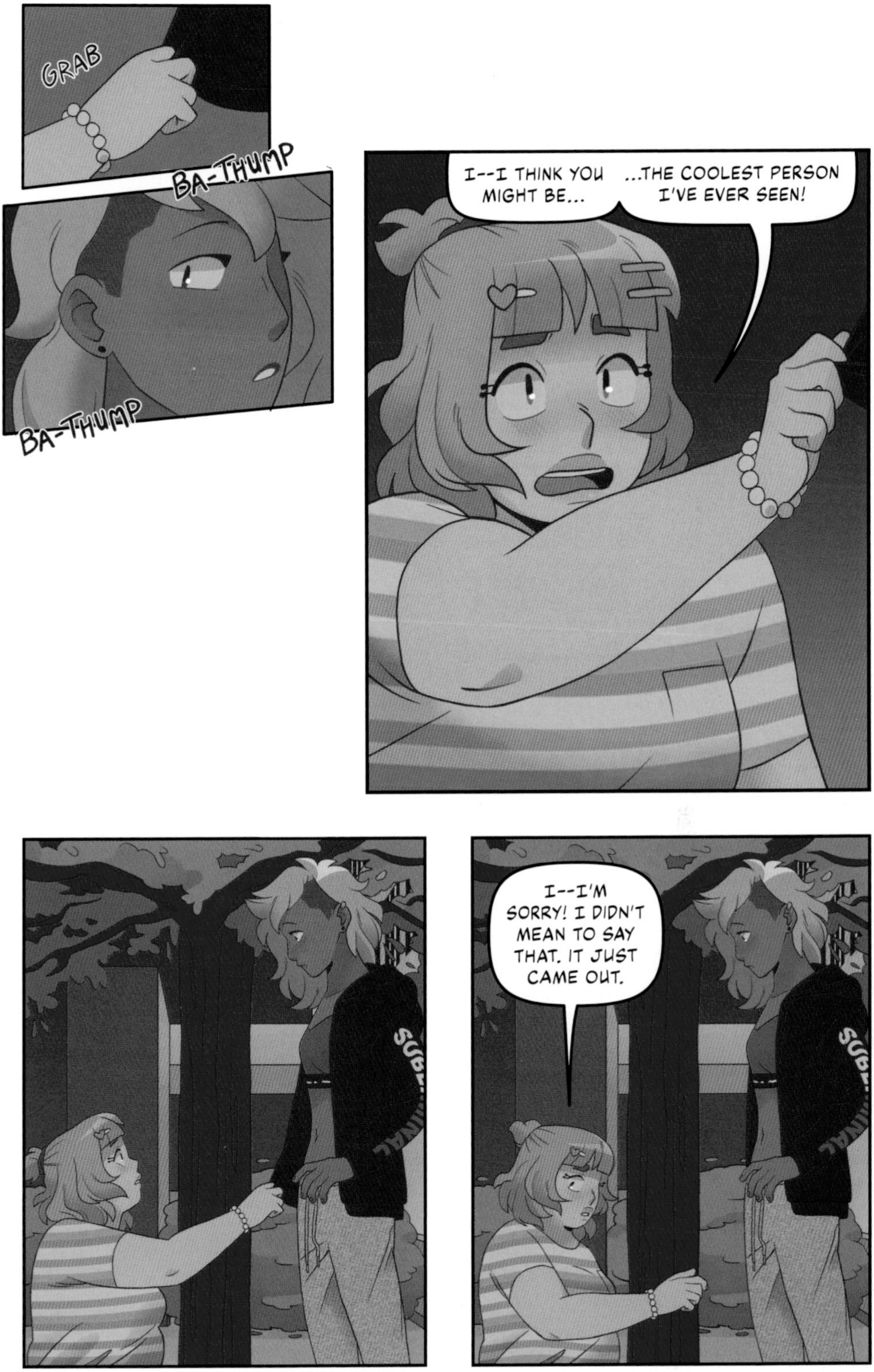
GRAB
BA-THUMP
BA-THUMP
I--I THINK YOU MIGHT BE...
...THE COOLEST PERSON I'VE EVER SEEN!
I--I'M SORRY! I DIDN'T MEAN TO SAY THAT. IT JUST CAME OUT.

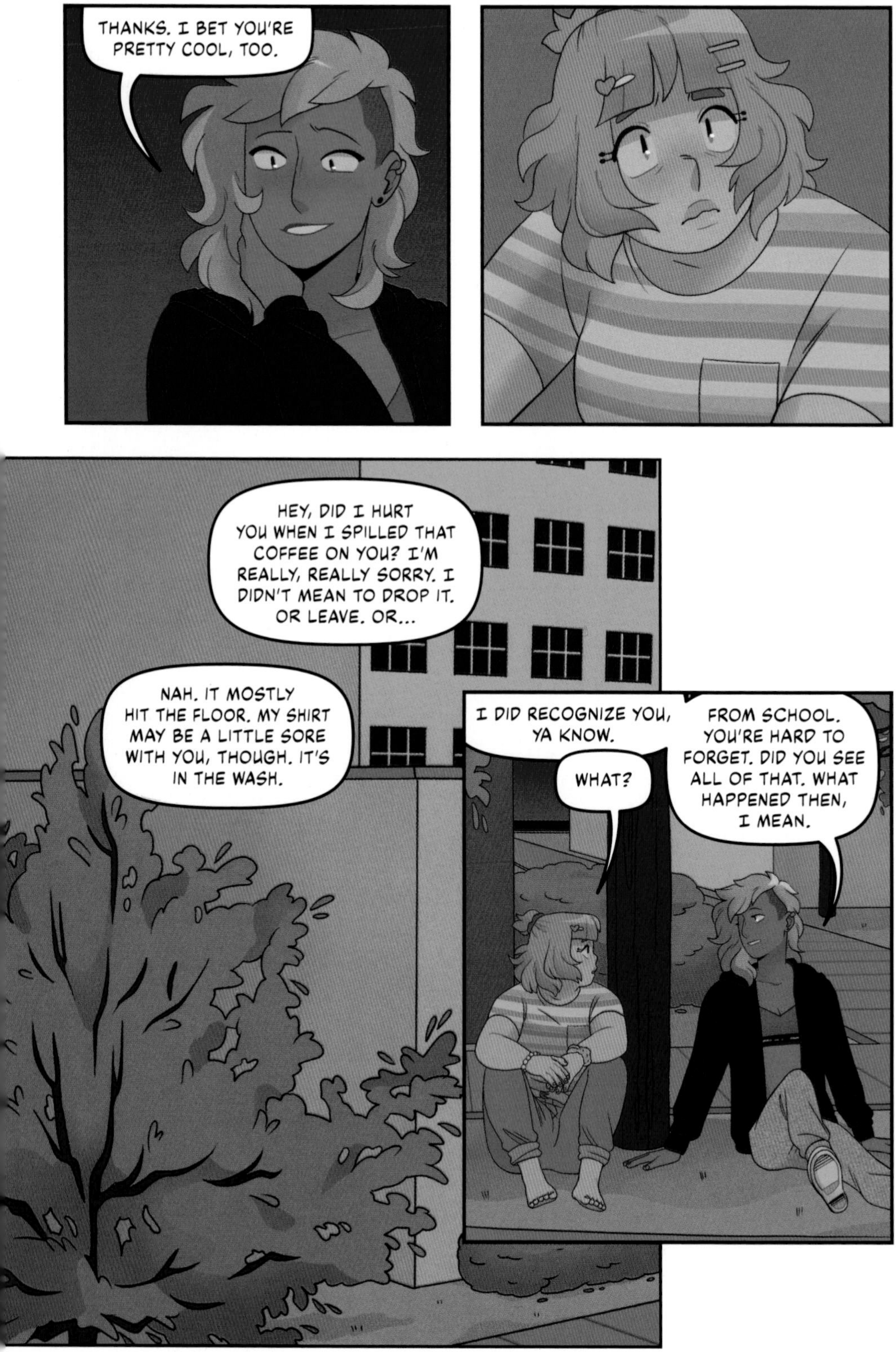
THANKS. I BET YOU'RE PRETTY COOL, TOO.
HEY, DID I HURT YOU WHEN I SPILLED THAT COFFEE ON YOU? I'M REALLY, REALLY SORRY. I DIDN'T MEAN TO DROP IT. OR LEAVE. OR...
NAH. IT MOSTLY HIT THE FLOOR. MY SHIRT MAY BE A LITTLE SORE WITH YOU, THOUGH. IT'S IN THE WASH.
I DID RECOGNIZE YOU, YA KNOW.
WHAT?
FROM SCHOOL. YOU'RE HARD TO FORGET. DID YOU SEE ALL OF THAT. WHAT HAPPENED THEN, I MEAN.

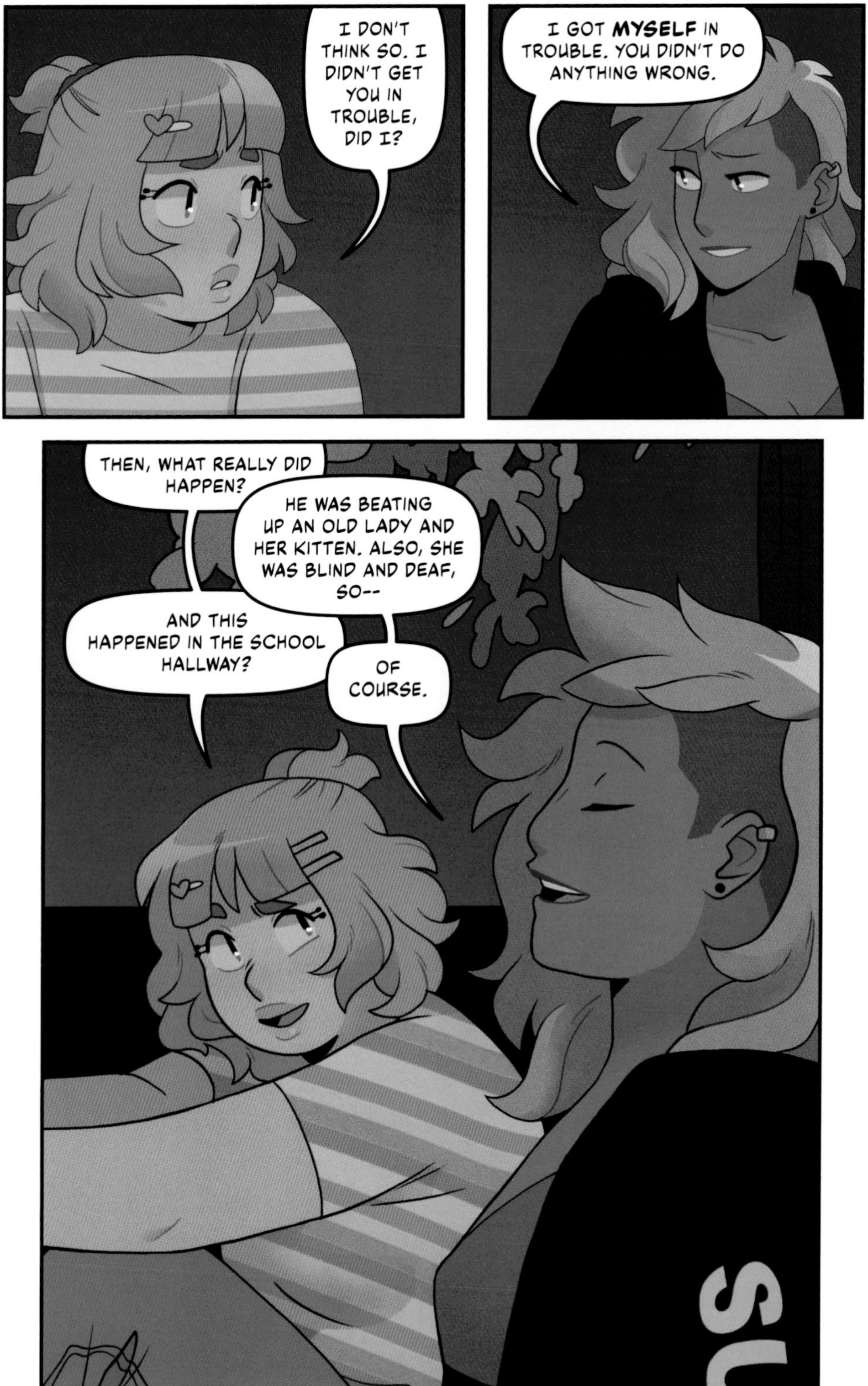
I DON'T THINK SO. I DIDN'T GET YOU IN TROUBLE, DID I?
I GOT **MYSELF** IN TROUBLE. YOU DIDN'T DO ANYTHING WRONG.
THEN, WHAT REALLY DID HAPPEN?
HE WAS BEATING UP AN OLD LADY AND HER KITTEN. ALSO, SHE WAS BLIND AND DEAF, SO--
AND THIS HAPPENED IN THE SCHOOL HALLWAY?
OF COURSE.

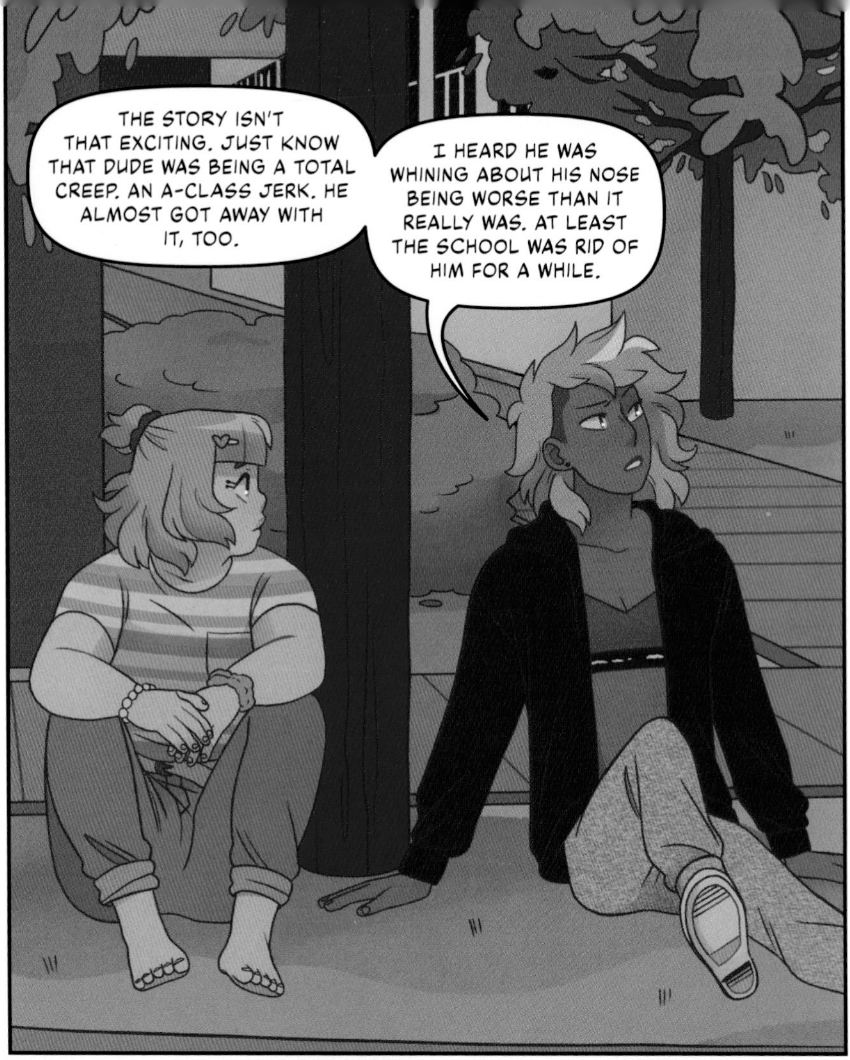
THE STORY ISN'T THAT EXCITING. JUST KNOW THAT DUDE WAS BEING A TOTAL CREEP. AN A-CLASS JERK. HE ALMOST GOT AWAY WITH IT, TOO.
I HEARD HE WAS WHINING ABOUT HIS NOSE BEING WORSE THAN IT REALLY WAS. AT LEAST THE SCHOOL WAS RID OF HIM FOR A WHILE.

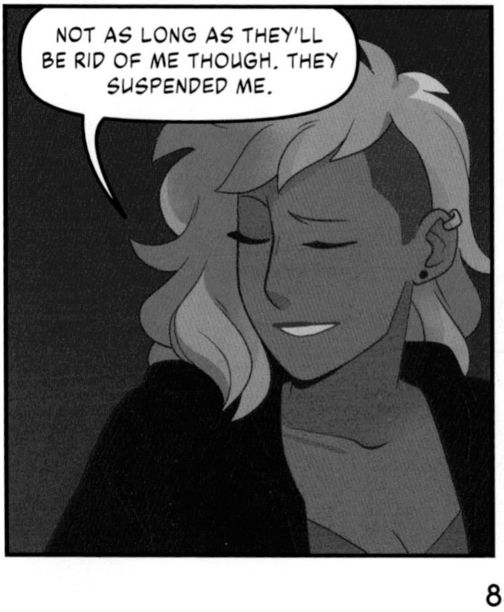
NOT AS LONG AS THEY'LL BE RID OF ME THOUGH. THEY SUSPENDED ME.

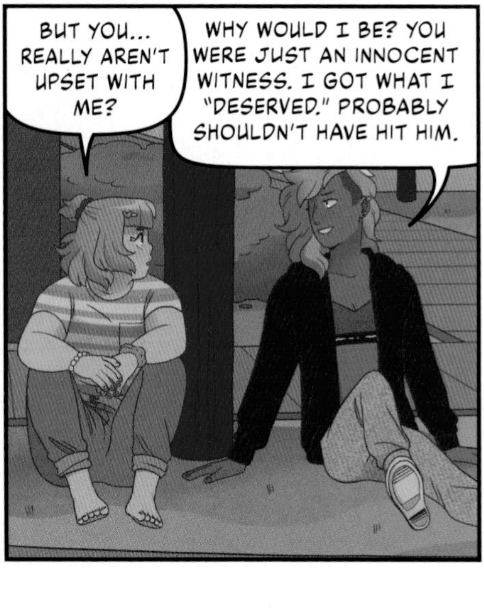
BUT YOU... REALLY AREN'T UPSET WITH ME?
WHY WOULD I BE? YOU WERE JUST AN INNOCENT WITNESS. I GOT WHAT I "DESERVED." PROBABLY SHOULDN'T HAVE HIT HIM.

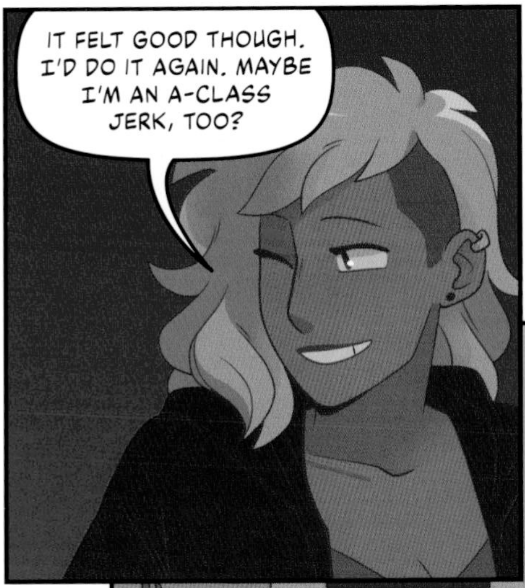
IT FELT GOOD THOUGH. I'D DO IT AGAIN. MAYBE I'M AN A-CLASS JERK, TOO?

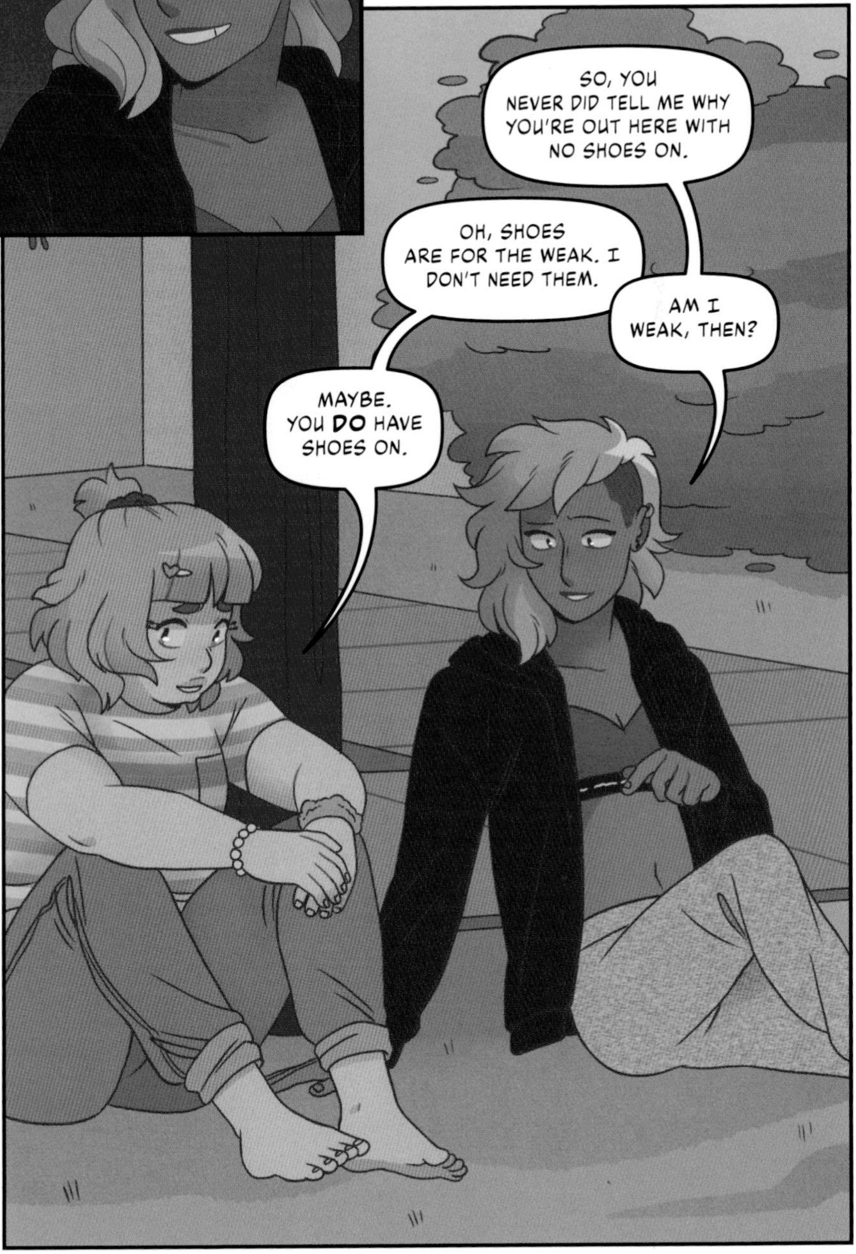
SO, YOU NEVER DID TELL ME WHY YOU'RE OUT HERE WITH NO SHOES ON.
OH, SHOES ARE FOR THE WEAK. I DON'T NEED THEM.
AM I WEAK, THEN?
MAYBE. YOU DO HAVE SHOES ON.

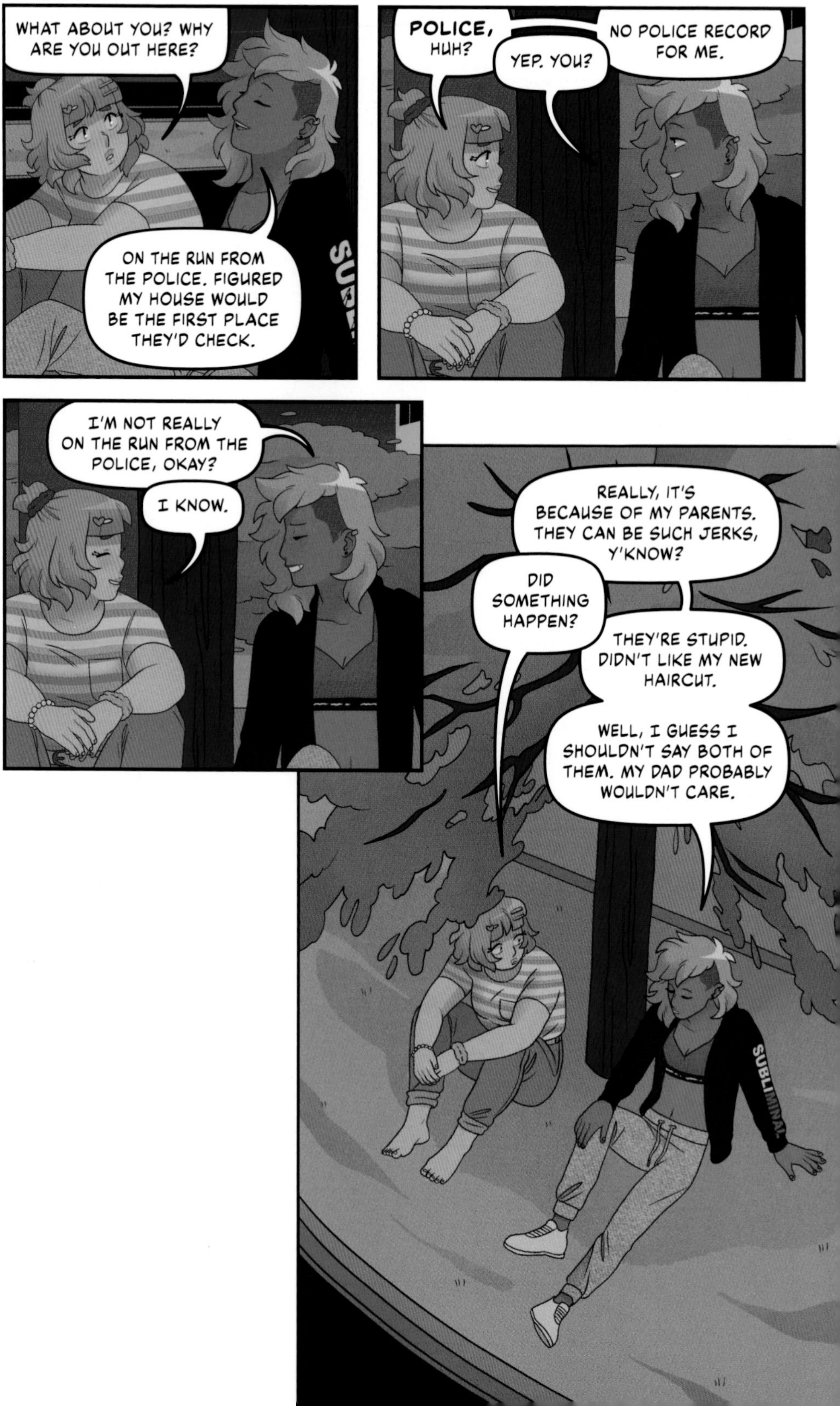
WHAT ABOUT YOU? WHY ARE YOU OUT HERE?
ON THE RUN FROM THE POLICE. FIGURED MY HOUSE WOULD BE THE FIRST PLACE THEY'D CHECK.
POLICE, HUH?
YEP. YOU?
NO POLICE RECORD FOR ME.
I'M NOT REALLY ON THE RUN FROM THE POLICE, OKAY?
I KNOW.
REALLY, IT'S BECAUSE OF MY PARENTS. THEY CAN BE SUCH JERKS, Y'KNOW?
DID SOMETHING HAPPEN?
THEY'RE STUPID. DIDN'T LIKE MY NEW HAIRCUT.
WELL, I GUESS I SHOULDN'T SAY BOTH OF THEM. MY DAD PROBABLY WOULDN'T CARE.
SUBLIMINAL

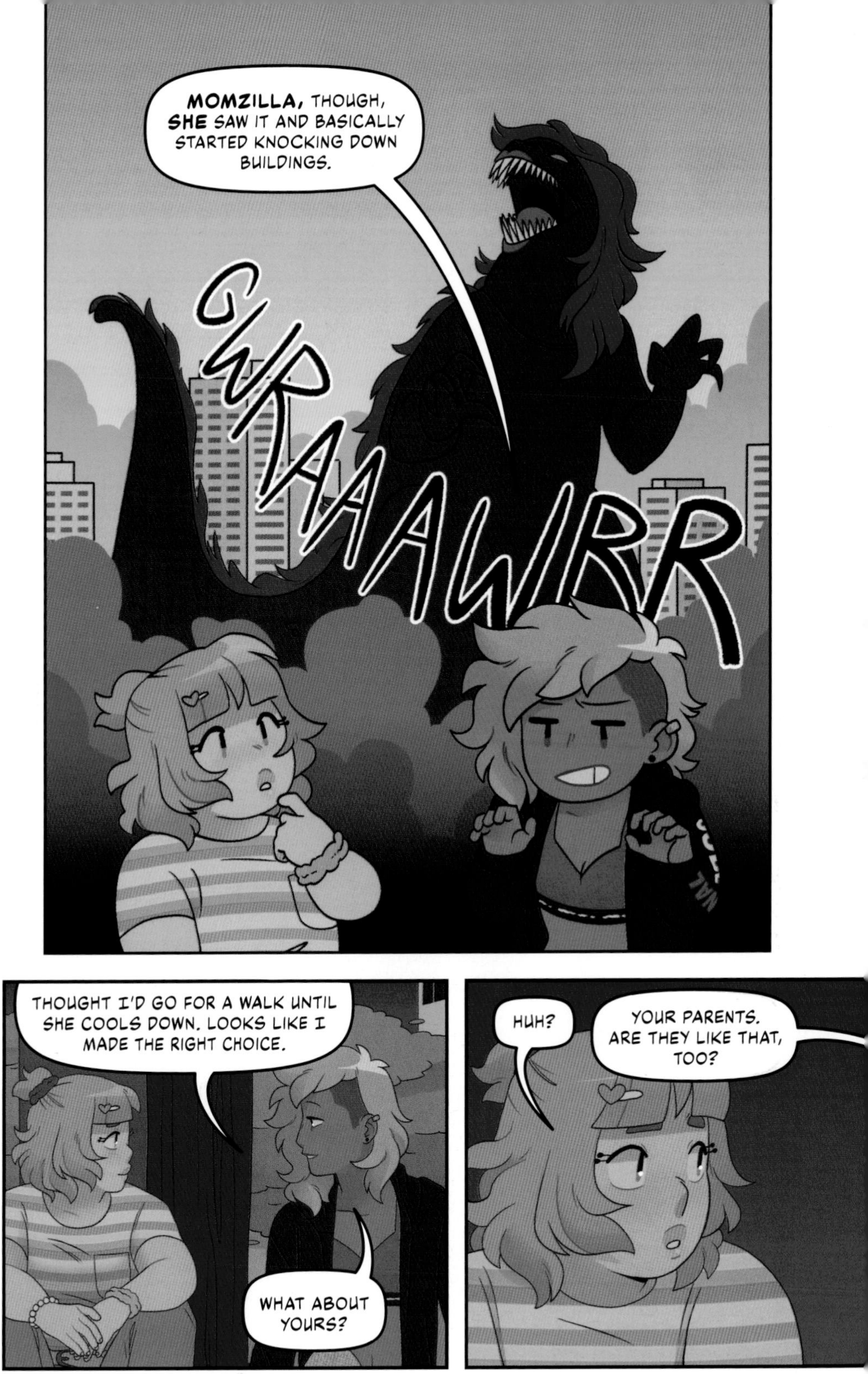
MOMZILLA, THOUGH, SHE SAW IT AND BASICALLY STARTED KNOCKING DOWN BUILDINGS.
GWRAAAWRR
THOUGHT I'D GO FOR A WALK UNTIL SHE COOLS DOWN. LOOKS LIKE I MADE THE RIGHT CHOICE.
WHAT ABOUT YOURS?
HUH?
YOUR PARENTS. ARE THEY LIKE THAT, TOO?

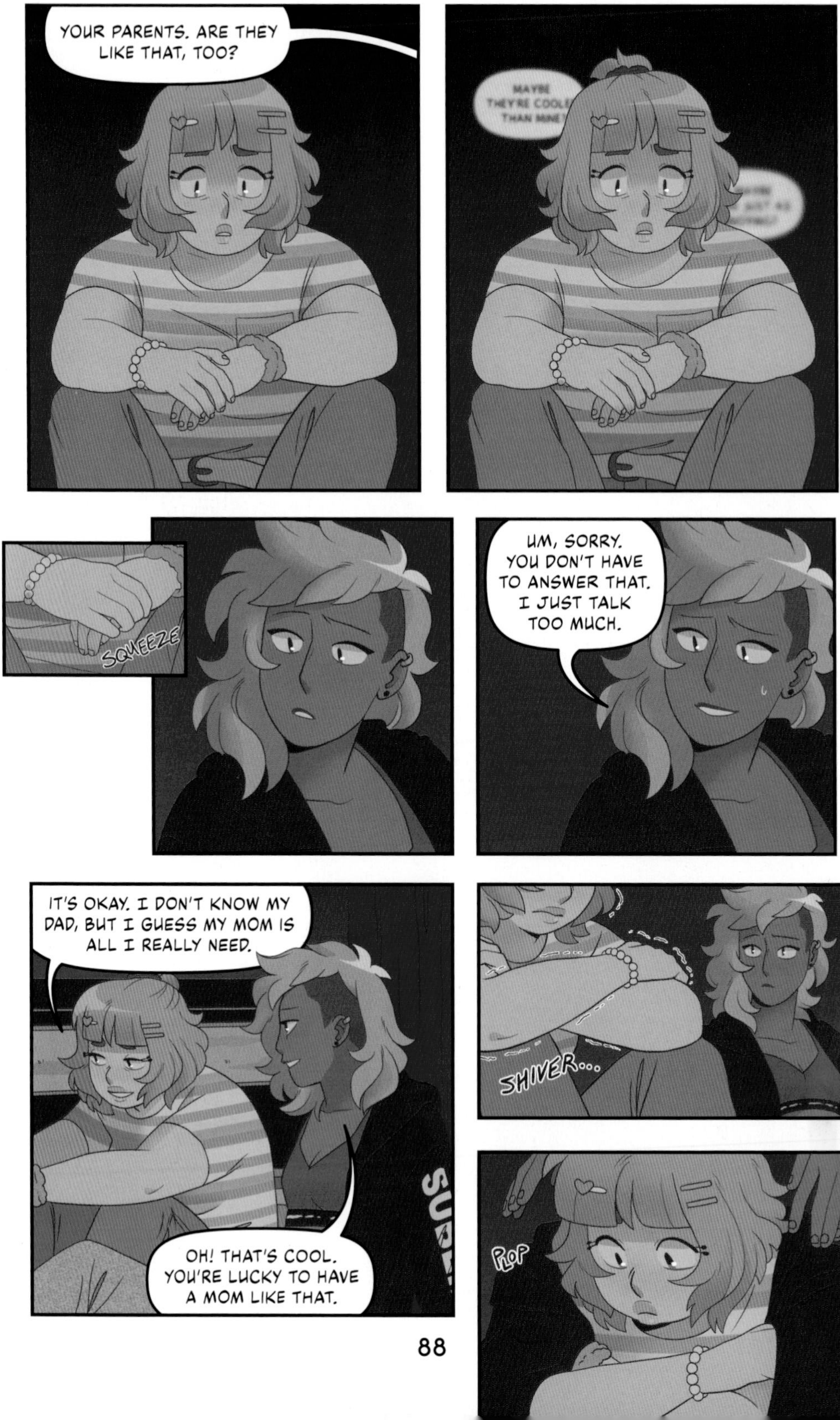

YOUR PARENTS. ARE THEY LIKE THAT, TOO?
MAYBE THEY'RE COOLE THAN MINE
SQUEEZE
UM, SORRY. YOU DON'T HAVE TO ANSWER THAT. I JUST TALK TOO MUCH.
IT'S OKAY. I DON'T KNOW MY DAD, BUT I GUESS MY MOM IS ALL I REALLY NEED.
OH! THAT'S COOL. YOU'RE LUCKY TO HAVE A MOM LIKE THAT.
SHIVER...
PLOP

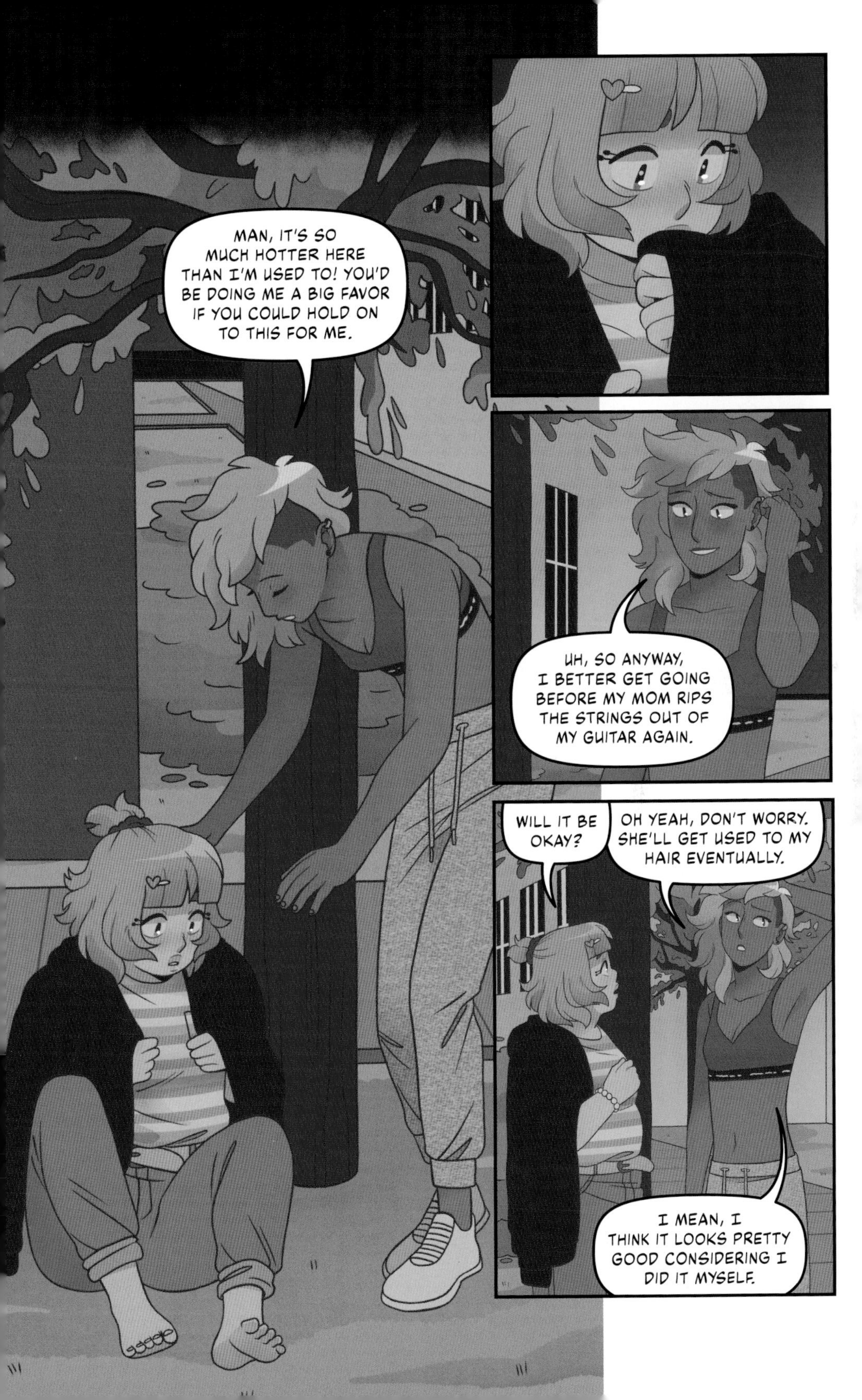
MAN, IT'S SO MUCH HOTTER HERE THAN I'M USED TO! YOU'D BE DOING ME A BIG FAVOR IF YOU COULD HOLD ON TO THIS FOR ME.
UH, SO ANYWAY, I BETTER GET GOING BEFORE MY MOM RIPS THE STRINGS OUT OF MY GUITAR AGAIN.
WILL IT BE OKAY?
OH YEAH, DON'T WORRY. SHE'LL GET USED TO MY HAIR EVENTUALLY.
I MEAN, I THINK IT LOOKS PRETTY GOOD CONSIDERING I DID IT MYSELF.

I THINK SO, TOO.

OH!

SO MUCH GUM...!?

CAN I USE YOUR BACK?

UM, SURE?

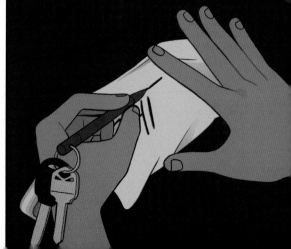

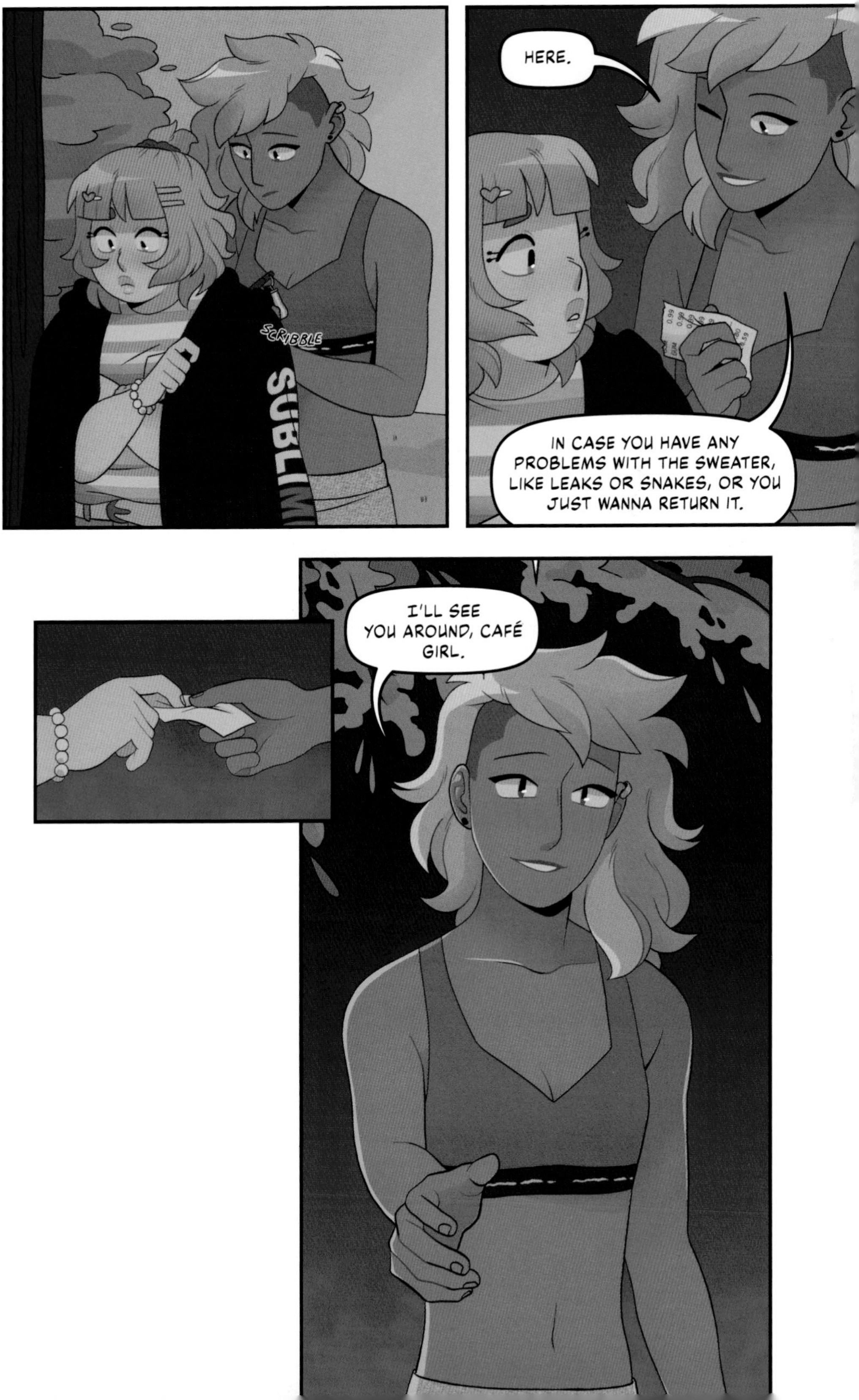
SCRIBBLE
SUBLIM
HERE.
IN CASE YOU HAVE ANY PROBLEMS WITH THE SWEATER, LIKE LEAKS OR SNAKES, OR YOU JUST WANNA RETURN IT.
I'LL SEE YOU AROUND, CAFÉ GIRL.

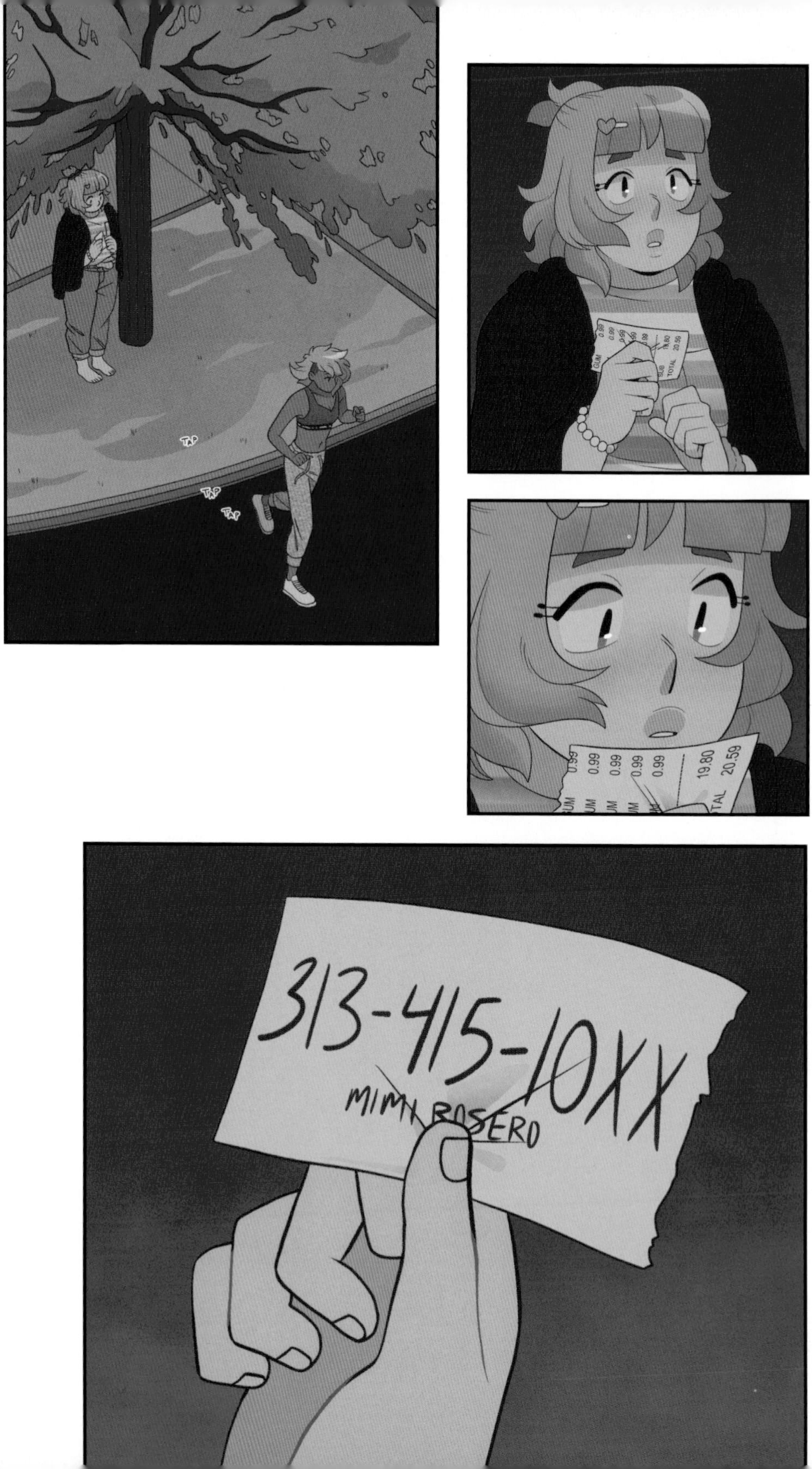
TAP
TAP
TAP
0.99
0.99
0.99
0.99
0.99
19.80
20.59
313-415-10XX
MIMI ROSERO

CHAPTER 3

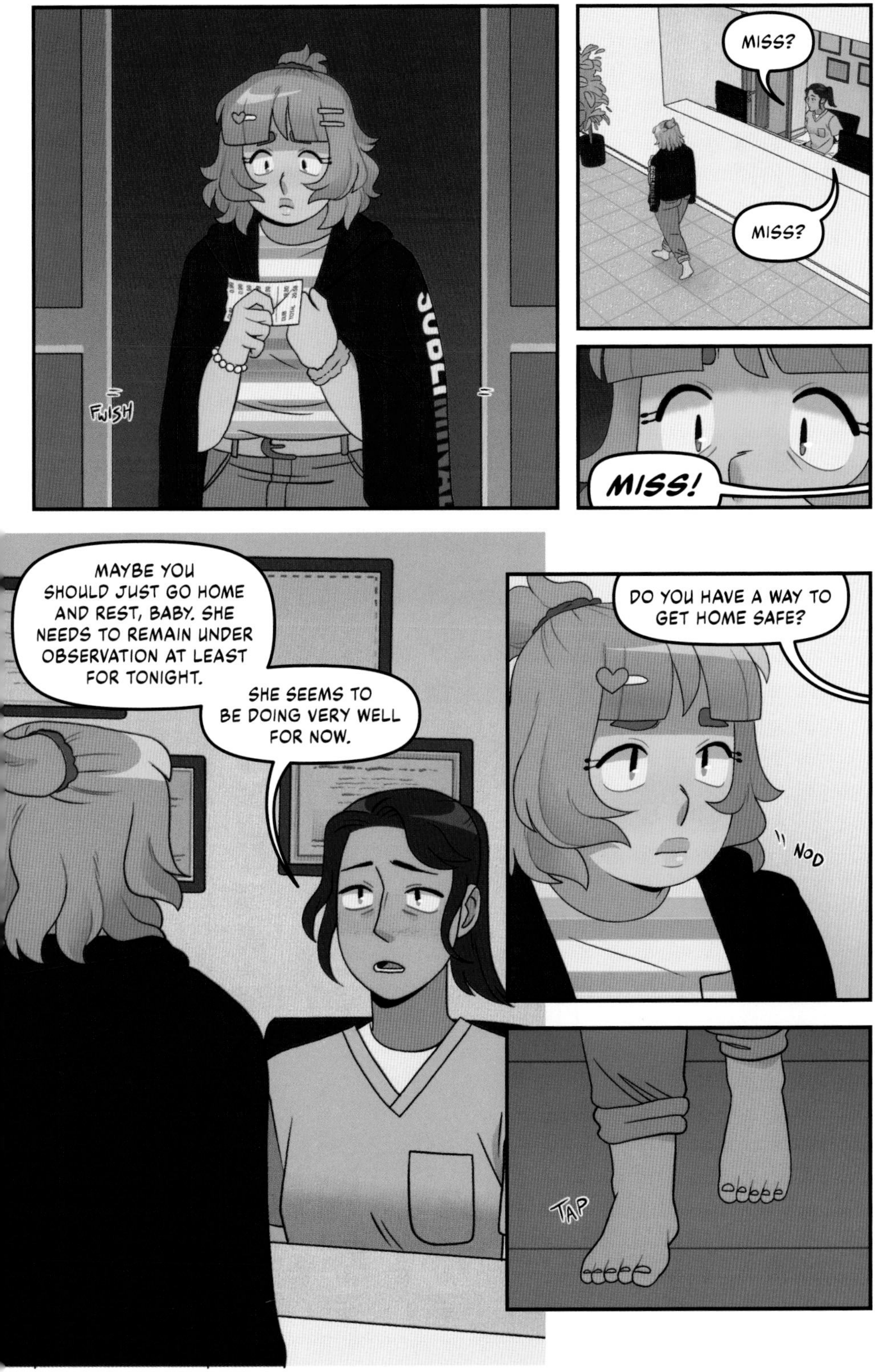
FWISH
MISS?
MISS?
MISS!
MAYBE YOU SHOULD JUST GO HOME AND REST, BABY. SHE NEEDS TO REMAIN UNDER OBSERVATION AT LEAST FOR TONIGHT.
SHE SEEMS TO BE DOING VERY WELL FOR NOW.
DO YOU HAVE A WAY TO GET HOME SAFE?
NOD
TAP

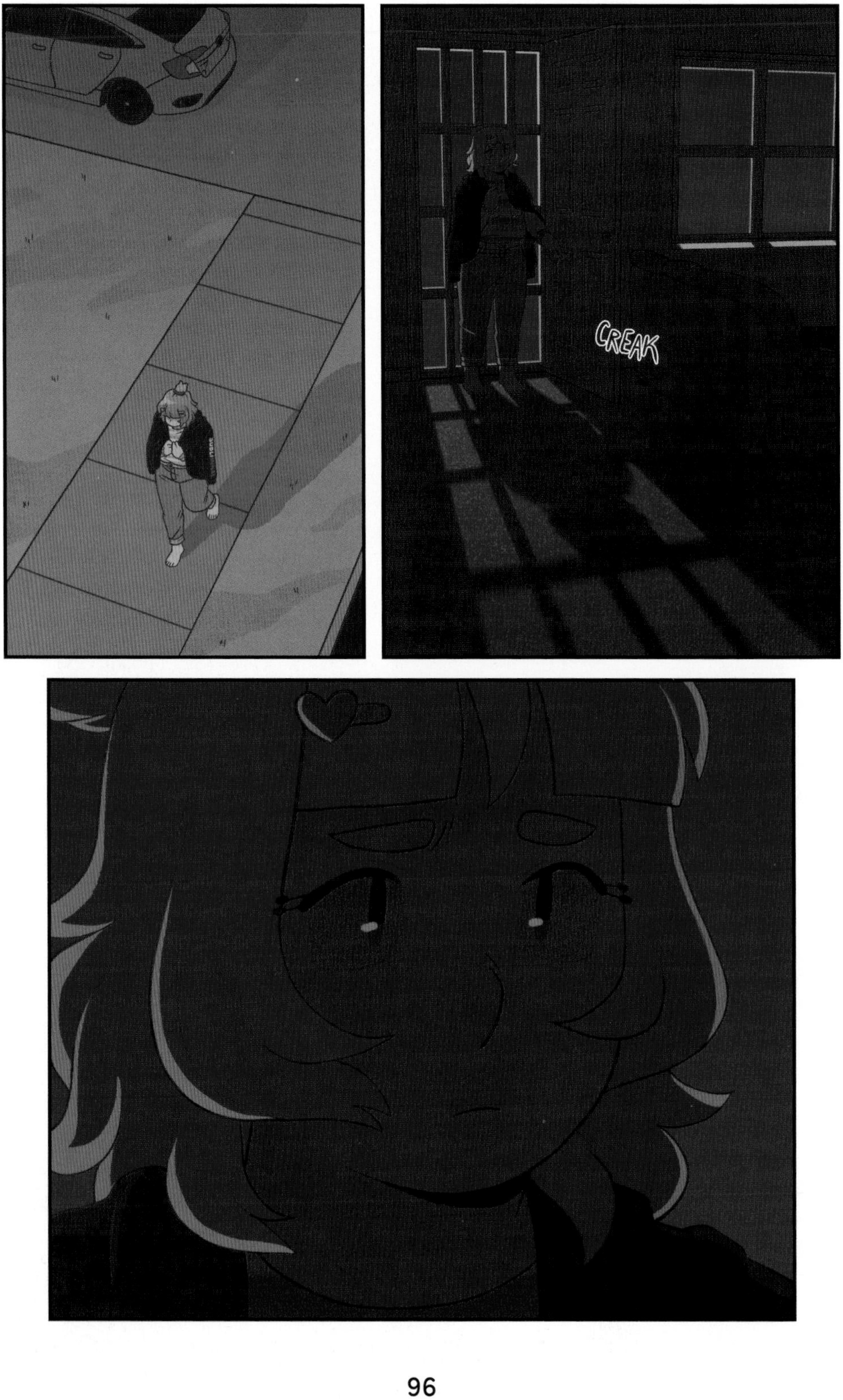
CREAK

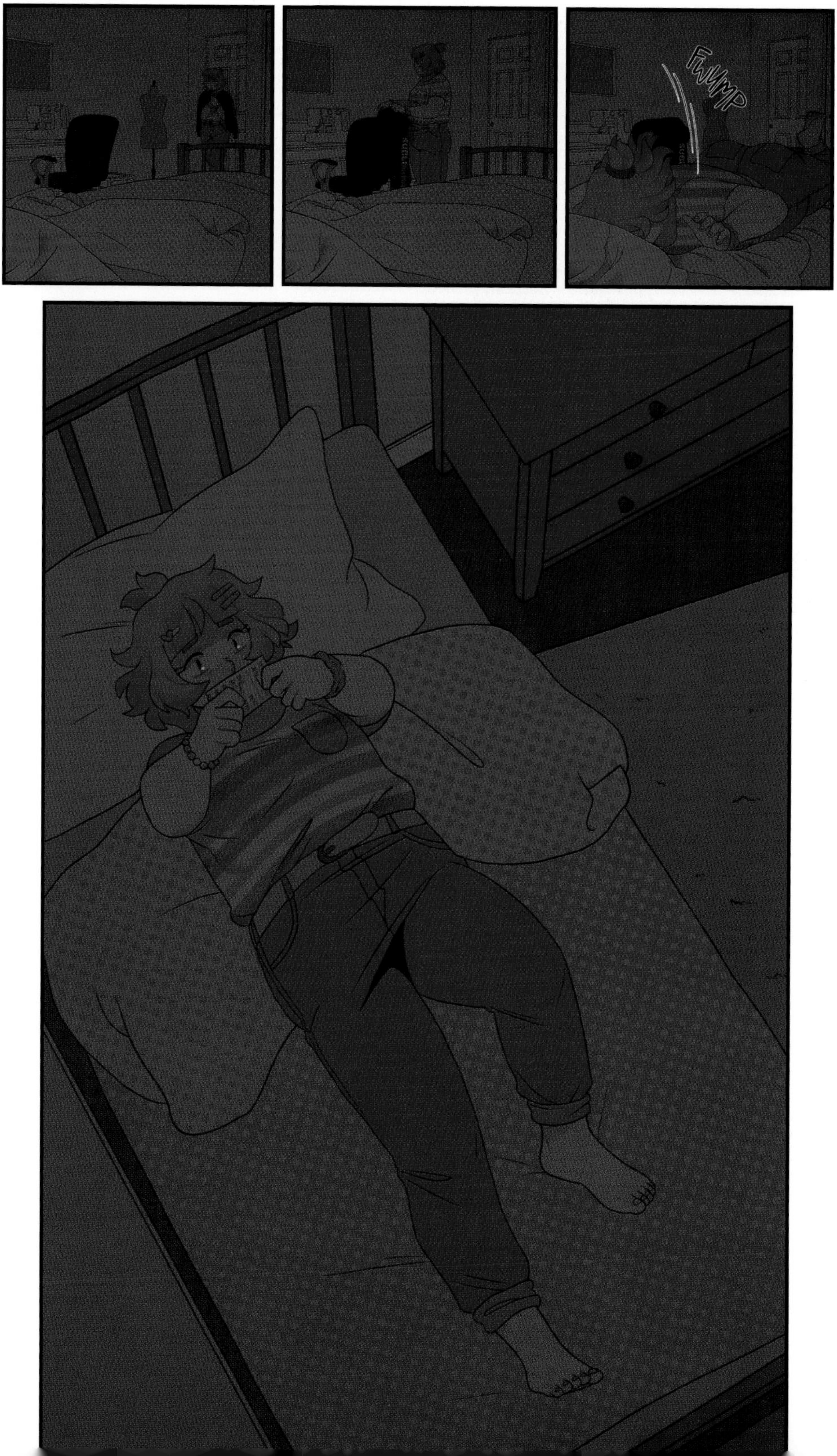
FWUMP

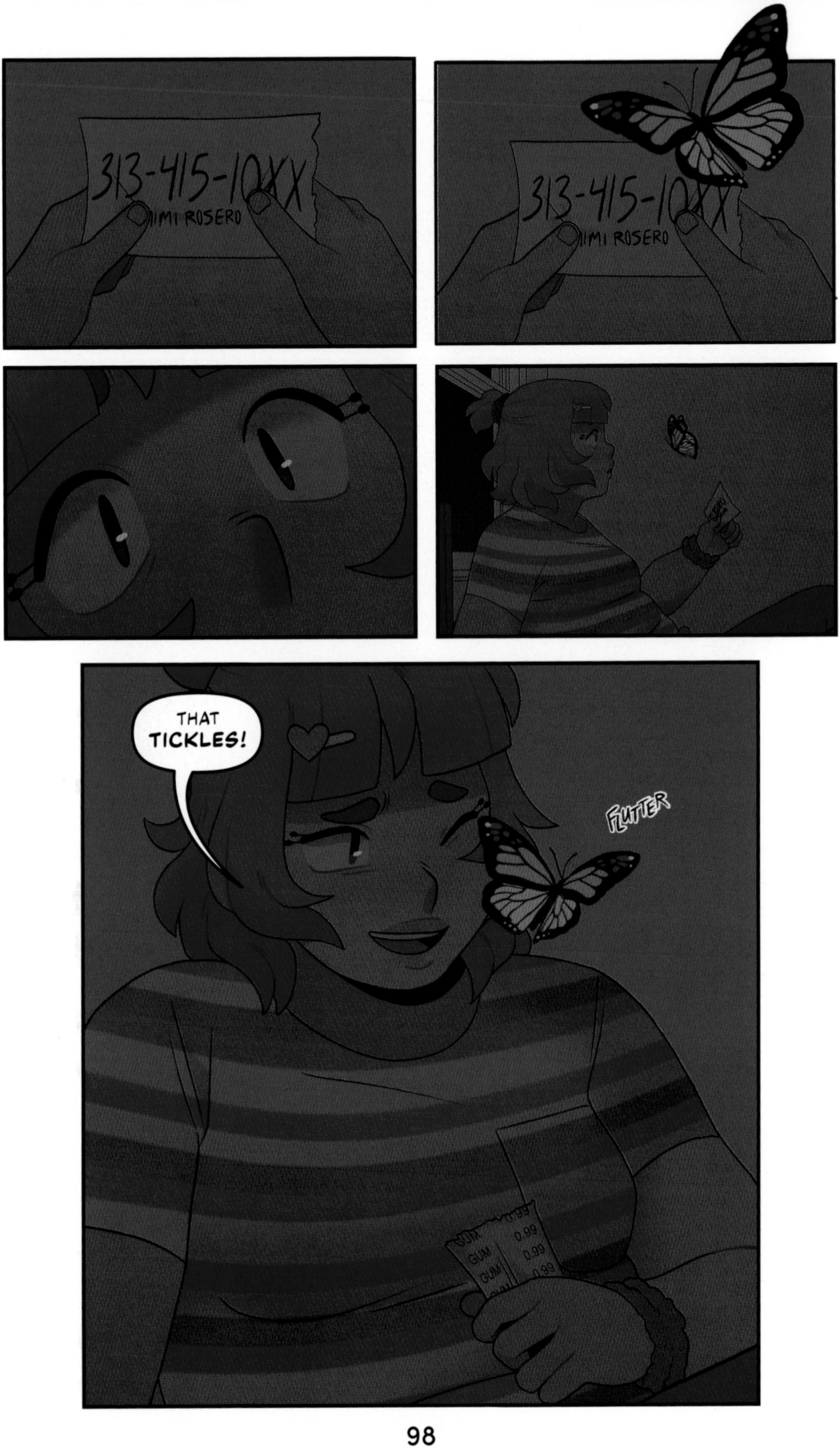
313-415-10XX
313-415-10XX
THAT TICKLES!
FLUTTER

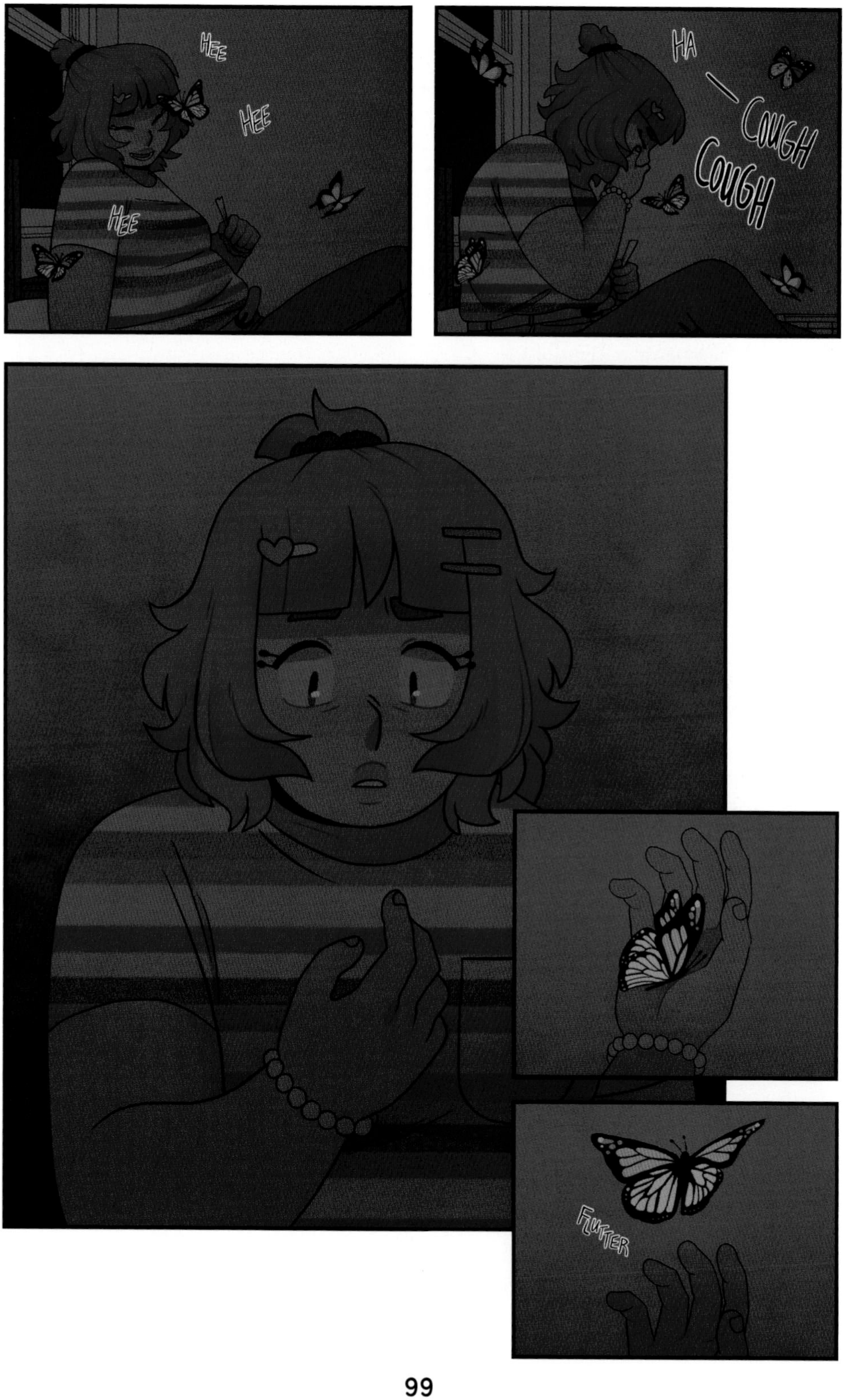
HEE
HEE
HEE
HA—COUGH
COUGH
FLUTTER

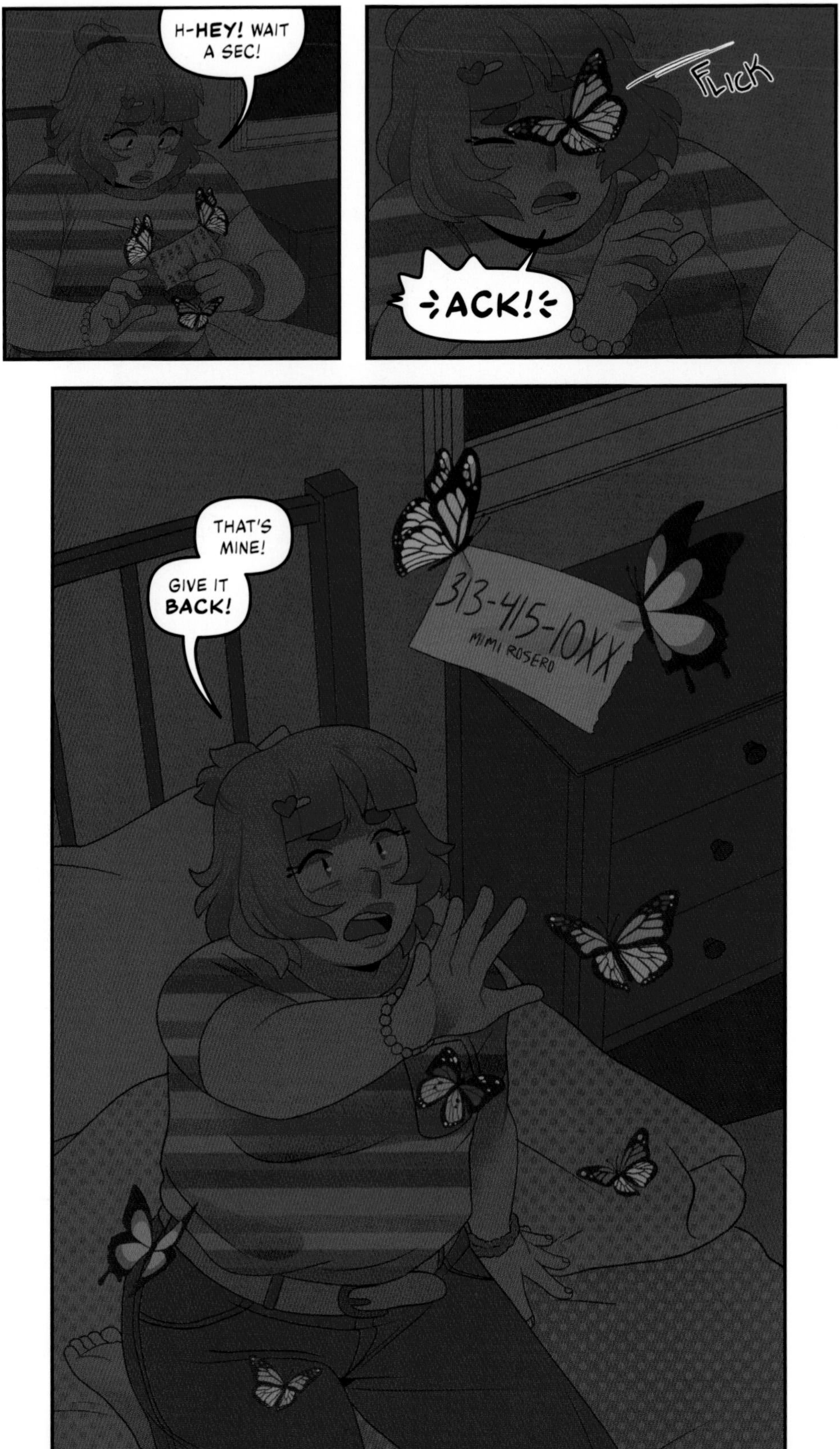
H-HEY! WAIT A SEC!
FLICK
ACK!
THAT'S MINE!
GIVE IT BACK!
313-415-10XX
MIMI ROSERO

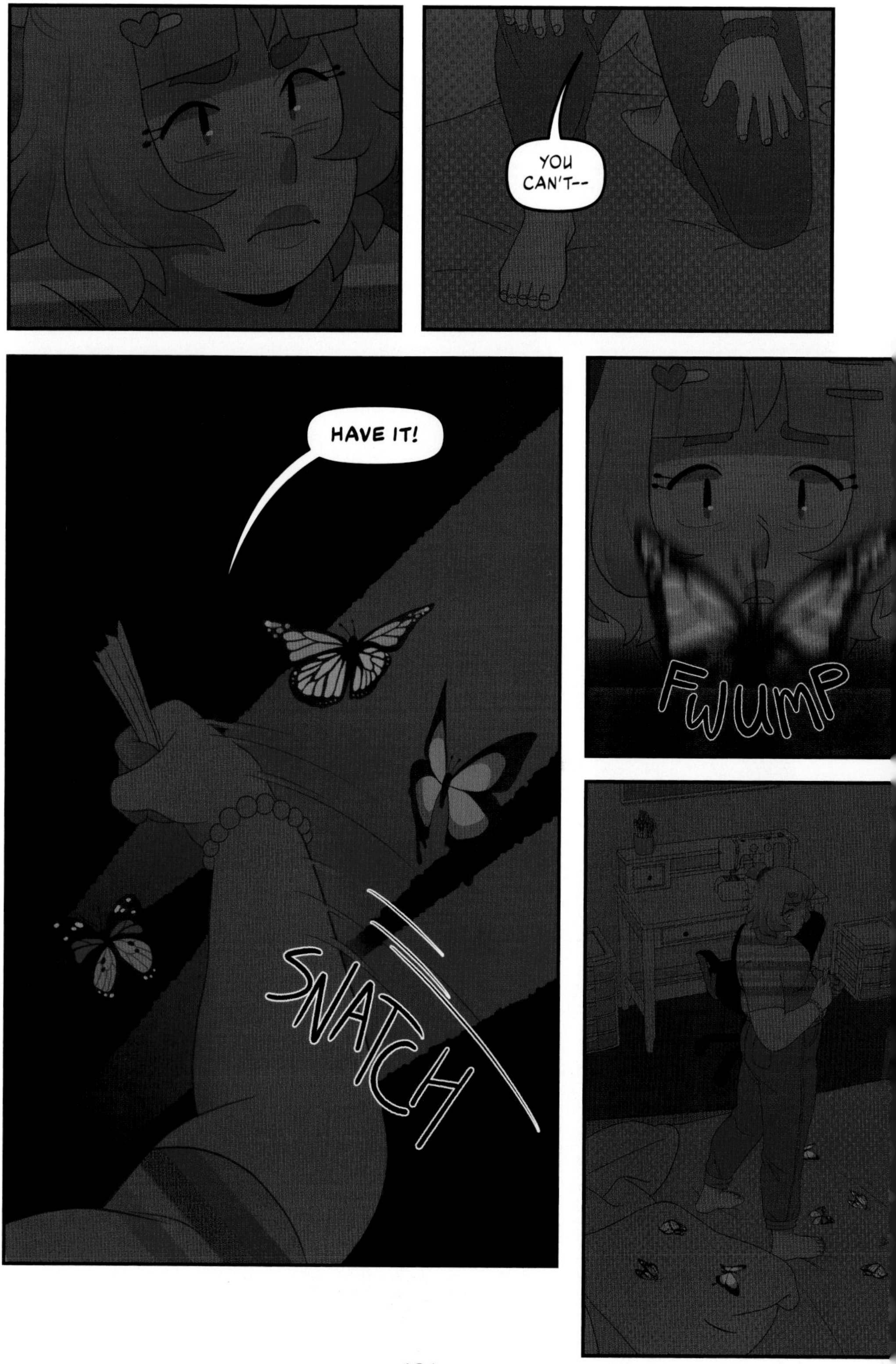
YOU CAN'T--
HAVE IT!
SNATCH
FWUMP

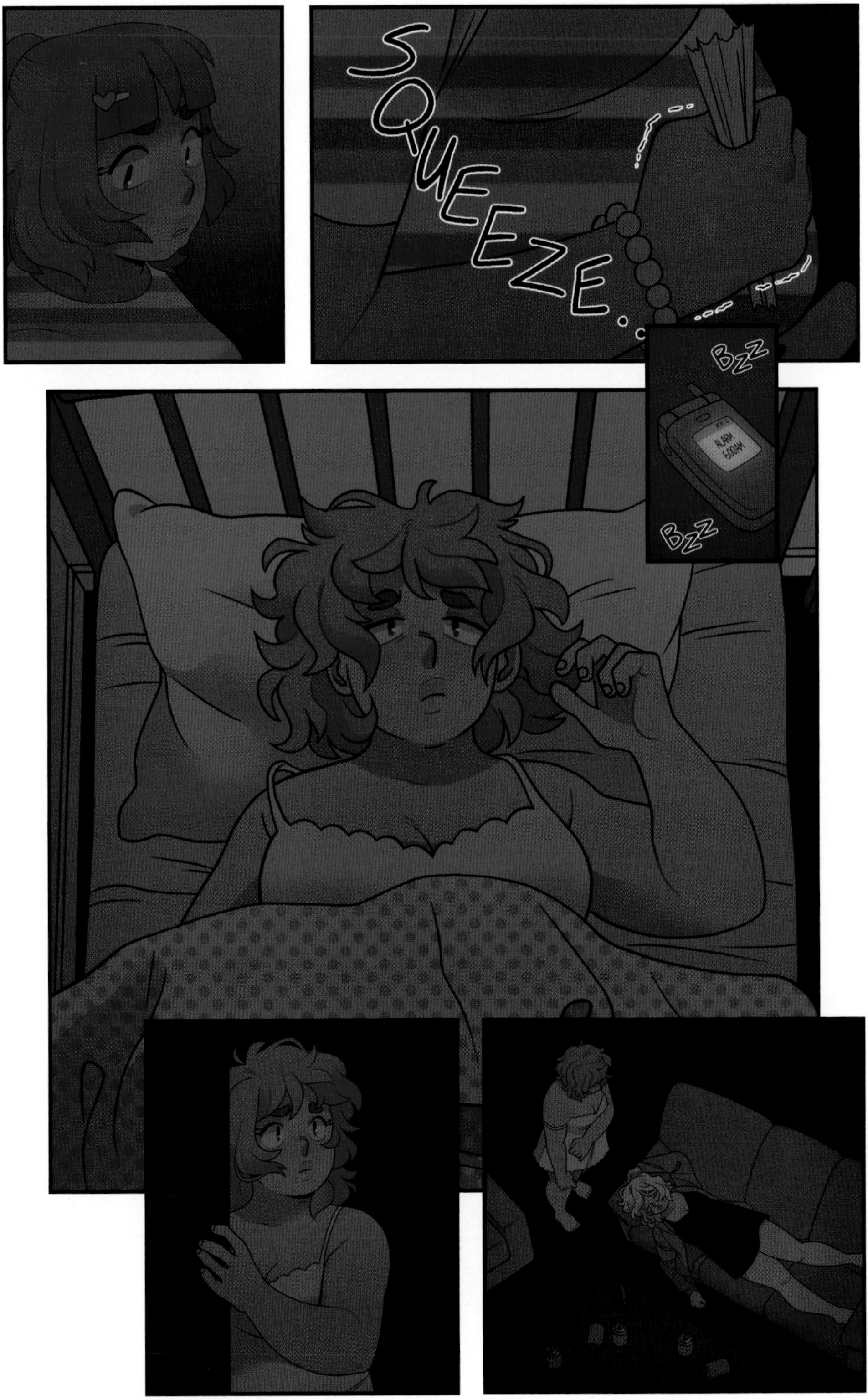
SQUEEZE...
Bzz
ALARM
6:00AM
Bzz

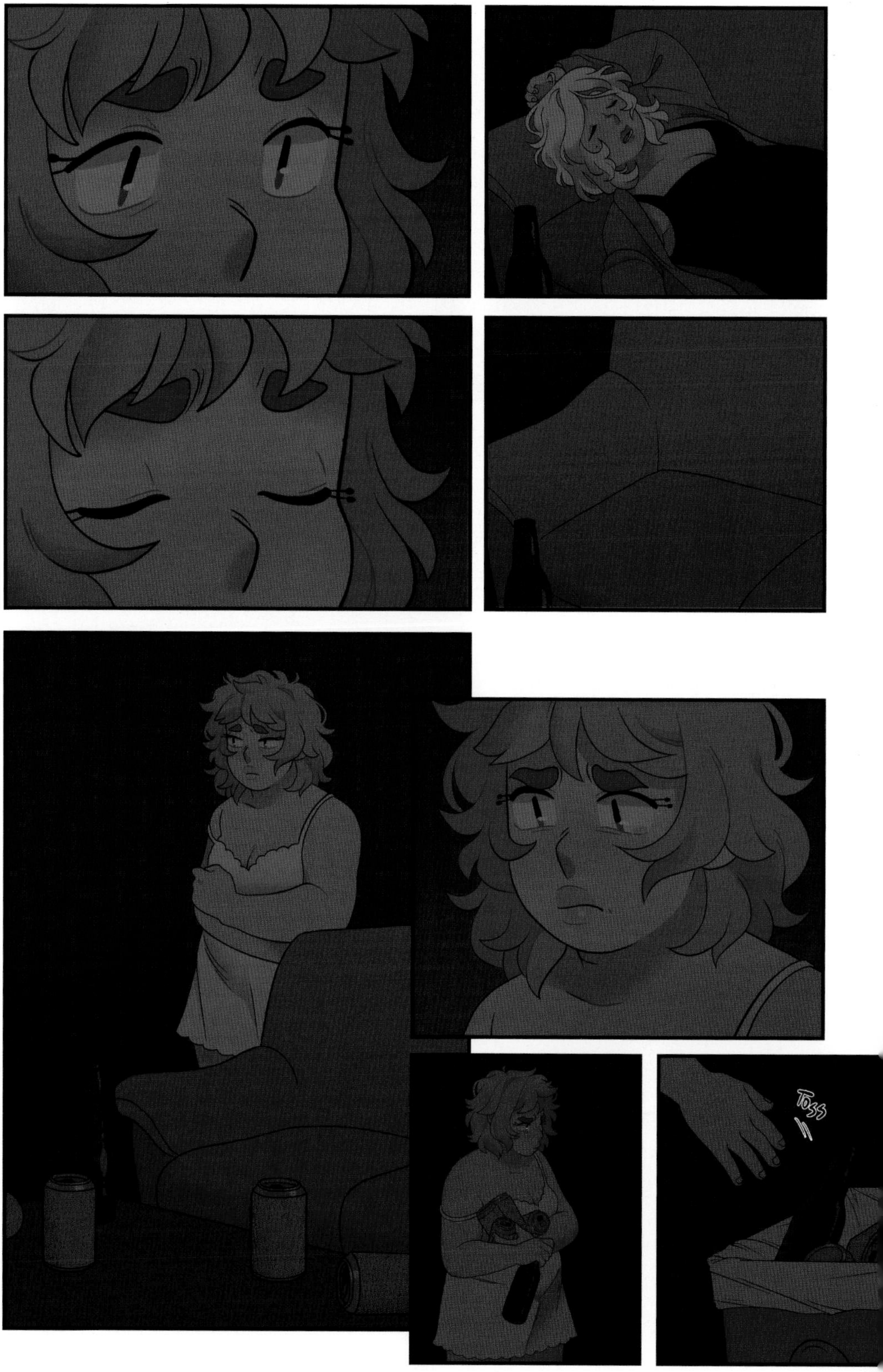
TOSS

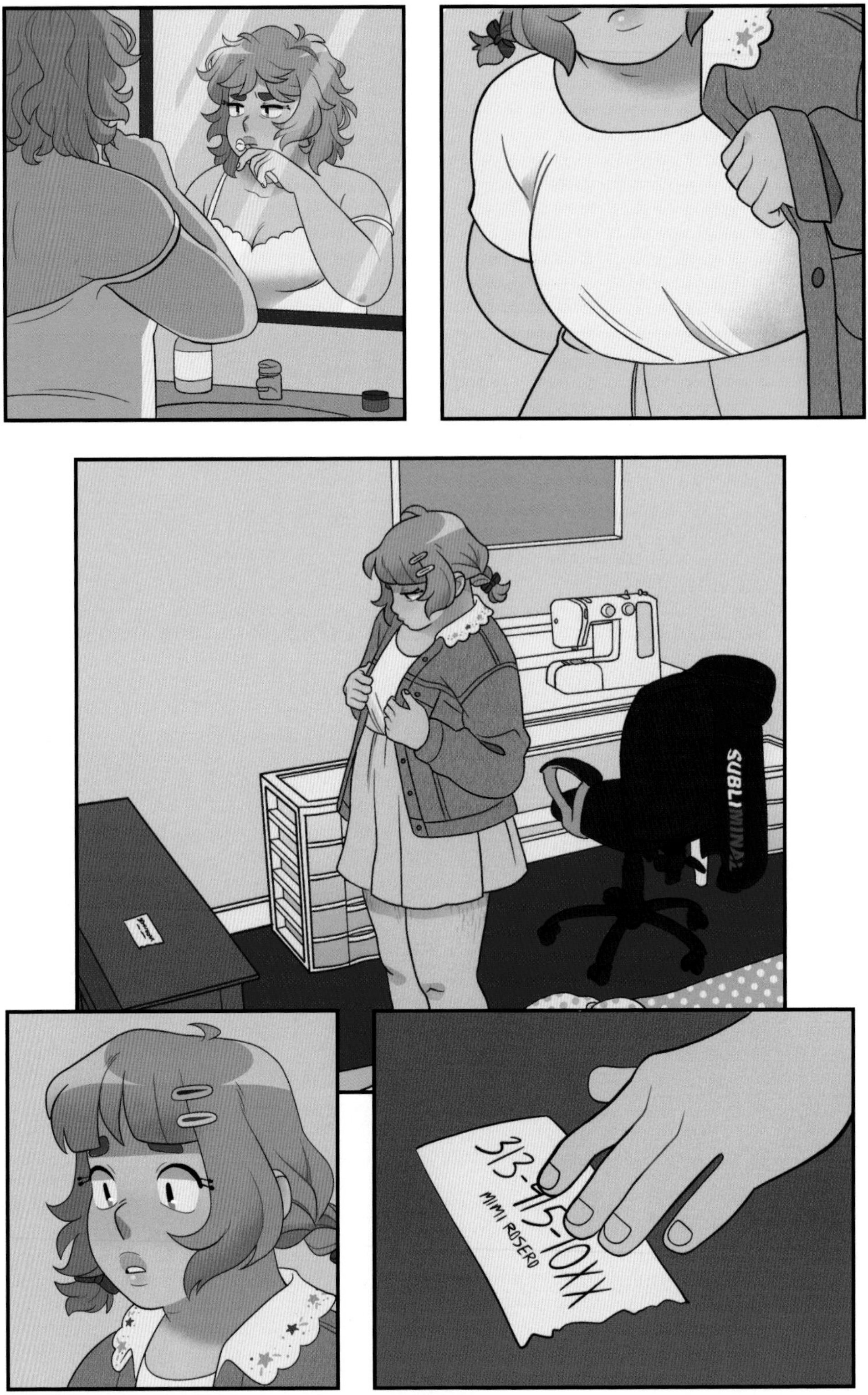
SUBLIMINAL
313-915-10XX
MIMI ROSERO

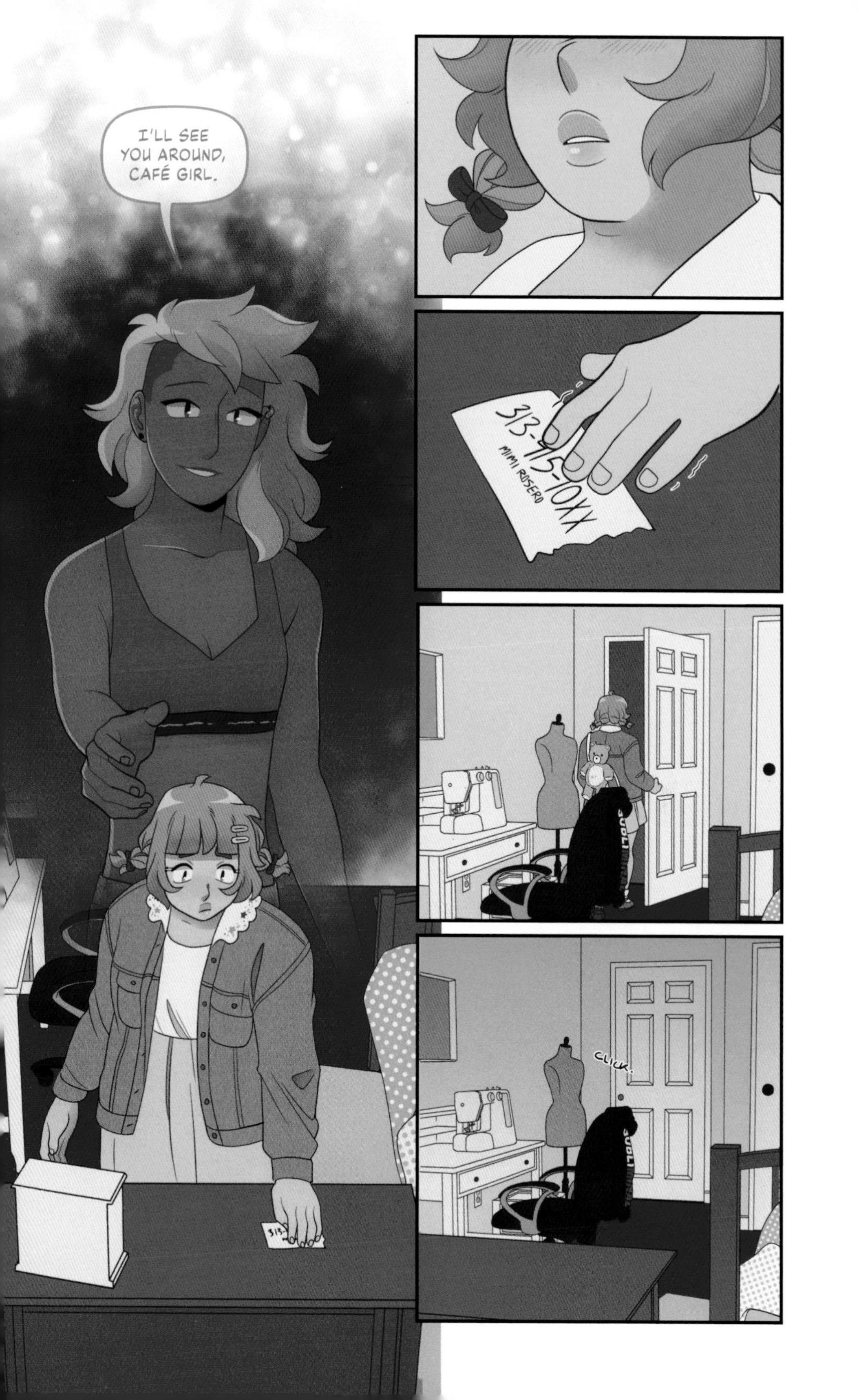
I'LL SEE YOU AROUND, CAFÉ GIRL.
MIMI ROSERO
CLICK.

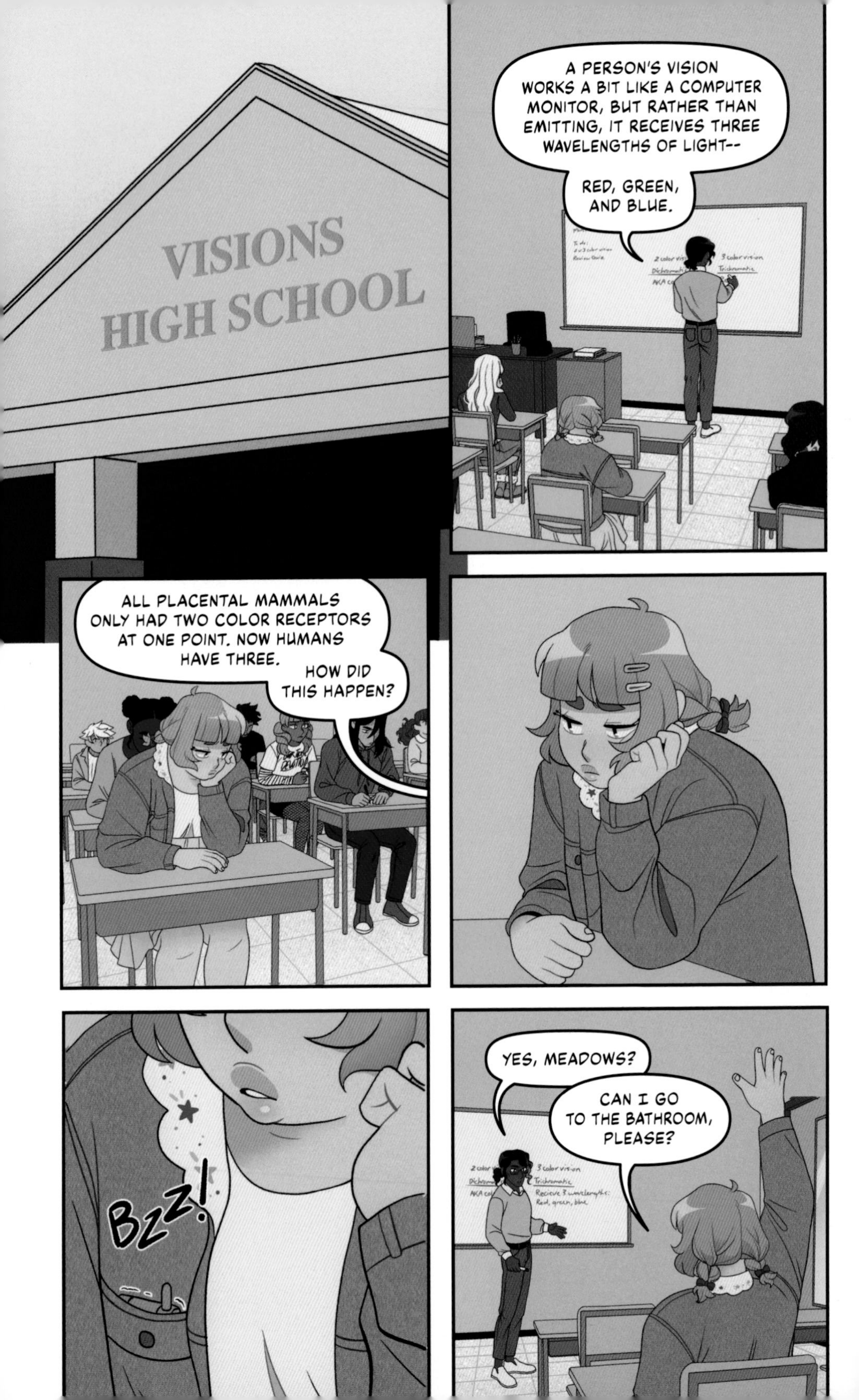
VISIONS HIGH SCHOOL
A PERSON'S VISION WORKS A BIT LIKE A COMPUTER MONITOR, BUT RATHER THAN EMITTING, IT RECEIVES THREE WAVELENGTHS OF LIGHT--
RED, GREEN, AND BLUE.
ALL PLACENTAL MAMMALS ONLY HAD TWO COLOR RECEPTORS AT ONE POINT. NOW HUMANS HAVE THREE.
HOW DID THIS HAPPEN?
BZZ!
YES, MEADOWS?
CAN I GO TO THE BATHROOM, PLEASE?

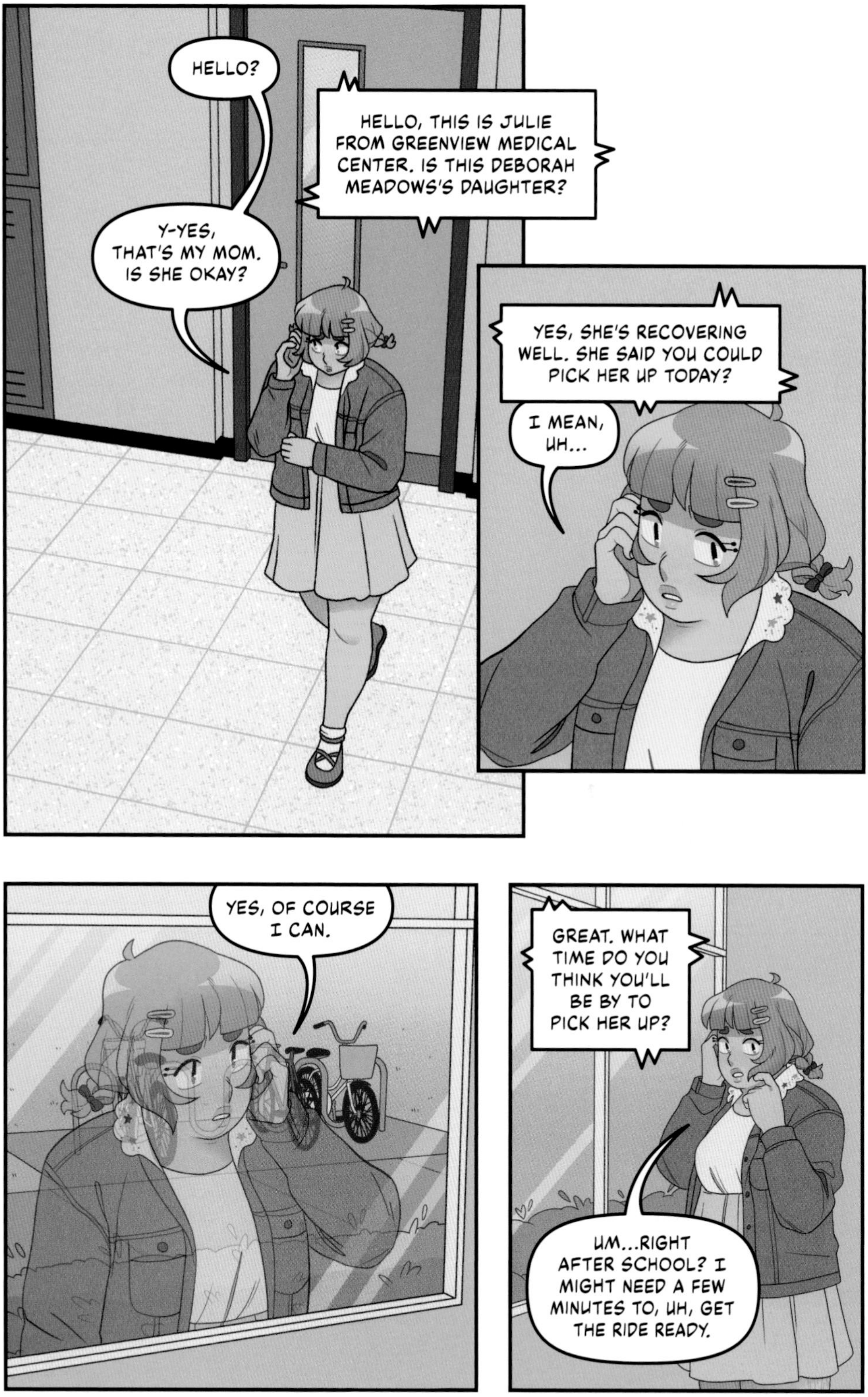
HELLO?
HELLO, THIS IS JULIE FROM GREENVIEW MEDICAL CENTER. IS THIS DEBORAH MEADOWS'S DAUGHTER?
Y-YES, THAT'S MY MOM. IS SHE OKAY?
YES, SHE'S RECOVERING WELL. SHE SAID YOU COULD PICK HER UP TODAY?
I MEAN, UH...
YES, OF COURSE I CAN.
GREAT. WHAT TIME DO YOU THINK YOU'LL BE BY TO PICK HER UP?
UM...RIGHT AFTER SCHOOL? I MIGHT NEED A FEW MINUTES TO, UH, GET THE RIDE READY.

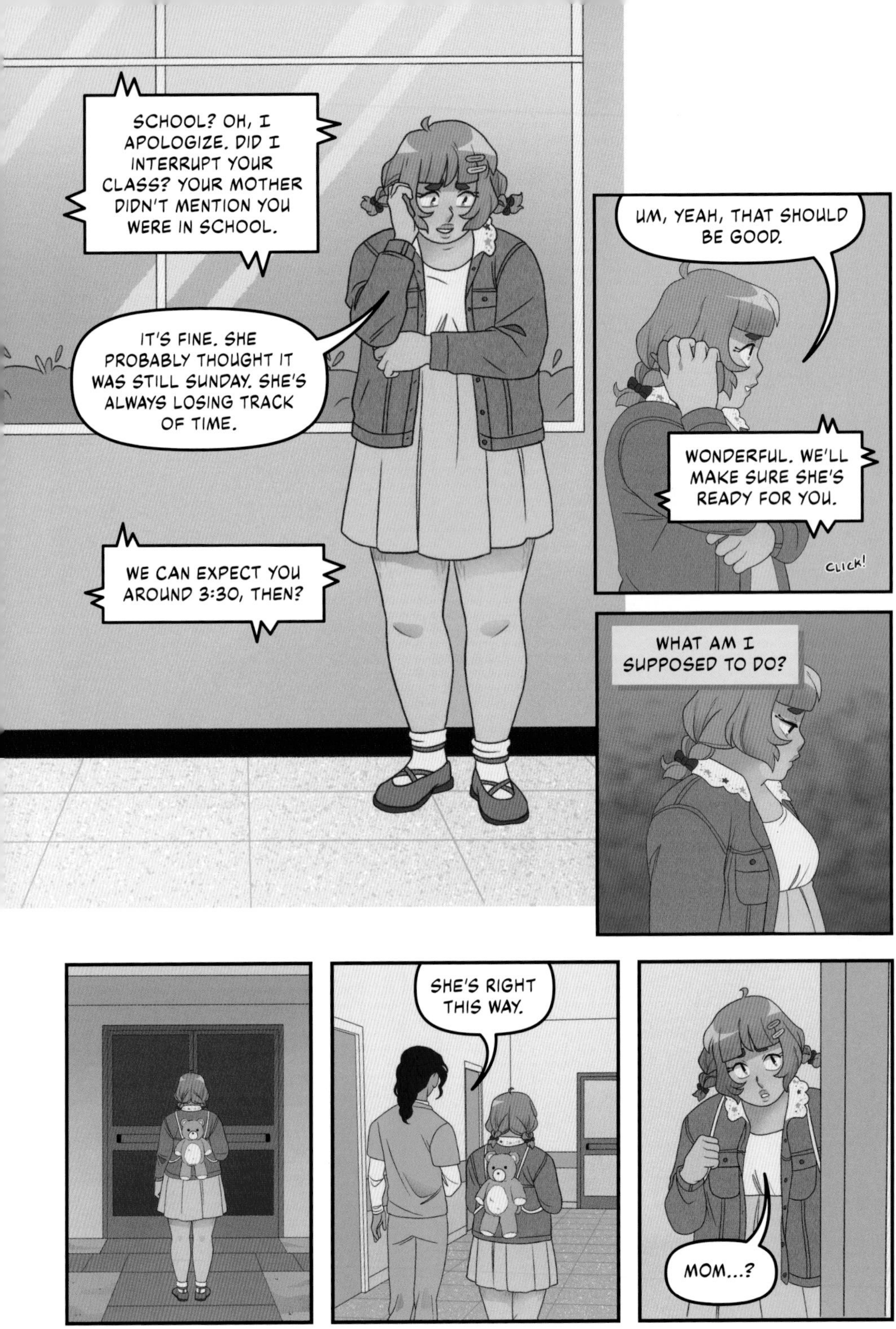
SCHOOL? OH, I APOLOGIZE. DID I INTERRUPT YOUR CLASS? YOUR MOTHER DIDN'T MENTION YOU WERE IN SCHOOL.
IT'S FINE. SHE PROBABLY THOUGHT IT WAS STILL SUNDAY. SHE'S ALWAYS LOSING TRACK OF TIME.
WE CAN EXPECT YOU AROUND 3:30, THEN?
UM, YEAH, THAT SHOULD BE GOOD.
WONDERFUL. WE'LL MAKE SURE SHE'S READY FOR YOU.
CLICK!
WHAT AM I SUPPOSED TO DO?
SHE'S RIGHT THIS WAY.
MOM...?

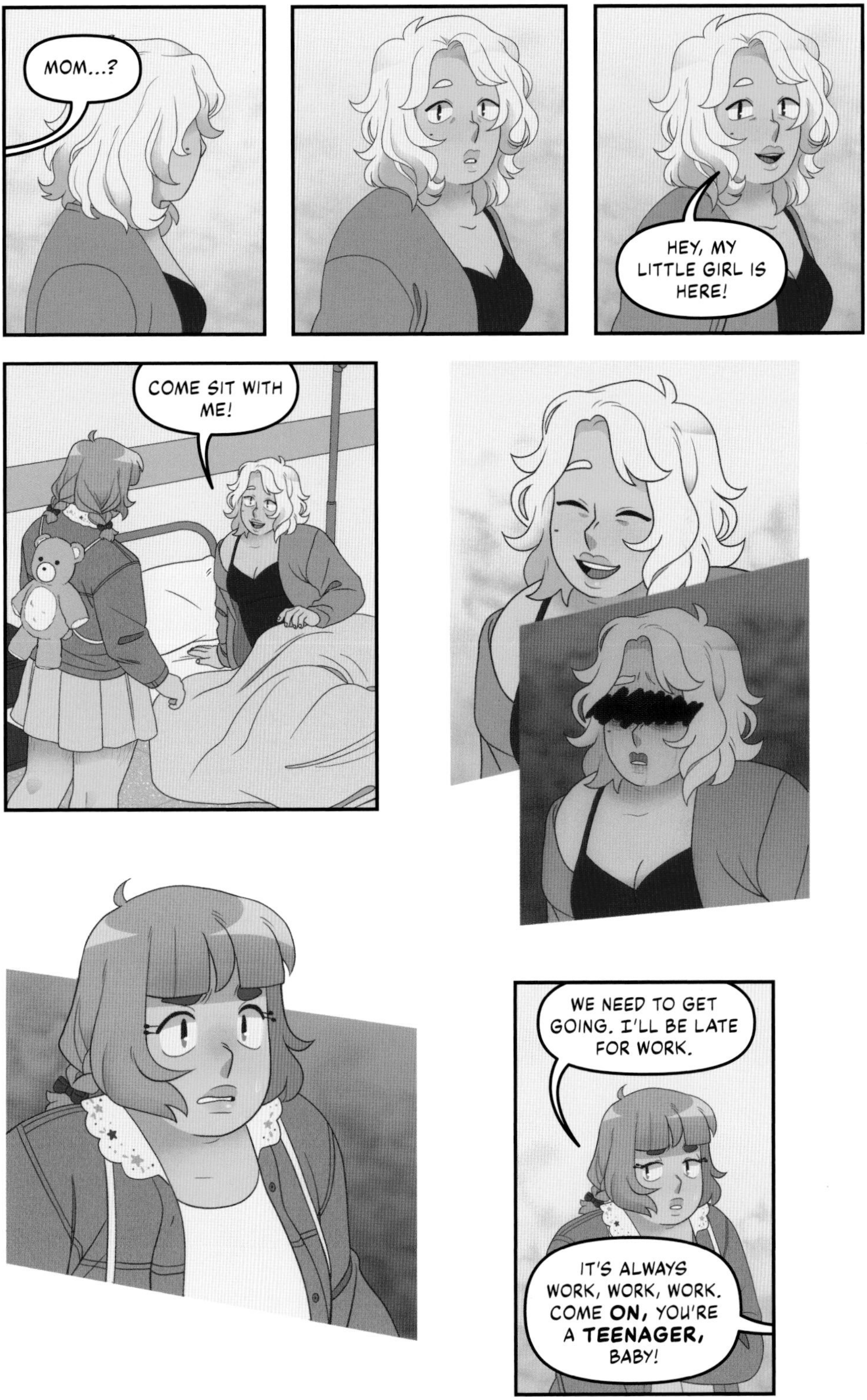
MOM...?
HEY, MY LITTLE GIRL IS HERE!
COME SIT WITH ME!
WE NEED TO GET GOING. I'LL BE LATE FOR WORK.
IT'S ALWAYS WORK, WORK, WORK. COME ON, YOU'RE A TEENAGER, BABY!

HUG—?

WHEN **I** WAS YOUR AGE--

I KNOW, MOM. COME ON.

FINE.

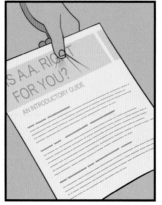

IS A.A. RIGHT FOR YOU?

AN INTRODUCTORY GUIDE

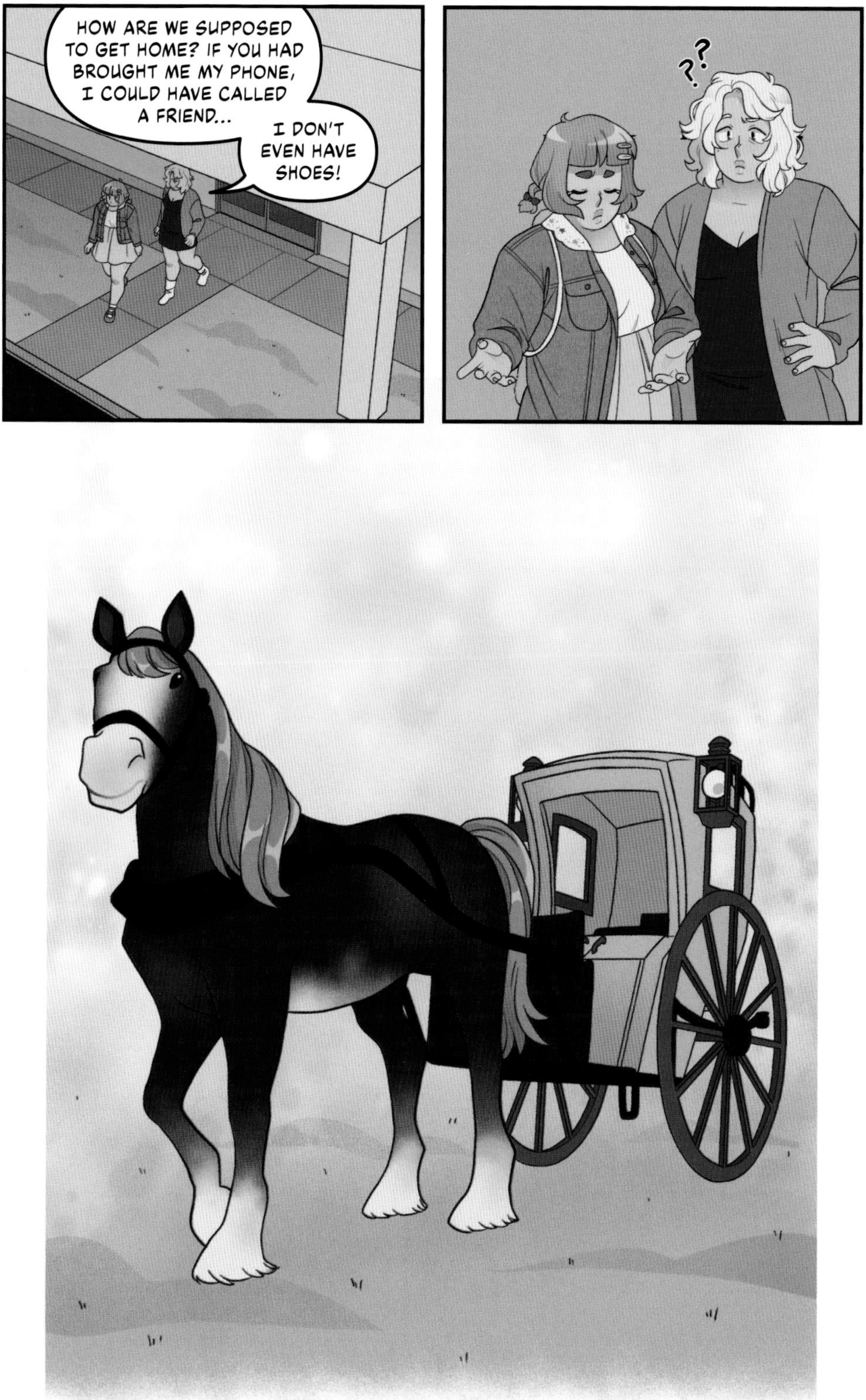
HOW ARE WE SUPPOSED TO GET HOME? IF YOU HAD BROUGHT ME MY PHONE, I COULD HAVE CALLED A FRIEND...
I DON'T EVEN HAVE SHOES!
??

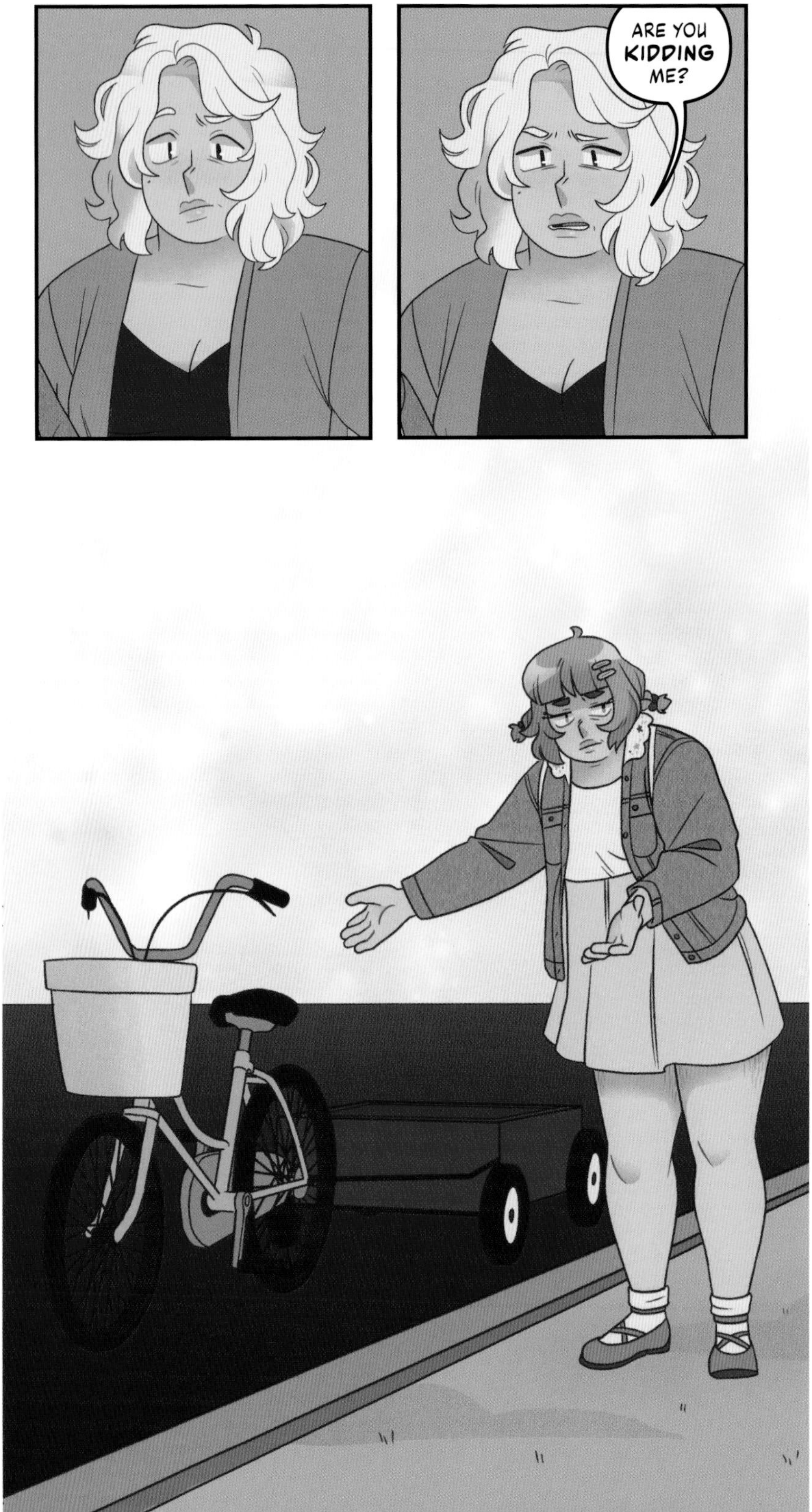
ARE YOU **KIDDING** ME?

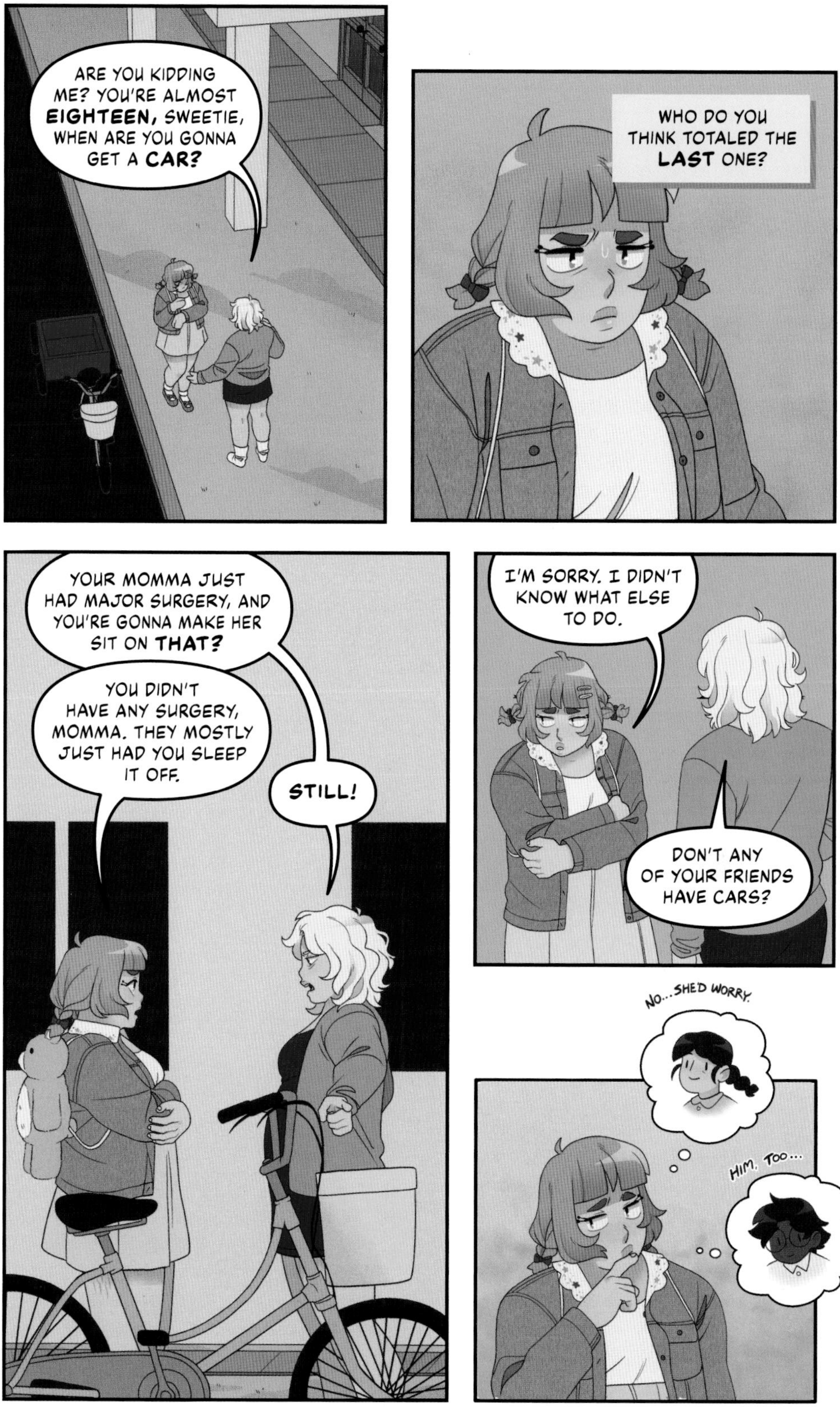
ARE YOU KIDDING ME? YOU'RE ALMOST EIGHTEEN, SWEETIE, WHEN ARE YOU GONNA GET A CAR?
WHO DO YOU THINK TOTALED THE LAST ONE?
YOUR MOMMA JUST HAD MAJOR SURGERY, AND YOU'RE GONNA MAKE HER SIT ON THAT?
YOU DIDN'T HAVE ANY SURGERY, MOMMA. THEY MOSTLY JUST HAD YOU SLEEP IT OFF.
STILL!
I'M SORRY. I DIDN'T KNOW WHAT ELSE TO DO.
DON'T ANY OF YOUR FRIENDS HAVE CARS?
NO...SHE'D WORRY.
HIM, TOO...

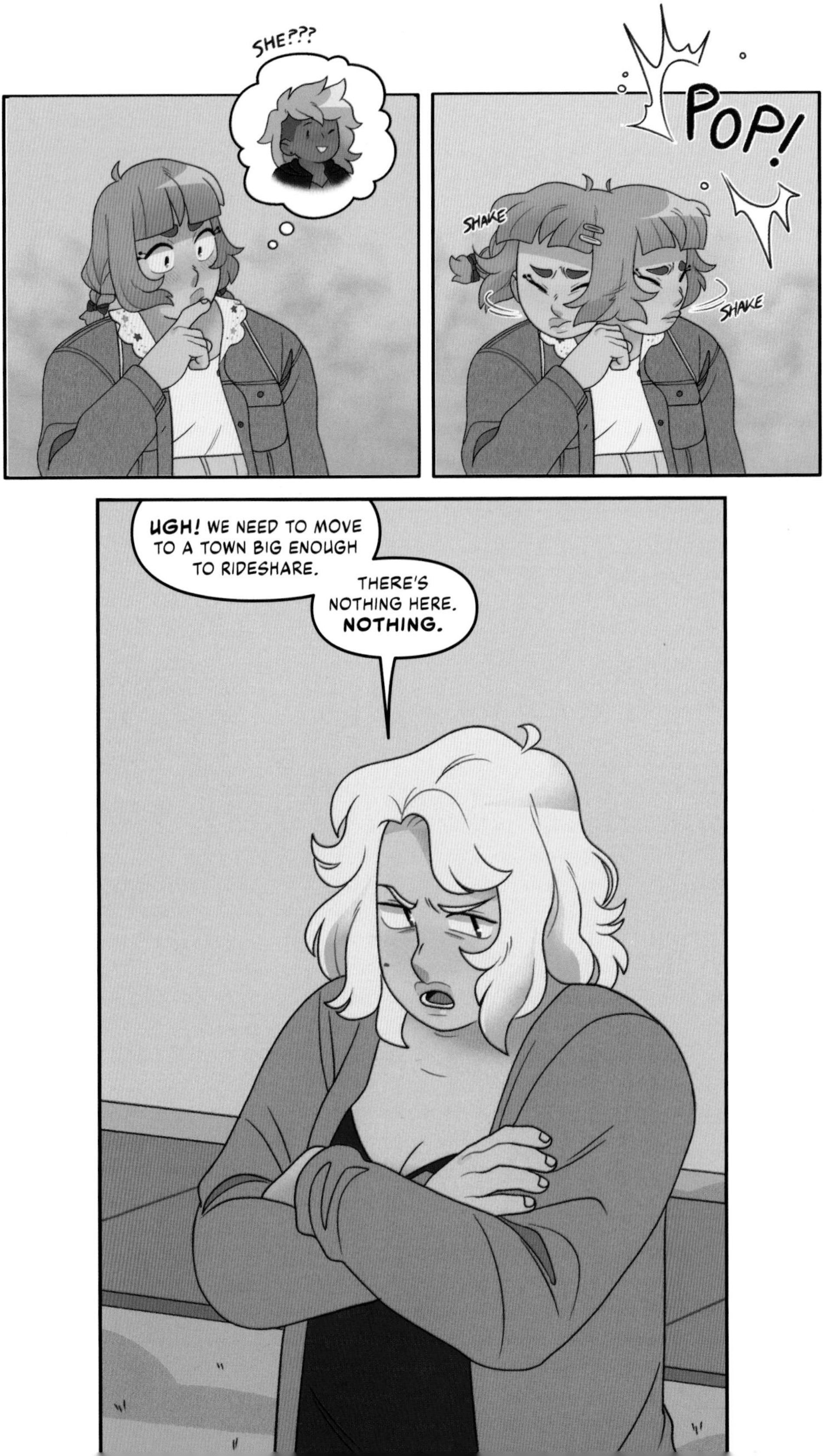
SHE???
POP!
SHAKE
SHAKE
UGH! WE NEED TO MOVE TO A TOWN BIG ENOUGH TO RIDESHARE.
THERE'S NOTHING HERE. **NOTHING.**

AT LEAST IT'S A SHORT RIDE...

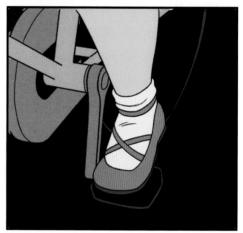

INHALE

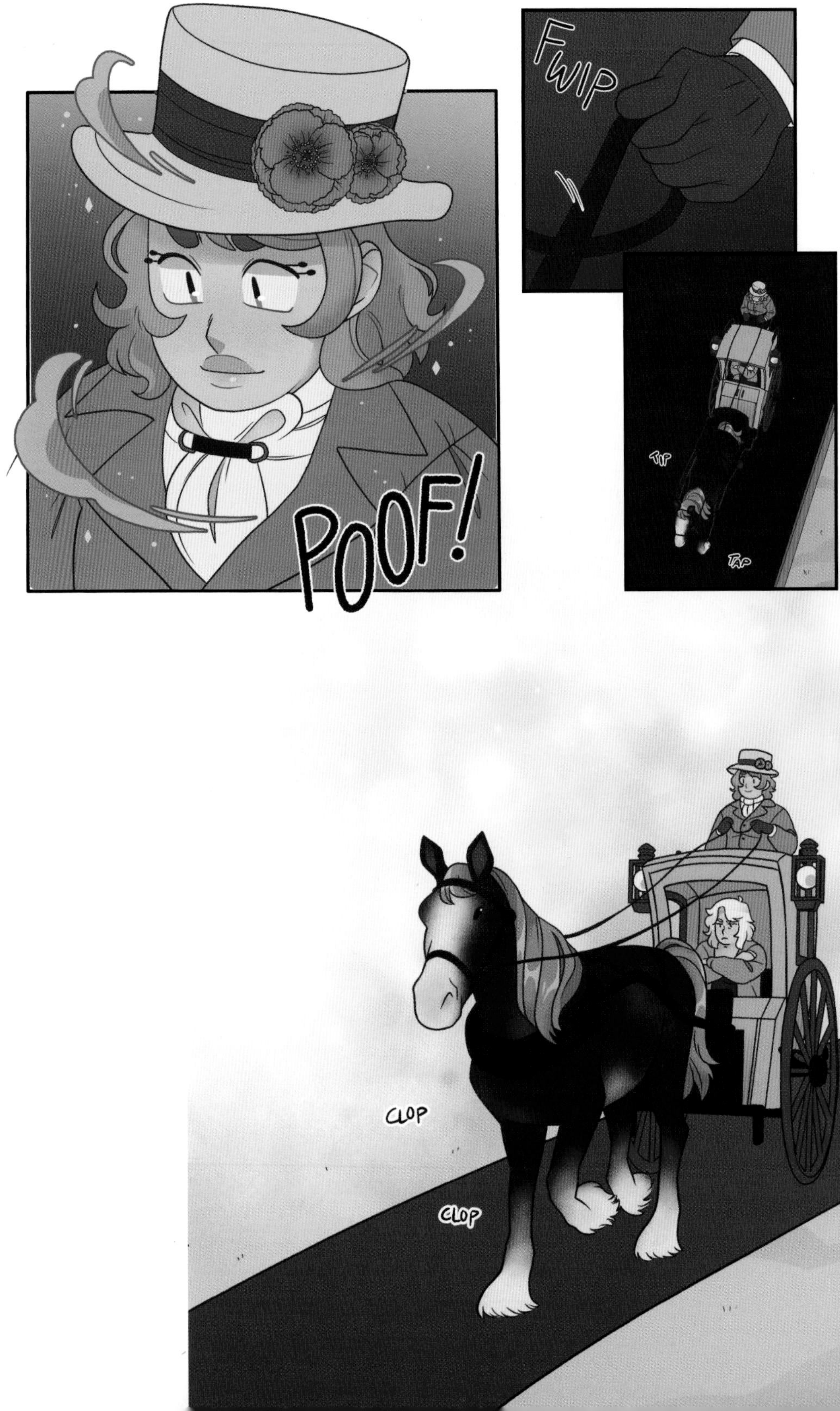
POOF!
FWIP
TIP
TAP
CLOP
CLOP

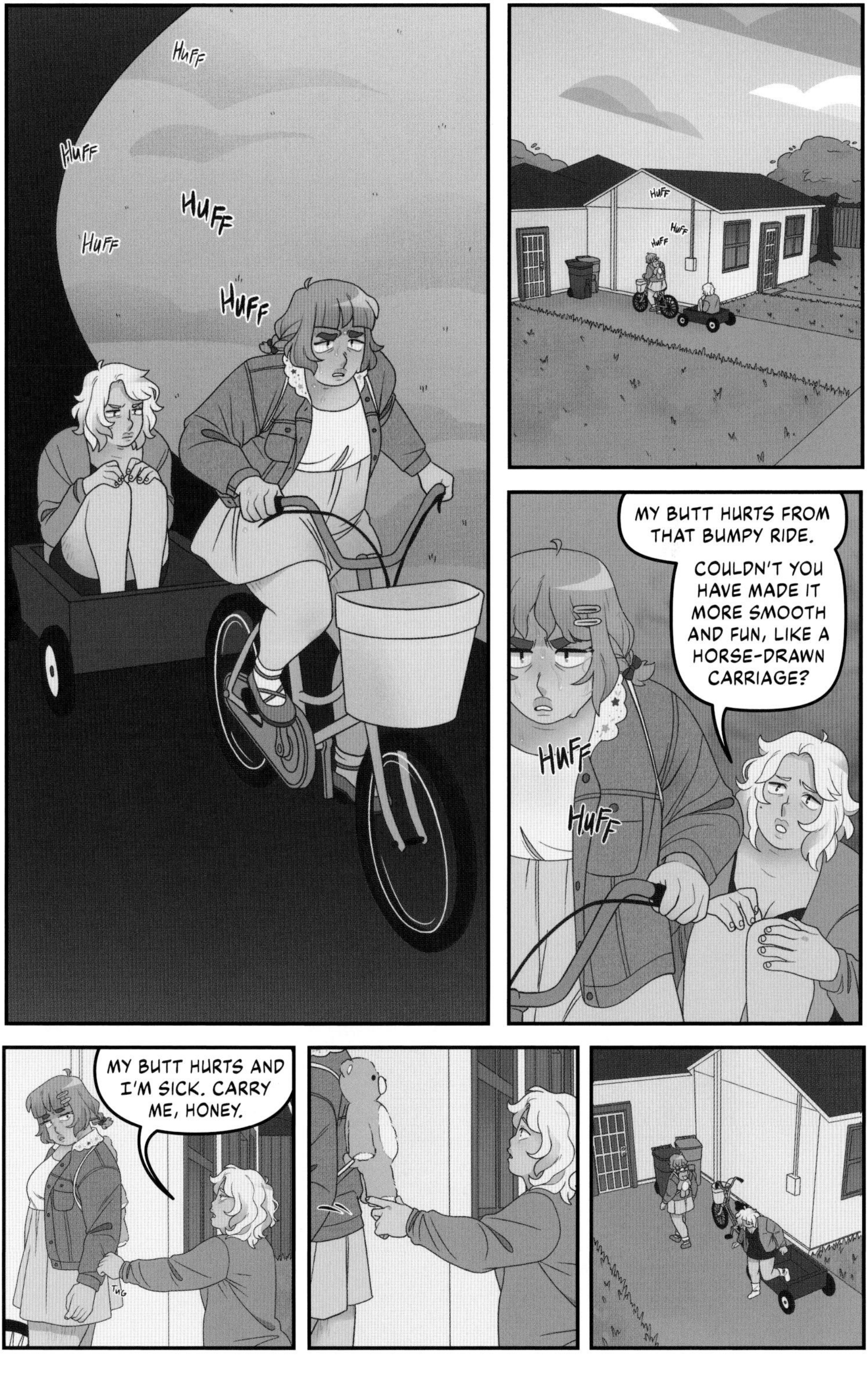
HUFF
HUFF
HUFF
HUFF
HUFF
HUFF
HUFF
HUFF
MY BUTT HURTS FROM THAT BUMPY RIDE.
COULDN'T YOU HAVE MADE IT MORE SMOOTH AND FUN, LIKE A HORSE-DRAWN CARRIAGE?
HUFF
HUFF
MY BUTT HURTS AND I'M SICK. CARRY ME, HONEY.
TUG

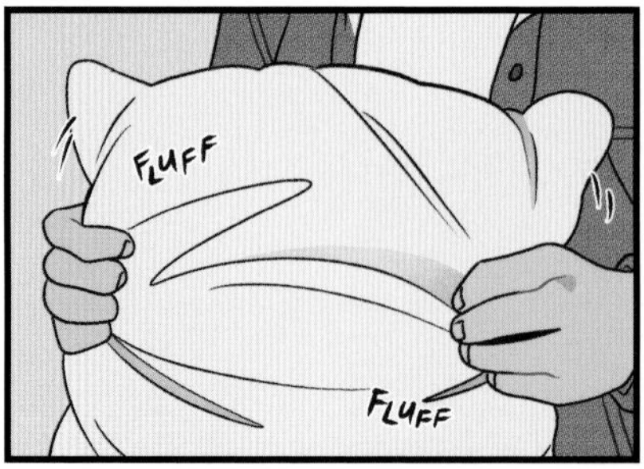
FLUFF
FLUFF

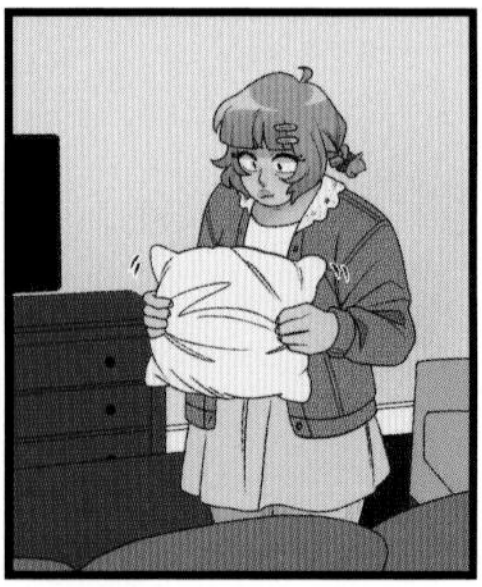

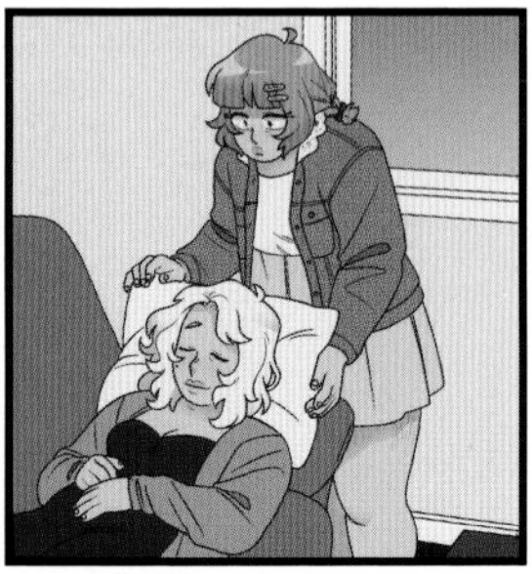

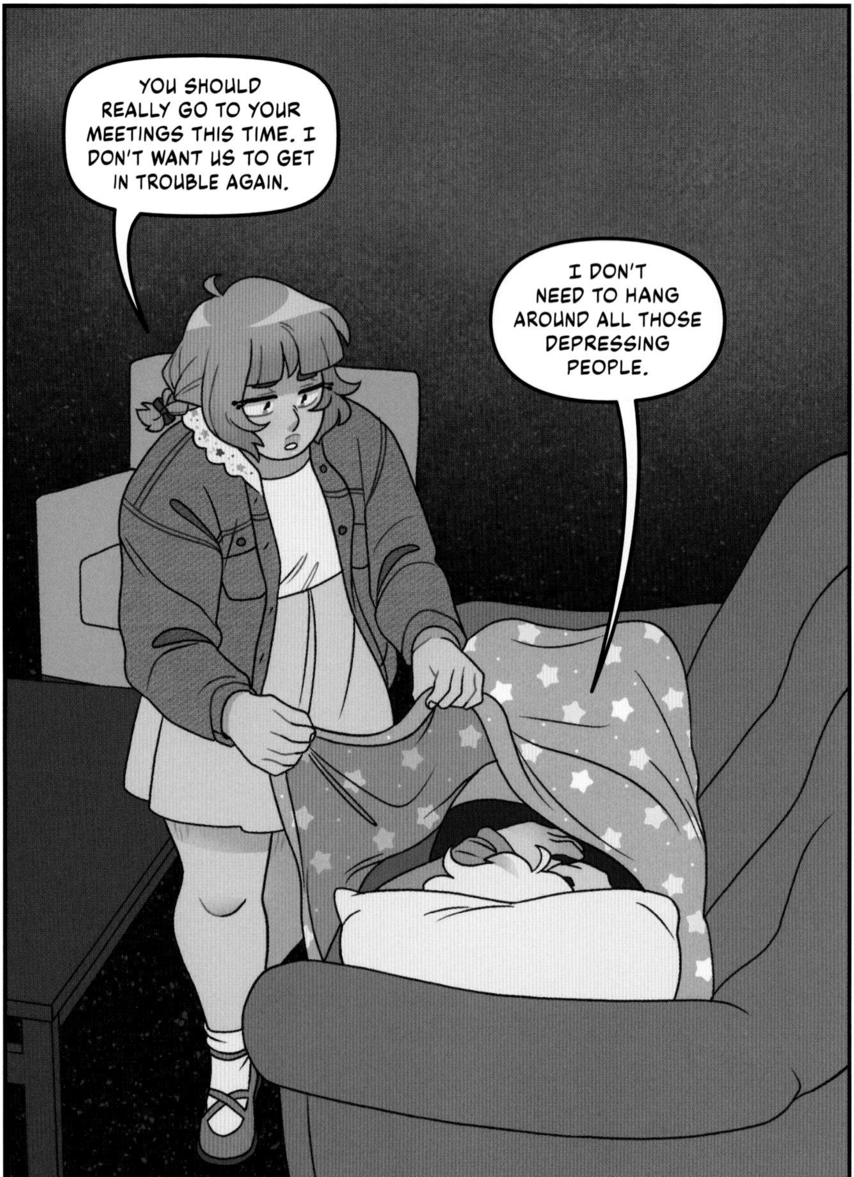
YOU SHOULD REALLY GO TO YOUR MEETINGS THIS TIME. I DON'T WANT US TO GET IN TROUBLE AGAIN.
I DON'T NEED TO HANG AROUND ALL THOSE DEPRESSING PEOPLE.

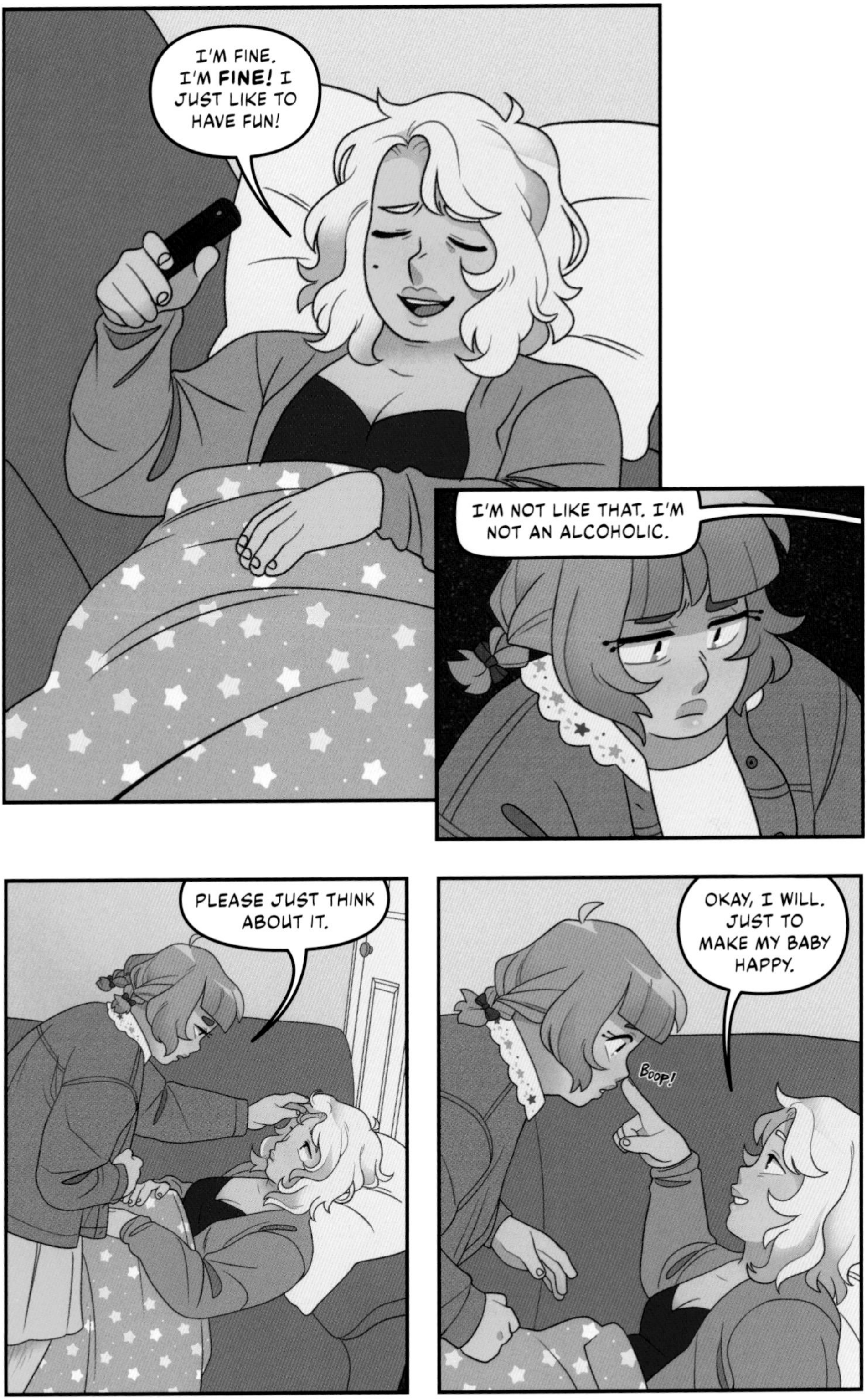
I'M FINE. I'M **FINE!** I JUST LIKE TO HAVE FUN!
I'M NOT LIKE THAT. I'M NOT AN ALCOHOLIC.
PLEASE JUST THINK ABOUT IT.
OKAY, I WILL. JUST TO MAKE MY BABY HAPPY.
BOOP!

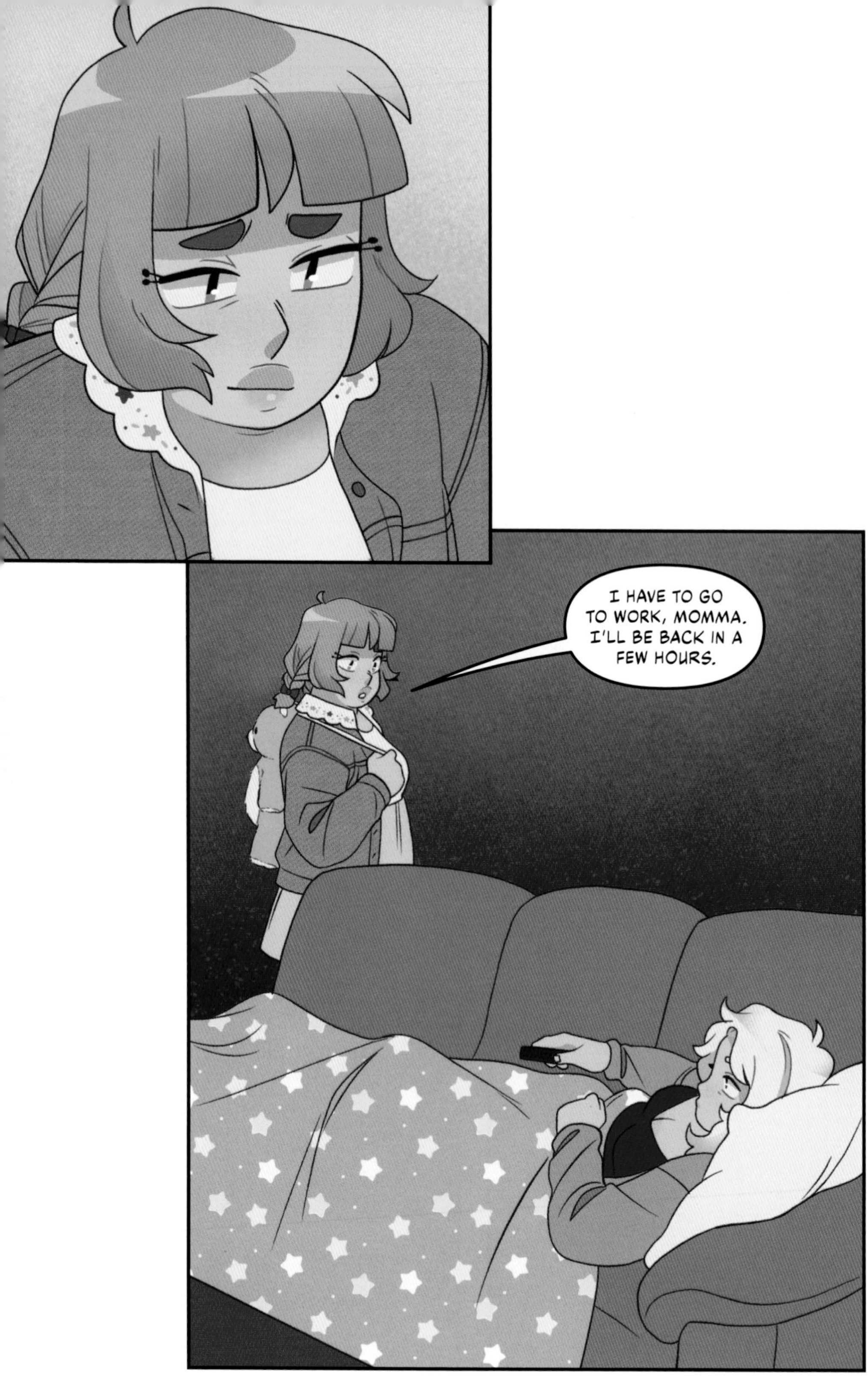
I HAVE TO GO TO WORK, MOMMA. I'LL BE BACK IN A FEW HOURS.

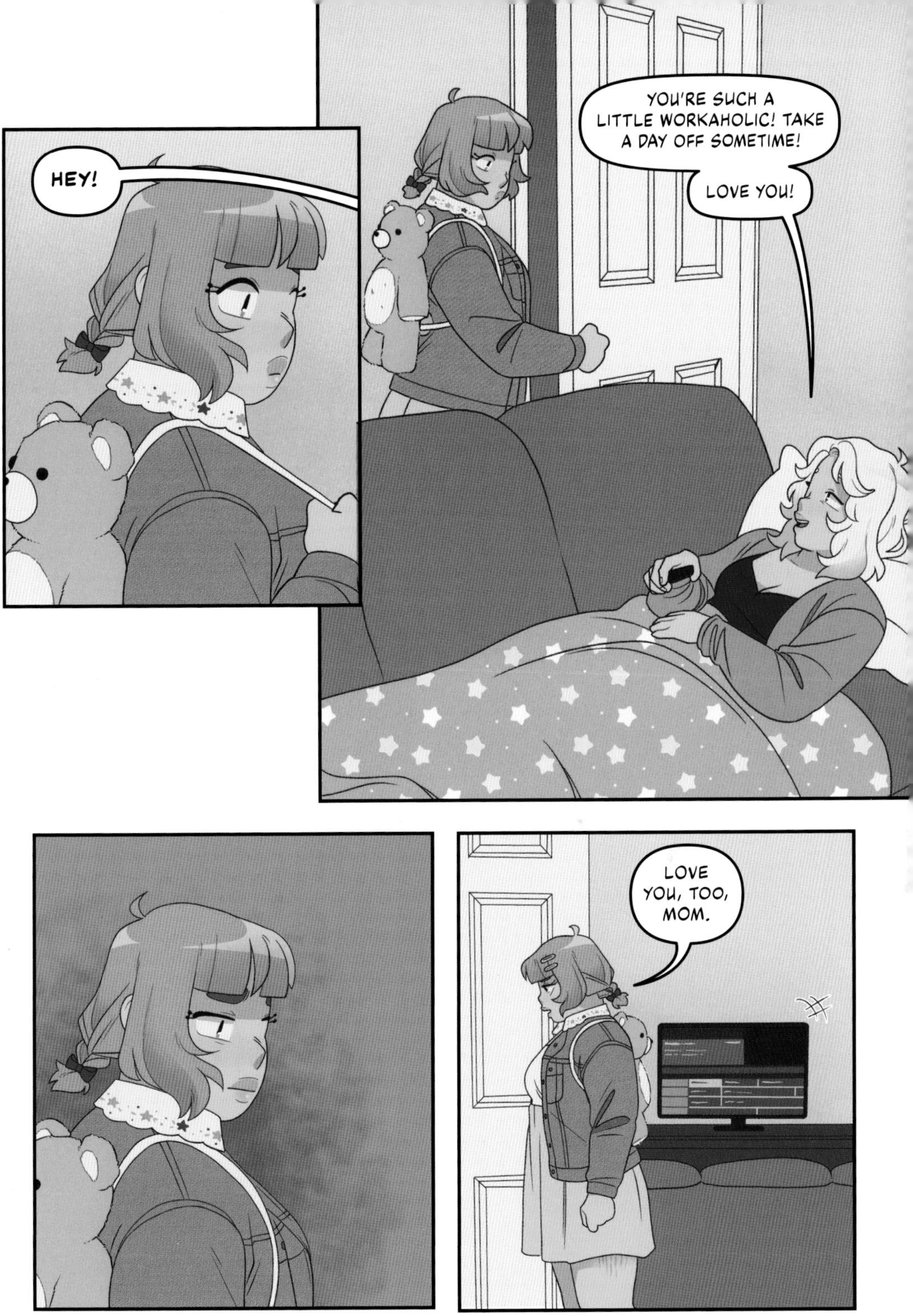
HEY!
YOU'RE SUCH A LITTLE WORKAHOLIC! TAKE A DAY OFF SOMETIME!
LOVE YOU!
LOVE YOU, TOO, MOM.

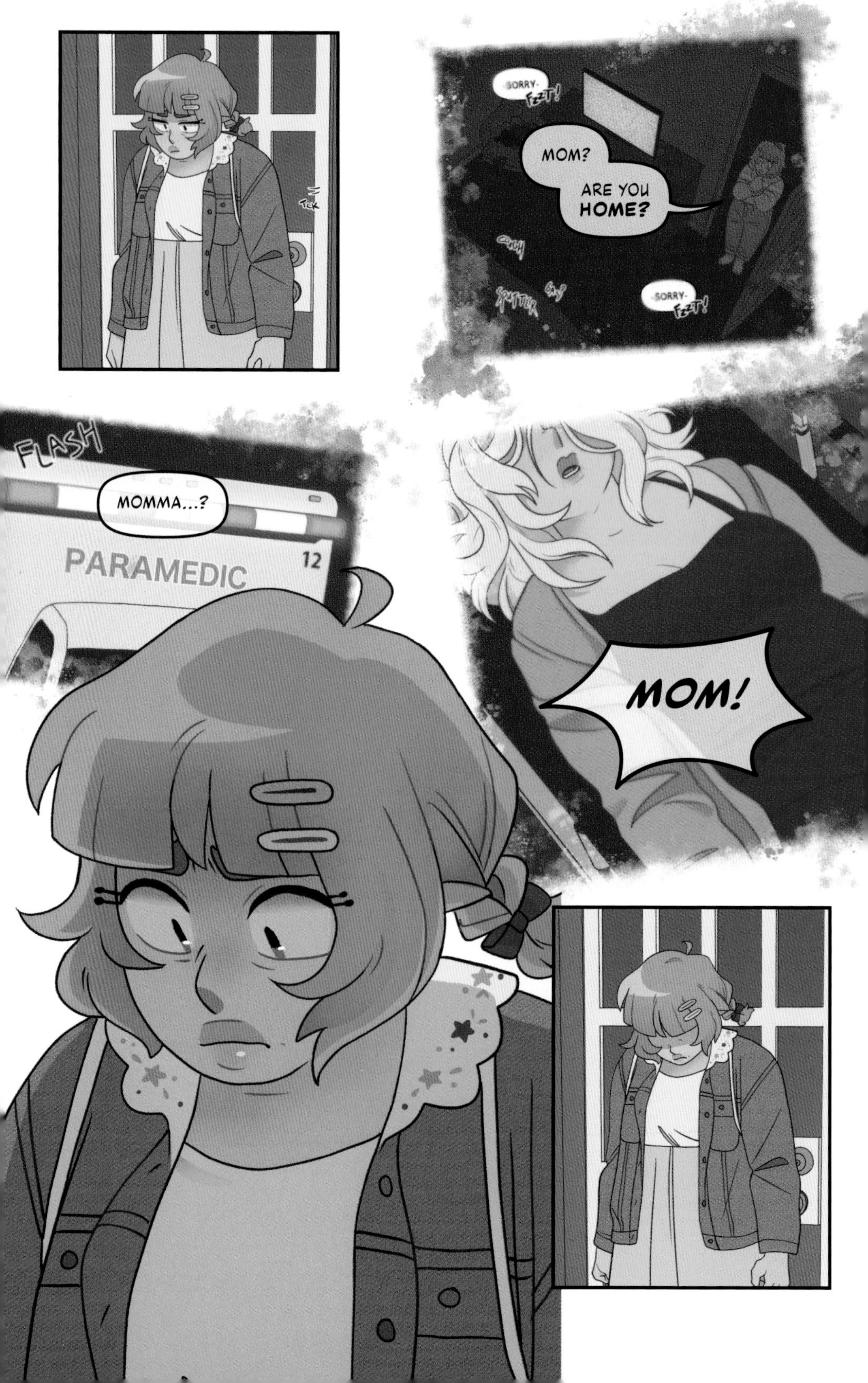
-SORRY-
FZZT!
MOM?
ARE YOU HOME?
COUGH
SPUTTER
GASP
-SORRY-
FZZT!
FLASH
MOMMA...?
PARAMEDIC
12
MOM!

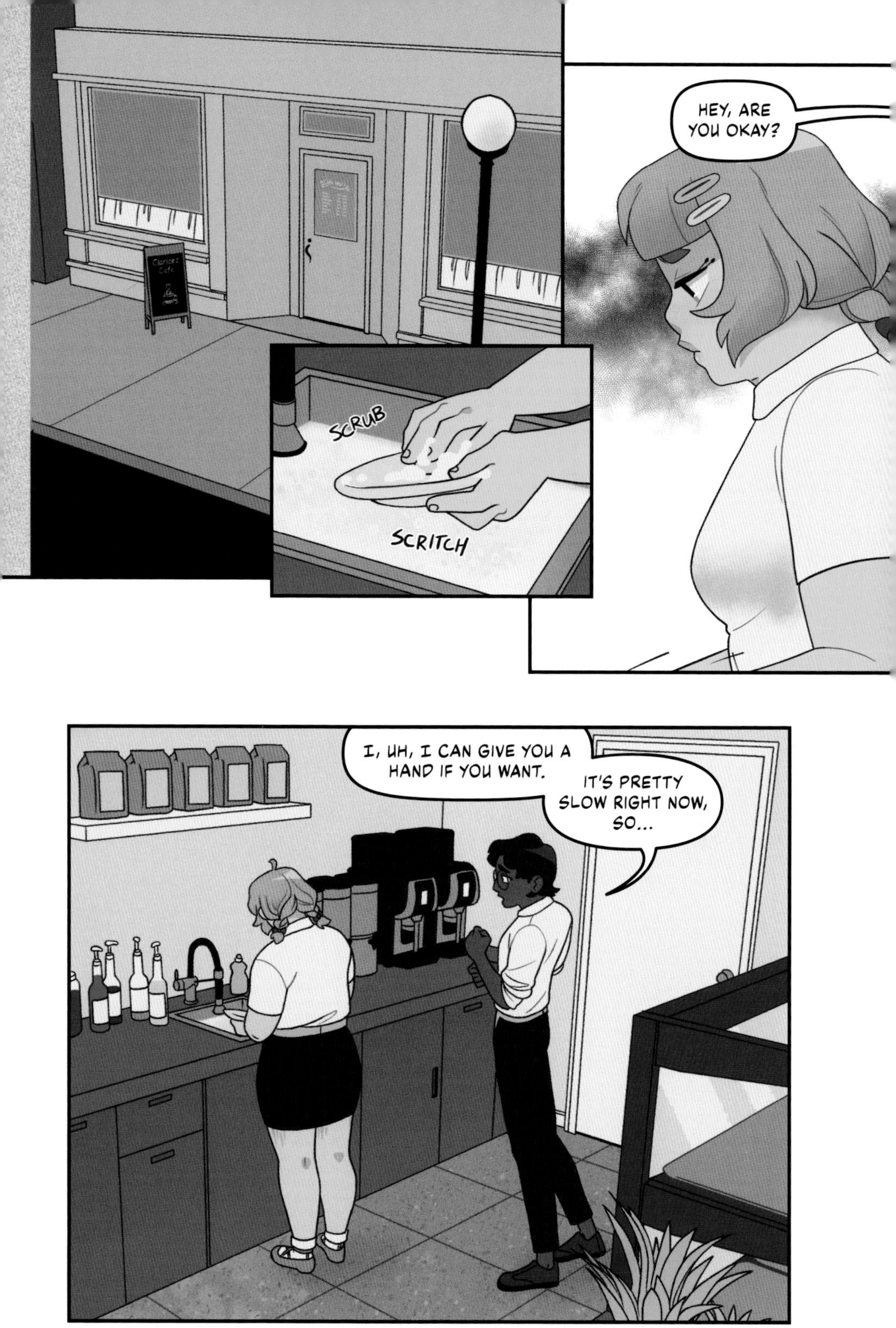
Clarice's Cafe
SCRUB
SCRITCH
HEY, ARE YOU OKAY?
I, UH, I CAN GIVE YOU A HAND IF YOU WANT.
IT'S PRETTY SLOW RIGHT NOW, SO...

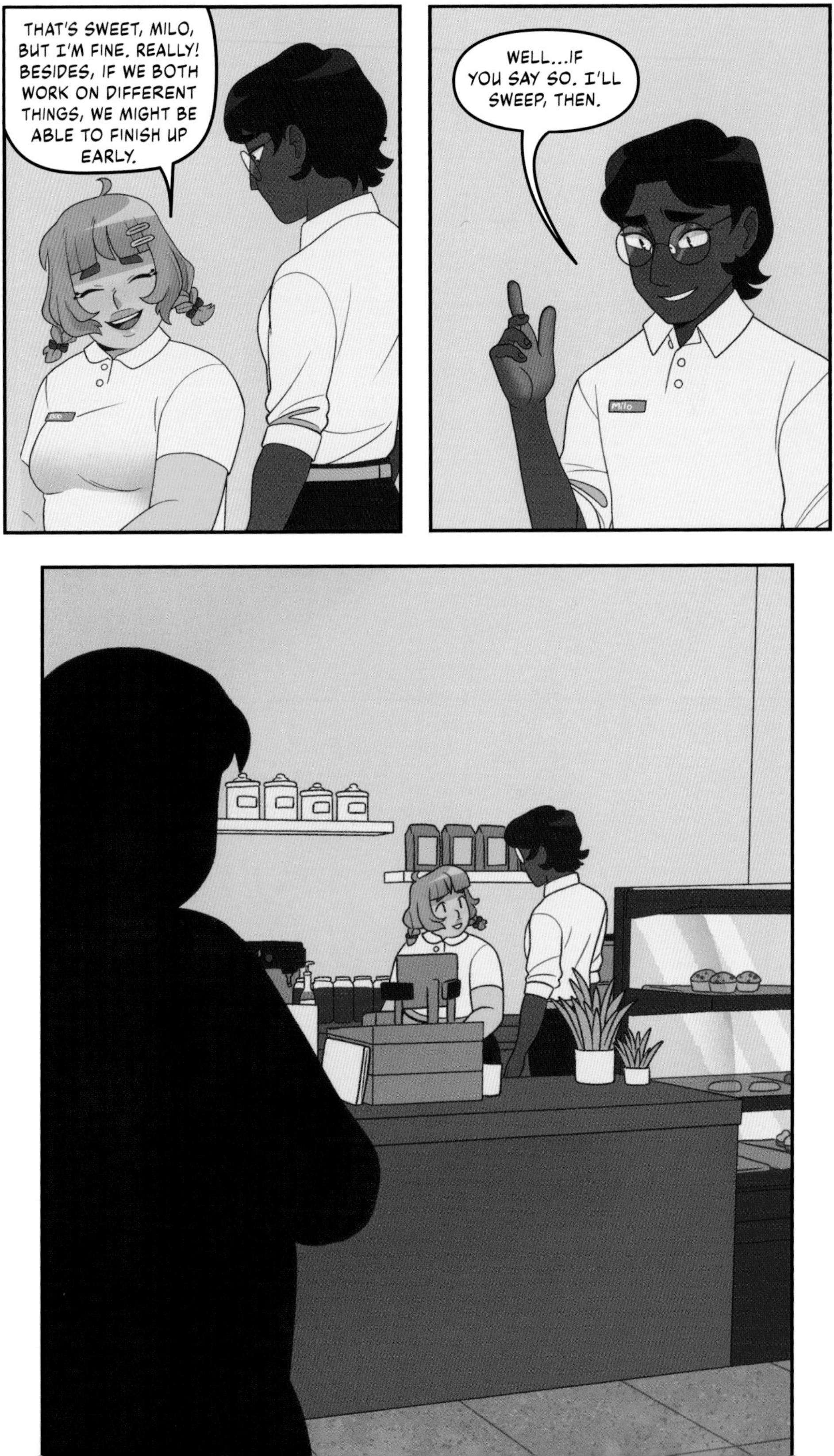
THAT'S SWEET, MILO, BUT I'M FINE. REALLY! BESIDES, IF WE BOTH WORK ON DIFFERENT THINGS, WE MIGHT BE ABLE TO FINISH UP EARLY.
WELL...IF YOU SAY SO. I'LL SWEEP, THEN.

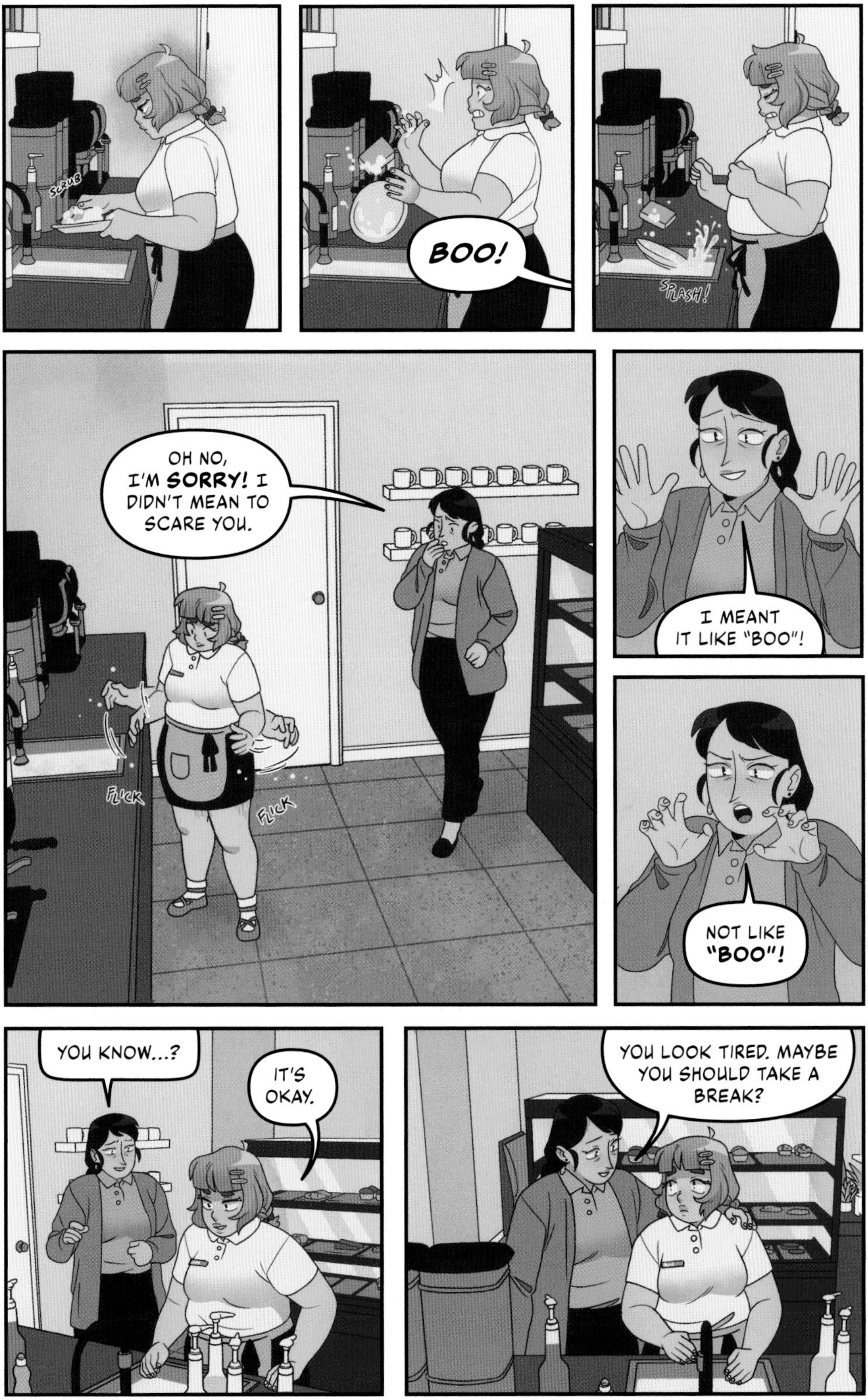
SCRUB
BOO!
SPLASH!
OH NO, I'M **SORRY!** I DIDN'T MEAN TO SCARE YOU.
FLICK
FLICK
I MEANT IT LIKE "BOO"!
NOT LIKE **"BOO"!**
YOU KNOW...?
IT'S OKAY.
YOU LOOK TIRED. MAYBE YOU SHOULD TAKE A BREAK?

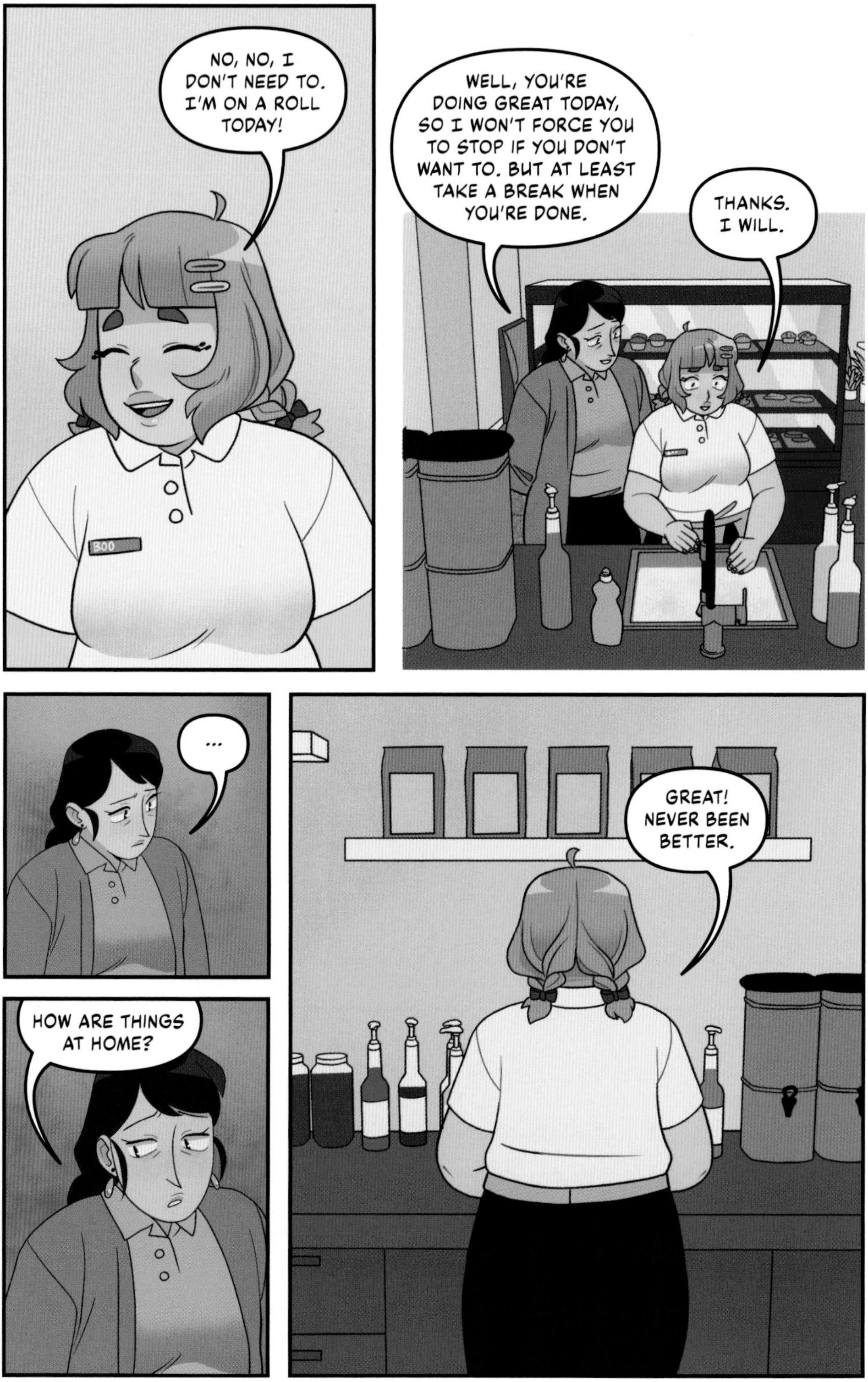
NO, NO, I DON'T NEED TO. I'M ON A ROLL TODAY!
BOO
WELL, YOU'RE DOING GREAT TODAY, SO I WON'T FORCE YOU TO STOP IF YOU DON'T WANT TO. BUT AT LEAST TAKE A BREAK WHEN YOU'RE DONE.
THANKS. I WILL.
...
HOW ARE THINGS AT HOME?
GREAT! NEVER BEEN BETTER.

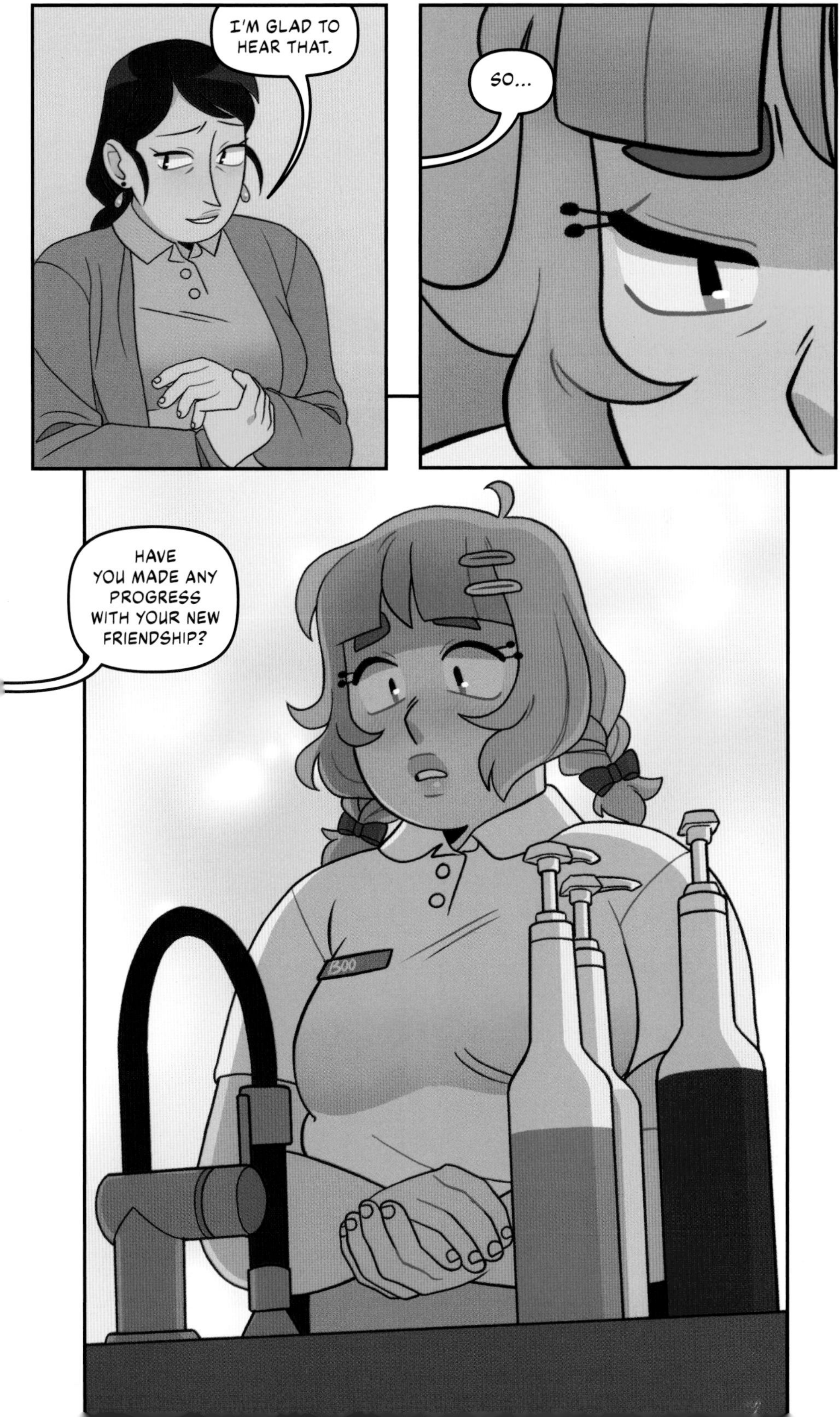
I'M GLAD TO HEAR THAT.
SO...
HAVE YOU MADE ANY PROGRESS WITH YOUR NEW FRIENDSHIP?
BOO

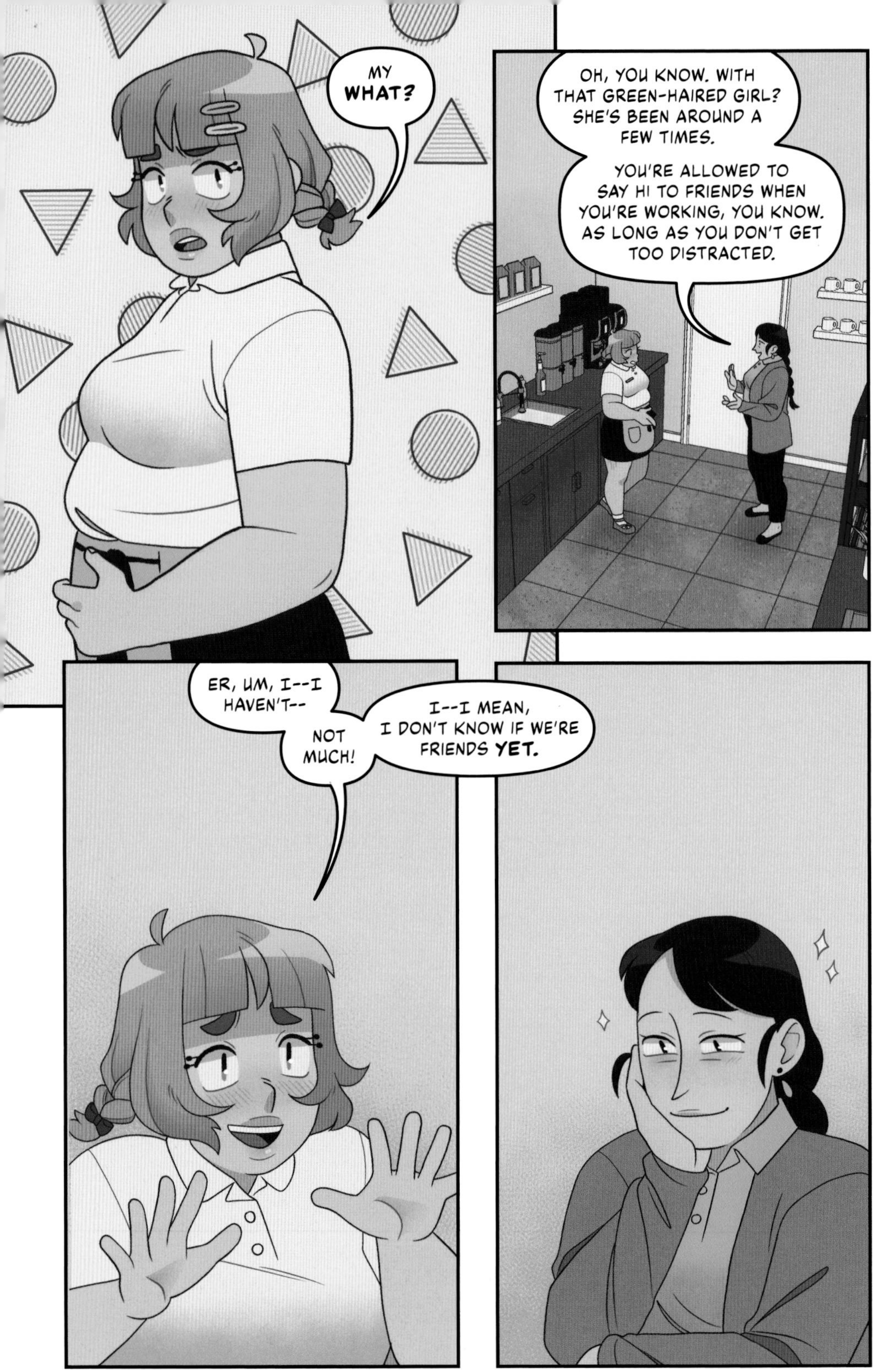
MY WHAT?
OH, YOU KNOW. WITH THAT GREEN-HAIRED GIRL? SHE'S BEEN AROUND A FEW TIMES.
YOU'RE ALLOWED TO SAY HI TO FRIENDS WHEN YOU'RE WORKING, YOU KNOW. AS LONG AS YOU DON'T GET TOO DISTRACTED.
ER, UM, I--I HAVEN'T--
NOT MUCH!
I--I MEAN, I DON'T KNOW IF WE'RE FRIENDS YET.

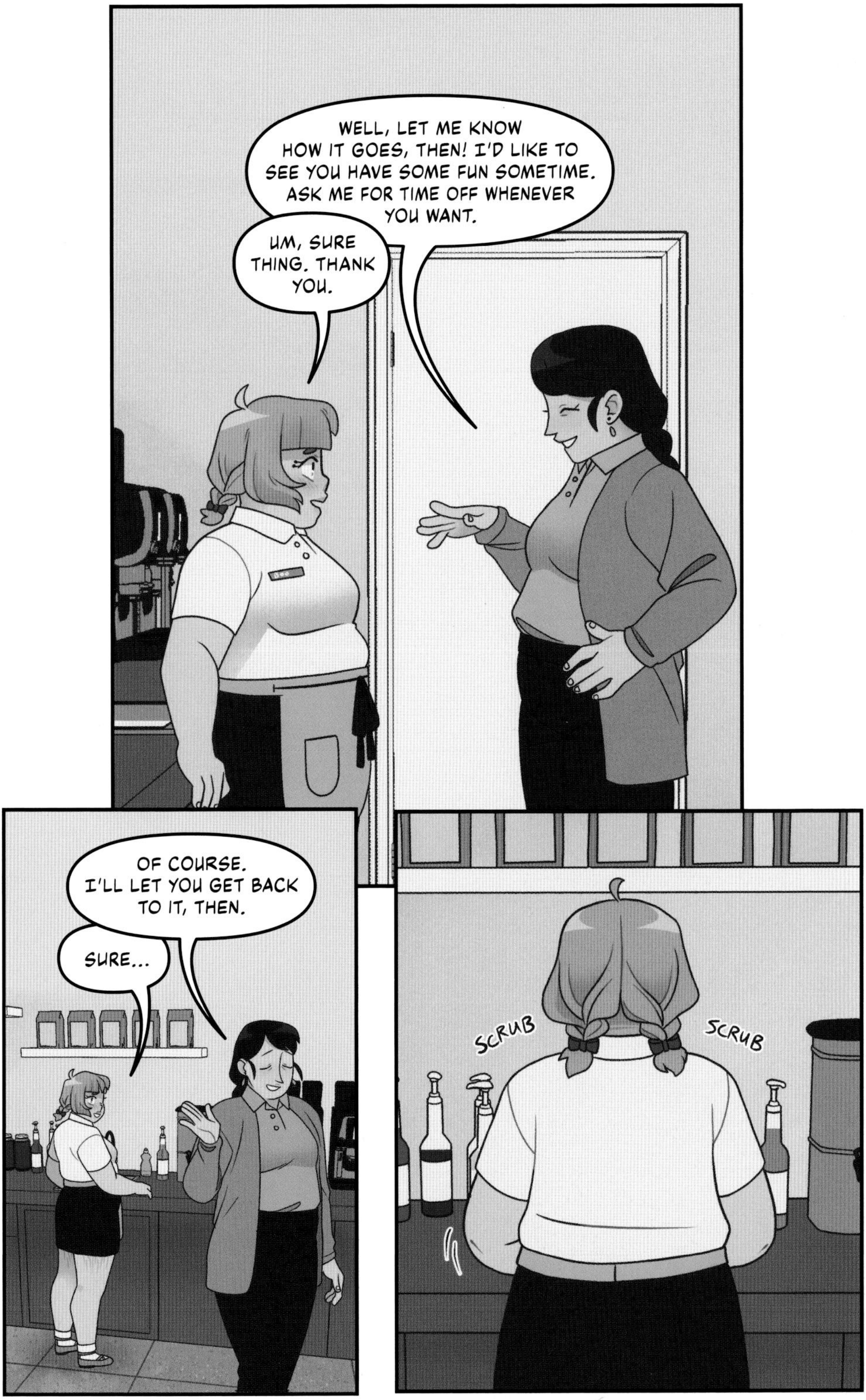
WELL, LET ME KNOW HOW IT GOES, THEN! I'D LIKE TO SEE YOU HAVE SOME FUN SOMETIME. ASK ME FOR TIME OFF WHENEVER YOU WANT.
UM, SURE THING. THANK YOU.
OF COURSE. I'LL LET YOU GET BACK TO IT, THEN.
SURE...
SCRUB
SCRUB

SORRY-
FZZT!

COUGH
HM!

SPUTTER

SORRY-
FZZT!

MOM!

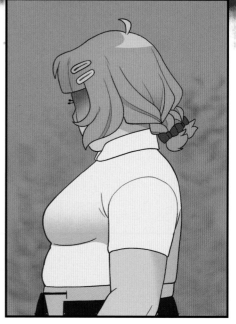

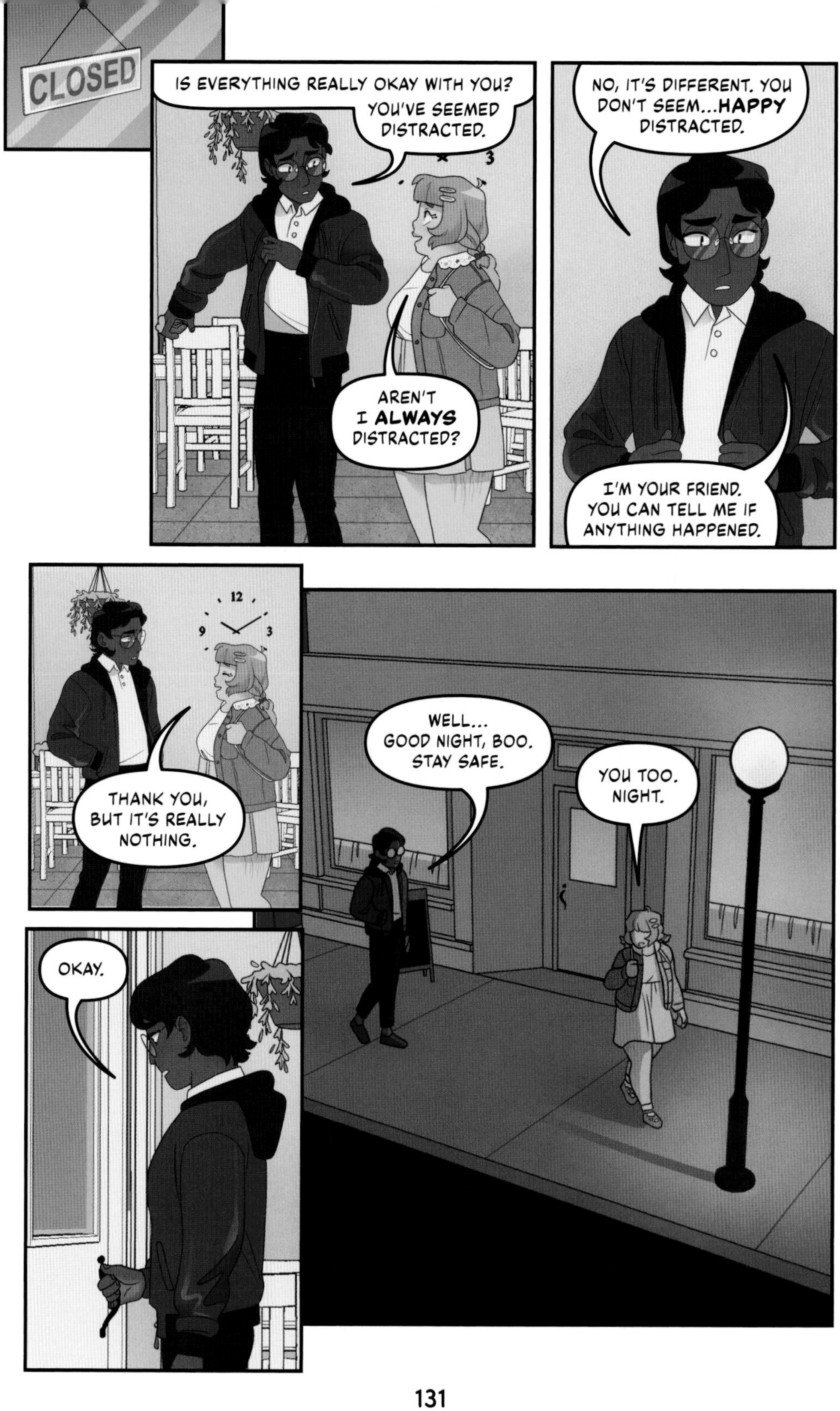
CLOSED
IS EVERYTHING REALLY OKAY WITH YOU? YOU'VE SEEMED DISTRACTED.
AREN'T I **ALWAYS** DISTRACTED?
NO, IT'S DIFFERENT. YOU DON'T SEEM...**HAPPY** DISTRACTED.
I'M YOUR FRIEND. YOU CAN TELL ME IF ANYTHING HAPPENED.
THANK YOU, BUT IT'S REALLY NOTHING.
OKAY.
WELL... GOOD NIGHT, BOO. STAY SAFE.
YOU TOO. NIGHT.

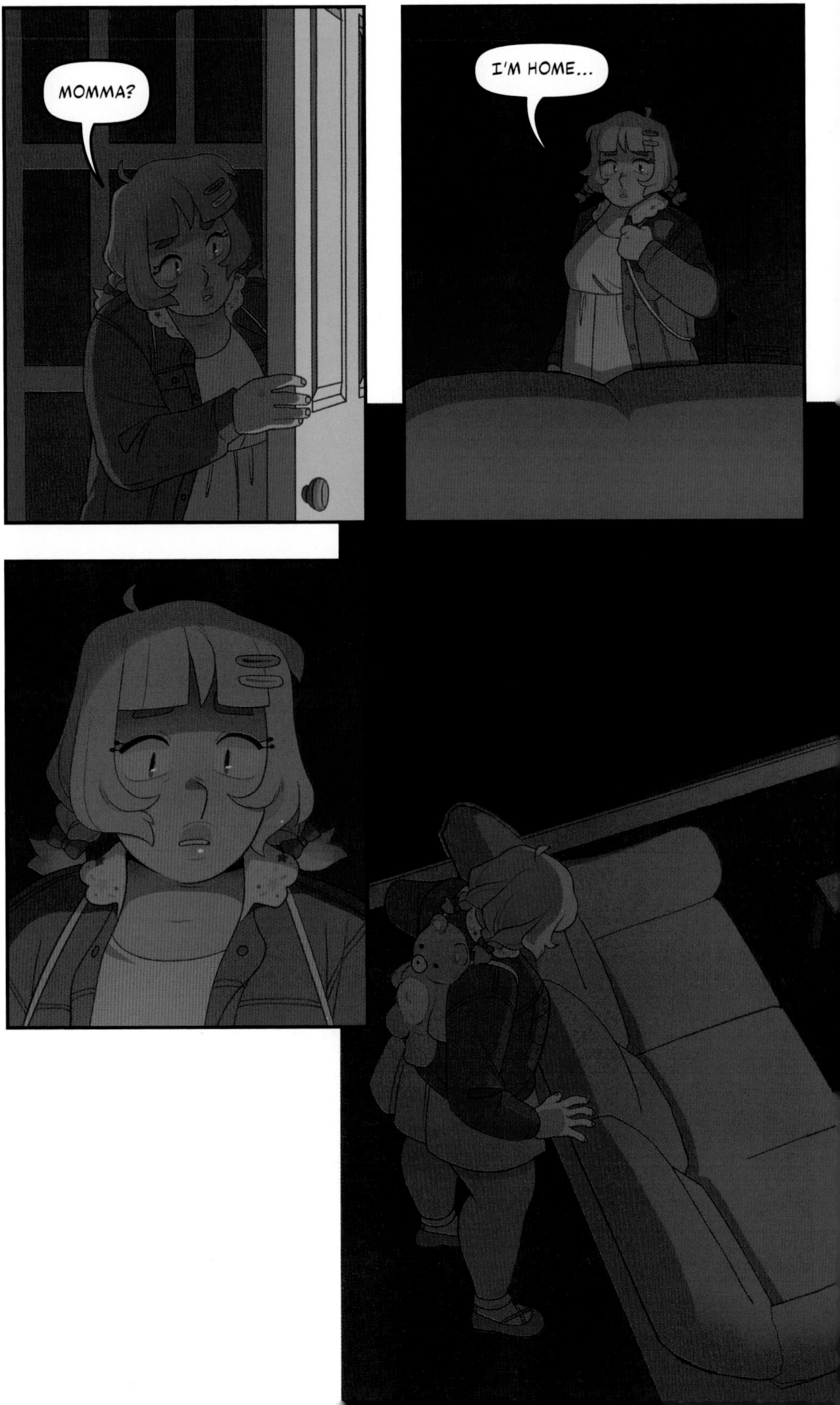
MOMMA?
I'M HOME...

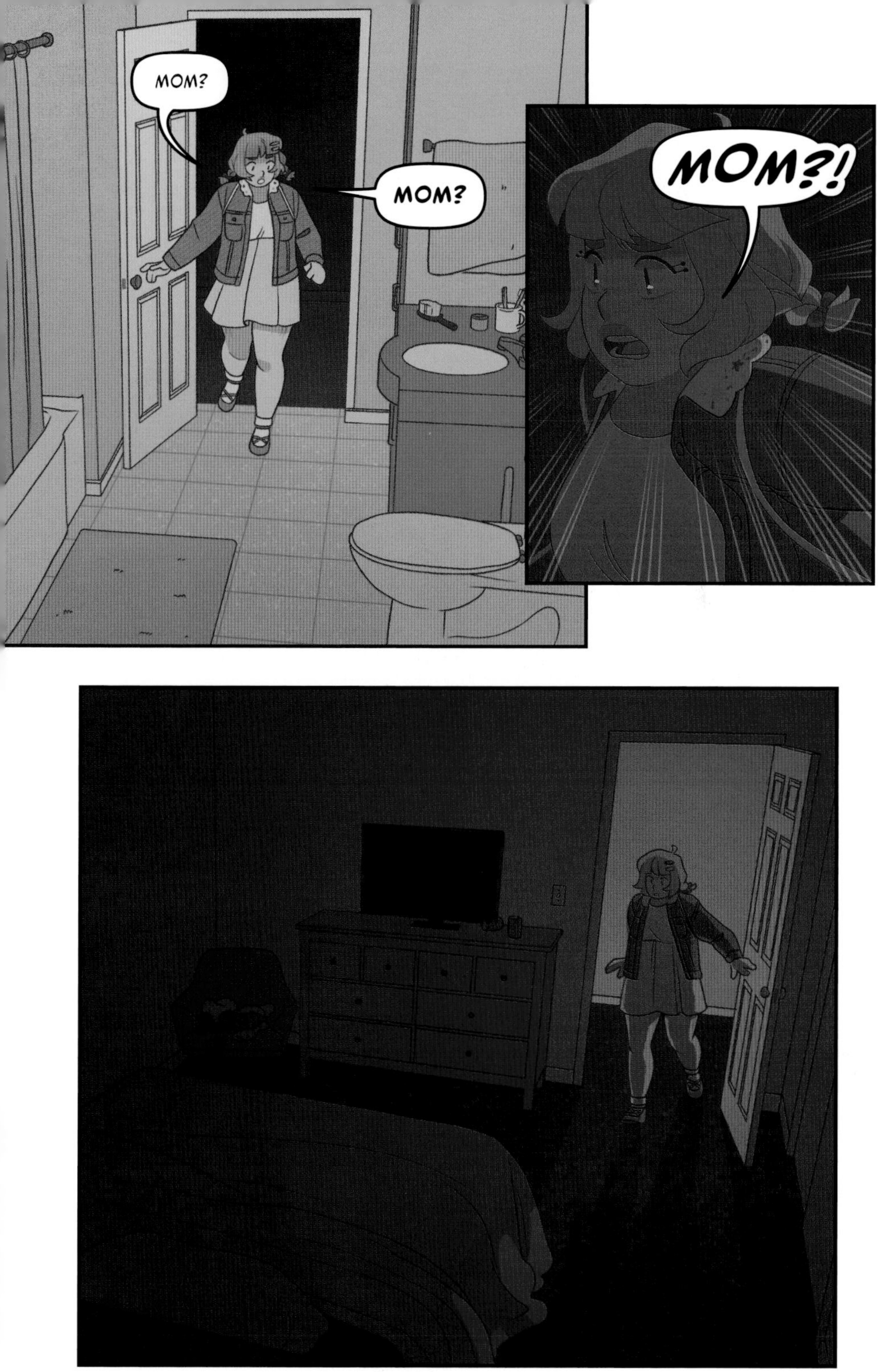
MOM?
MOM?
MOM?!

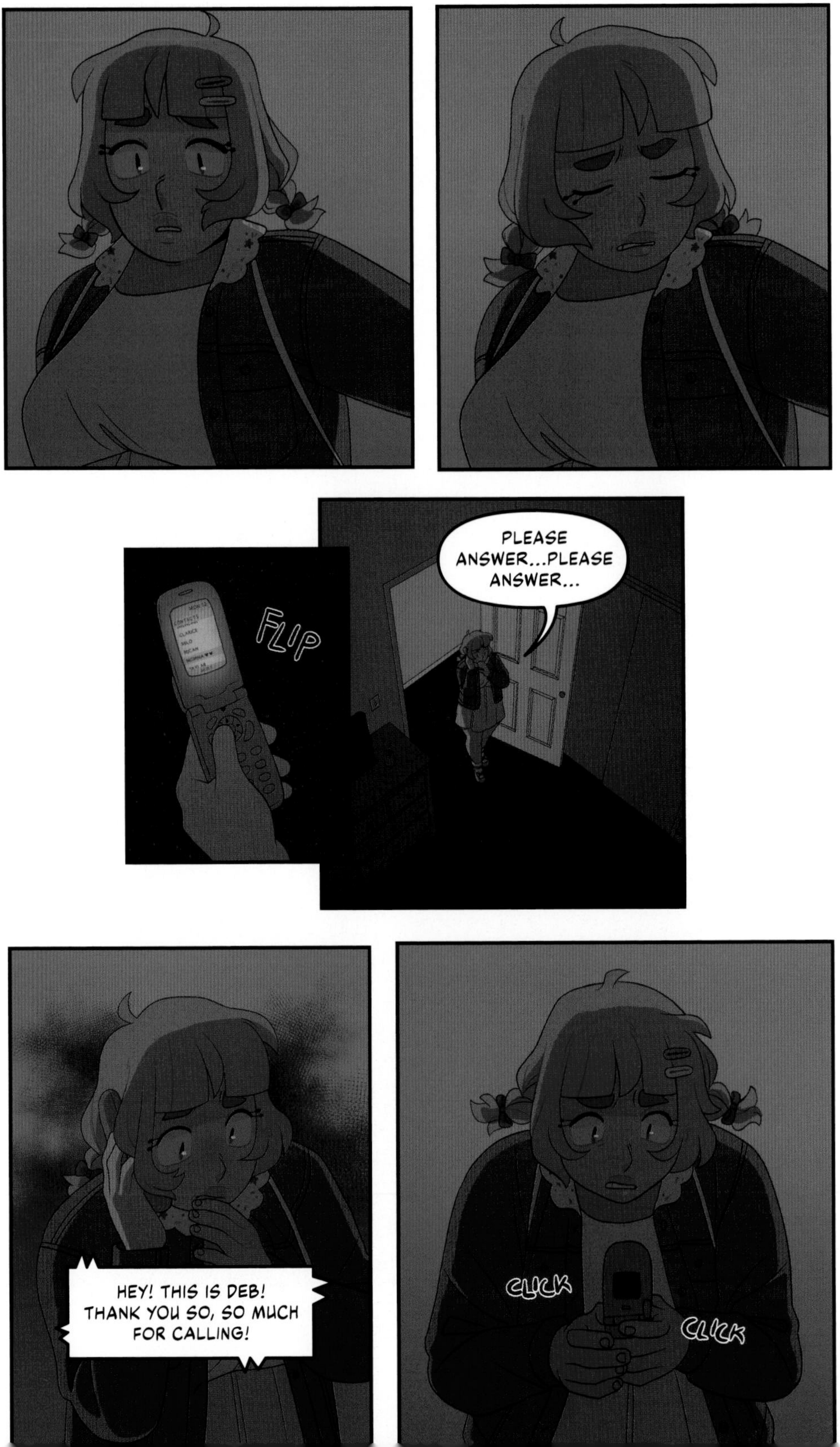
FLIP
PLEASE ANSWER...PLEASE ANSWER...
HEY! THIS IS DEB! THANK YOU SO, SO MUCH FOR CALLING!
CLICK
CLICK

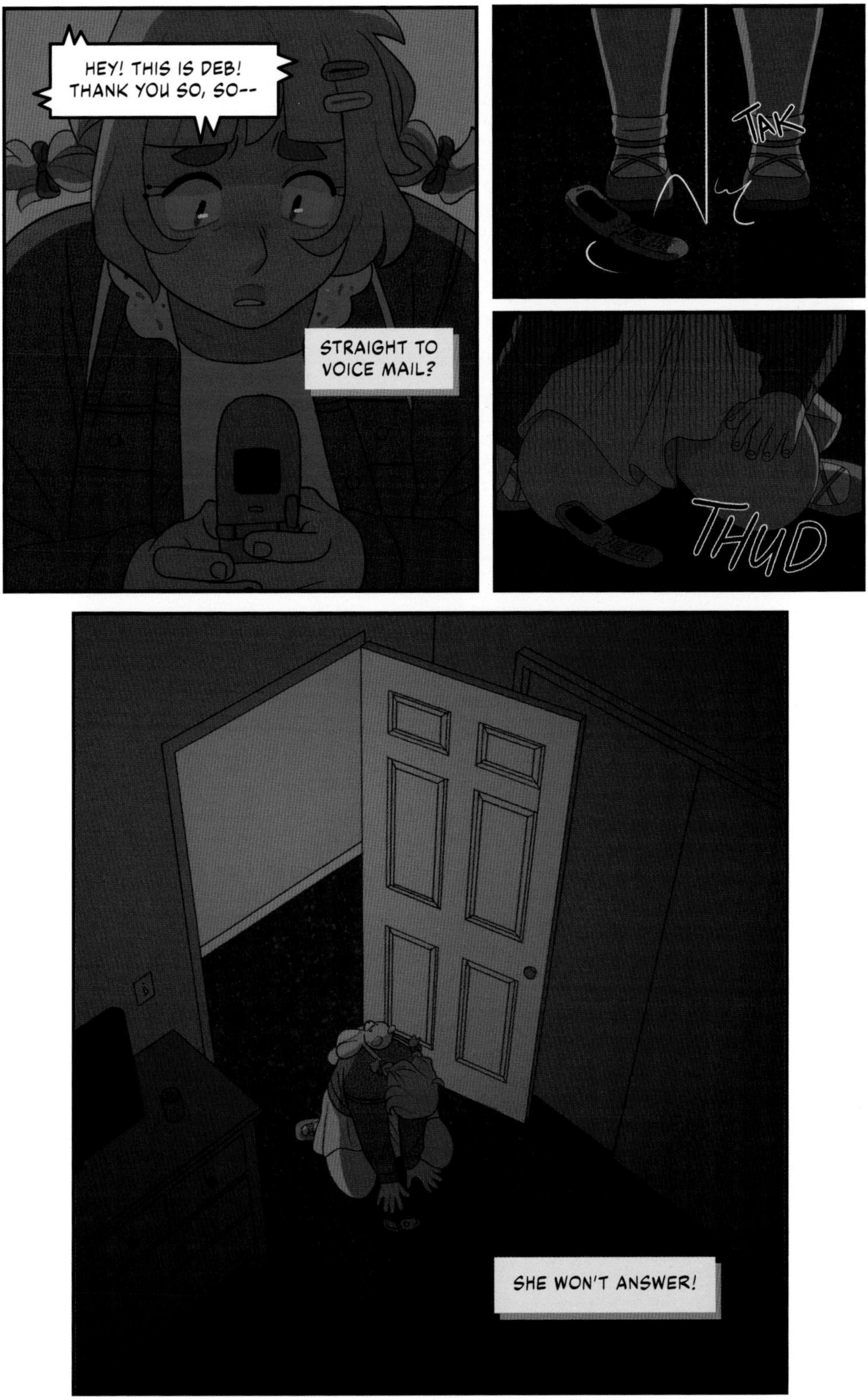
HEY! THIS IS DEB!
THANK YOU SO, SO--
STRAIGHT TO
VOICE MAIL?
TAK
THUD
SHE WON'T ANSWER!

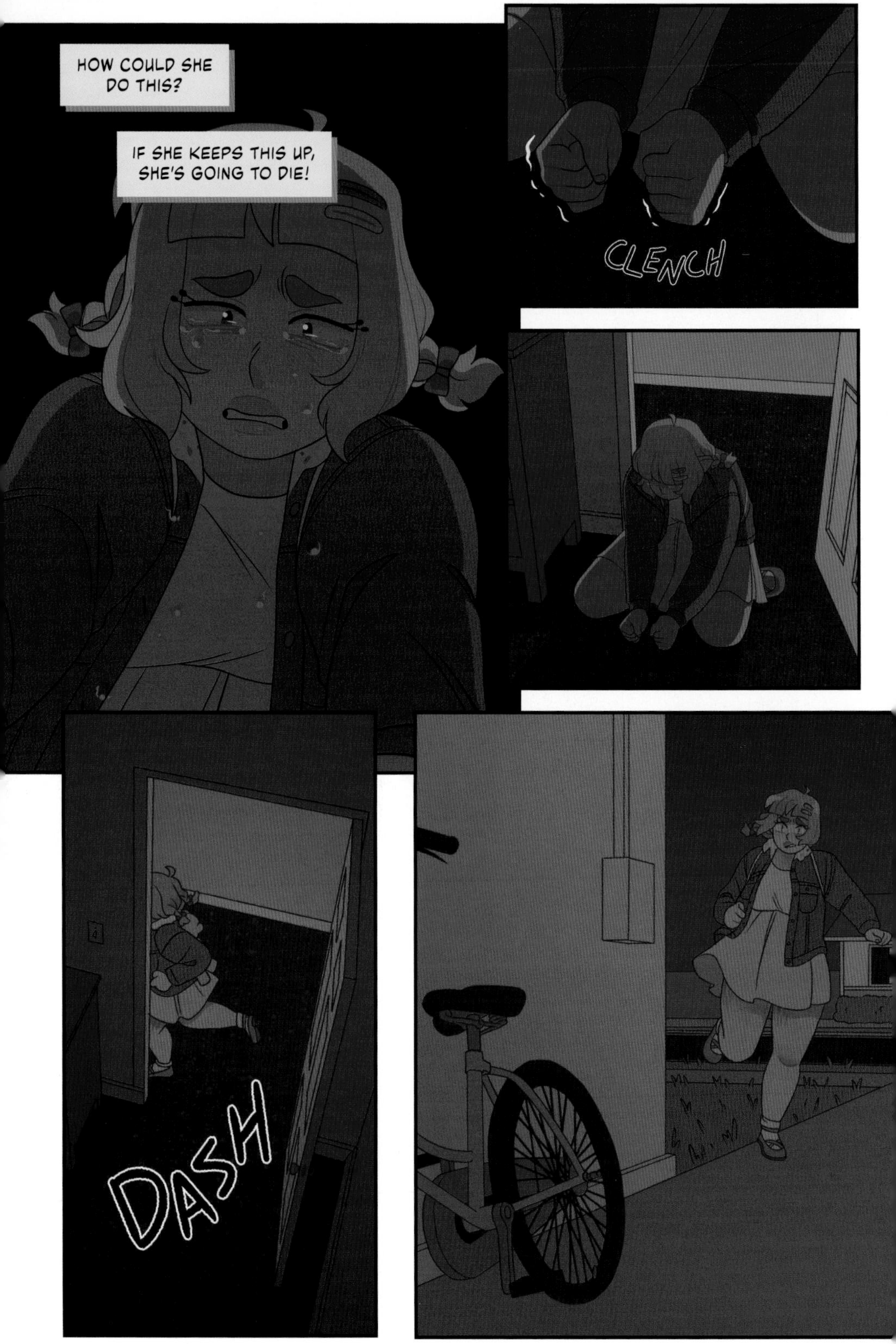
HOW COULD SHE DO THIS?
IF SHE KEEPS THIS UP, SHE'S GOING TO DIE!
CLENCH
DASH

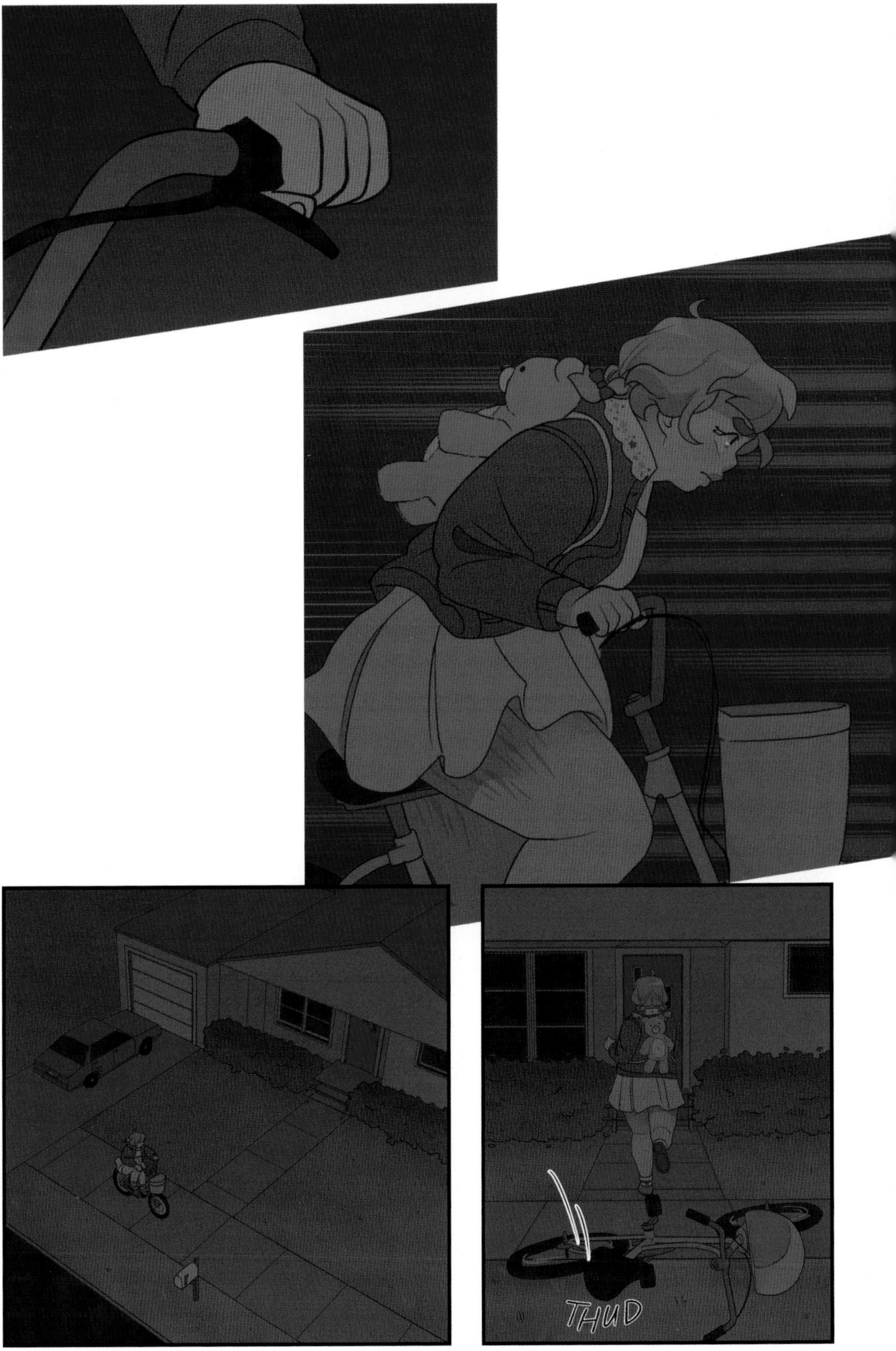
THUD

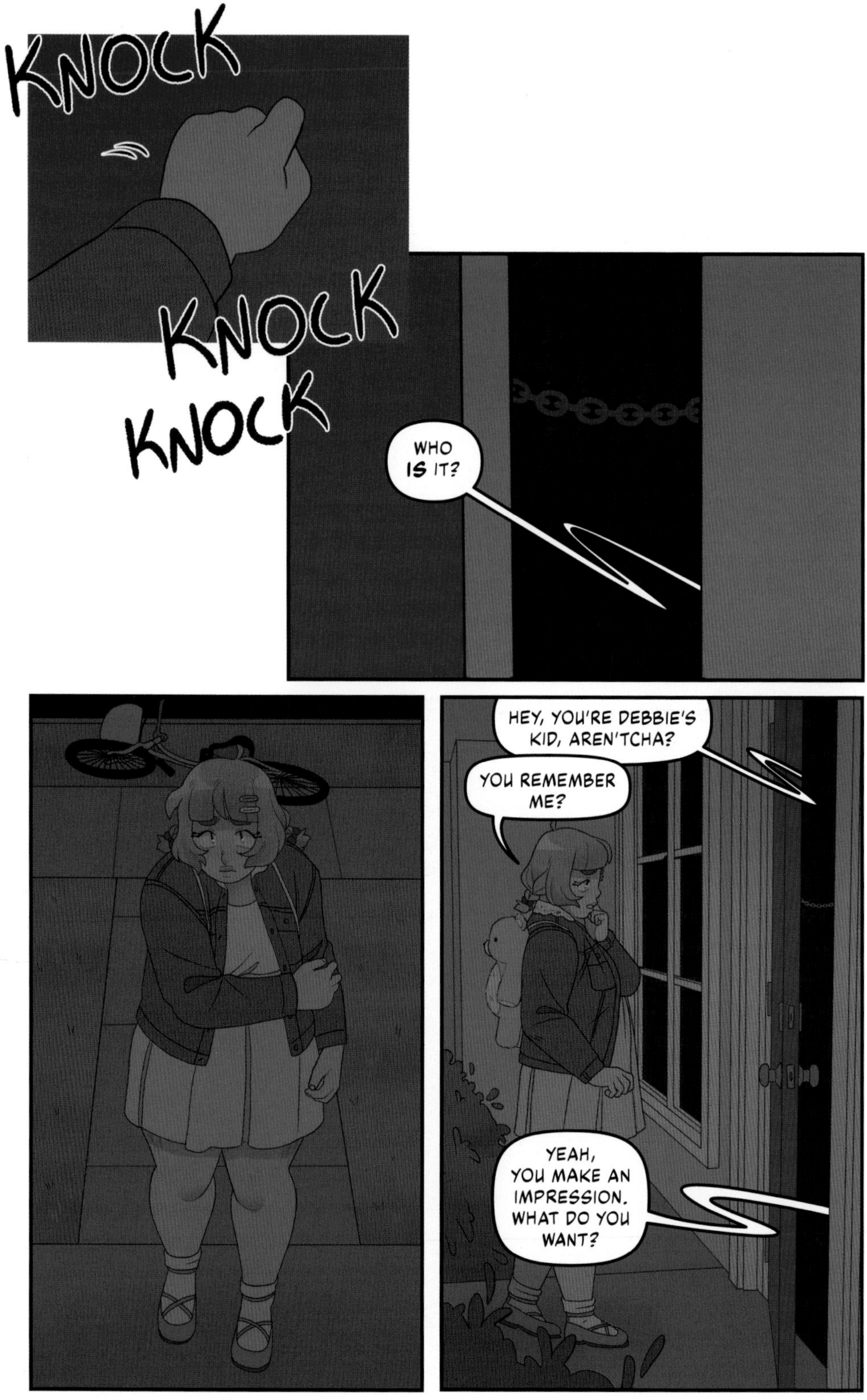
KNOCK
KNOCK
KNOCK
WHO IS IT?
HEY, YOU'RE DEBBIE'S KID, AREN'TCHA?
YOU REMEMBER ME?
YEAH, YOU MAKE AN IMPRESSION. WHAT DO YOU WANT?

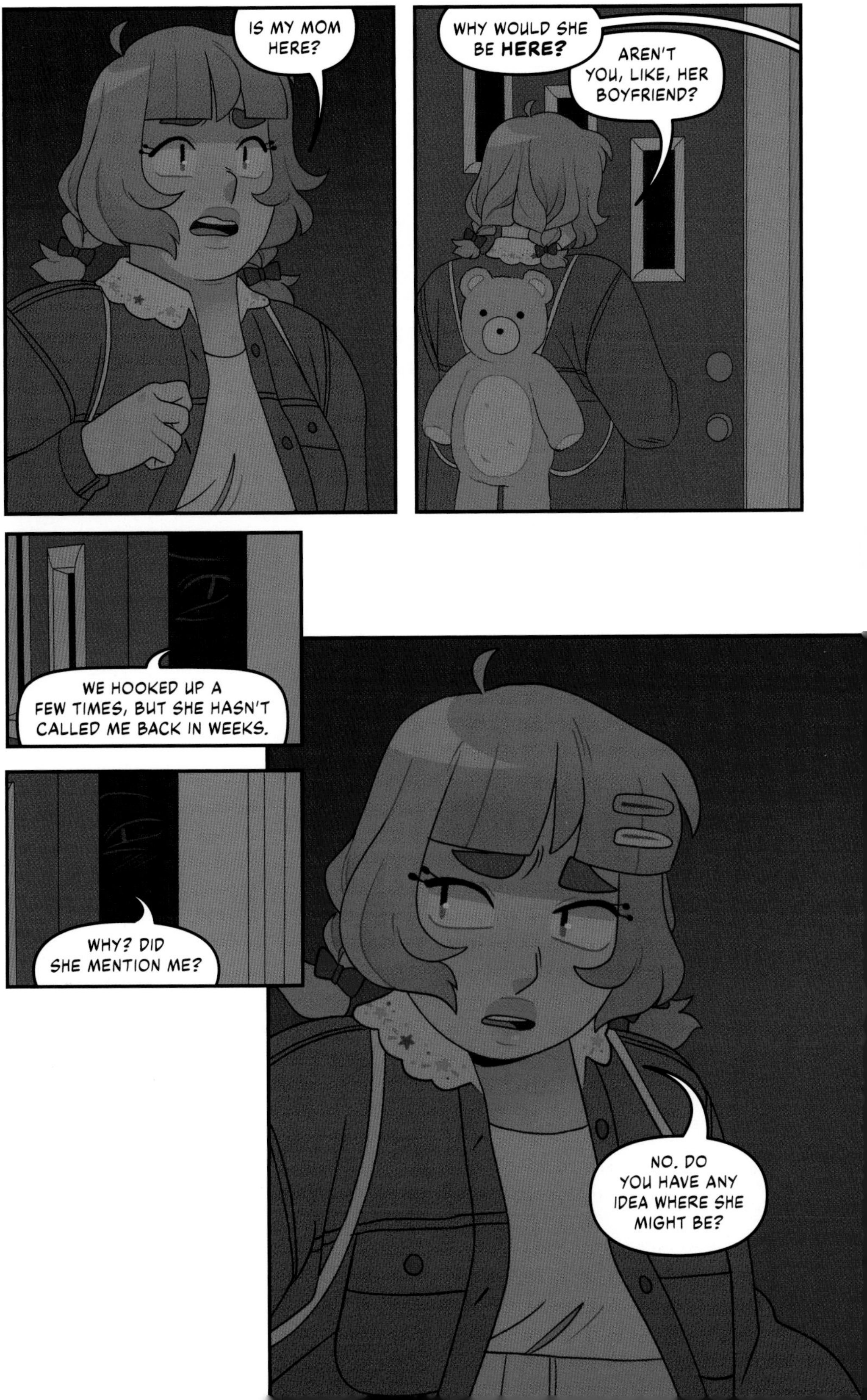
IS MY MOM HERE?
WHY WOULD SHE BE **HERE?**
AREN'T YOU, LIKE, HER BOYFRIEND?
WE HOOKED UP A FEW TIMES, BUT SHE HASN'T CALLED ME BACK IN WEEKS.
WHY? DID SHE MENTION ME?
NO. DO YOU HAVE ANY IDEA WHERE SHE MIGHT BE?

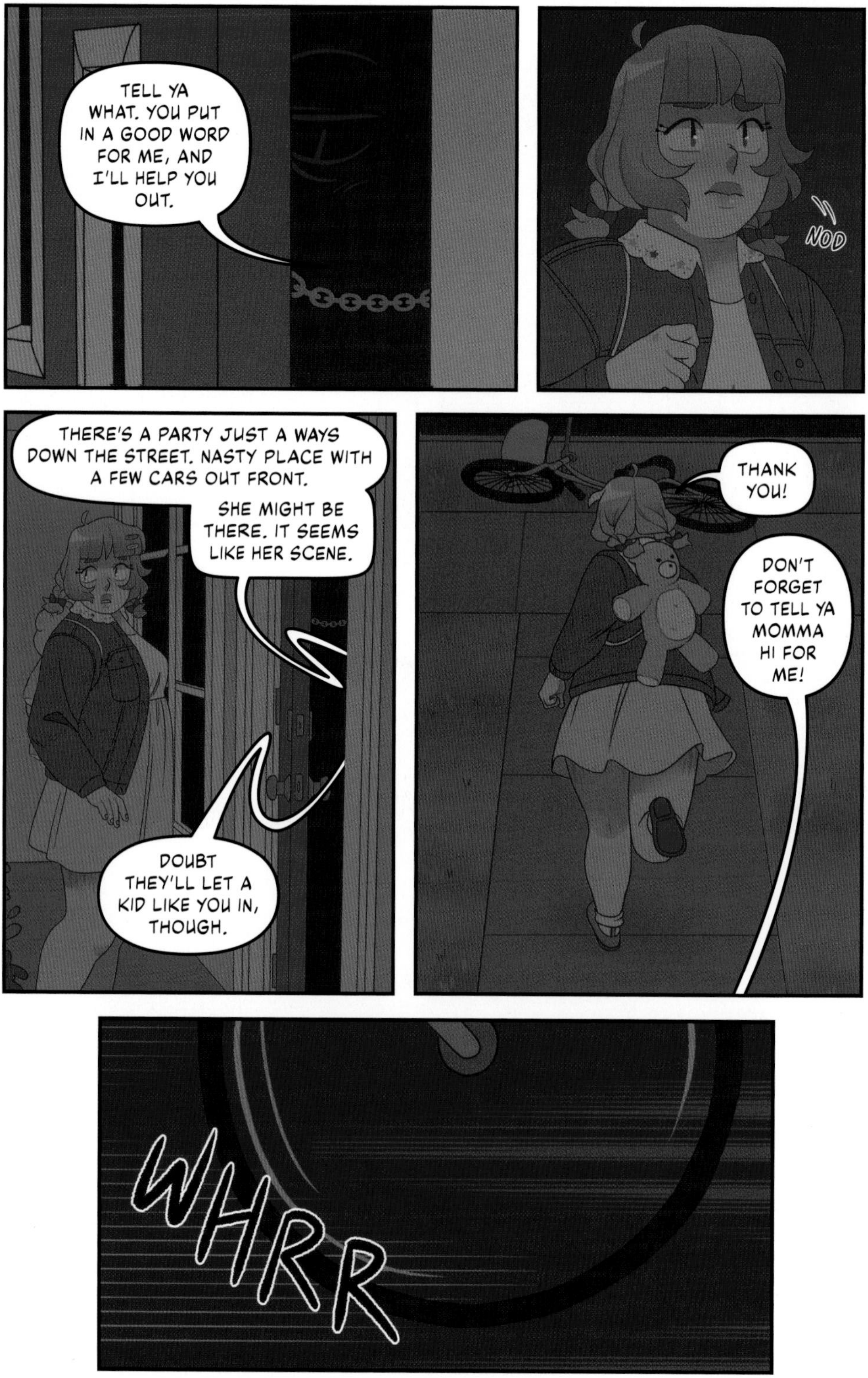

TELL YA WHAT. YOU PUT IN A GOOD WORD FOR ME, AND I'LL HELP YOU OUT.
NOD
THERE'S A PARTY JUST A WAYS DOWN THE STREET. NASTY PLACE WITH A FEW CARS OUT FRONT.
SHE MIGHT BE THERE. IT SEEMS LIKE HER SCENE.
DOUBT THEY'LL LET A KID LIKE YOU IN, THOUGH.
THANK YOU!
DON'T FORGET TO TELL YA MOMMA HI FOR ME!
WHRR

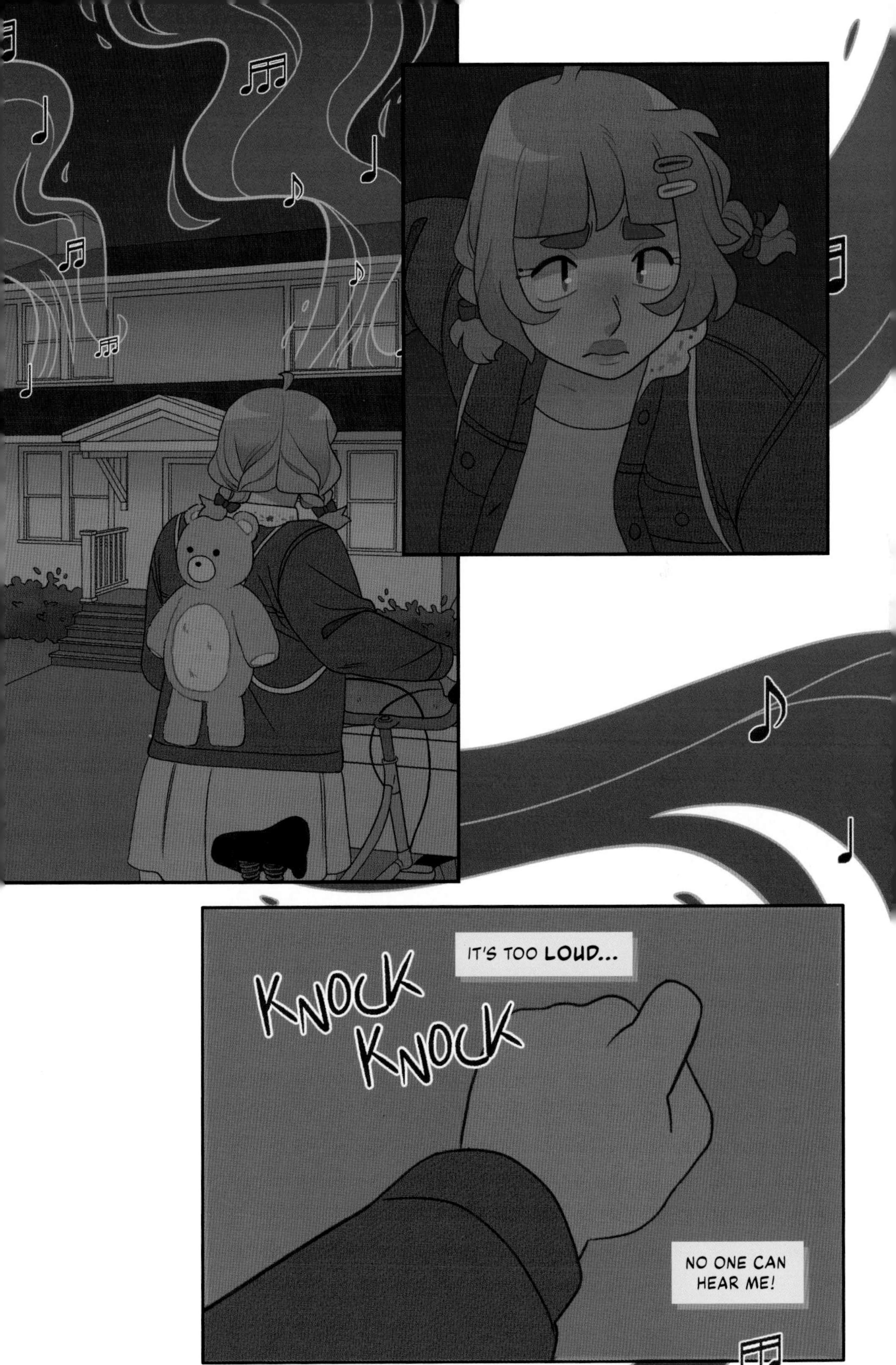
IT'S TOO LOUD...
KNOCK KNOCK
NO ONE CAN HEAR ME!

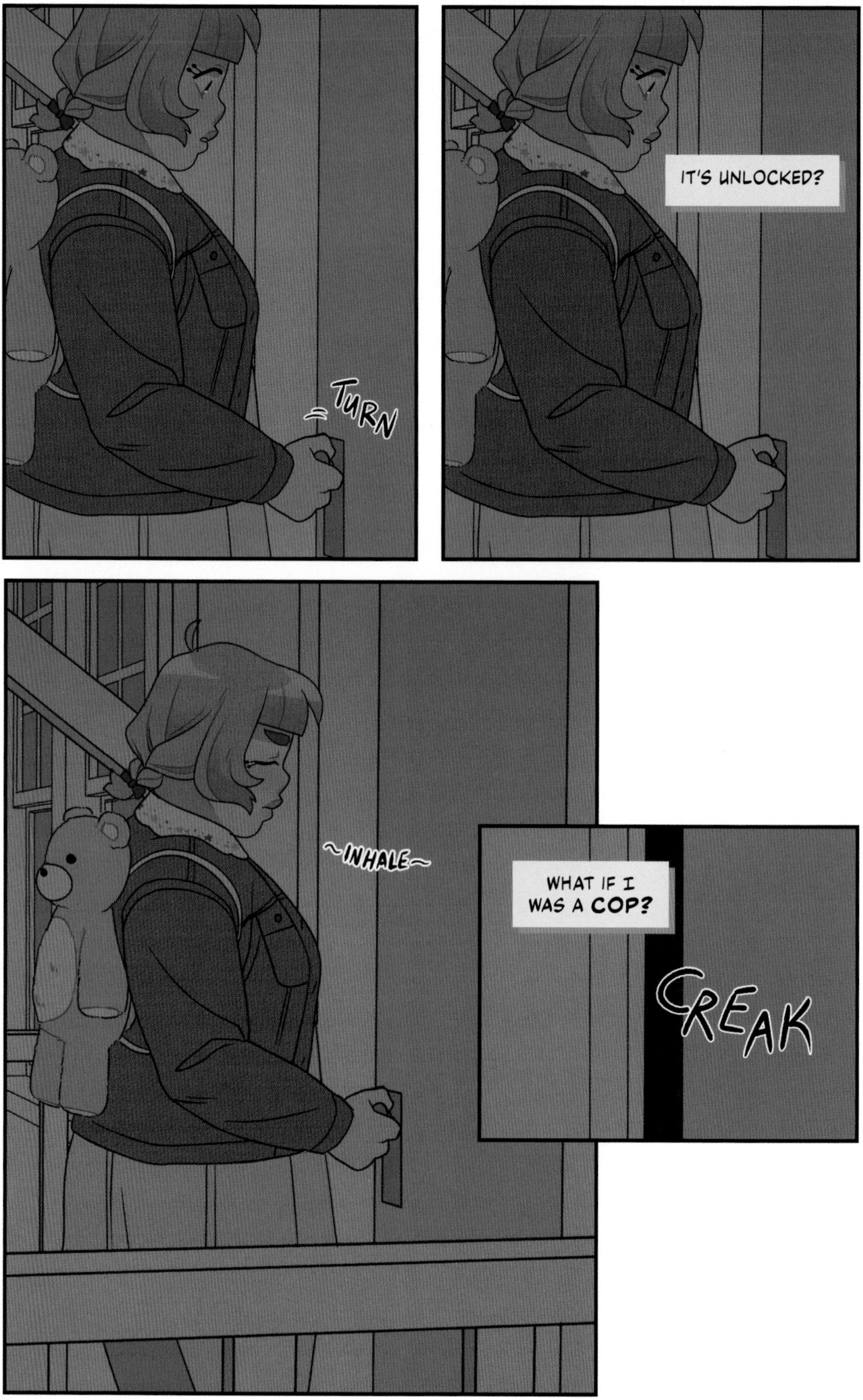
TURN
IT'S UNLOCKED?
~INHALE~
WHAT IF I WAS A COP?
CREAK

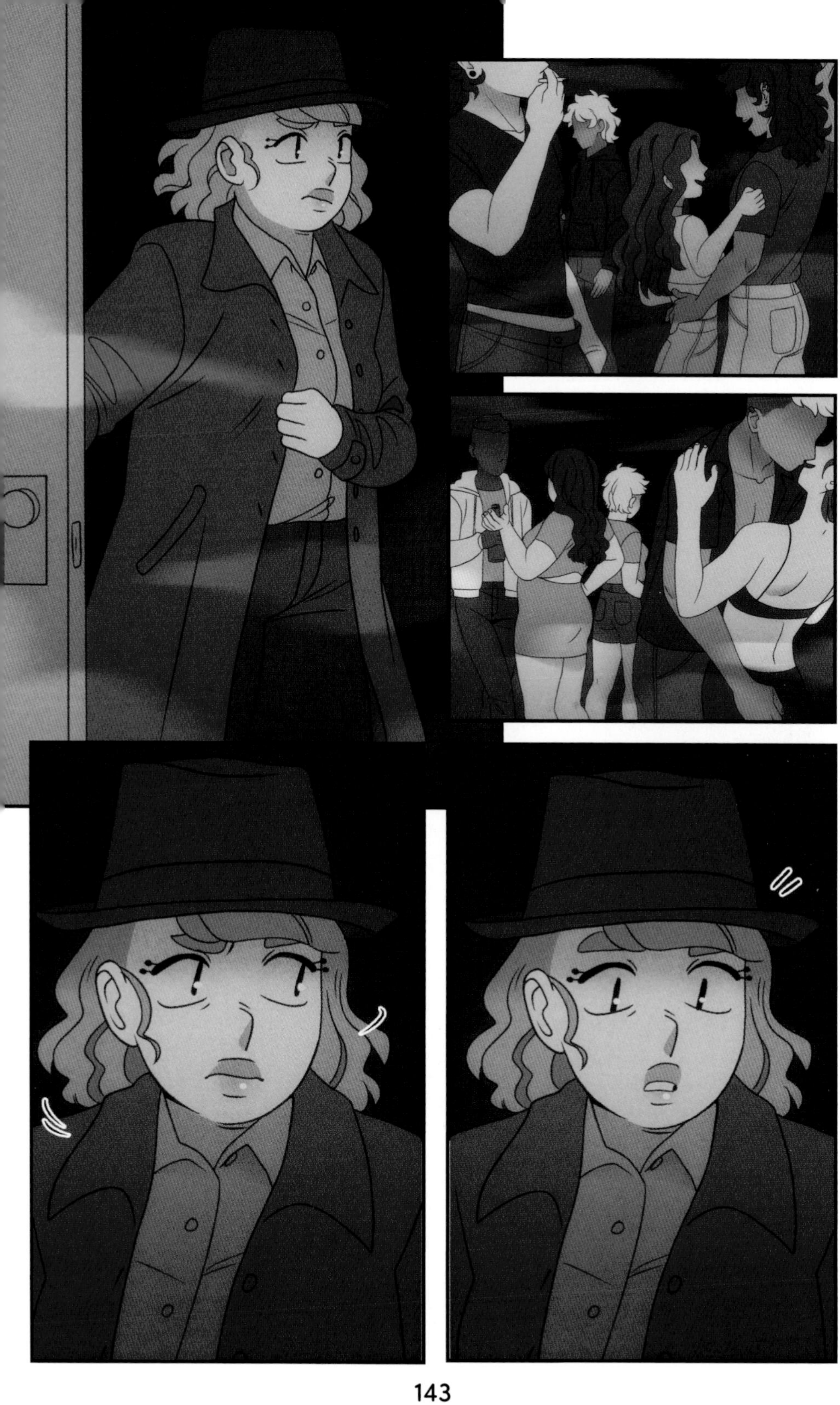

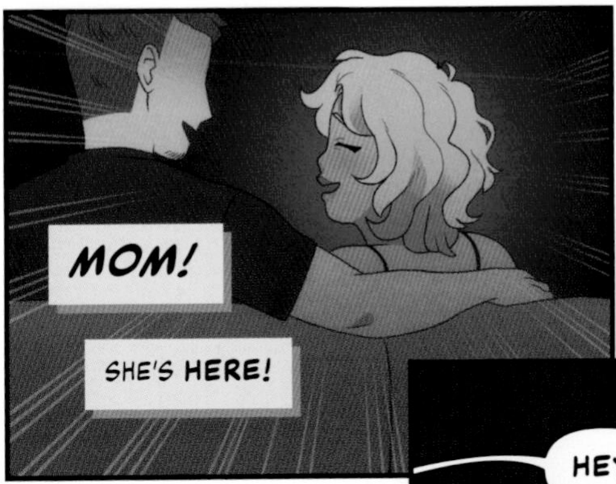
MOM!
SHE'S HERE!

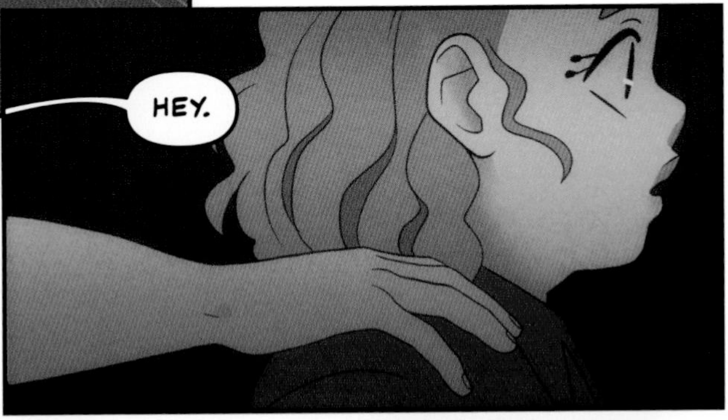
HEY.

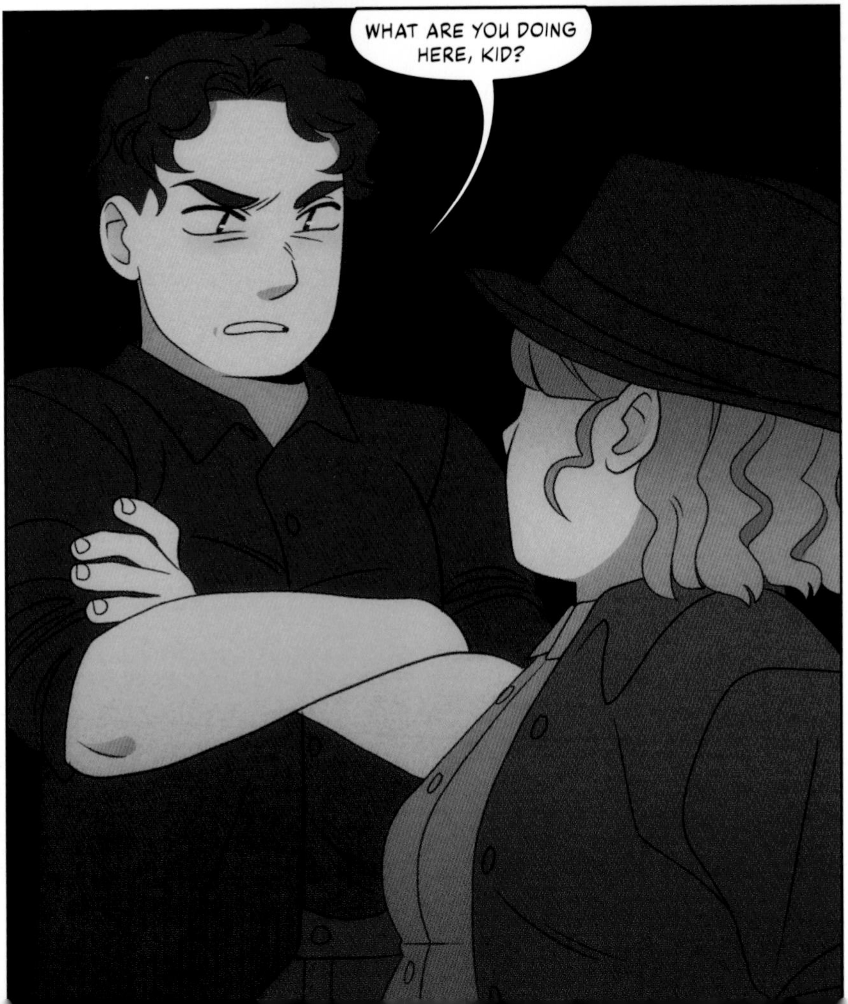
WHAT ARE YOU DOING HERE, KID?

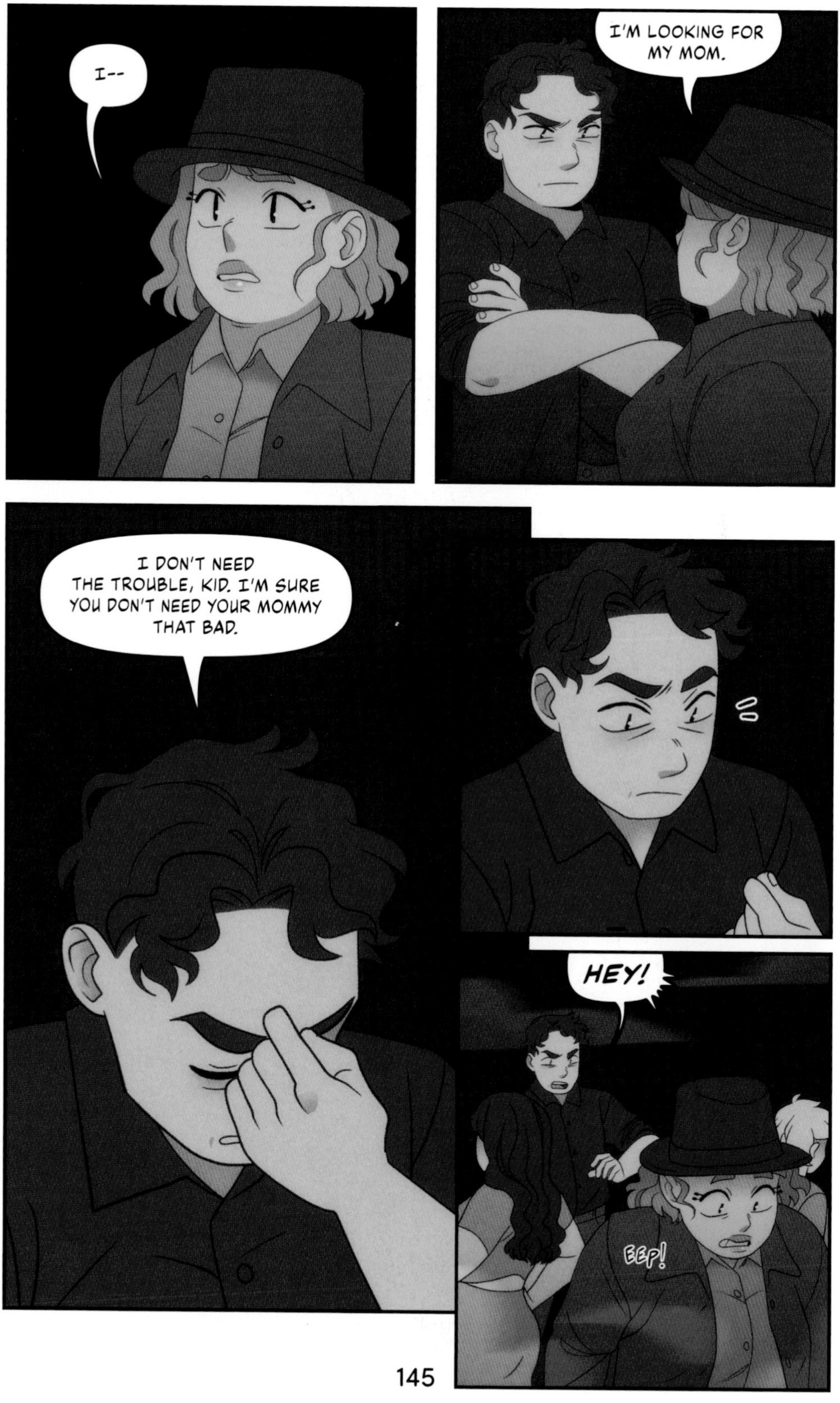
I--
I'M LOOKING FOR MY MOM.
I DON'T NEED THE TROUBLE, KID. I'M SURE YOU DON'T NEED YOUR MOMMY THAT BAD.
HEY!
EEP!

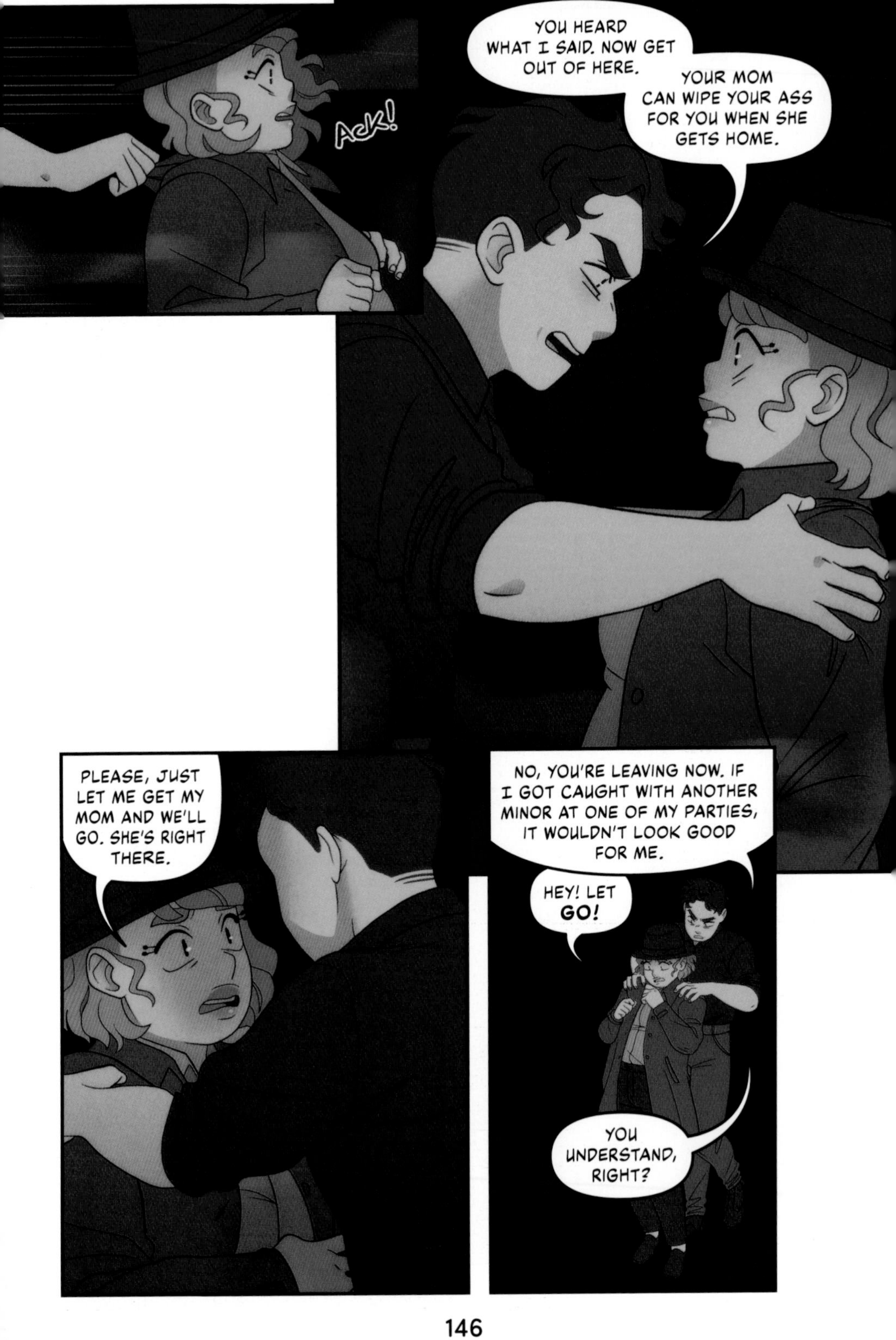
Ack!
YOU HEARD WHAT I SAID. NOW GET OUT OF HERE.
YOUR MOM CAN WIPE YOUR ASS FOR YOU WHEN SHE GETS HOME.
PLEASE, JUST LET ME GET MY MOM AND WE'LL GO. SHE'S RIGHT THERE.
NO, YOU'RE LEAVING NOW. IF I GOT CAUGHT WITH ANOTHER MINOR AT ONE OF MY PARTIES, IT WOULDN'T LOOK GOOD FOR ME.
HEY! LET GO!
YOU UNDERSTAND, RIGHT?

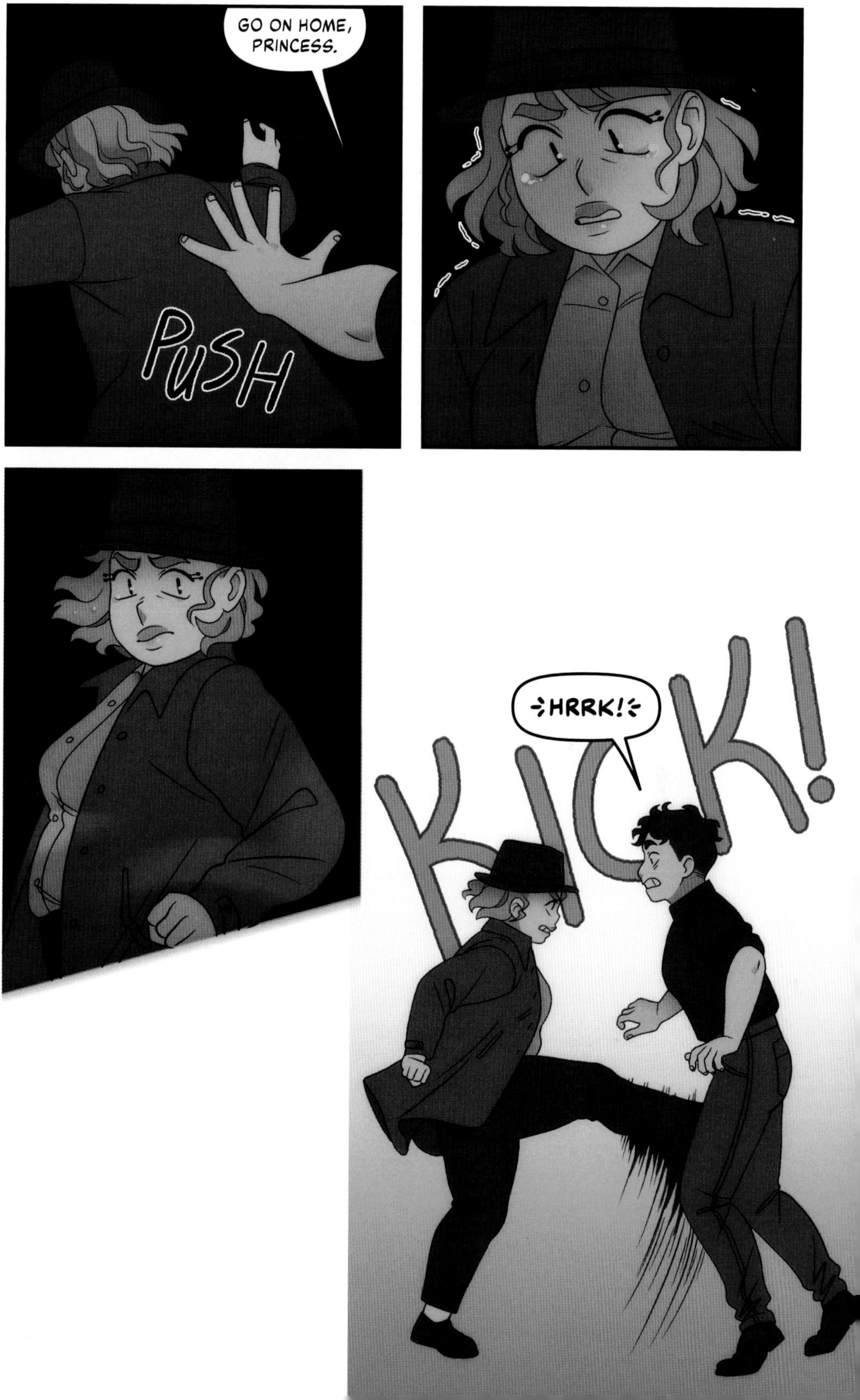
GO ON HOME, PRINCESS.
PUSH
HRRK!
KICK!

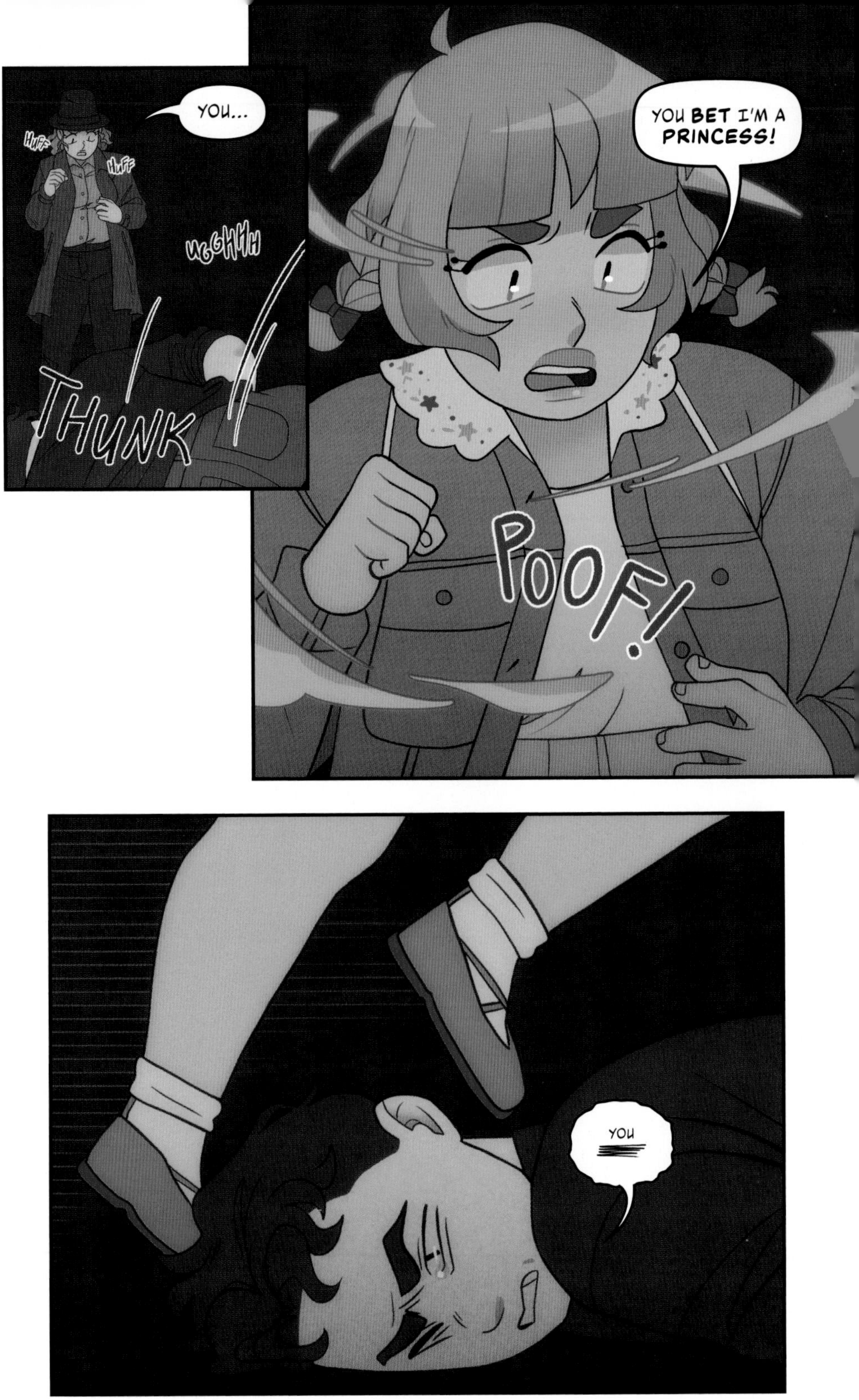
HUFF
HUFF
YOU...
UGGHHH
THUNK
YOU BET I'M A PRINCESS!
POOF!
YOU

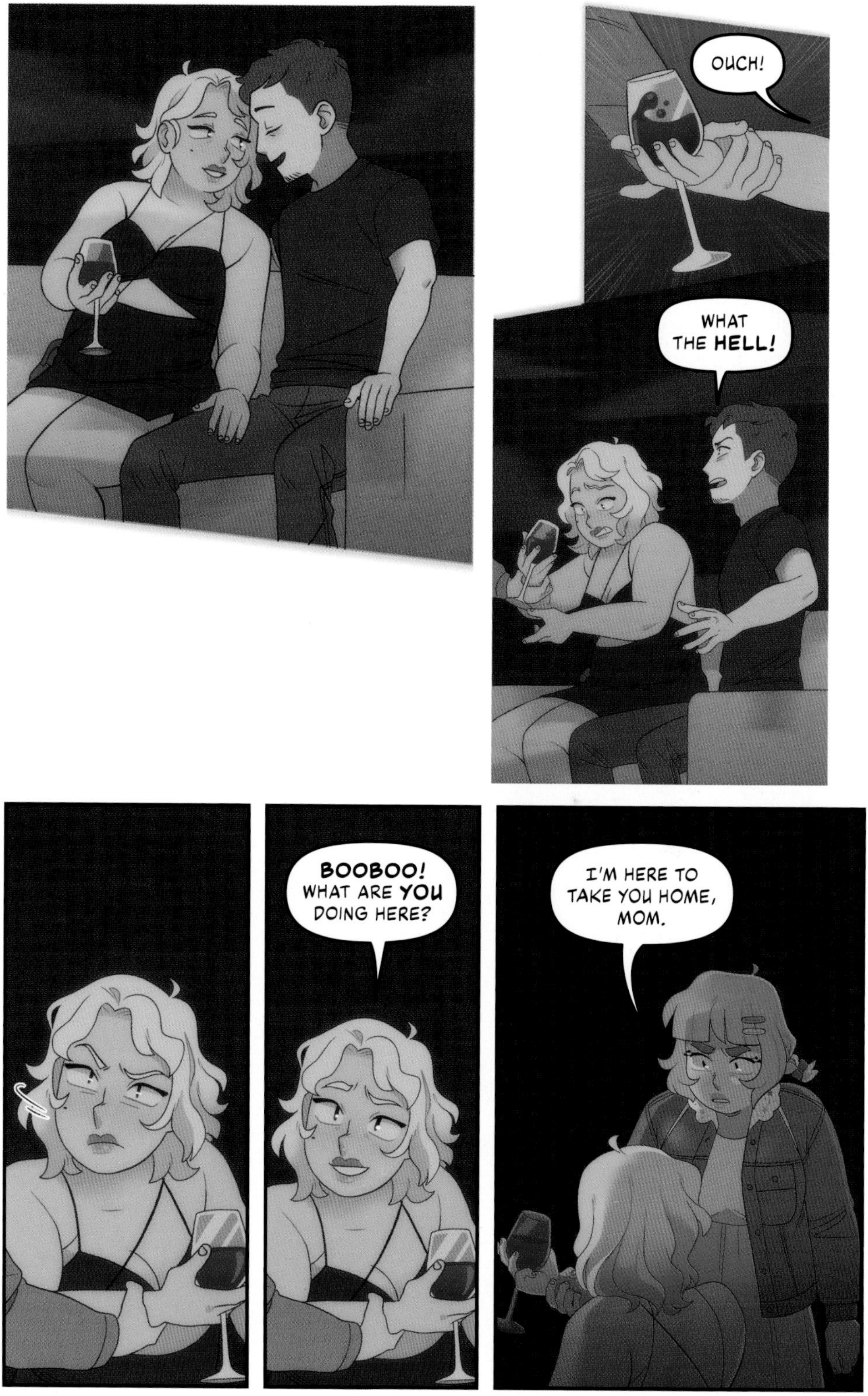
OUCH!
WHAT THE **HELL!**
BOOBOO! WHAT ARE **YOU** DOING HERE?
I'M HERE TO TAKE YOU HOME, MOM.

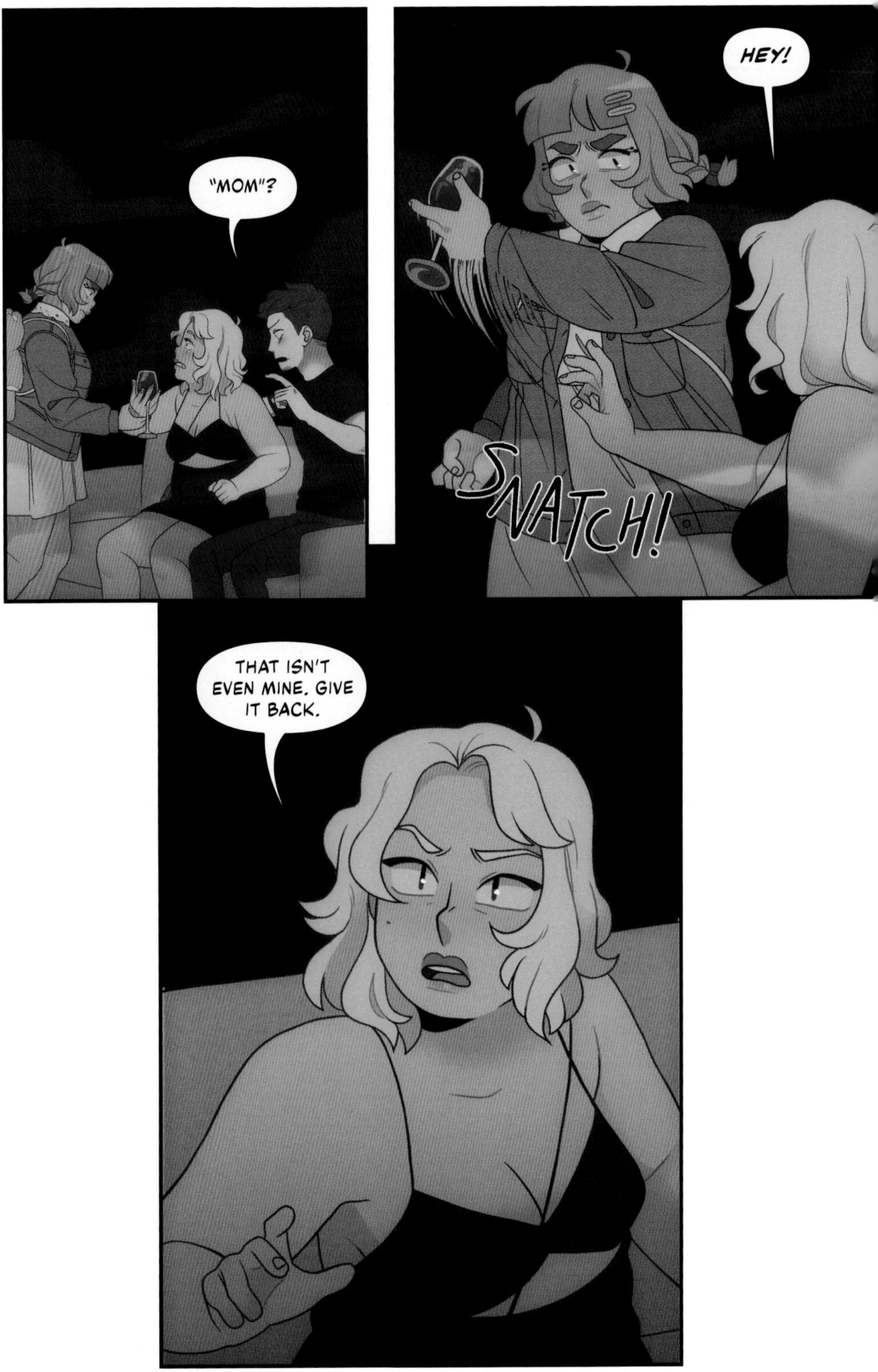
"MOM"?
HEY!
SNATCH!
THAT ISN'T EVEN MINE. GIVE IT BACK.

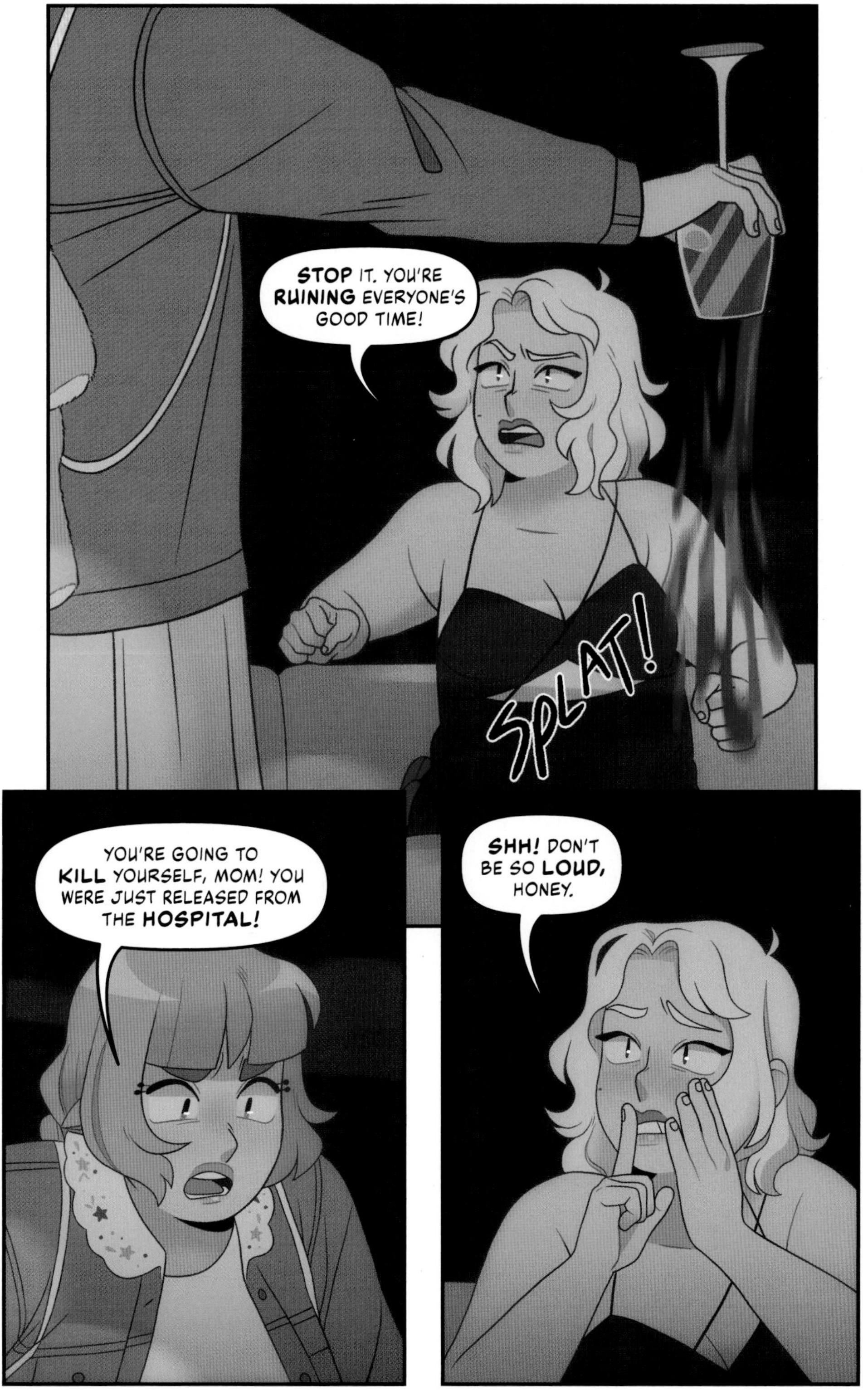
STOP IT. YOU'RE RUINING EVERYONE'S GOOD TIME!
SPLAT!
YOU'RE GOING TO KILL YOURSELF, MOM! YOU WERE JUST RELEASED FROM THE HOSPITAL!
SHH! DON'T BE SO LOUD, HONEY.

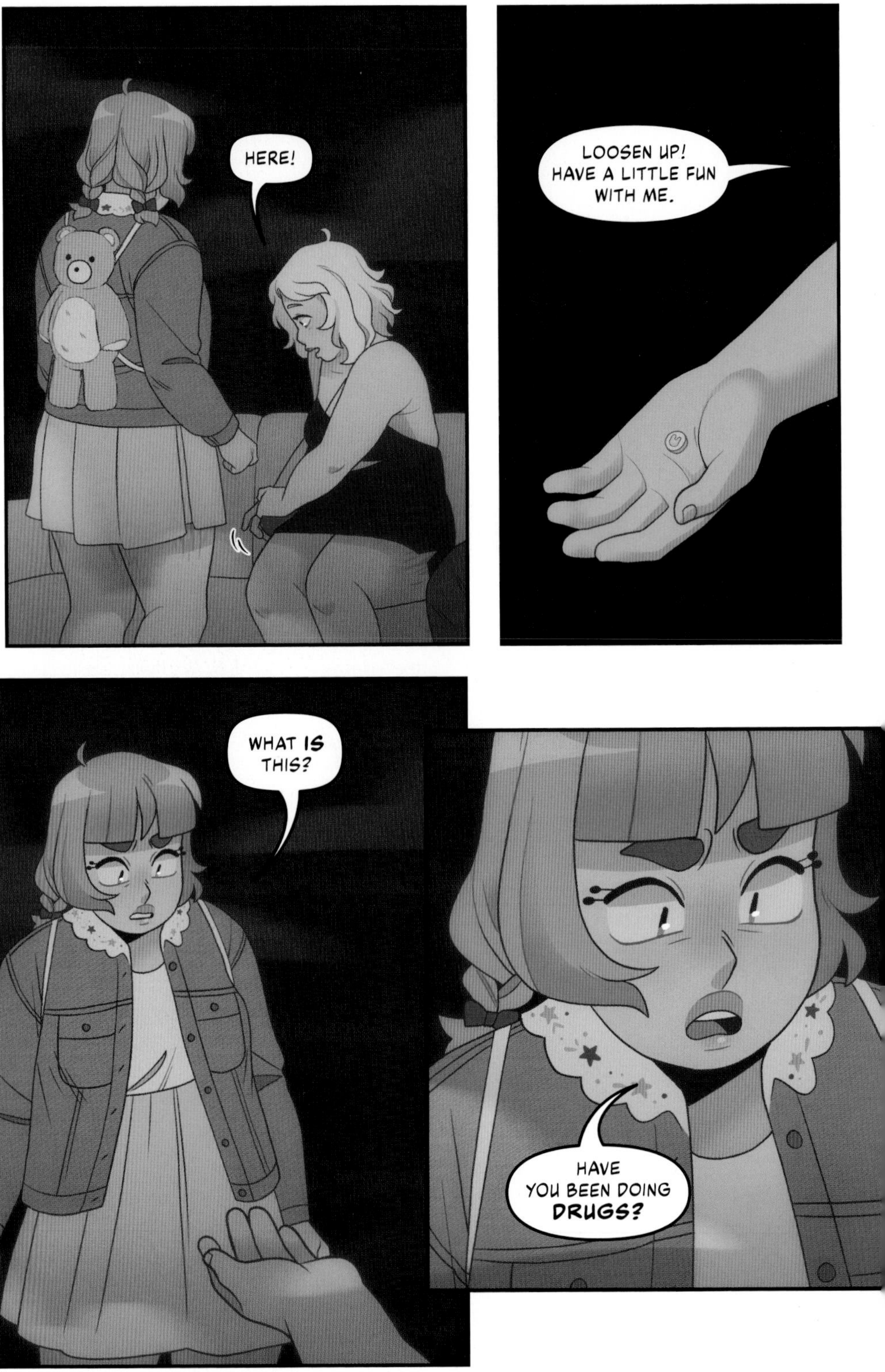
HERE!
LOOSEN UP! HAVE A LITTLE FUN WITH ME.
WHAT **IS** THIS?
HAVE YOU BEEN DOING **DRUGS?**

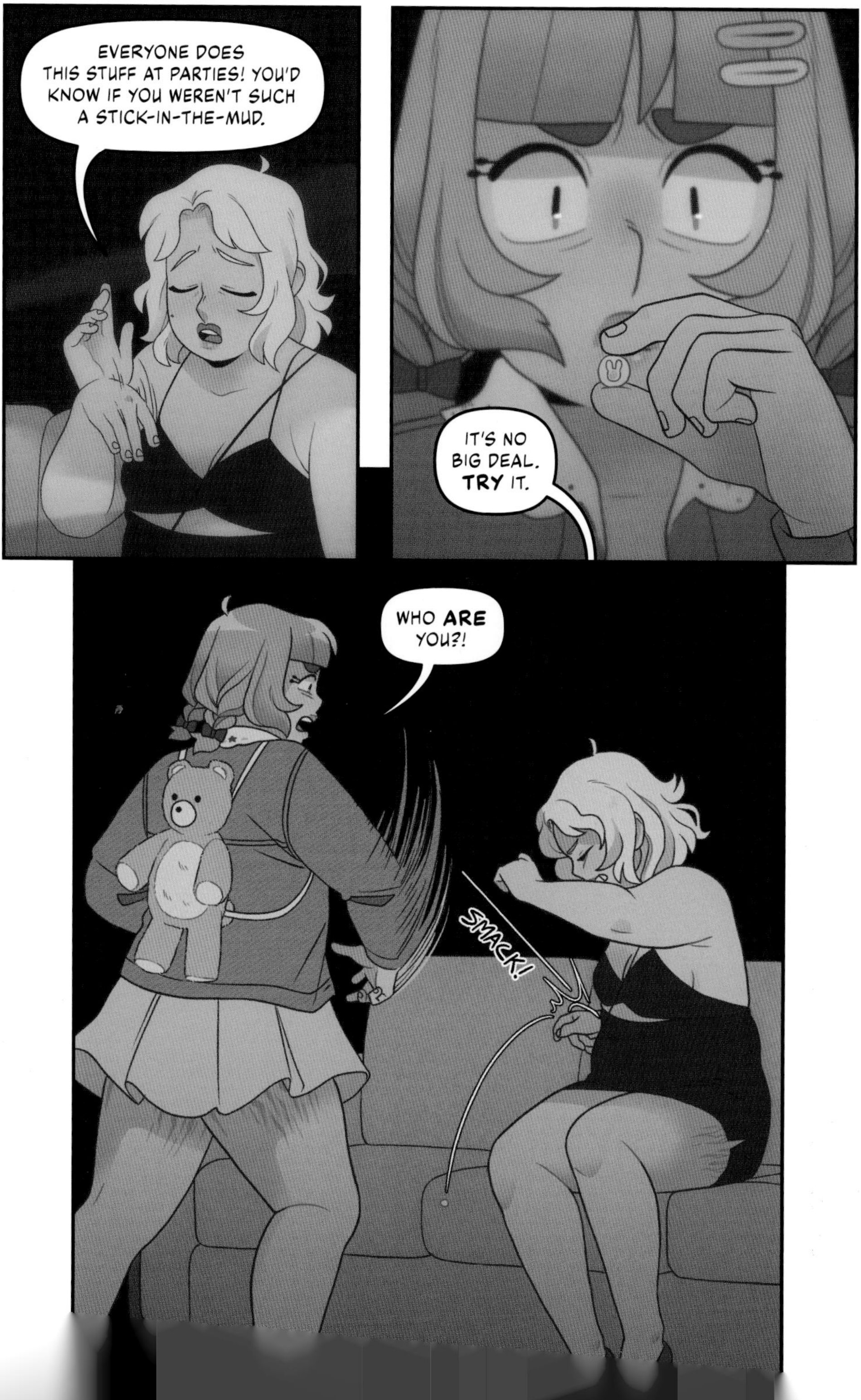
EVERYONE DOES THIS STUFF AT PARTIES! YOU'D KNOW IF YOU WEREN'T SUCH A STICK-IN-THE-MUD.
IT'S NO BIG DEAL. **TRY** IT.
WHO **ARE** YOU?!
SMACK!

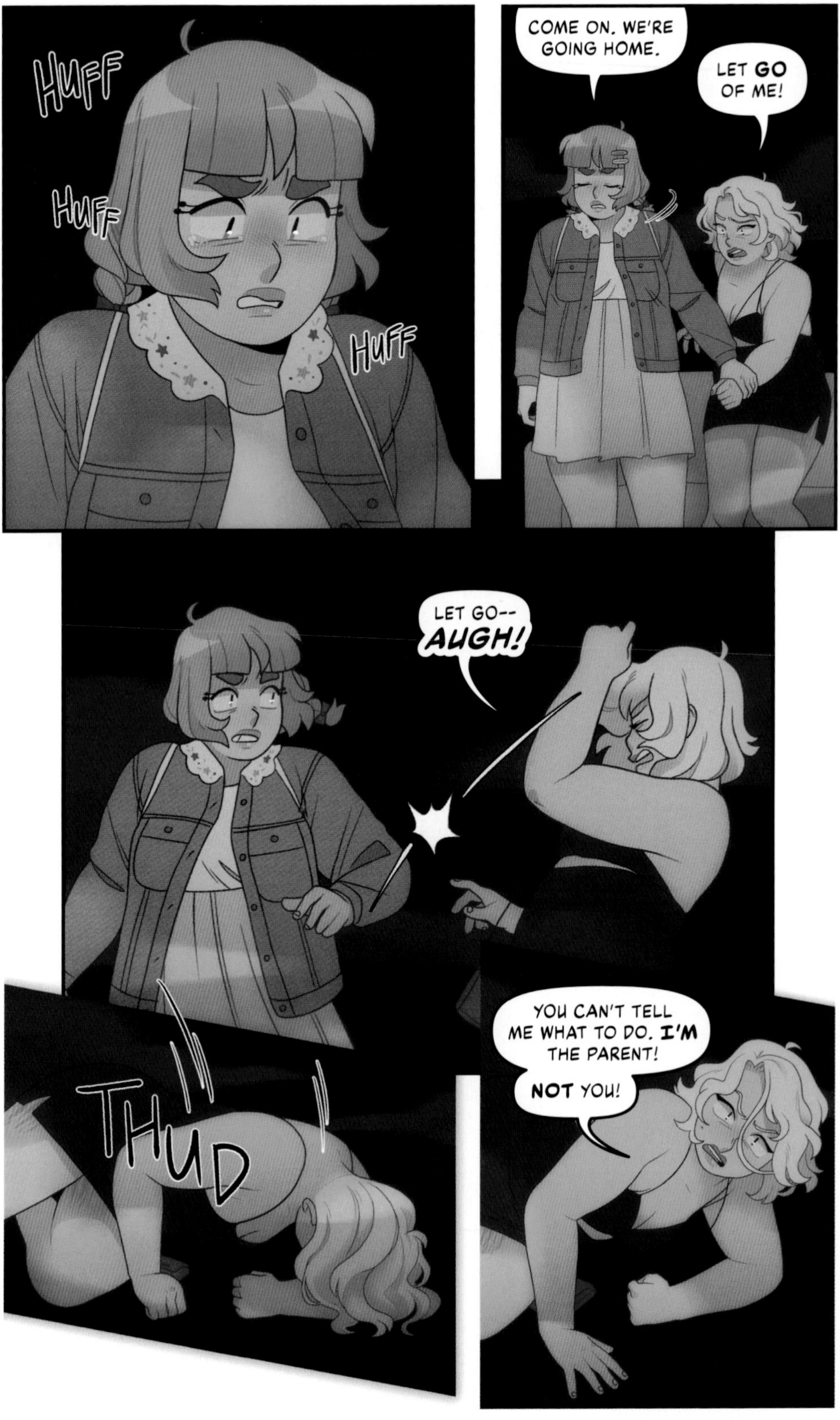
HUFF
HUFF
HUFF
COME ON. WE'RE GOING HOME.
LET **GO** OF ME!
LET GO--
AUGH!
THUD
YOU CAN'T TELL ME WHAT TO DO. **I'M** THE PARENT!
NOT YOU!

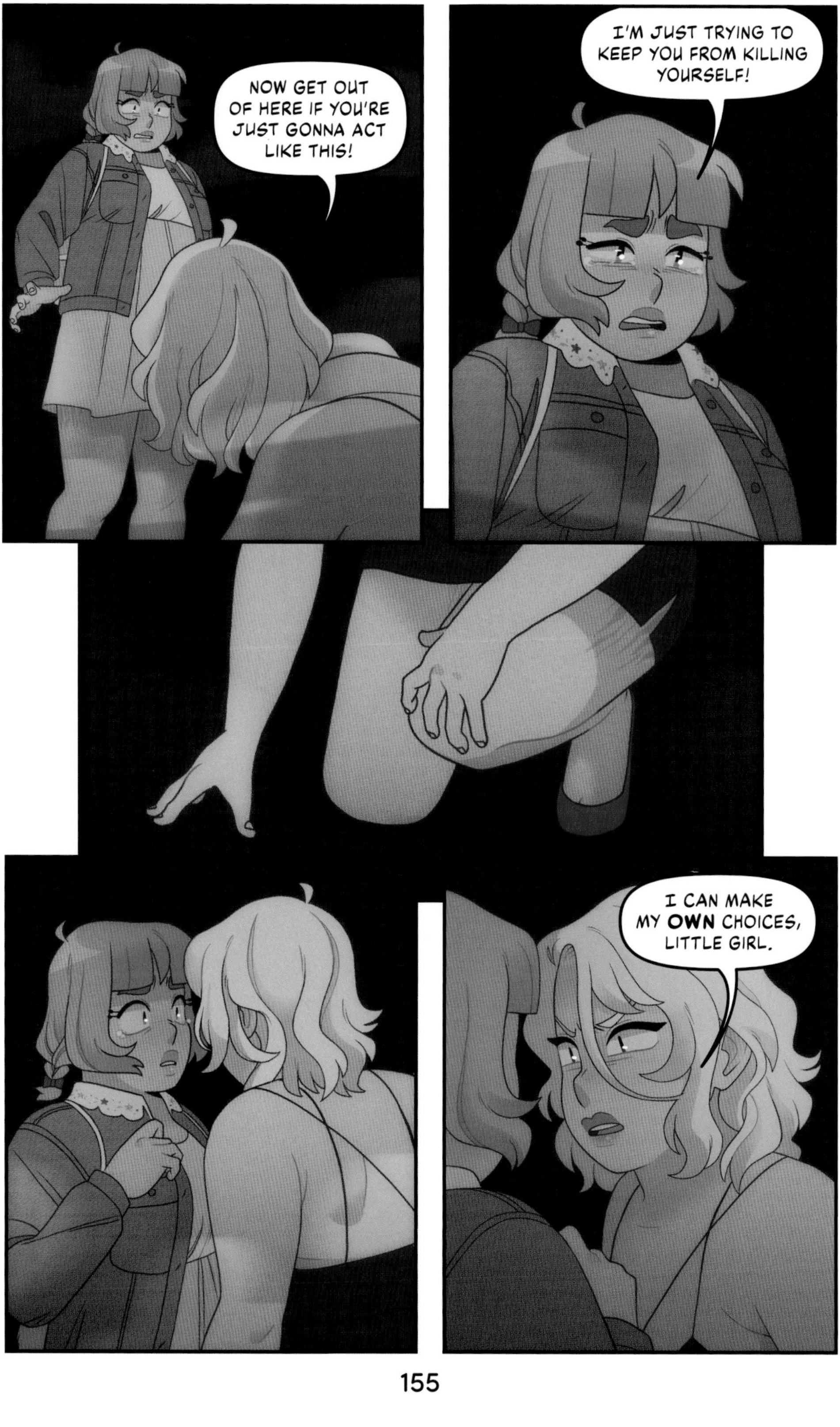
NOW GET OUT OF HERE IF YOU'RE JUST GONNA ACT LIKE THIS!
I'M JUST TRYING TO KEEP YOU FROM KILLING YOURSELF!
I CAN MAKE MY **OWN** CHOICES, LITTLE GIRL.

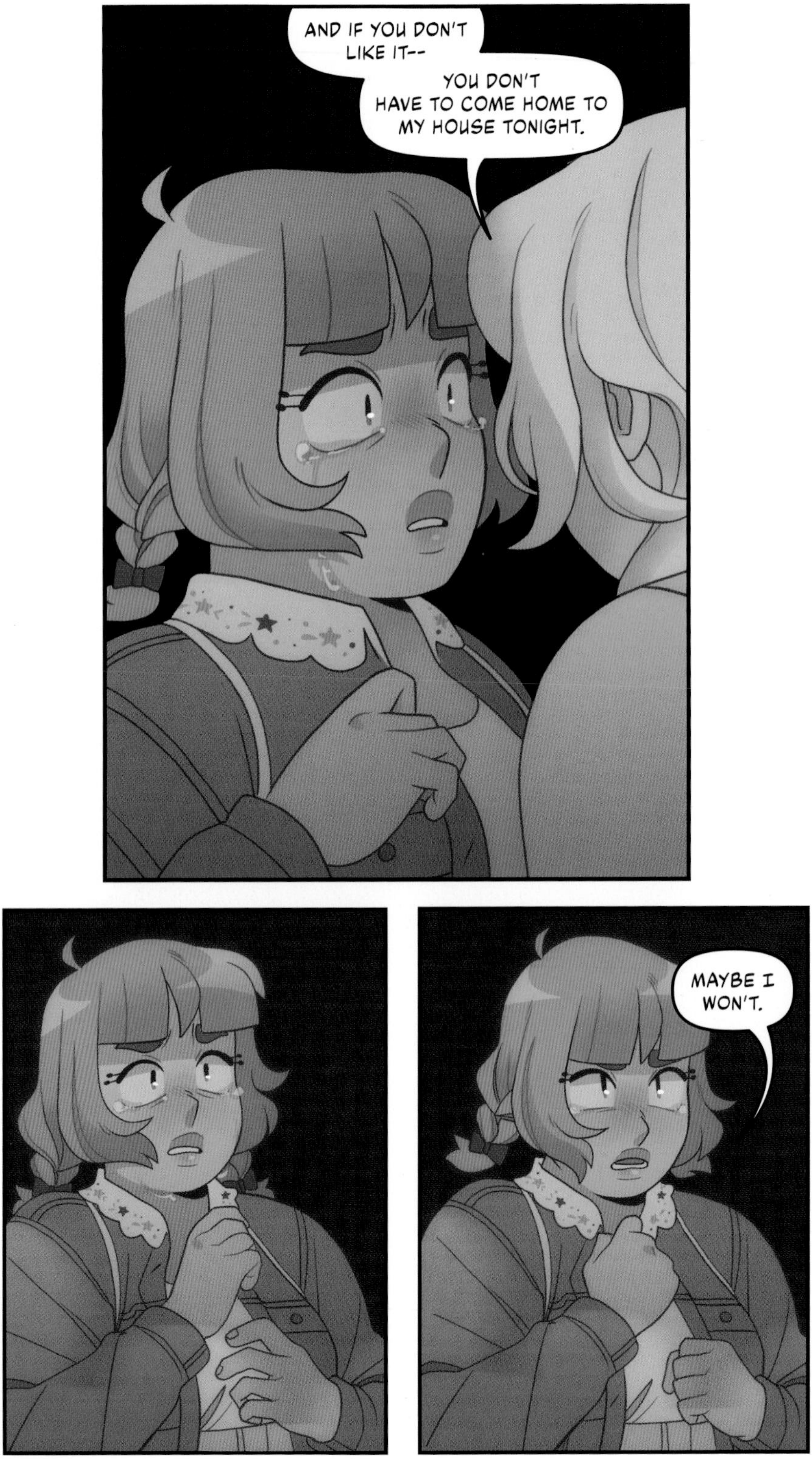
AND IF YOU DON'T LIKE IT--
YOU DON'T HAVE TO COME HOME TO MY HOUSE TONIGHT.
MAYBE I WON'T.

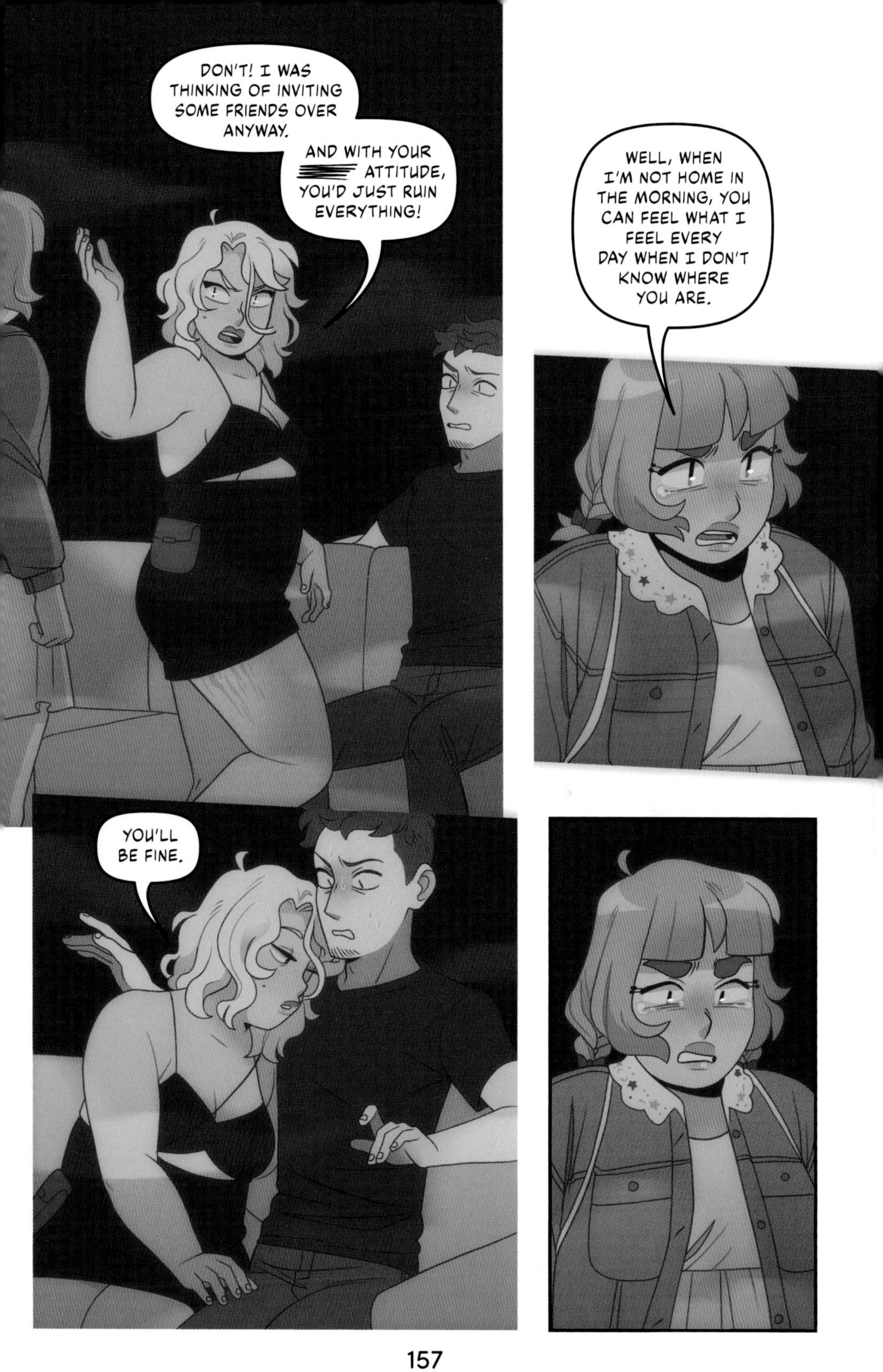
DON'T! I WAS THINKING OF INVITING SOME FRIENDS OVER ANYWAY.
AND WITH YOUR [redacted] ATTITUDE, YOU'D JUST RUIN EVERYTHING!
WELL, WHEN I'M NOT HOME IN THE MORNING, YOU CAN FEEL WHAT I FEEL EVERY DAY WHEN I DON'T KNOW WHERE YOU ARE.
YOU'LL BE FINE.

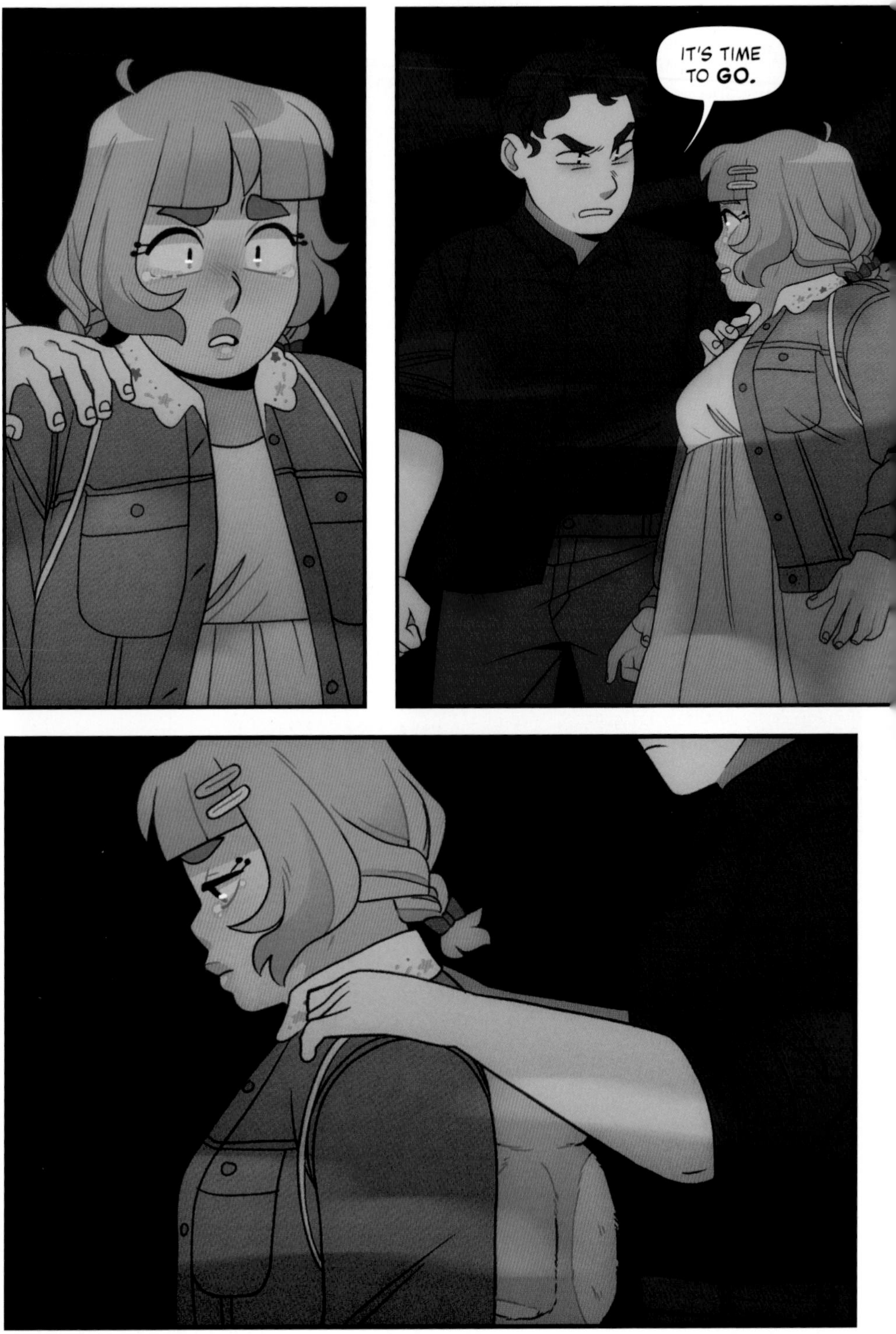
IT'S TIME TO GO.

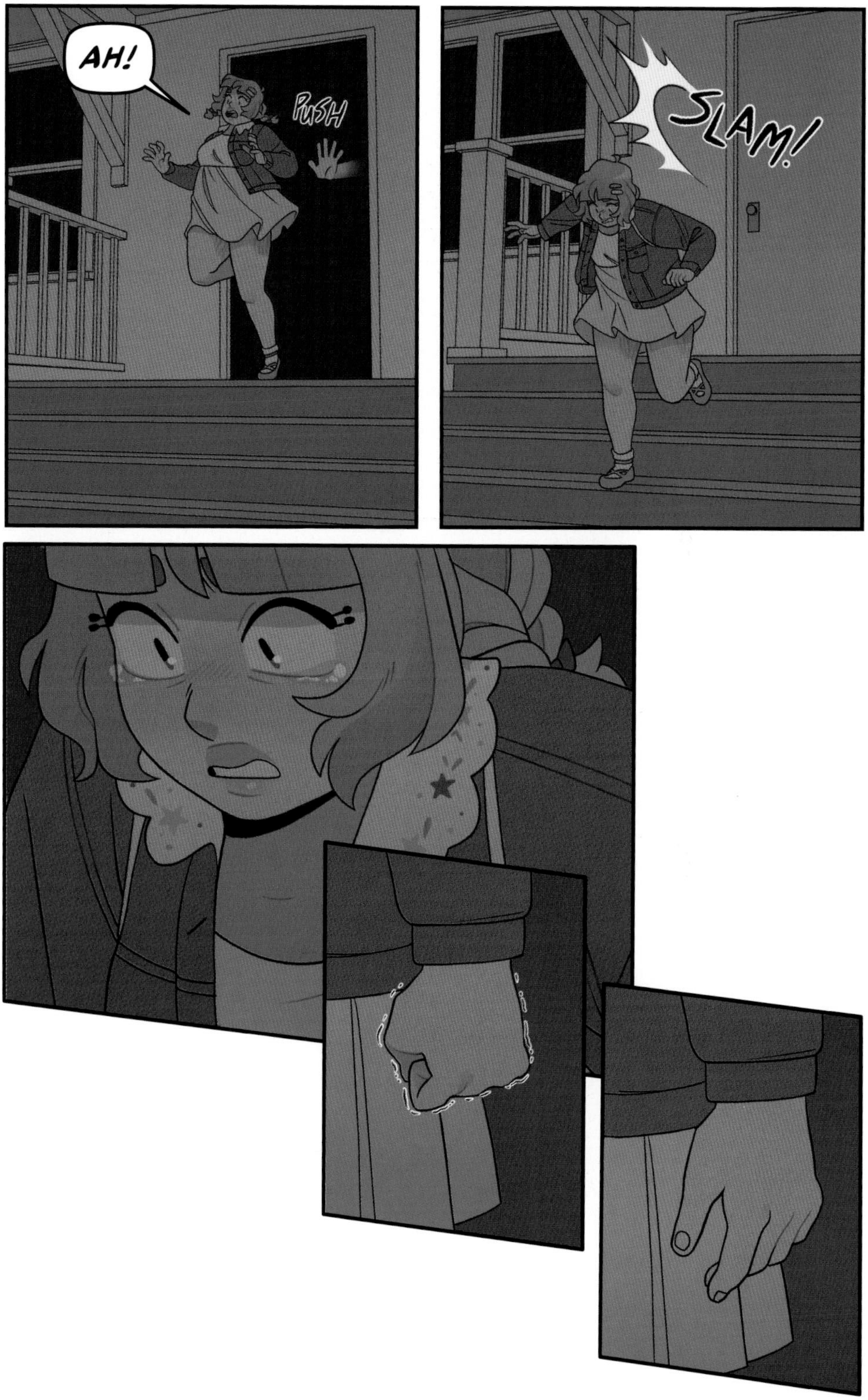
AH!
PUSH
SLAM!

TURN

NO, I CAN'T
GO HOME.

IF I GO HOME,
SHE WINS.

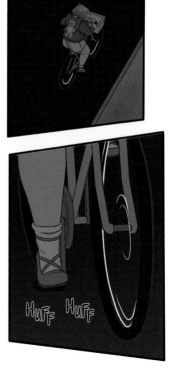

HUFF   HUFF

160

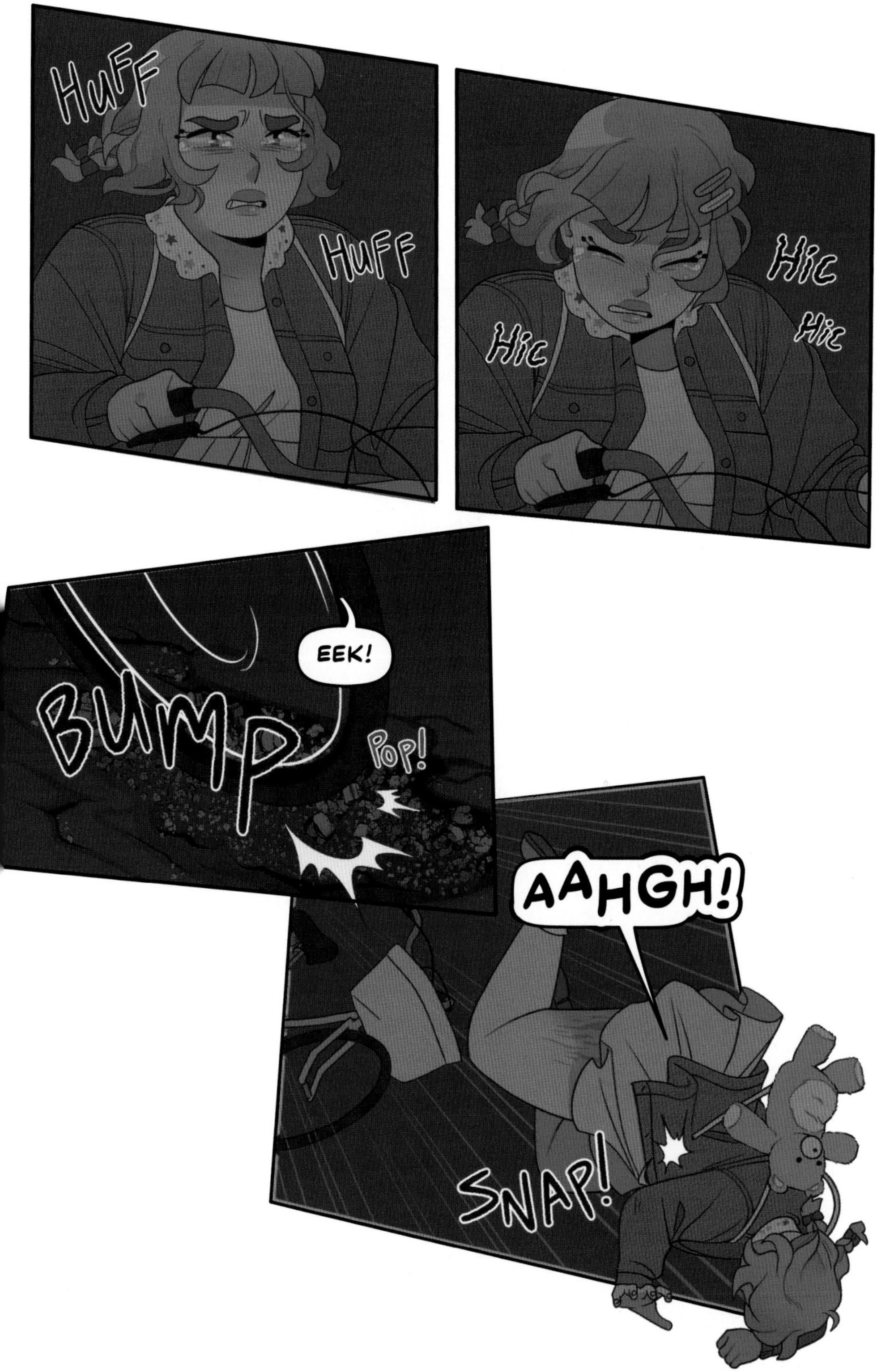
HUFF
HUFF
HIC
HIC
HIC
EEK!
BUMP
POP!
AAHGH!
SNAP!

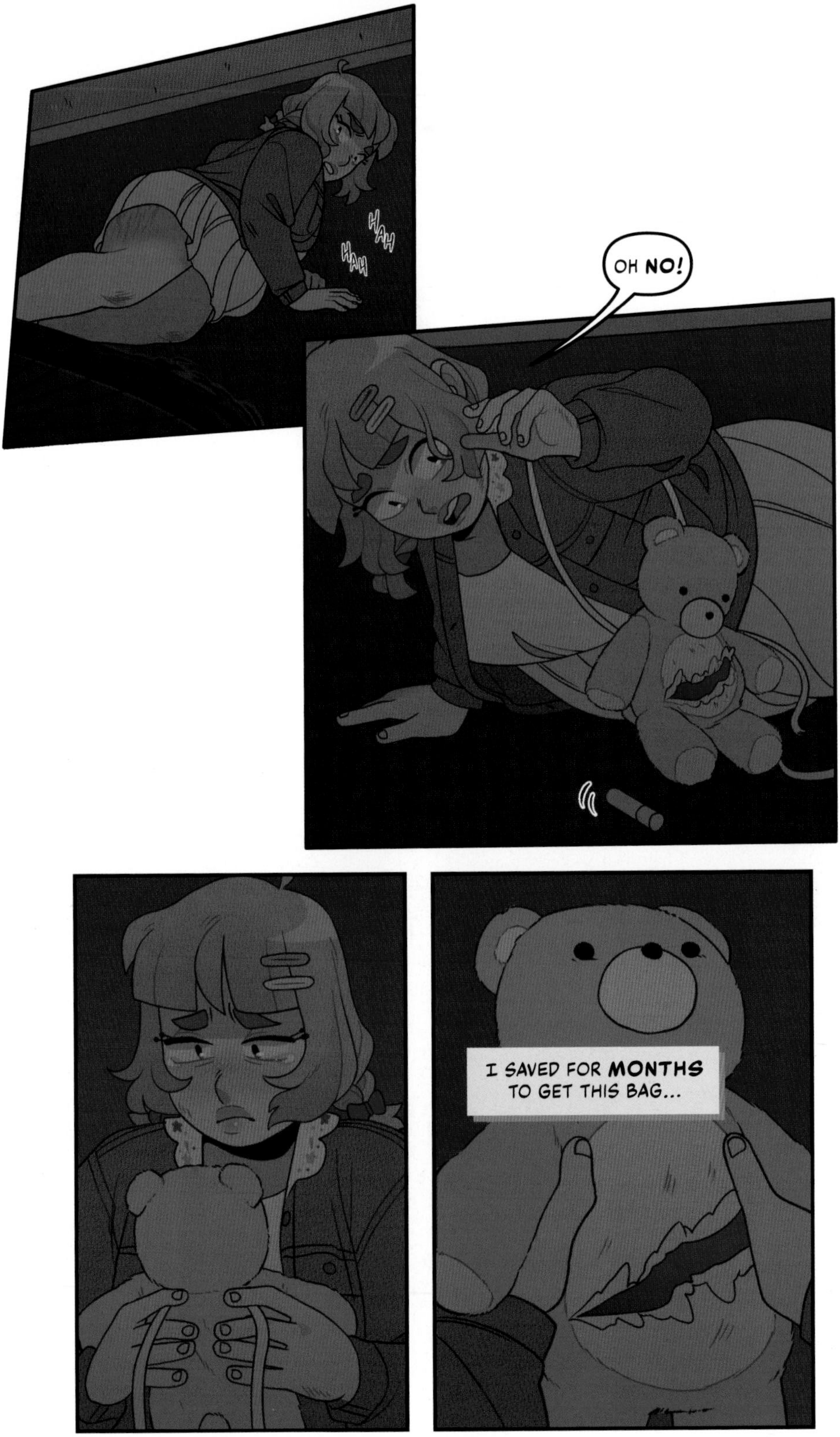
HAH
HAH
OH NO!
I SAVED FOR MONTHS TO GET THIS BAG...

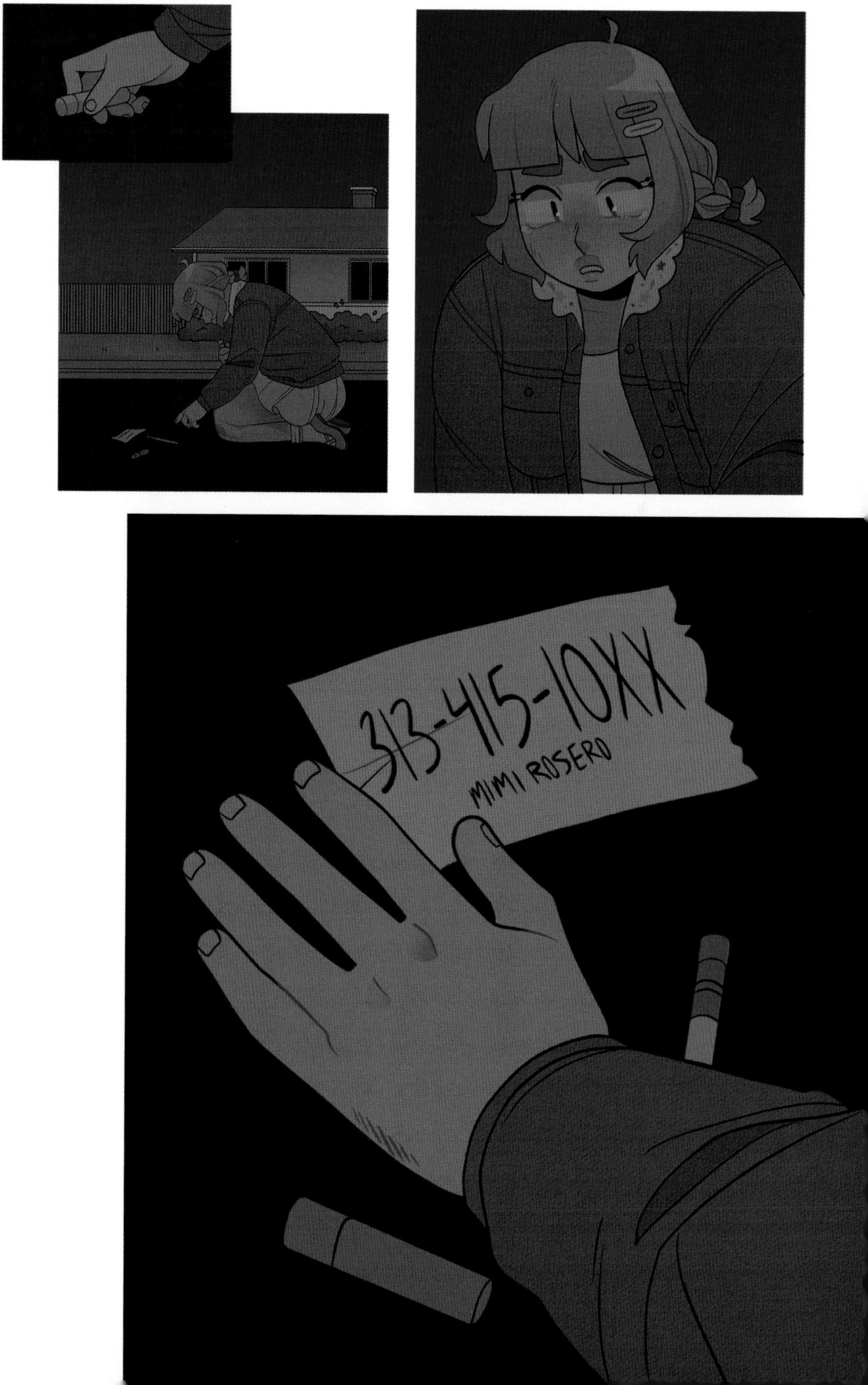
313-415-10XX
MIMI ROSERO

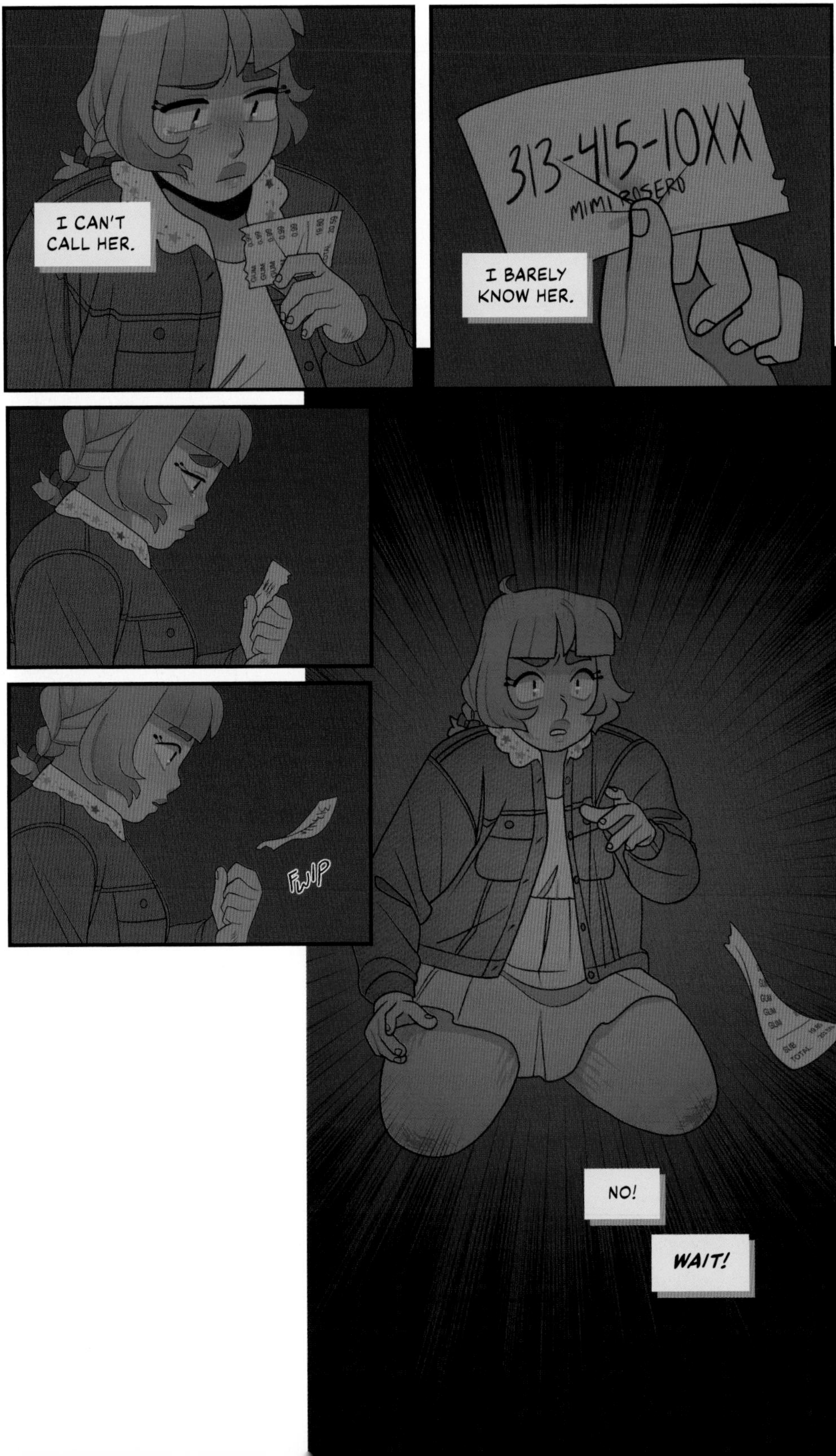
I CAN'T CALL HER.
313-415-10XX
MIMI ROSERO
I BARELY KNOW HER.
FWIP
NO!
WAIT!

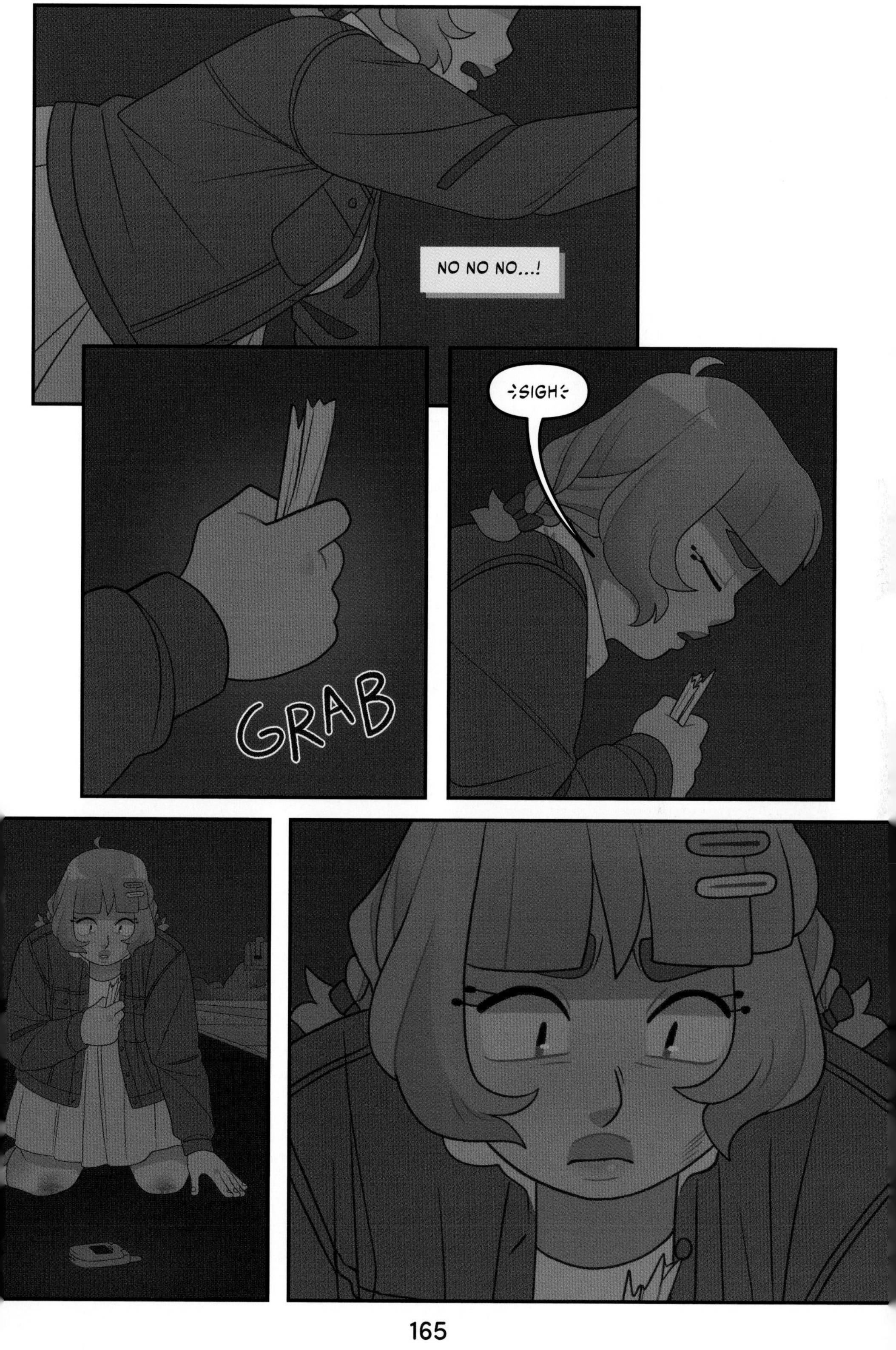
NO NO NO...!
GRAB
SIGH

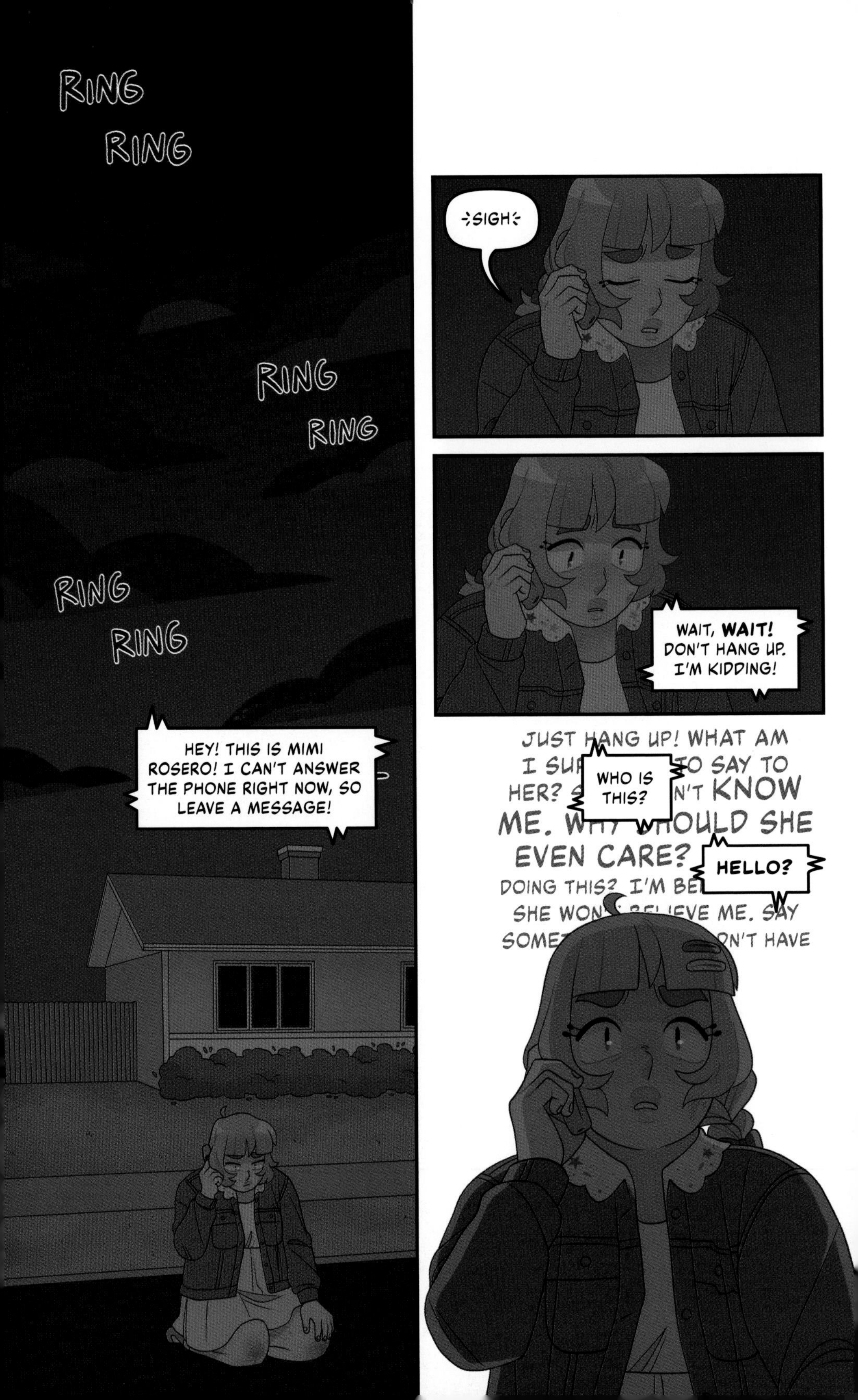
RING
RING
RING
RING
RING
RING
HEY! THIS IS MIMI ROSERO! I CAN'T ANSWER THE PHONE RIGHT NOW, SO LEAVE A MESSAGE!
-SIGH-
WAIT, WAIT! DON'T HANG UP. I'M KIDDING!
JUST HANG UP! WHAT AM
I SU
TO SAY TO
HER?
N'T KNOW
ME.
HOULD SHE
EVEN CARE?
DOING THIS? I'M BE
SHE WON
IEVE ME. SAY
SOME
ON'T HAVE
WHO IS THIS?
HELLO?

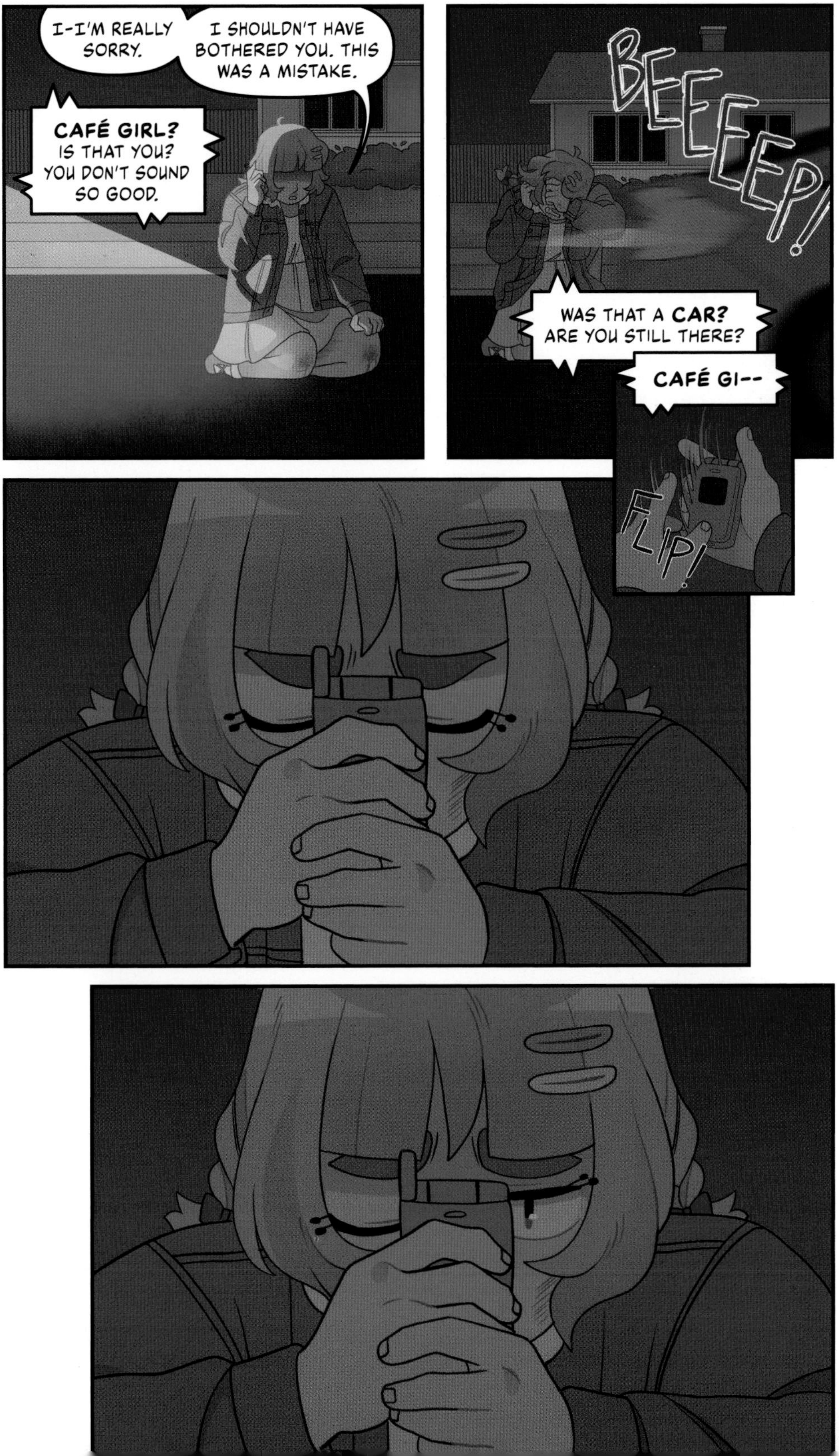

I-I'M REALLY SORRY.
I SHOULDN'T HAVE BOTHERED YOU. THIS WAS A MISTAKE.
CAFÉ GIRL? IS THAT YOU? YOU DON'T SOUND SO GOOD.
BEEEEEP!
WAS THAT A CAR? ARE YOU STILL THERE?
CAFÉ GI--
FLIP!

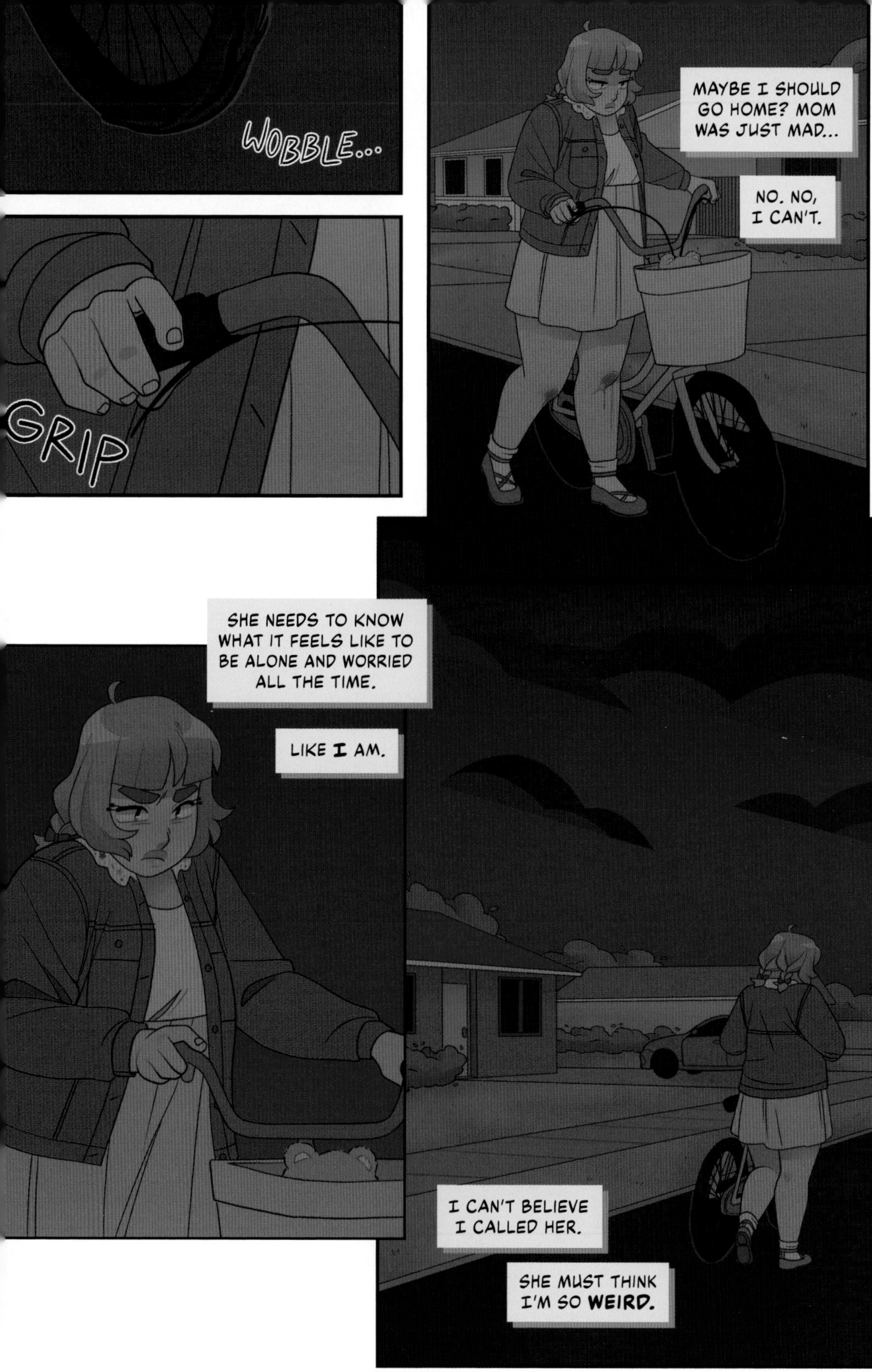
WOBBLE...
GRIP
MAYBE I SHOULD GO HOME? MOM WAS JUST MAD...
NO. NO, I CAN'T.
SHE NEEDS TO KNOW WHAT IT FEELS LIKE TO BE ALONE AND WORRIED ALL THE TIME.
LIKE I AM.
I CAN'T BELIEVE I CALLED HER.
SHE MUST THINK I'M SO WEIRD.

CHAPTER 4

HOW LONG HAVE I BEEN WALKING?
I NEED TO FIND A PLACE TO SLEEP.
BUT IF I ASK CLARICE OR MILO...
I CAN'T...
BEEP!!
EEK!
TRIP!

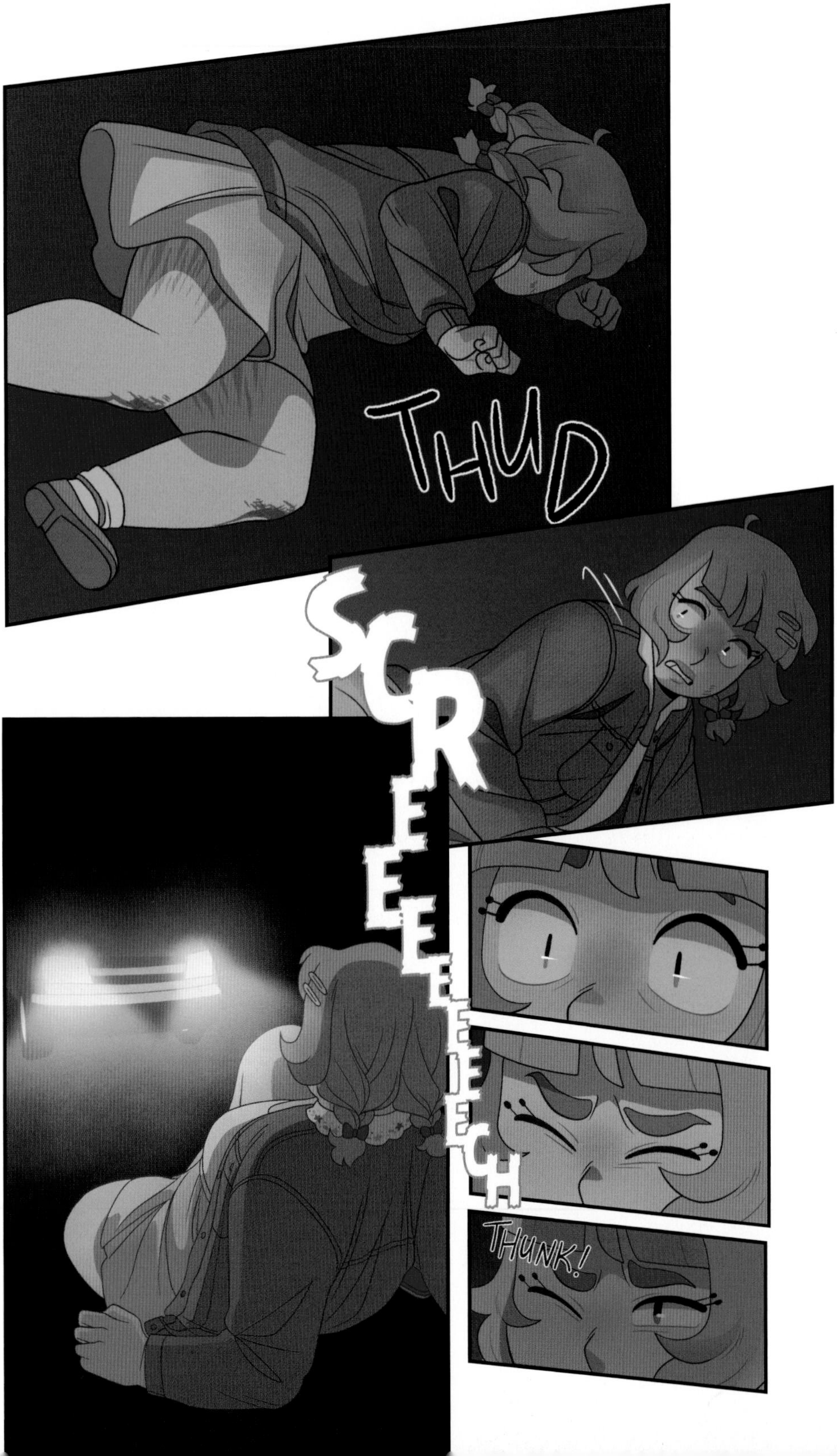
THUD
SCREEEEEEEECH
THUNK!

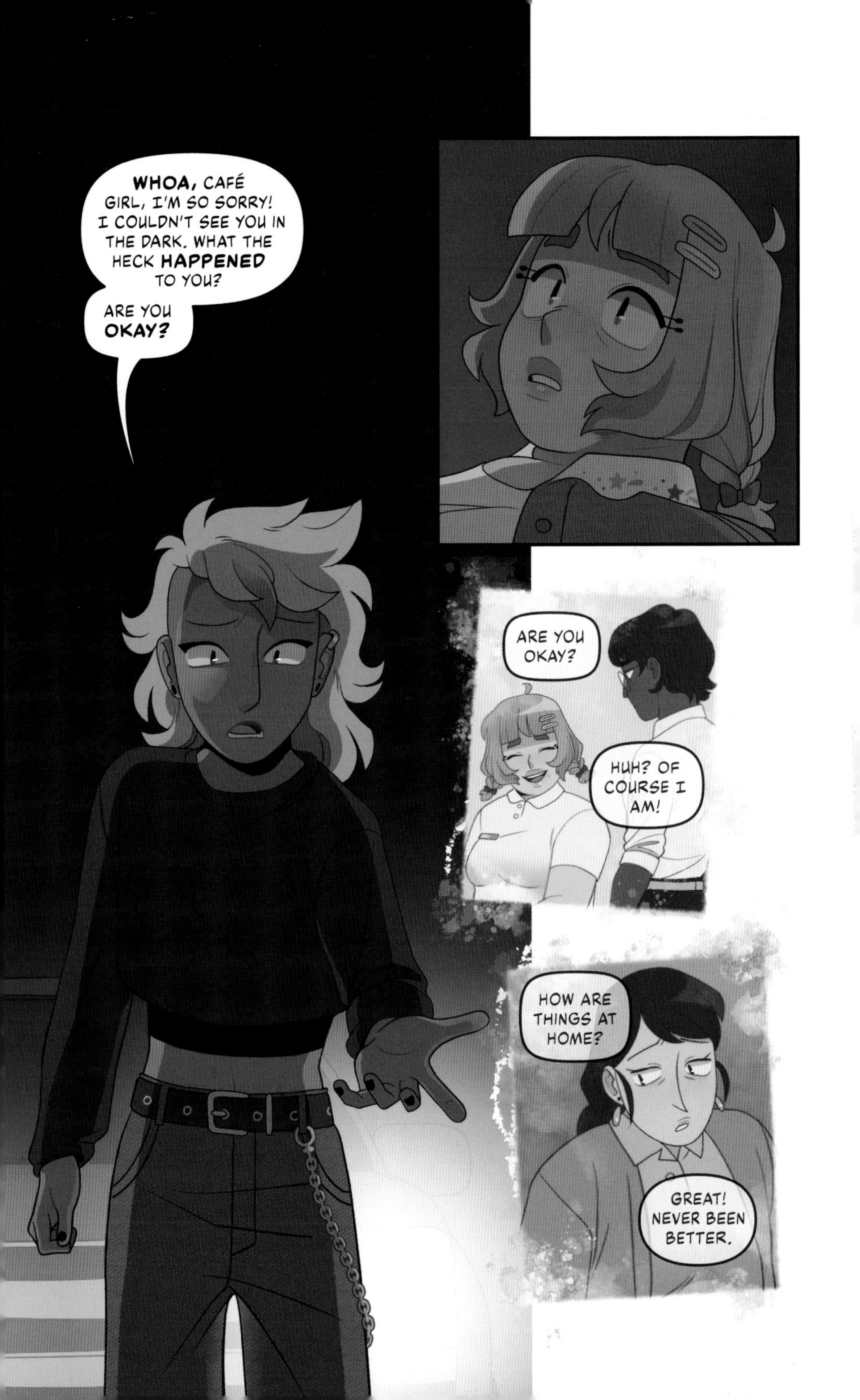
WHOA, CAFÉ GIRL, I'M SO SORRY! I COULDN'T SEE YOU IN THE DARK. WHAT THE HECK HAPPENED TO YOU?
ARE YOU OKAY?
ARE YOU OKAY?
HUH? OF COURSE I AM!
HOW ARE THINGS AT HOME?
GREAT! NEVER BEEN BETTER.

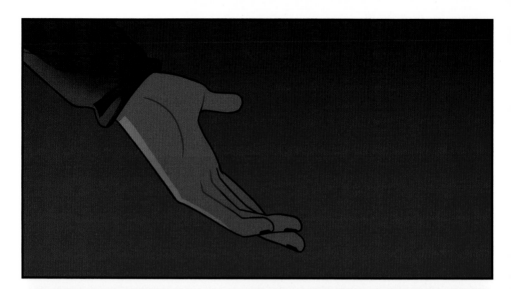

THERE YOU GO...

COME ON. YOU CAN SIT IN MY TRUCK OUT OF THE COLD FOR A SEC. I MEAN, IF YOU WANT TO.

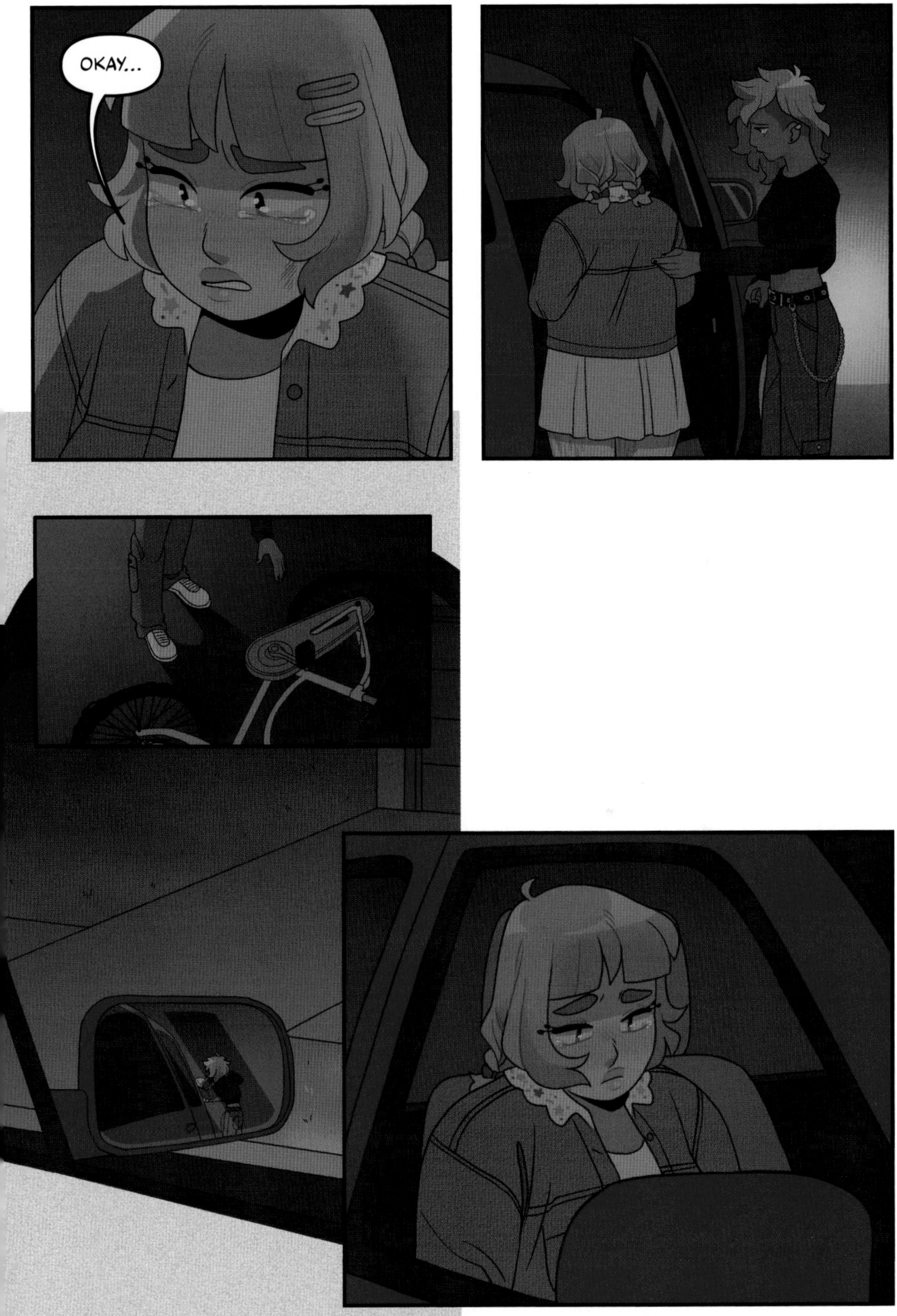
OKAY...

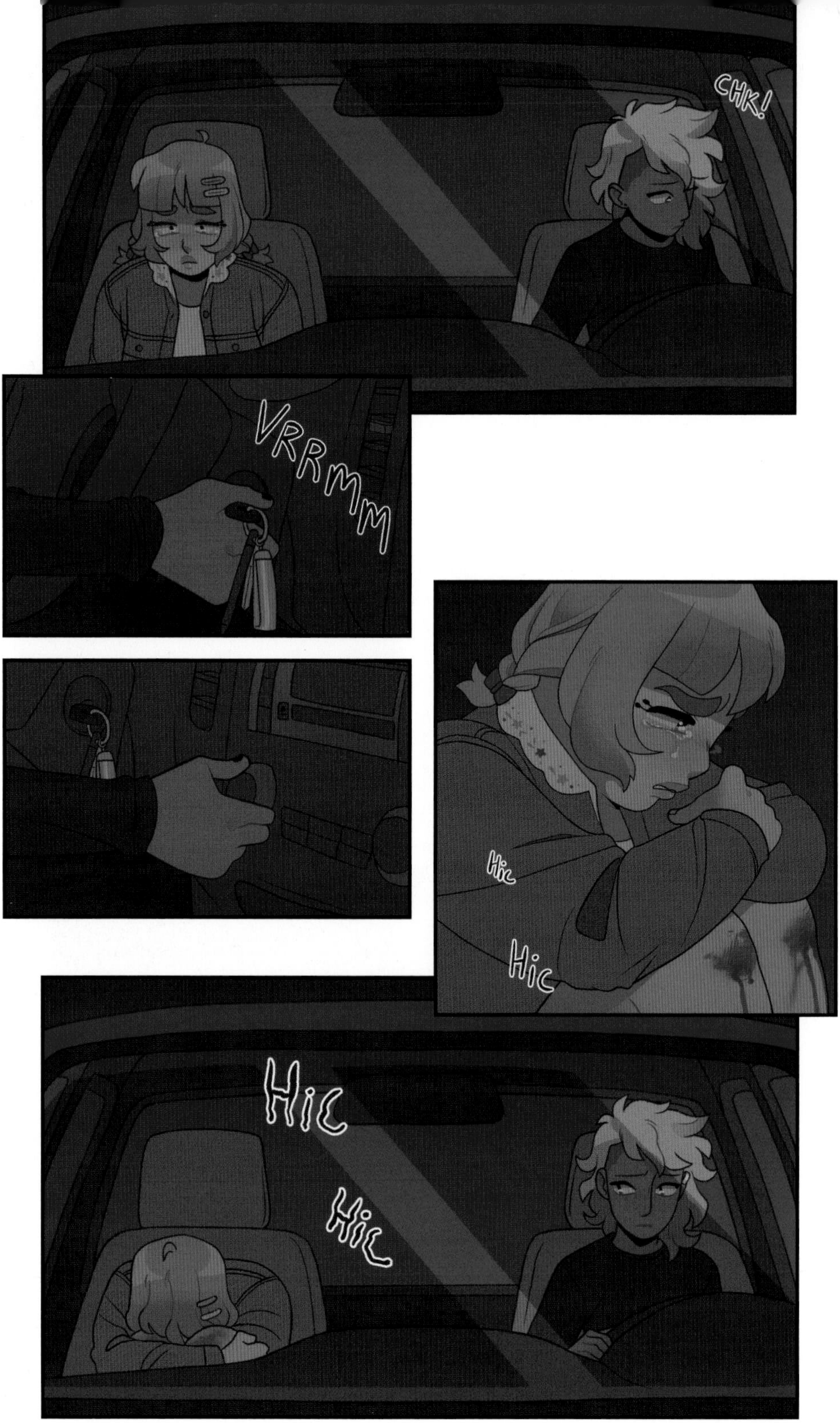
CHK!
VRRMMM
Hic
Hic
Hic
Hic

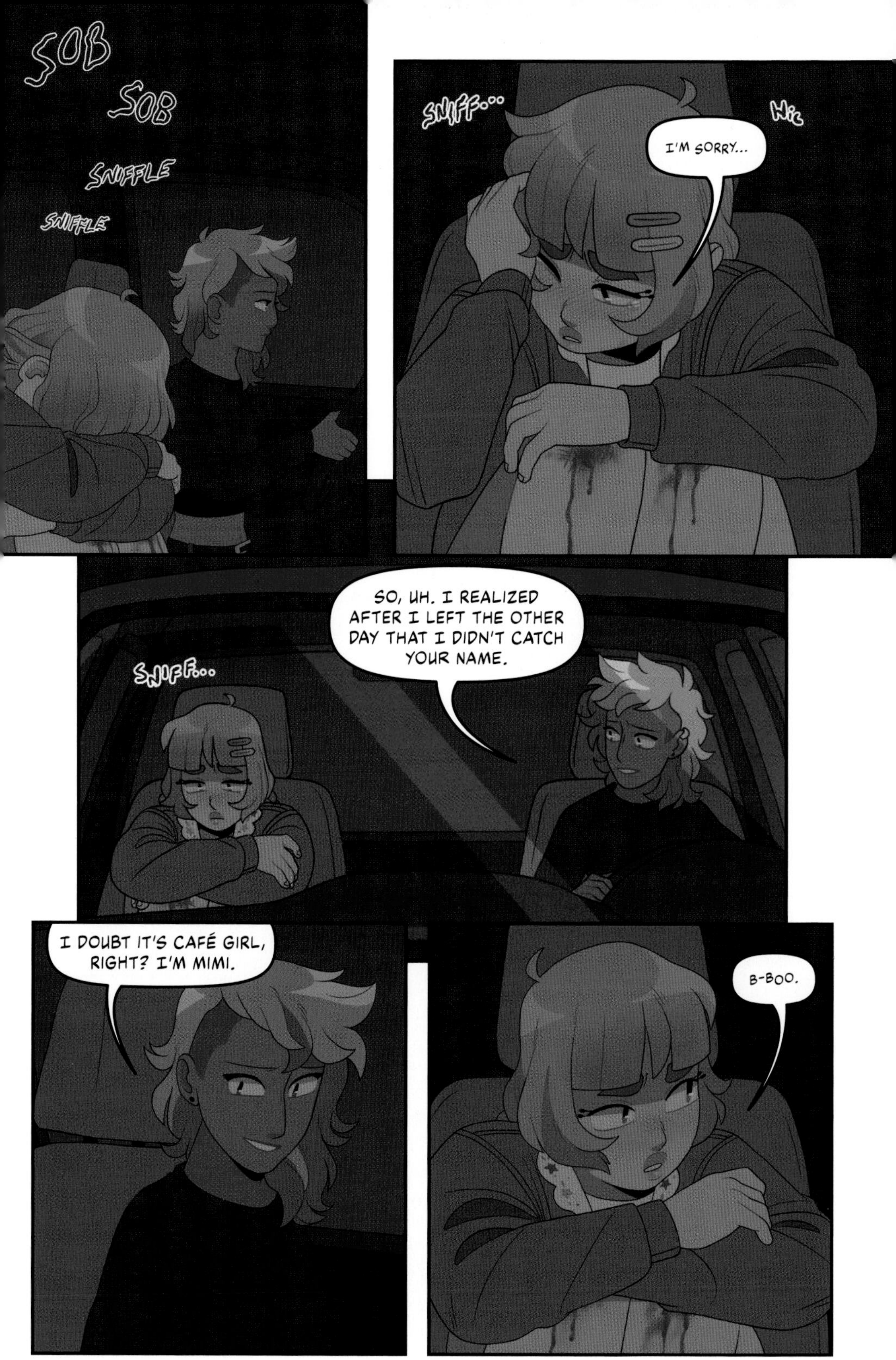
SOB
SOB
SNIFFLE
SNIFFLE
SNIFF...
HIC
I'M SORRY...
SNIFF...
SO, UH. I REALIZED AFTER I LEFT THE OTHER DAY THAT I DIDN'T CATCH YOUR NAME.
I DOUBT IT'S CAFÉ GIRL, RIGHT? I'M MIMI.
B-BOO.

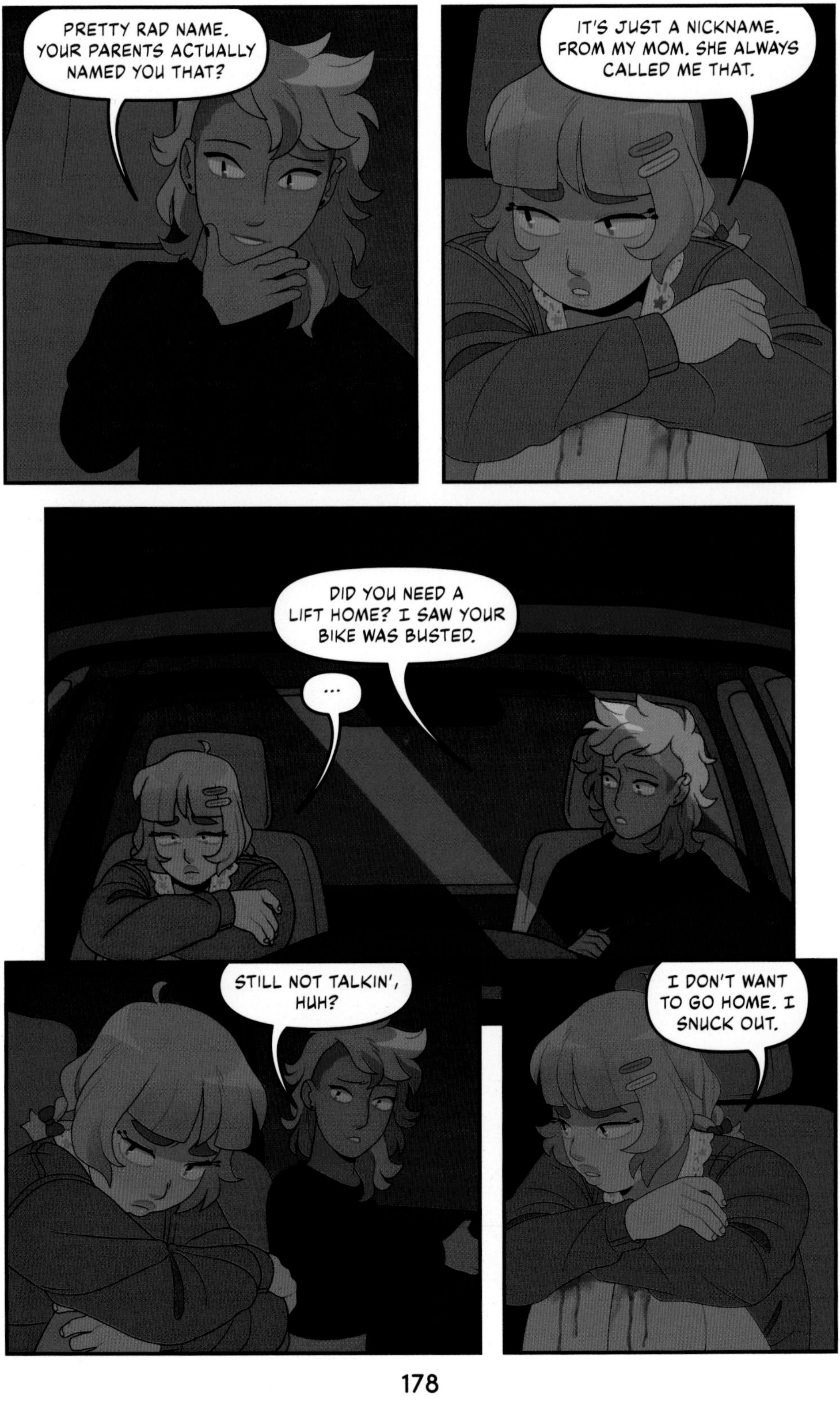
PRETTY RAD NAME. YOUR PARENTS ACTUALLY NAMED YOU THAT?
IT'S JUST A NICKNAME. FROM MY MOM. SHE ALWAYS CALLED ME THAT.
DID YOU NEED A LIFT HOME? I SAW YOUR BIKE WAS BUSTED.
...
STILL NOT TALKIN', HUH?
I DON'T WANT TO GO HOME. I SNUCK OUT.

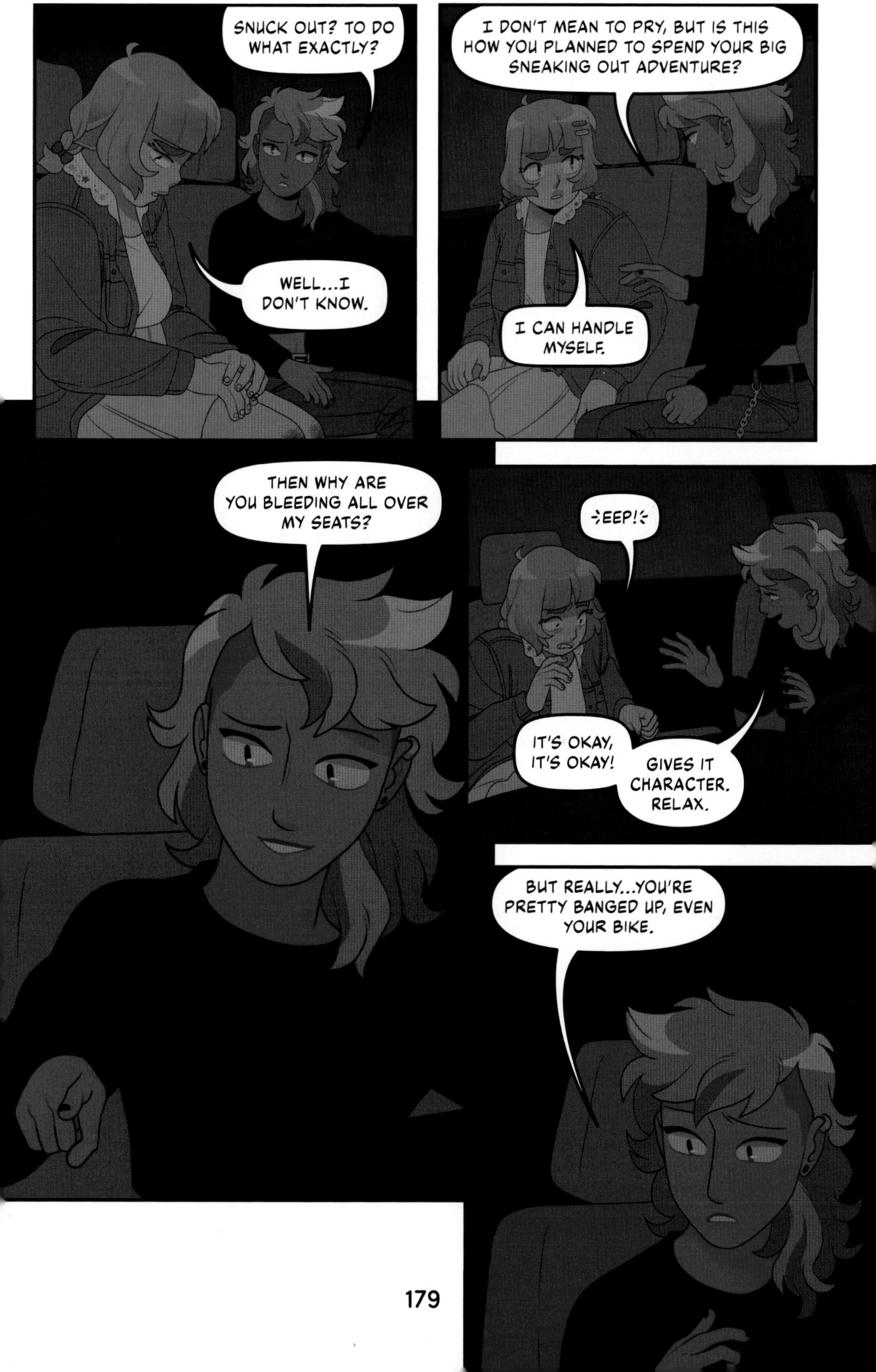
SNUCK OUT? TO DO WHAT EXACTLY?
WELL...I DON'T KNOW.
I DON'T MEAN TO PRY, BUT IS THIS HOW YOU PLANNED TO SPEND YOUR BIG SNEAKING OUT ADVENTURE?
I CAN HANDLE MYSELF.
THEN WHY ARE YOU BLEEDING ALL OVER MY SEATS?
EEP!
IT'S OKAY, IT'S OKAY!
GIVES IT CHARACTER. RELAX.
BUT REALLY...YOU'RE PRETTY BANGED UP, EVEN YOUR BIKE.

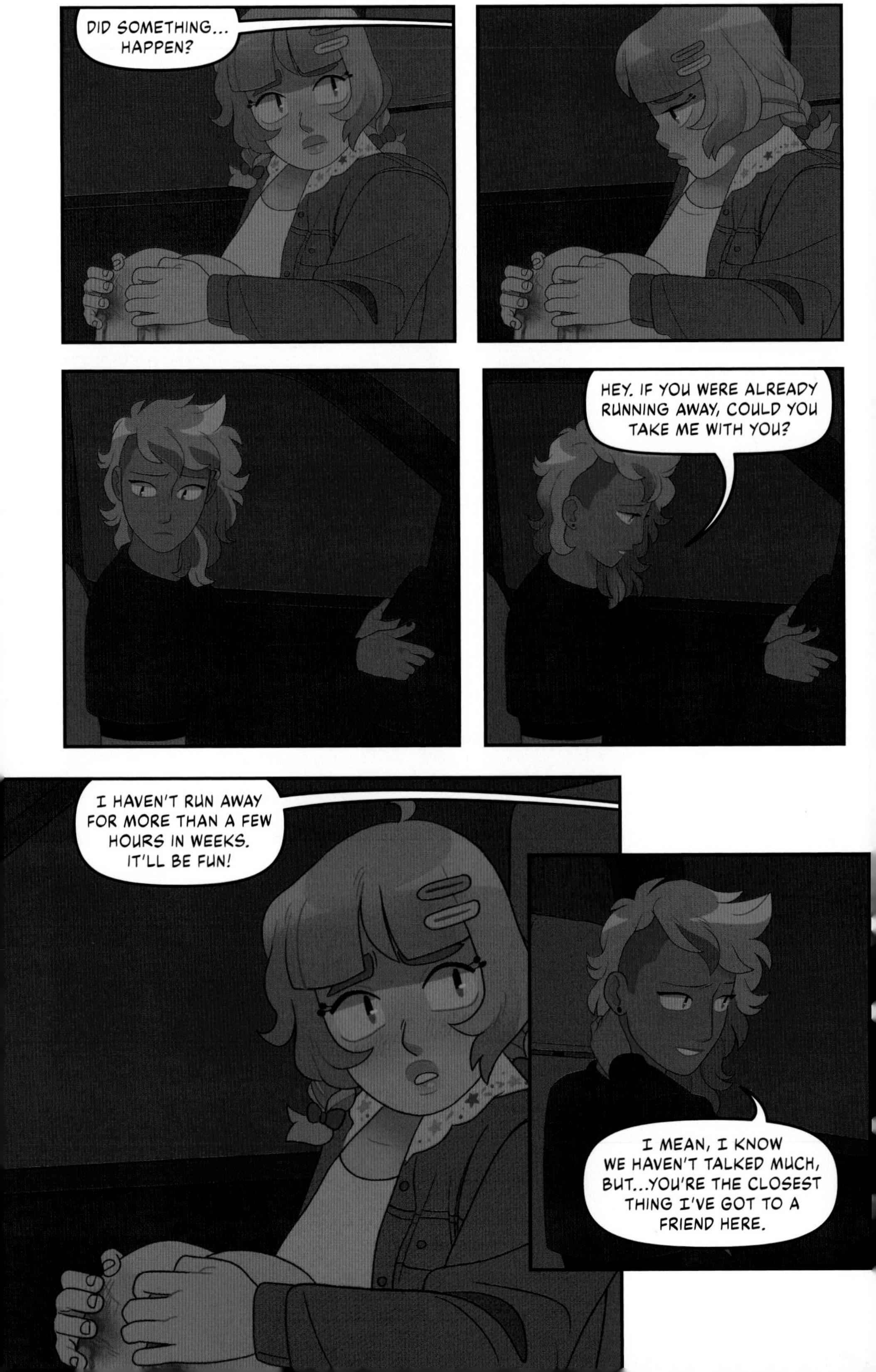
DID SOMETHING... HAPPEN?
HEY. IF YOU WERE ALREADY RUNNING AWAY, COULD YOU TAKE ME WITH YOU?
I HAVEN'T RUN AWAY FOR MORE THAN A FEW HOURS IN WEEKS. IT'LL BE FUN!
I MEAN, I KNOW WE HAVEN'T TALKED MUCH, BUT...YOU'RE THE CLOSEST THING I'VE GOT TO A FRIEND HERE.

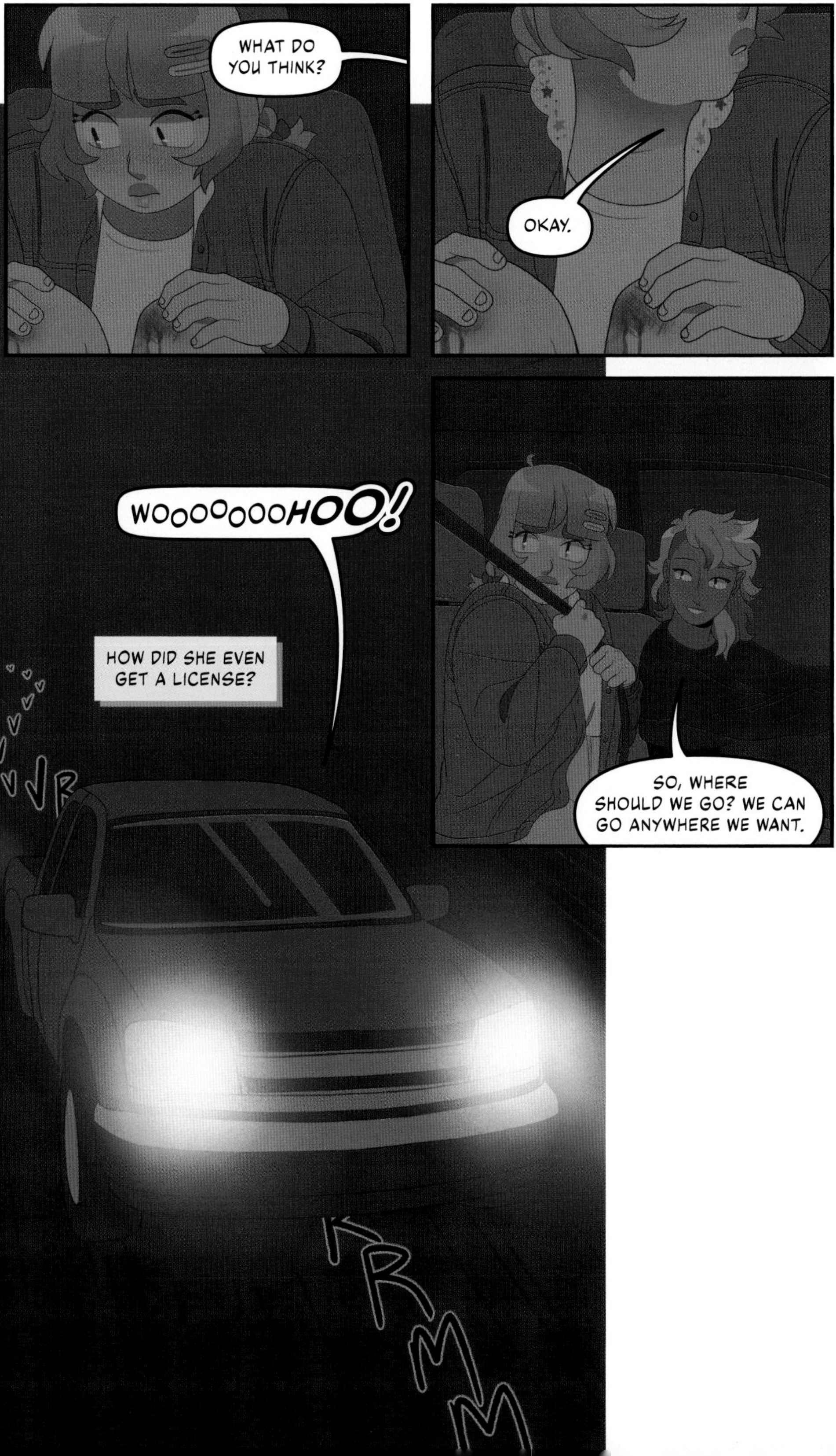
WHAT DO YOU THINK?
OKAY.
SO, WHERE SHOULD WE GO? WE CAN GO ANYWHERE WE WANT.
WOOOOOOOHOO!
HOW DID SHE EVEN GET A LICENSE?
KRMM

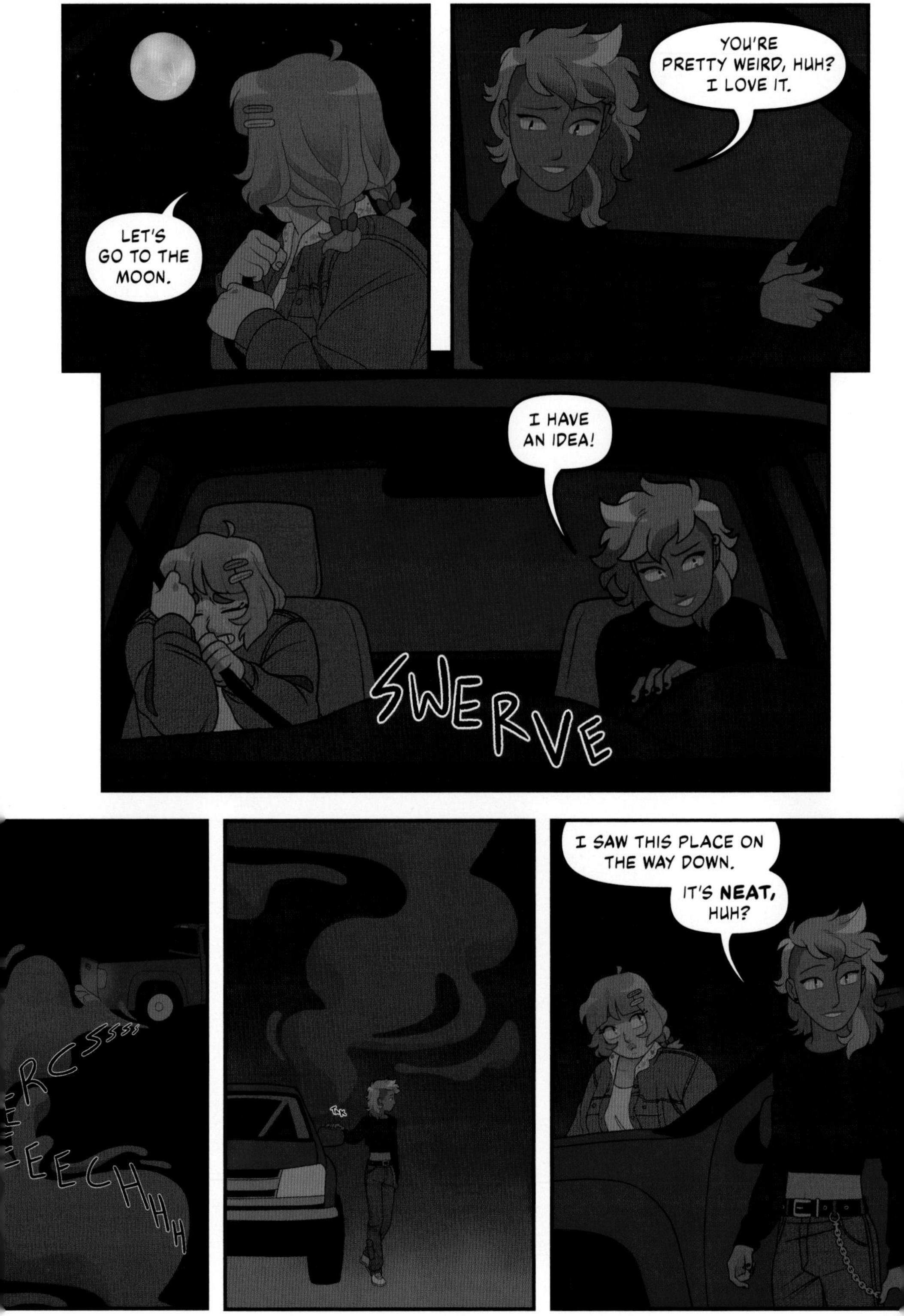
LET'S GO TO THE MOON.
YOU'RE PRETTY WEIRD, HUH? I LOVE IT.
I HAVE AN IDEA!
SWERVE
RCSsss
EECHHHH
TAK
I SAW THIS PLACE ON THE WAY DOWN.
IT'S **NEAT,** HUH?

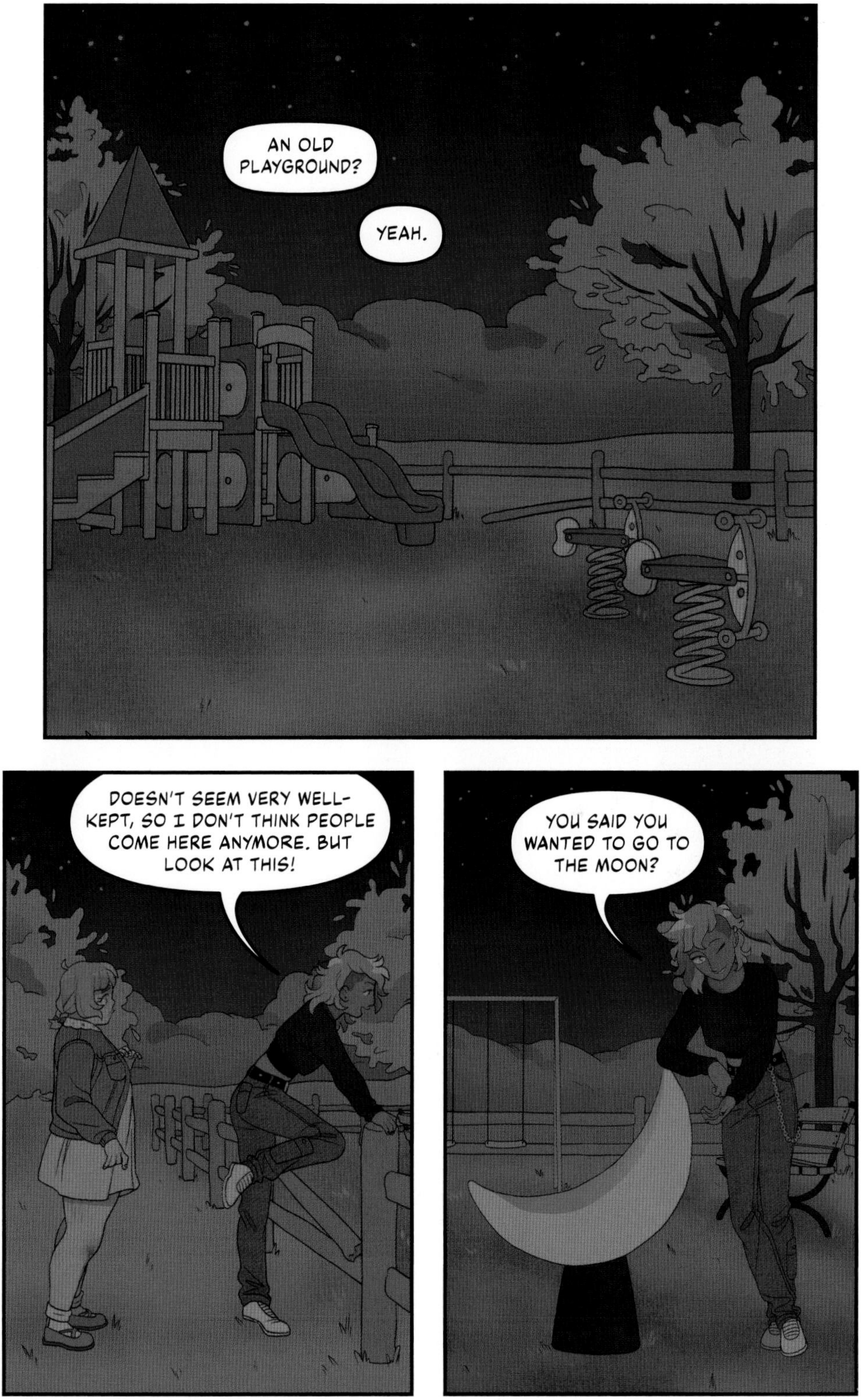
AN OLD PLAYGROUND?
YEAH.
DOESN'T SEEM VERY WELL-KEPT, SO I DON'T THINK PEOPLE COME HERE ANYMORE. BUT LOOK AT THIS!
YOU SAID YOU WANTED TO GO TO THE MOON?

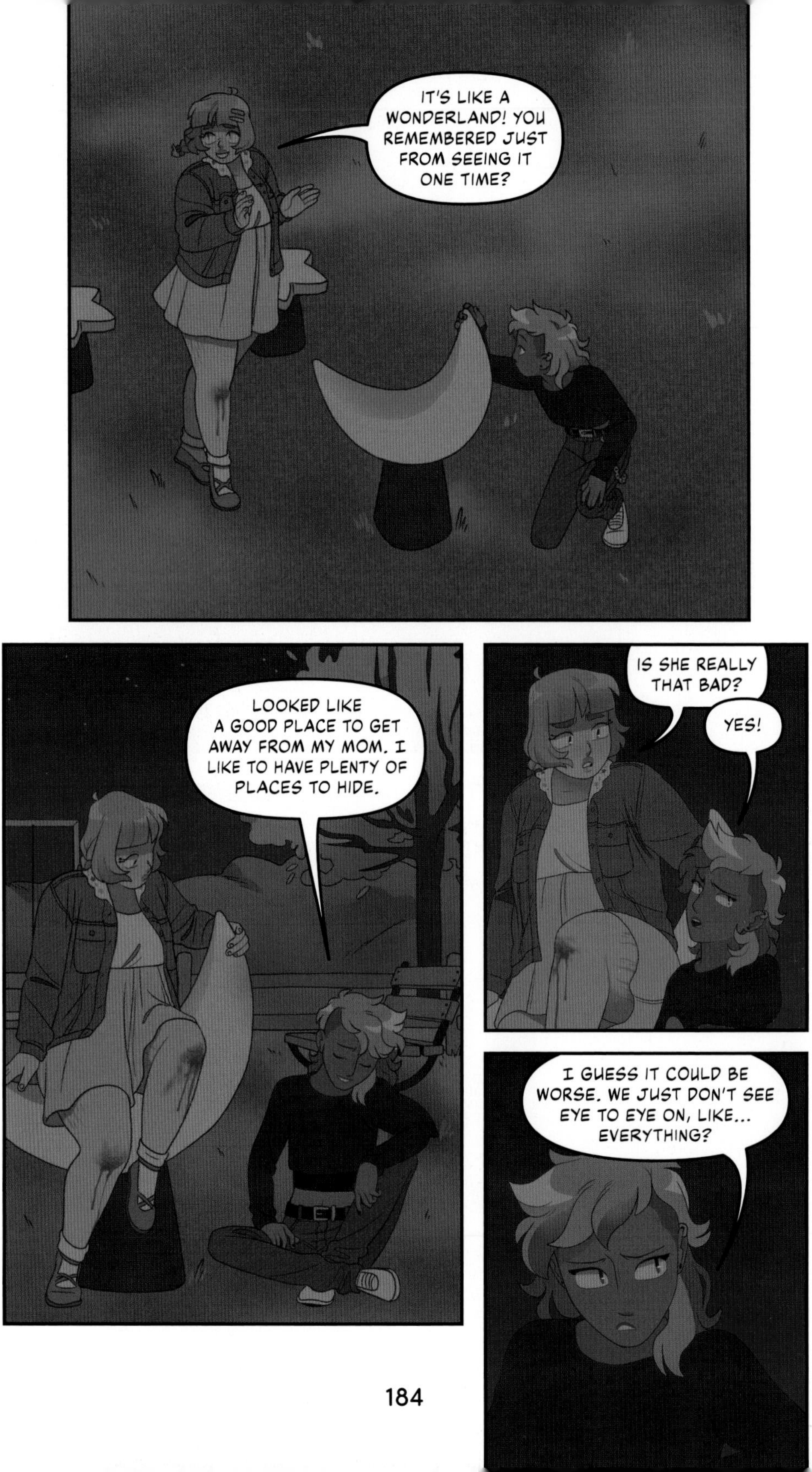
IT'S LIKE A WONDERLAND! YOU REMEMBERED JUST FROM SEEING IT ONE TIME?
LOOKED LIKE A GOOD PLACE TO GET AWAY FROM MY MOM. I LIKE TO HAVE PLENTY OF PLACES TO HIDE.
IS SHE REALLY THAT BAD?
YES!
I GUESS IT COULD BE WORSE. WE JUST DON'T SEE EYE TO EYE ON, LIKE... EVERYTHING?

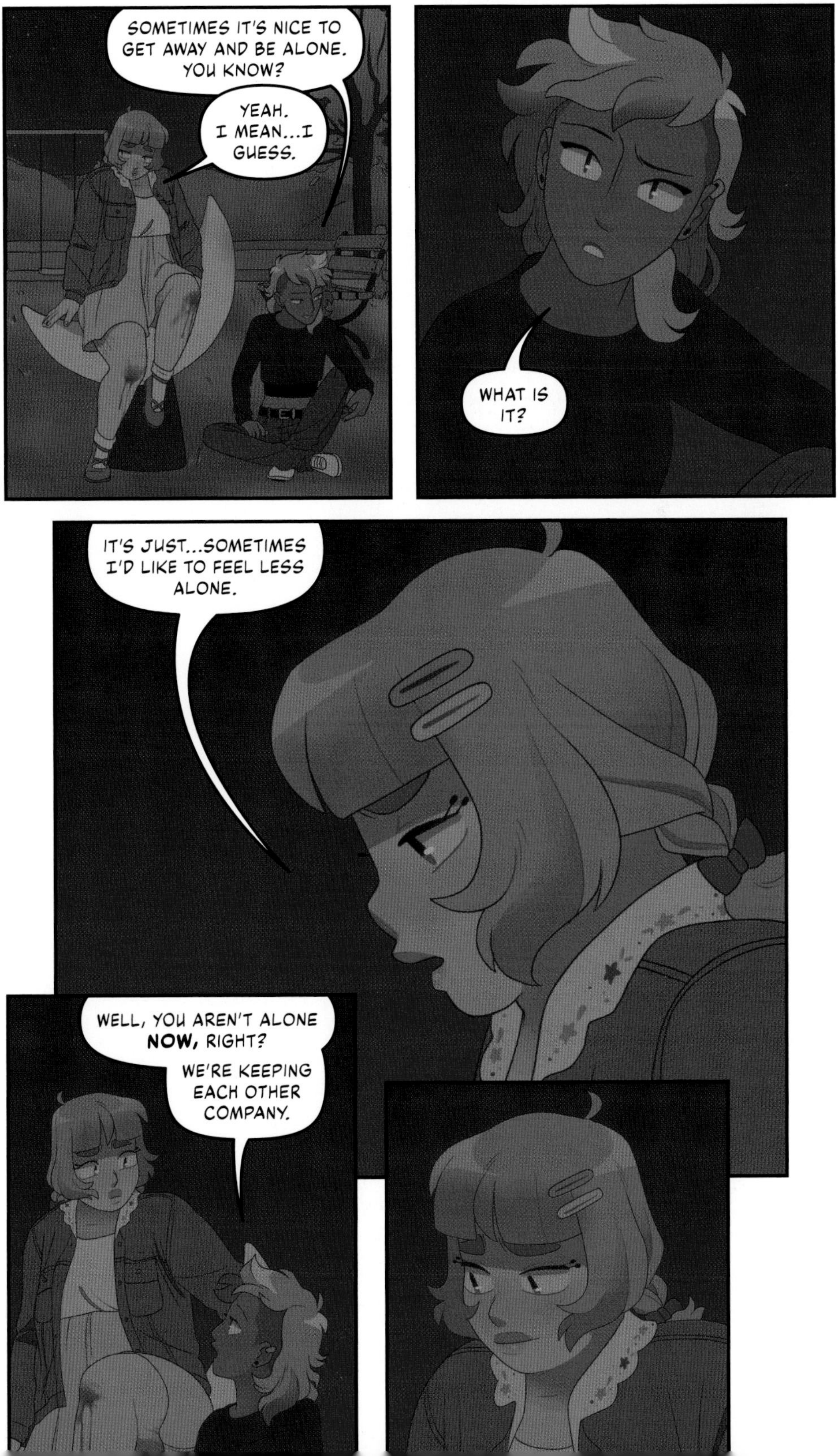
SOMETIMES IT'S NICE TO GET AWAY AND BE ALONE. YOU KNOW?
YEAH. I MEAN...I GUESS.
WHAT IS IT?
IT'S JUST...SOMETIMES I'D LIKE TO FEEL LESS ALONE.
WELL, YOU AREN'T ALONE **NOW,** RIGHT?
WE'RE KEEPING EACH OTHER COMPANY.

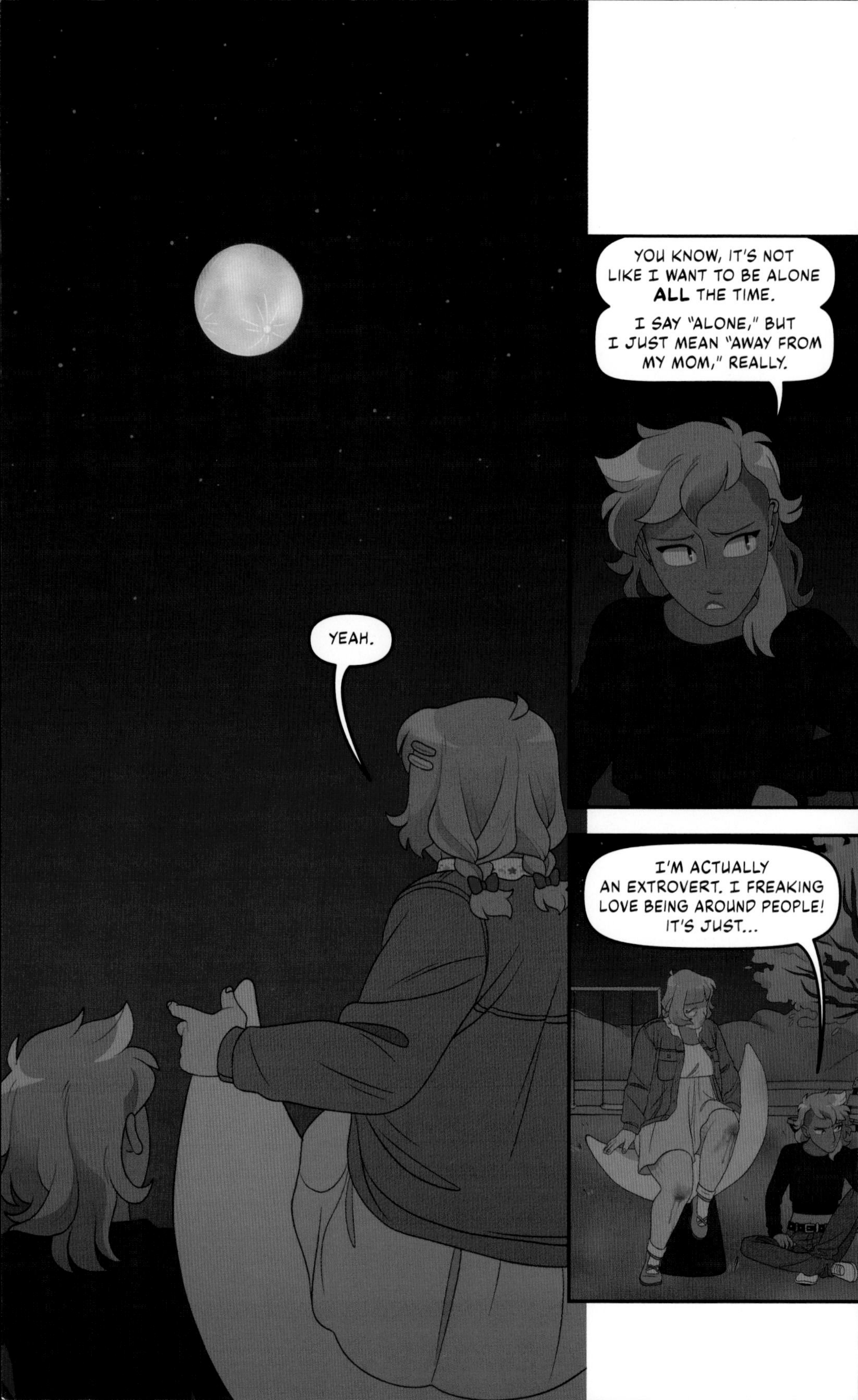
YEAH.
YOU KNOW, IT'S NOT LIKE I WANT TO BE ALONE **ALL** THE TIME.
I SAY "ALONE," BUT I JUST MEAN "AWAY FROM MY MOM," REALLY.
I'M ACTUALLY AN EXTROVERT. I FREAKING LOVE BEING AROUND PEOPLE! IT'S JUST...

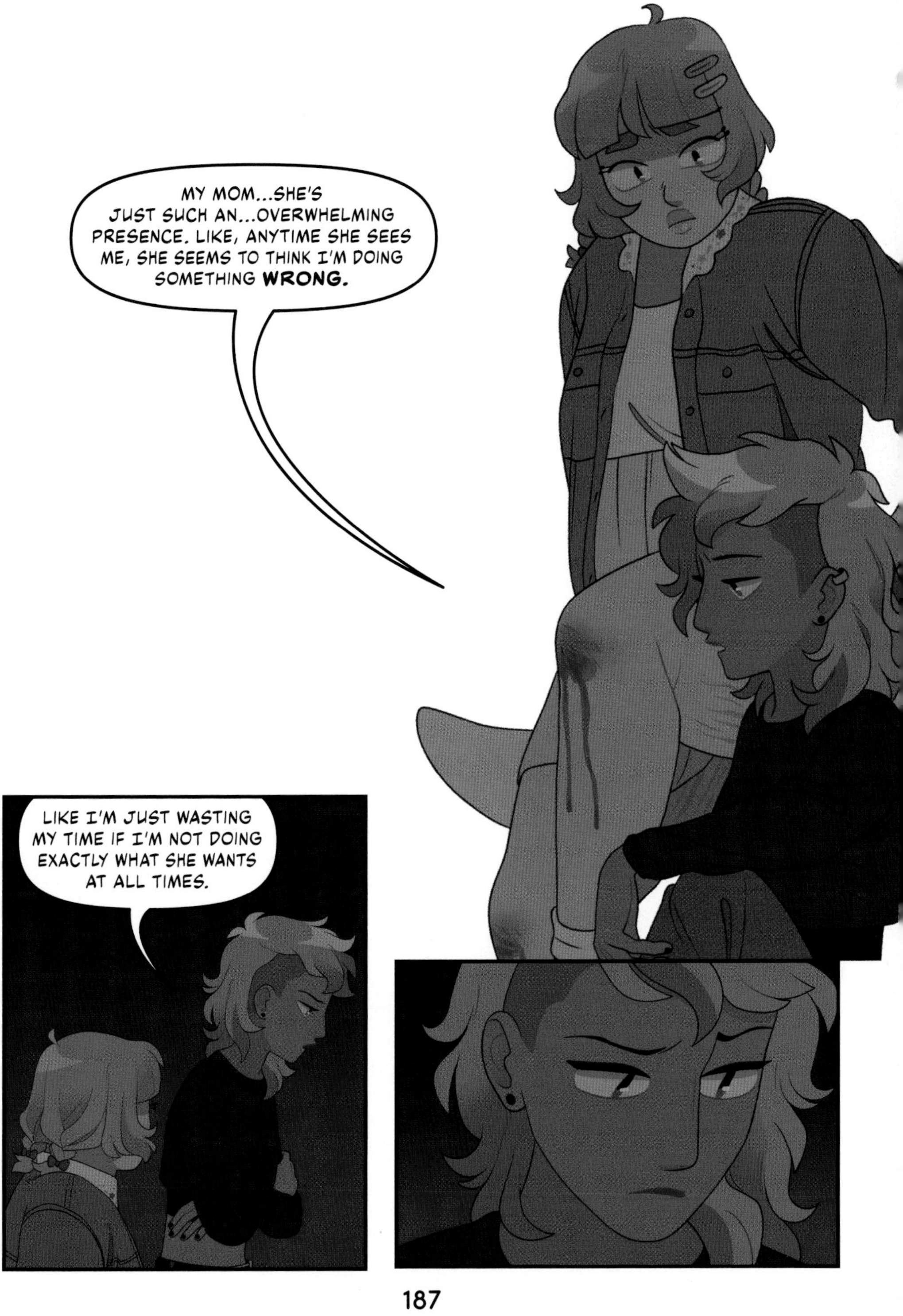
MY MOM...SHE'S JUST SUCH AN...OVERWHELMING PRESENCE. LIKE, ANYTIME SHE SEES ME, SHE SEEMS TO THINK I'M DOING SOMETHING **WRONG.**
LIKE I'M JUST WASTING MY TIME IF I'M NOT DOING EXACTLY WHAT SHE WANTS AT ALL TIMES.

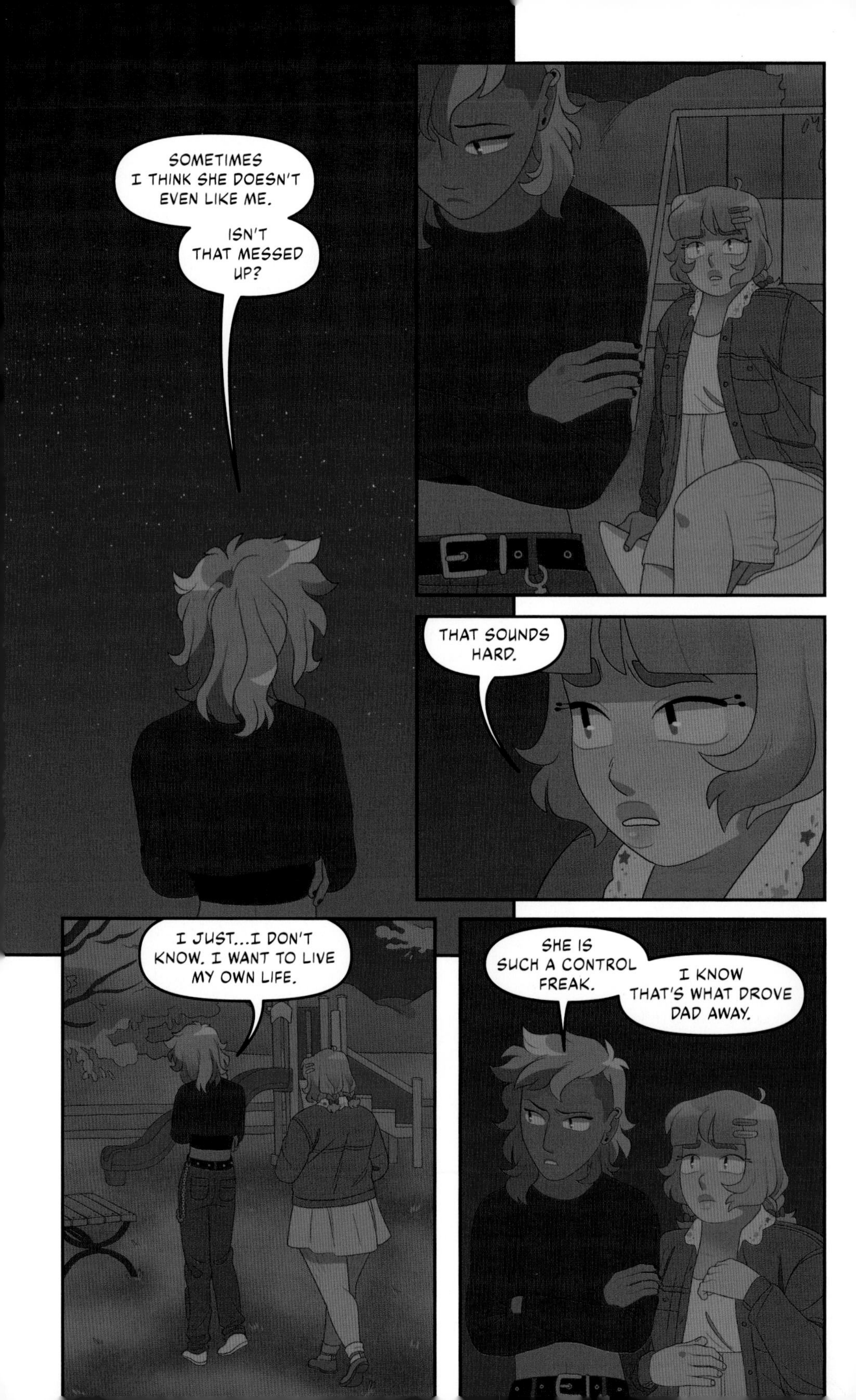
SOMETIMES I THINK SHE DOESN'T EVEN LIKE ME.
ISN'T THAT MESSED UP?
THAT SOUNDS HARD.
I JUST...I DON'T KNOW. I WANT TO LIVE MY OWN LIFE.
SHE IS SUCH A CONTROL FREAK.
I KNOW THAT'S WHAT DROVE DAD AWAY.

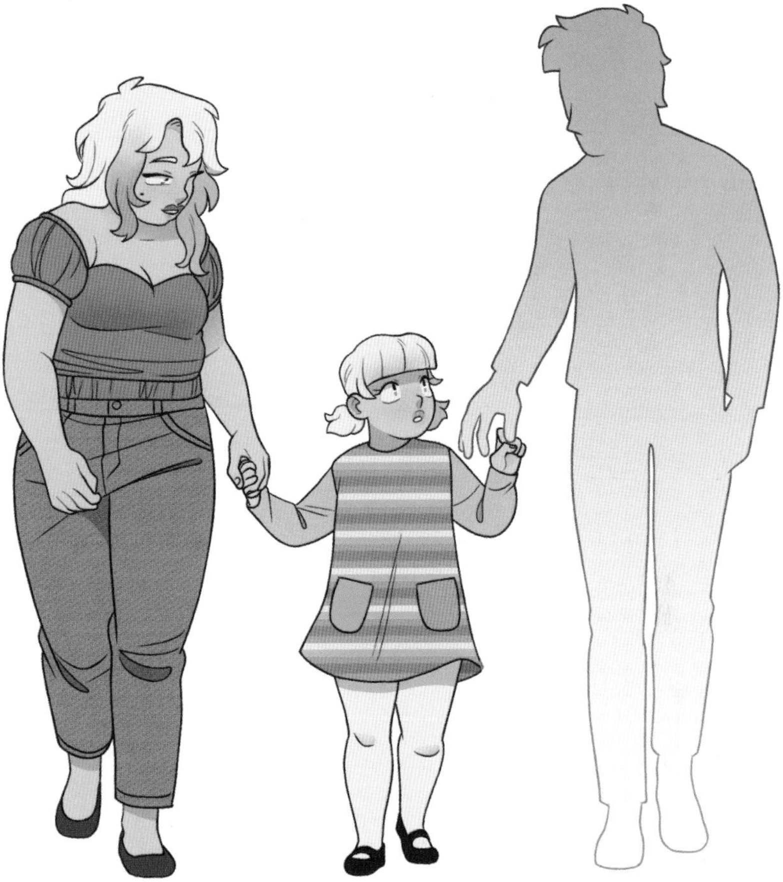

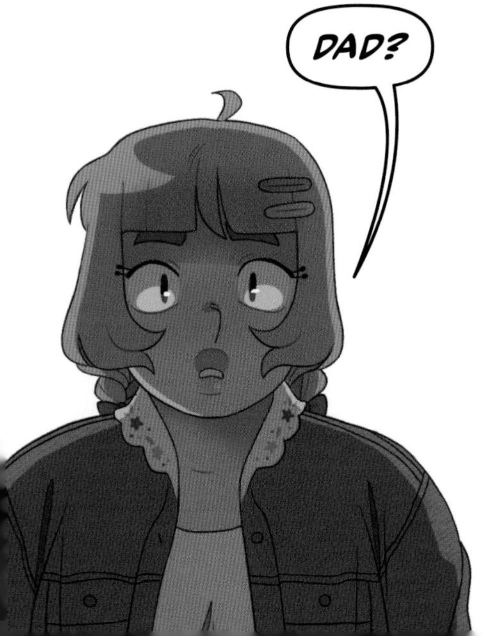
DAD?

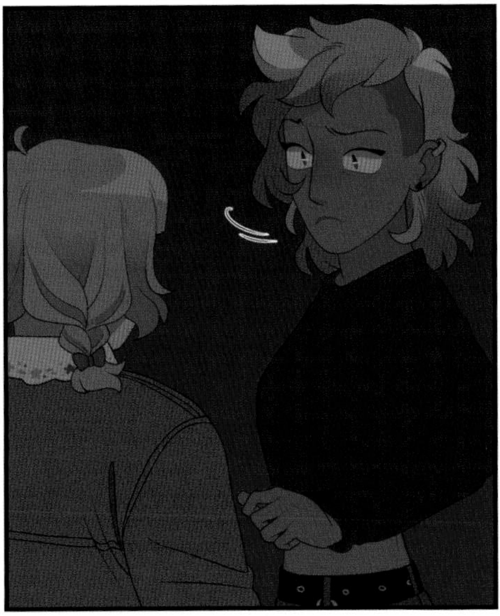

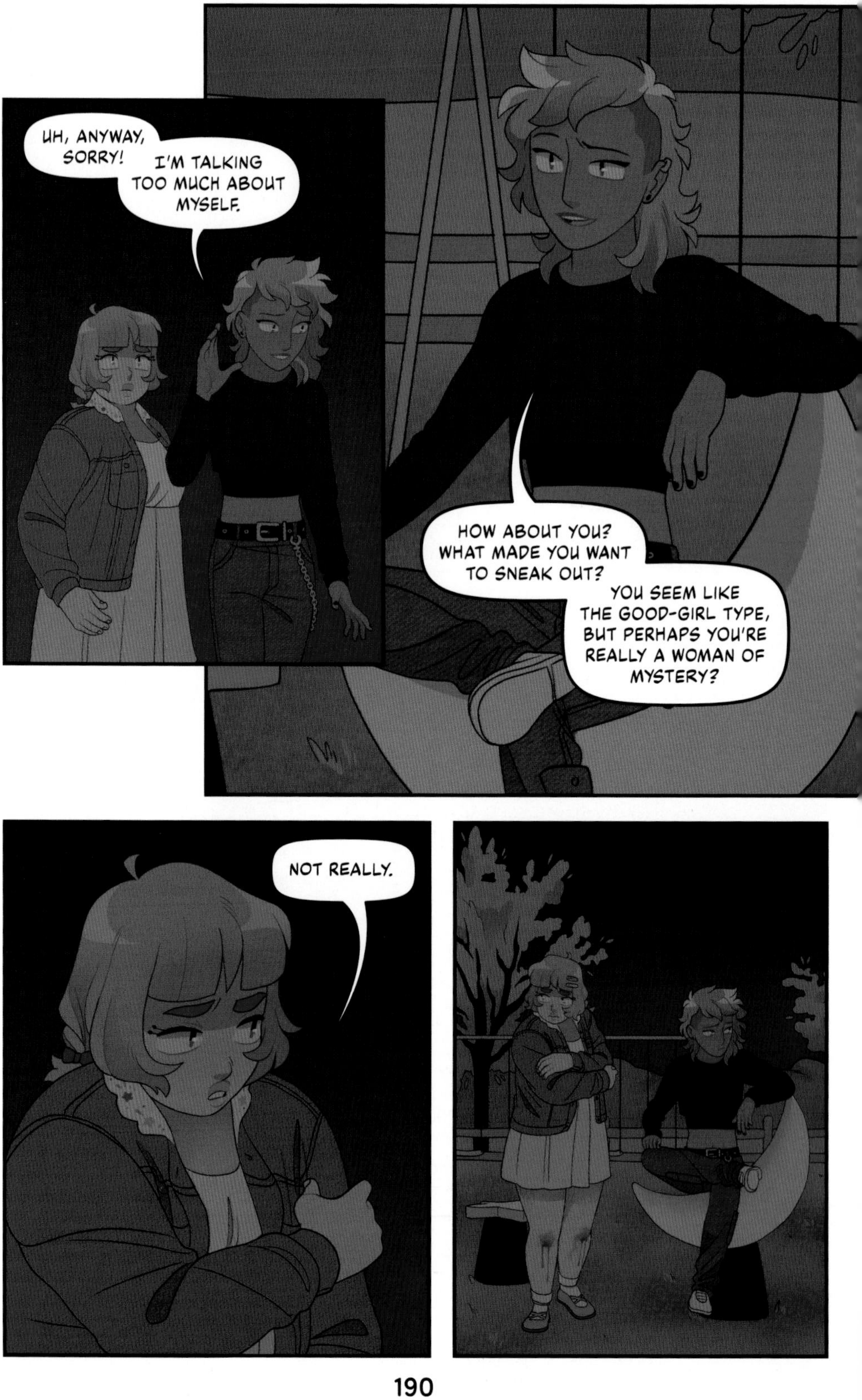
UH, ANYWAY, SORRY!
I'M TALKING TOO MUCH ABOUT MYSELF.
HOW ABOUT YOU? WHAT MADE YOU WANT TO SNEAK OUT?
YOU SEEM LIKE THE GOOD-GIRL TYPE, BUT PERHAPS YOU'RE REALLY A WOMAN OF MYSTERY?
NOT REALLY.

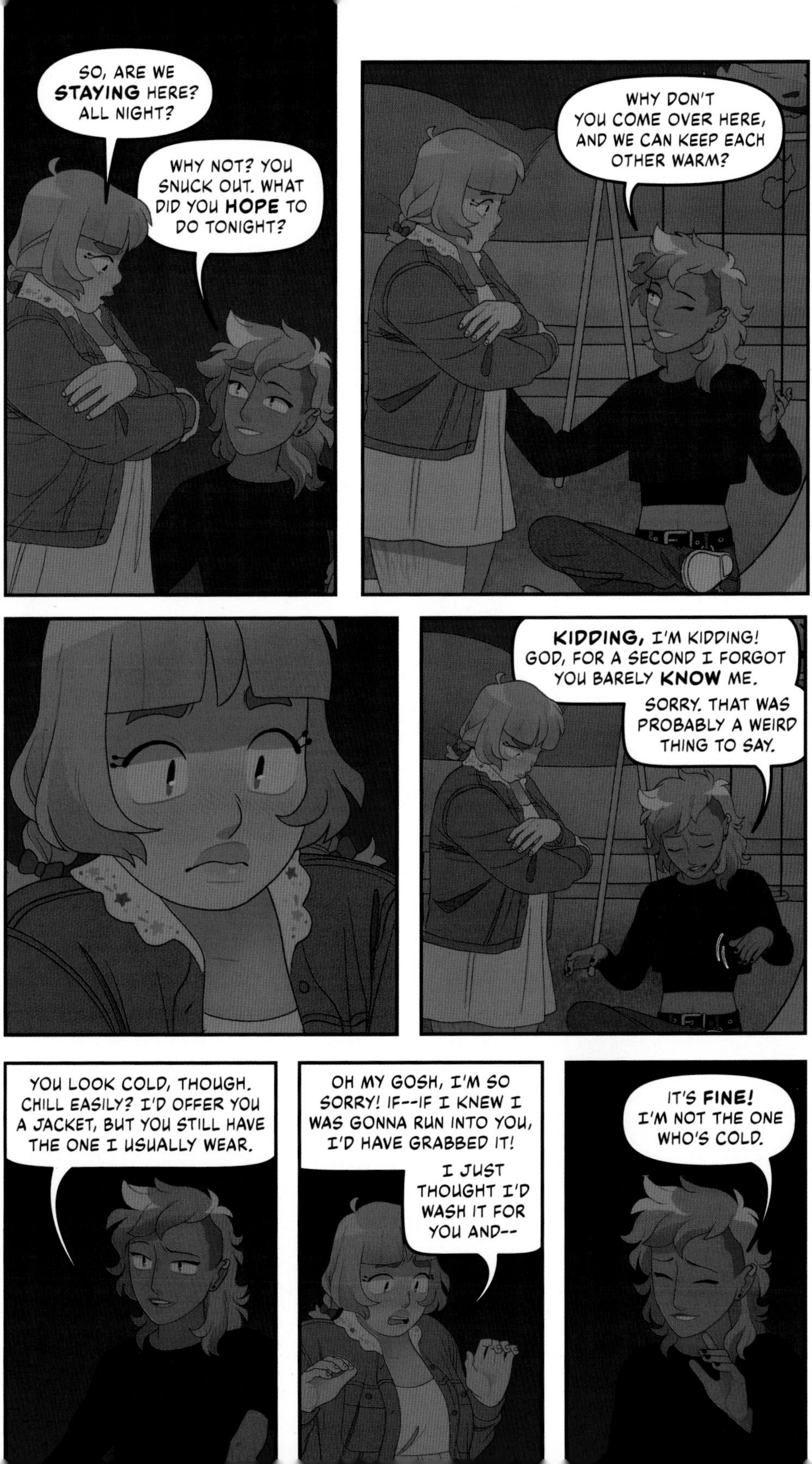
SO, ARE WE STAYING HERE? ALL NIGHT?
WHY NOT? YOU SNUCK OUT. WHAT DID YOU HOPE TO DO TONIGHT?
WHY DON'T YOU COME OVER HERE, AND WE CAN KEEP EACH OTHER WARM?
KIDDING, I'M KIDDING! GOD, FOR A SECOND I FORGOT YOU BARELY KNOW ME.
SORRY. THAT WAS PROBABLY A WEIRD THING TO SAY.
YOU LOOK COLD, THOUGH. CHILL EASILY? I'D OFFER YOU A JACKET, BUT YOU STILL HAVE THE ONE I USUALLY WEAR.
OH MY GOSH, I'M SO SORRY! IF--IF I KNEW I WAS GONNA RUN INTO YOU, I'D HAVE GRABBED IT!
I JUST THOUGHT I'D WASH IT FOR YOU AND--
IT'S FINE! I'M NOT THE ONE WHO'S COLD.

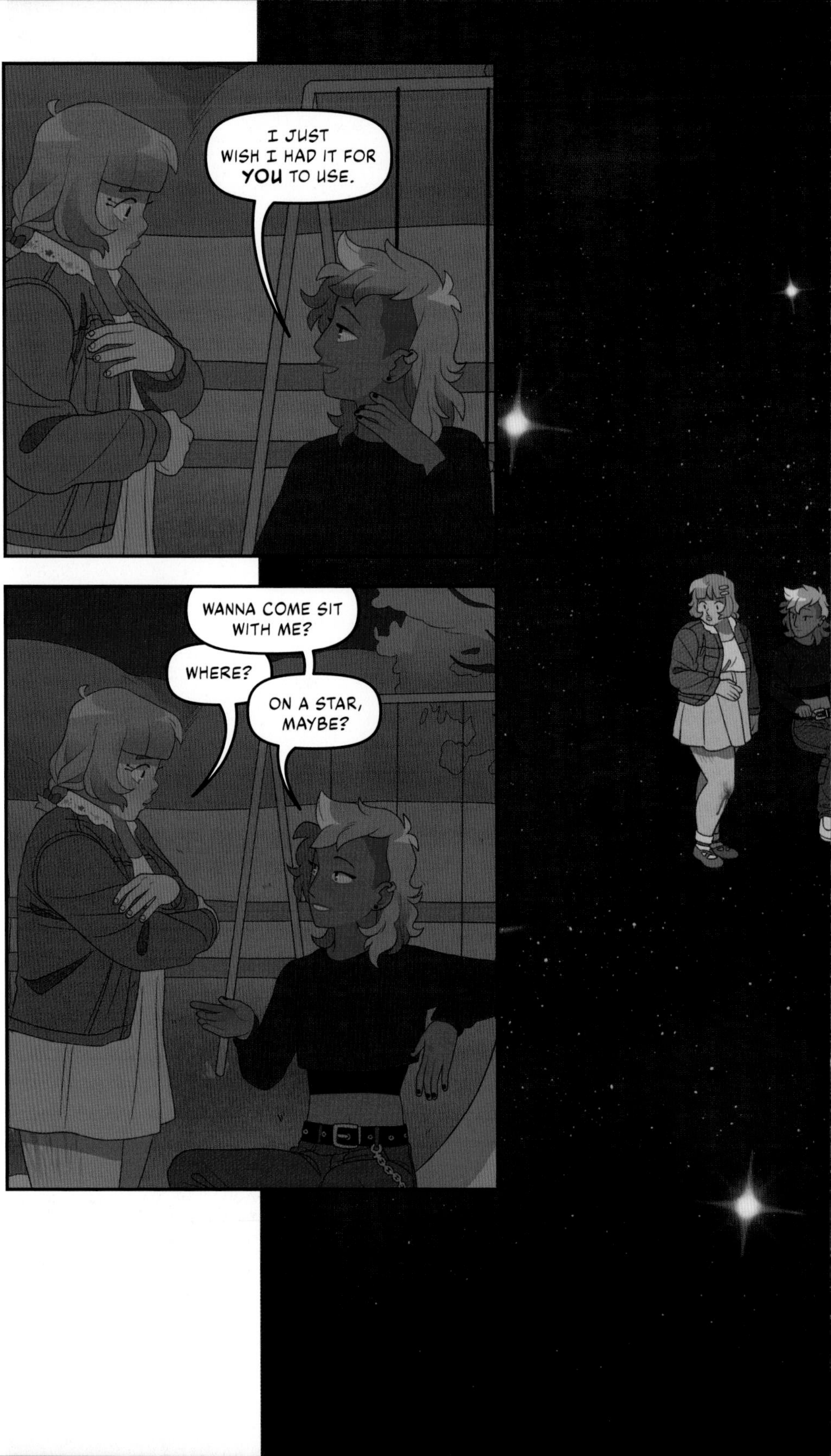
I JUST WISH I HAD IT FOR YOU TO USE.
WANNA COME SIT WITH ME?
WHERE?
ON A STAR, MAYBE?

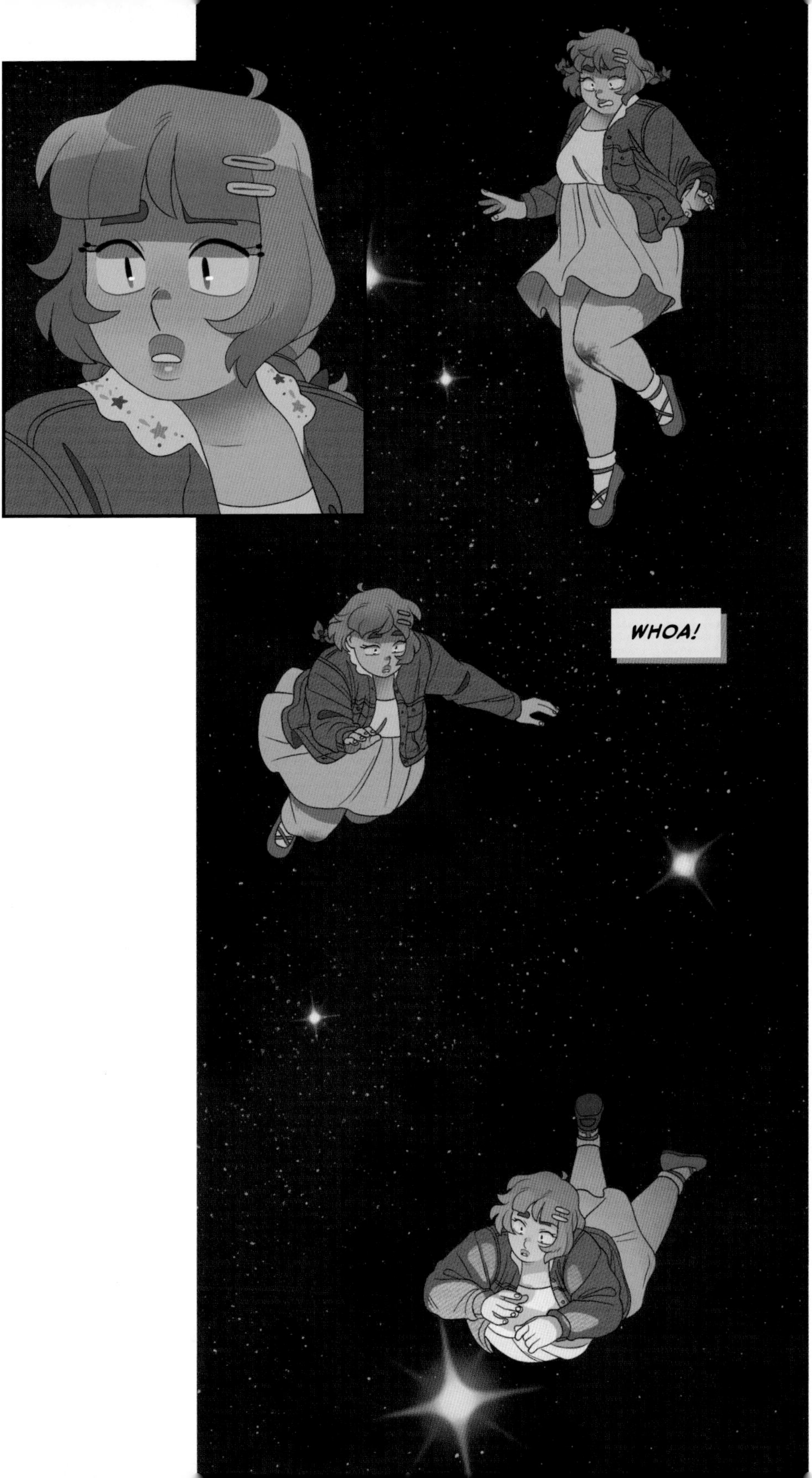
WHOA!

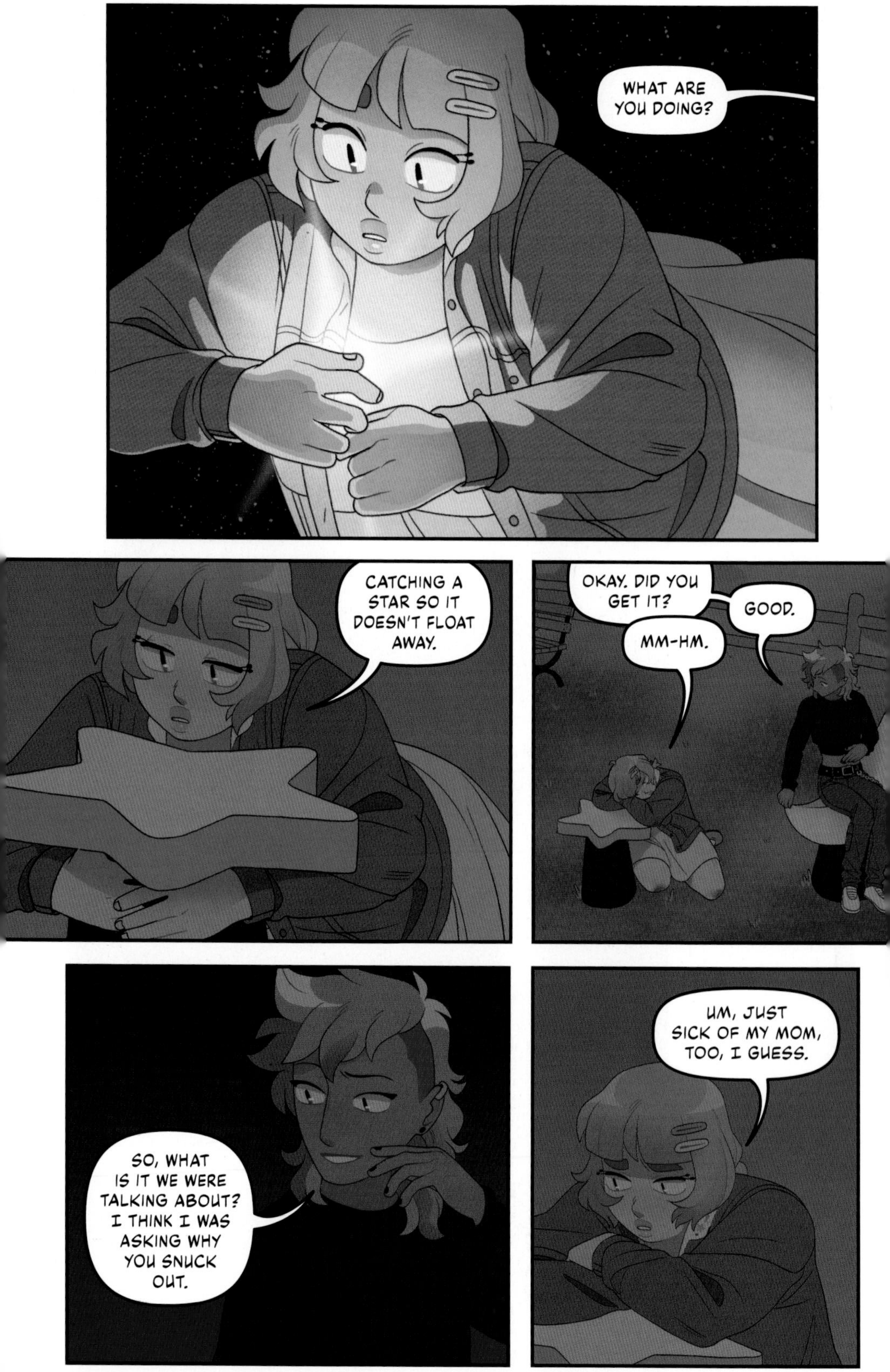
WHAT ARE YOU DOING?
CATCHING A STAR SO IT DOESN'T FLOAT AWAY.
OKAY. DID YOU GET IT?
MM-HM.
GOOD.
SO, WHAT IS IT WE WERE TALKING ABOUT? I THINK I WAS ASKING WHY YOU SNUCK OUT.
UM, JUST SICK OF MY MOM, TOO, I GUESS.

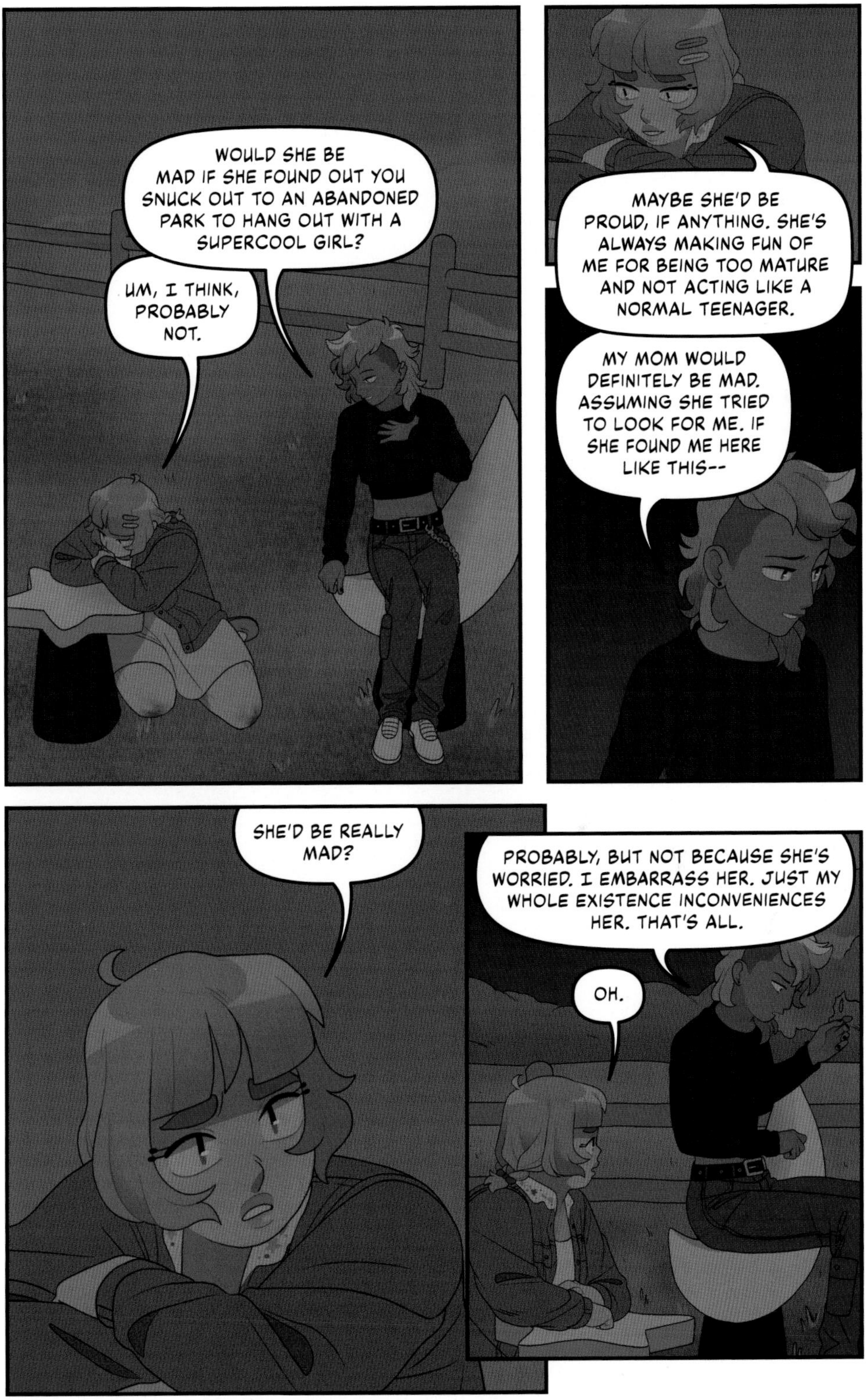
WOULD SHE BE MAD IF SHE FOUND OUT YOU SNUCK OUT TO AN ABANDONED PARK TO HANG OUT WITH A SUPERCOOL GIRL?
UM, I THINK, PROBABLY NOT.
MAYBE SHE'D BE PROUD, IF ANYTHING. SHE'S ALWAYS MAKING FUN OF ME FOR BEING TOO MATURE AND NOT ACTING LIKE A NORMAL TEENAGER.
MY MOM WOULD DEFINITELY BE MAD. ASSUMING SHE TRIED TO LOOK FOR ME. IF SHE FOUND ME HERE LIKE THIS--
SHE'D BE REALLY MAD?
PROBABLY, BUT NOT BECAUSE SHE'S WORRIED. I EMBARRASS HER. JUST MY WHOLE EXISTENCE INCONVENIENCES HER. THAT'S ALL.
OH.

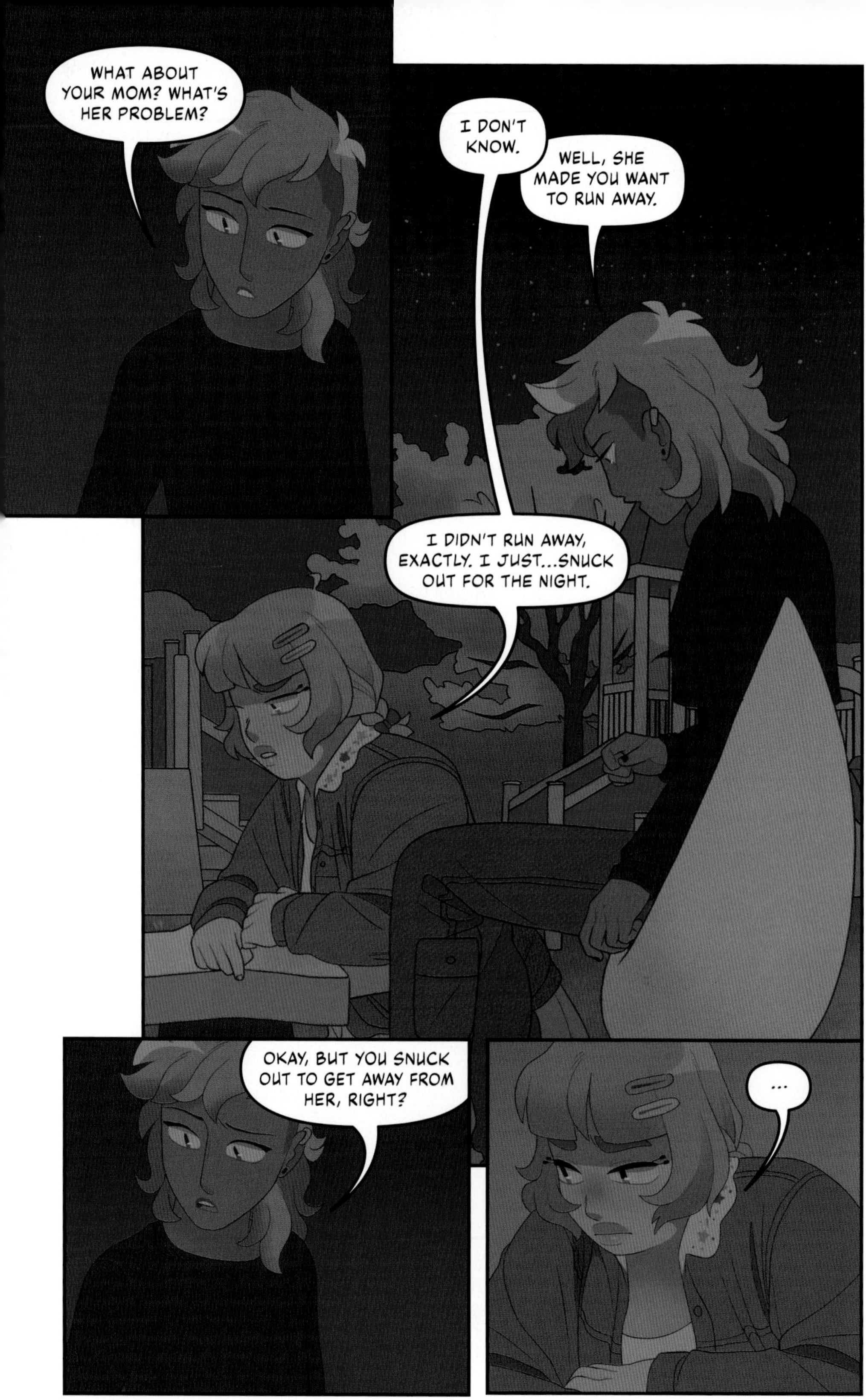
WHAT ABOUT YOUR MOM? WHAT'S HER PROBLEM?
I DON'T KNOW.
WELL, SHE MADE YOU WANT TO RUN AWAY.
I DIDN'T RUN AWAY, EXACTLY. I JUST...SNUCK OUT FOR THE NIGHT.
OKAY, BUT YOU SNUCK OUT TO GET AWAY FROM HER, RIGHT?
...

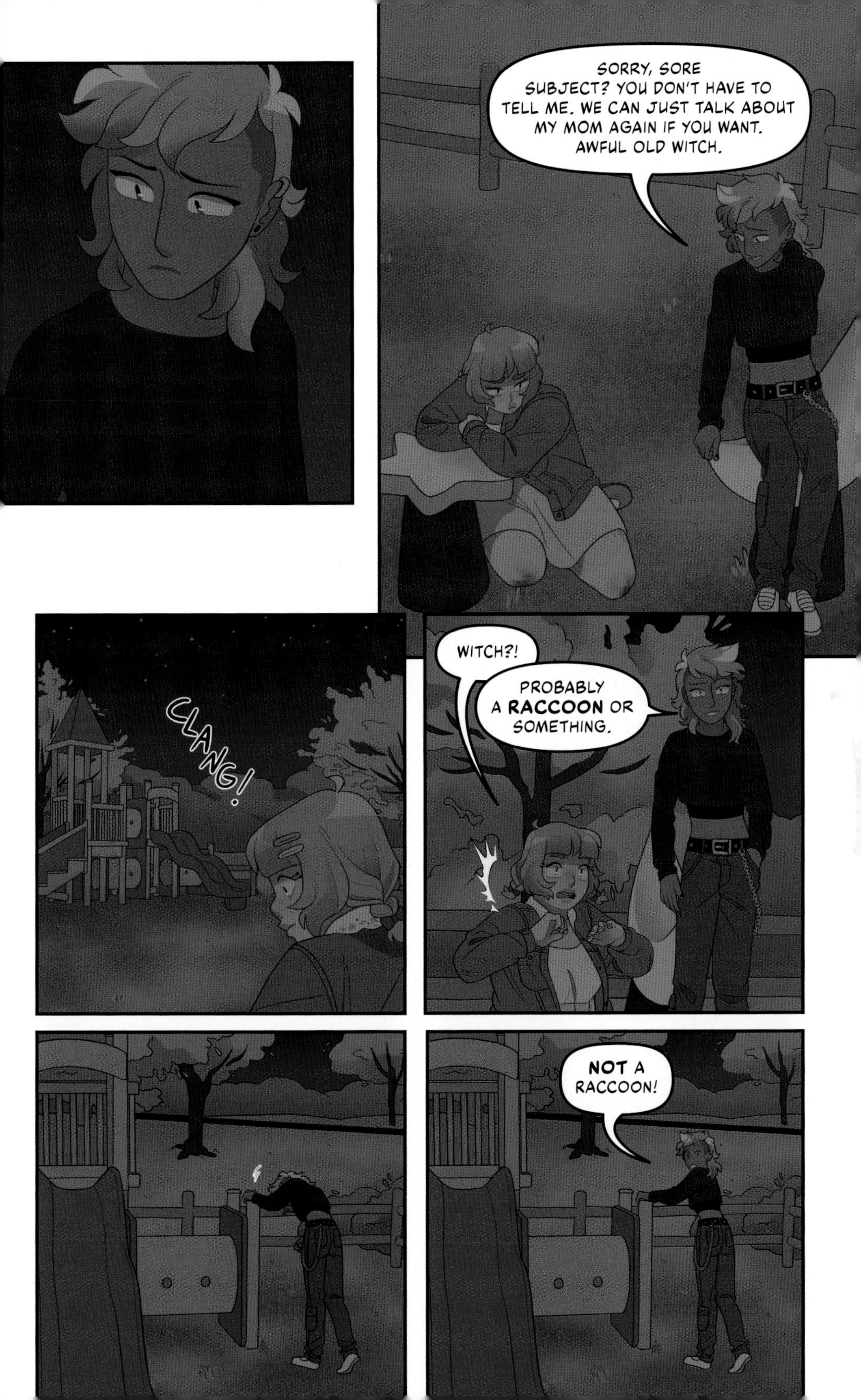
SORRY, SORE SUBJECT? YOU DON'T HAVE TO TELL ME. WE CAN JUST TALK ABOUT MY MOM AGAIN IF YOU WANT. AWFUL OLD WITCH.
CLANG!
WITCH?!
PROBABLY A **RACCOON** OR SOMETHING.
NOT A RACCOON!

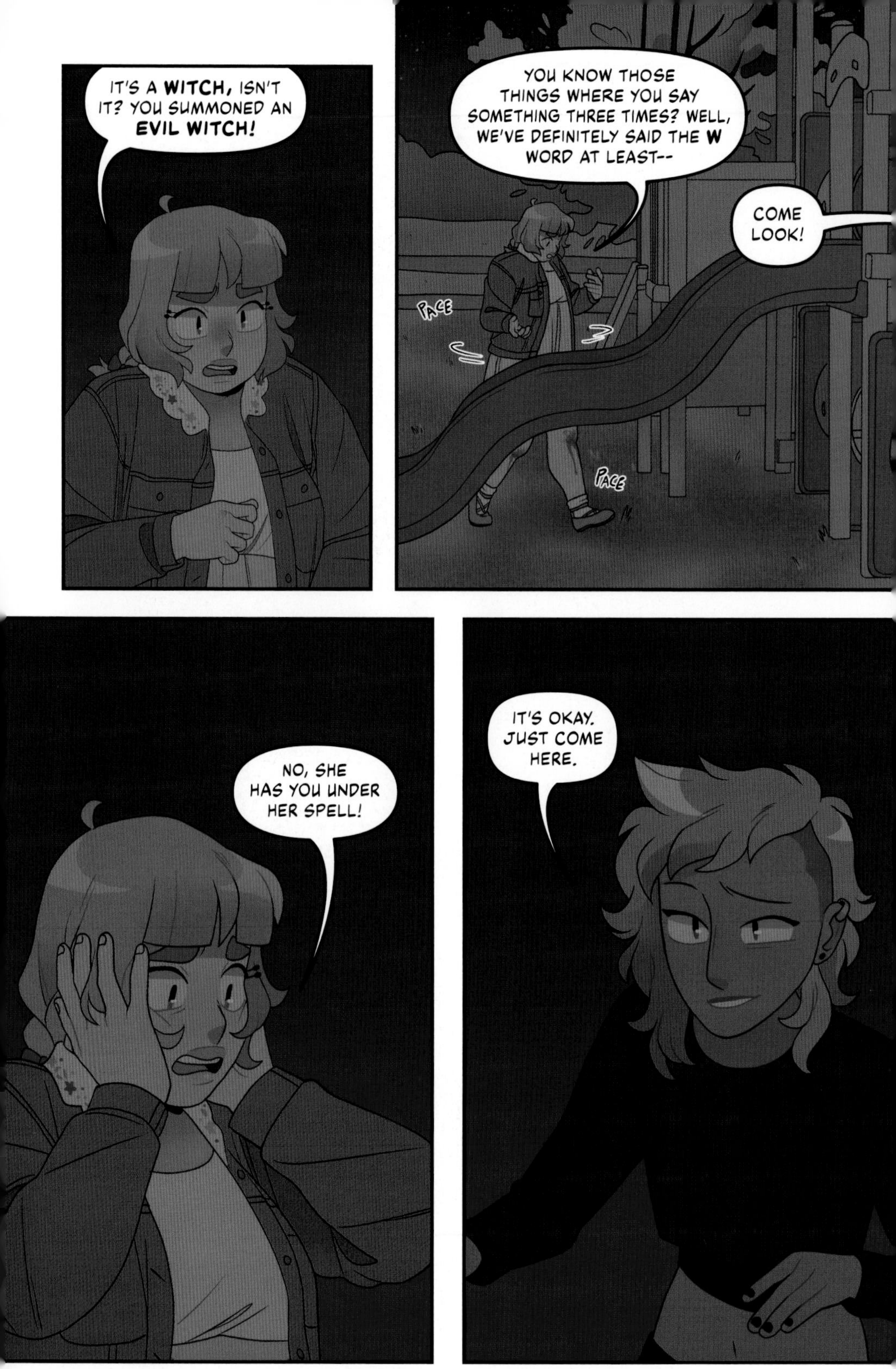
IT'S A **WITCH,** ISN'T IT? YOU SUMMONED AN **EVIL WITCH!**
YOU KNOW THOSE THINGS WHERE YOU SAY SOMETHING THREE TIMES? WELL, WE'VE DEFINITELY SAID THE **W** WORD AT LEAST--
PACE
PACE
COME LOOK!
NO, SHE HAS YOU UNDER HER SPELL!
IT'S OKAY. JUST COME HERE.

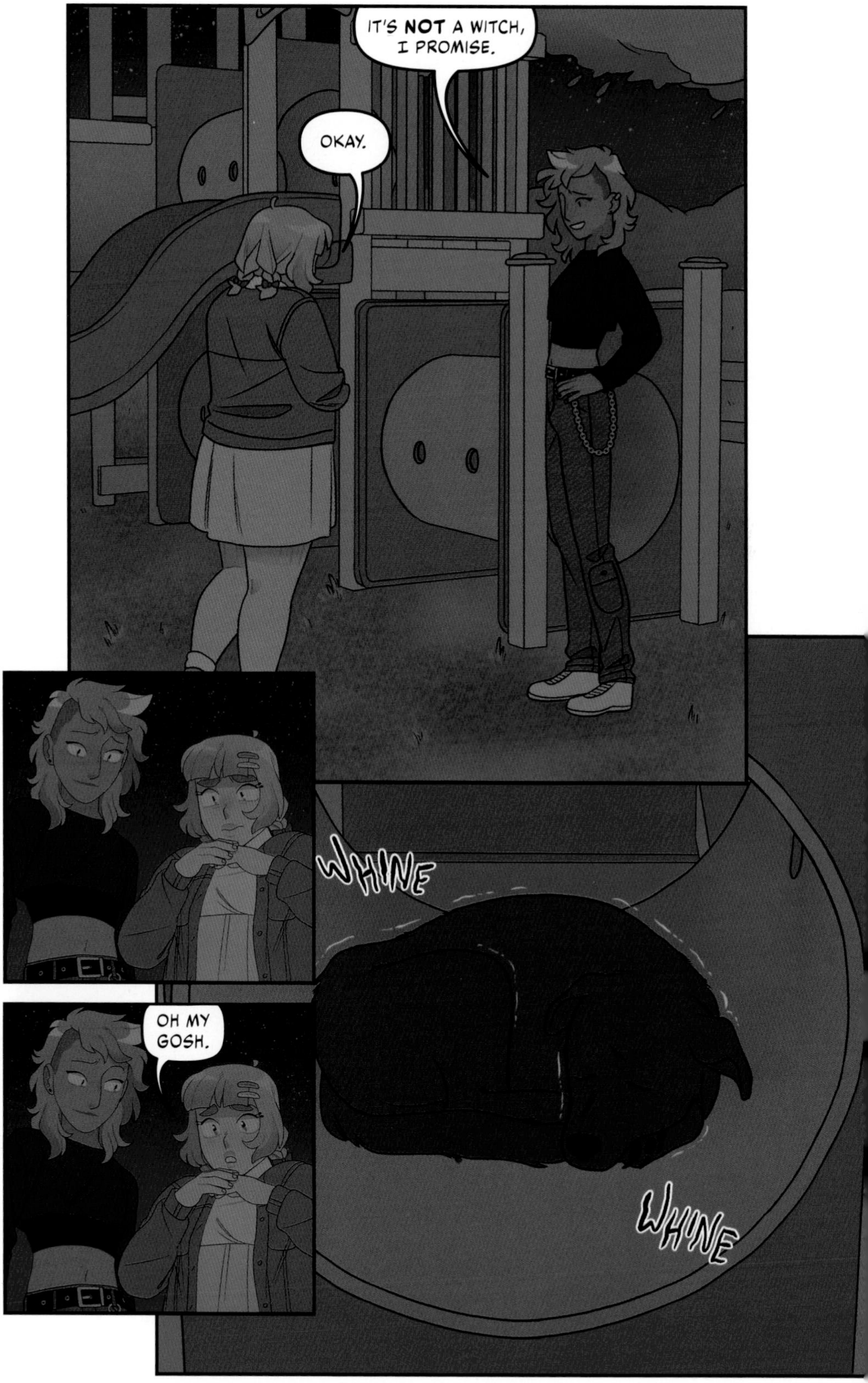
IT'S NOT A WITCH, I PROMISE.
OKAY.
WHINE
OH MY GOSH.
WHINE

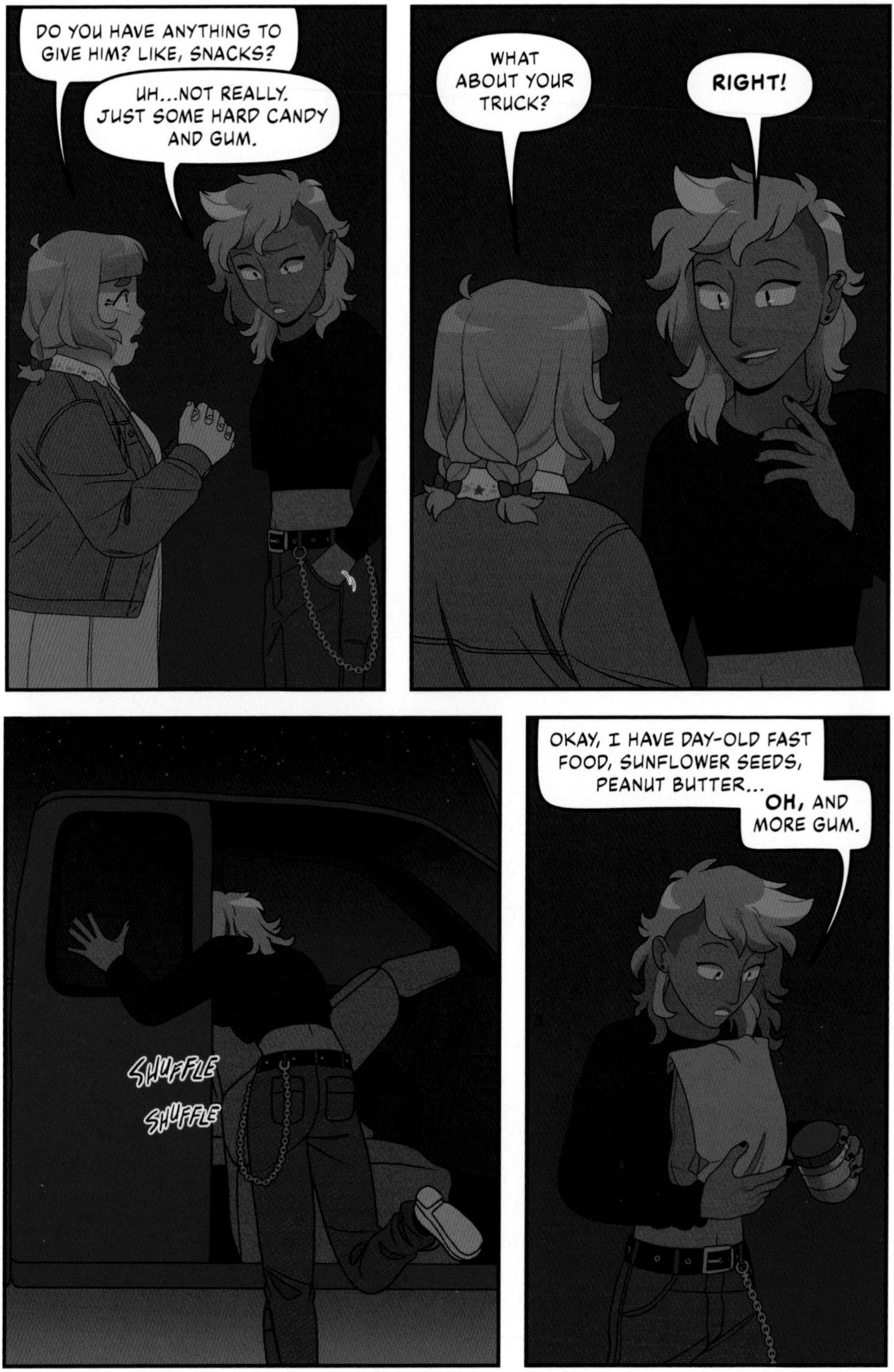
DO YOU HAVE ANYTHING TO GIVE HIM? LIKE, SNACKS?
UH...NOT REALLY. JUST SOME HARD CANDY AND GUM.
WHAT ABOUT YOUR TRUCK?
RIGHT!
SHUFFLE
SHUFFLE
OKAY, I HAVE DAY-OLD FAST FOOD, SUNFLOWER SEEDS, PEANUT BUTTER... OH, AND MORE GUM.

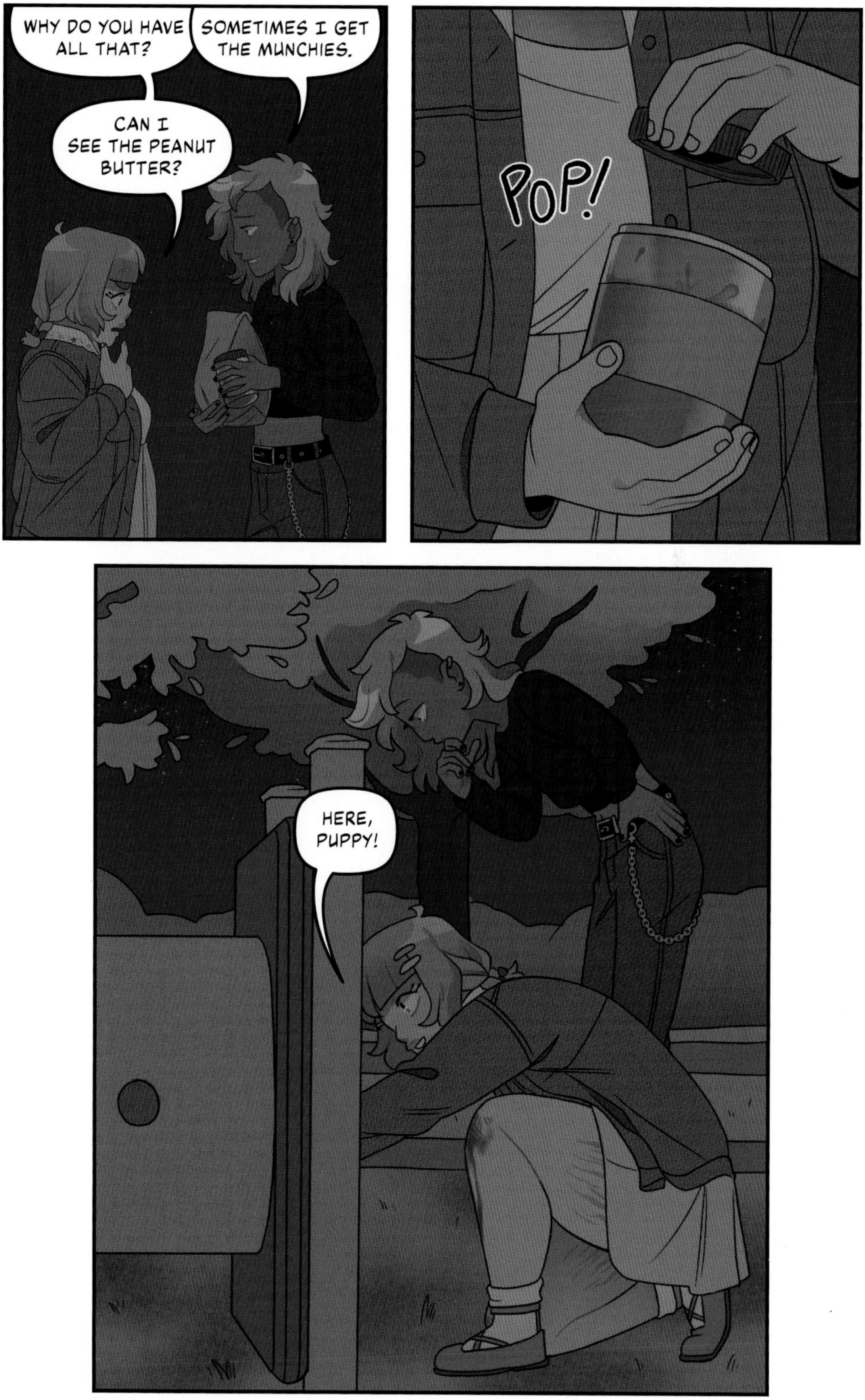
WHY DO YOU HAVE ALL THAT?
SOMETIMES I GET THE MUNCHIES.
CAN I SEE THE PEANUT BUTTER?
POP!
HERE, PUPPY!

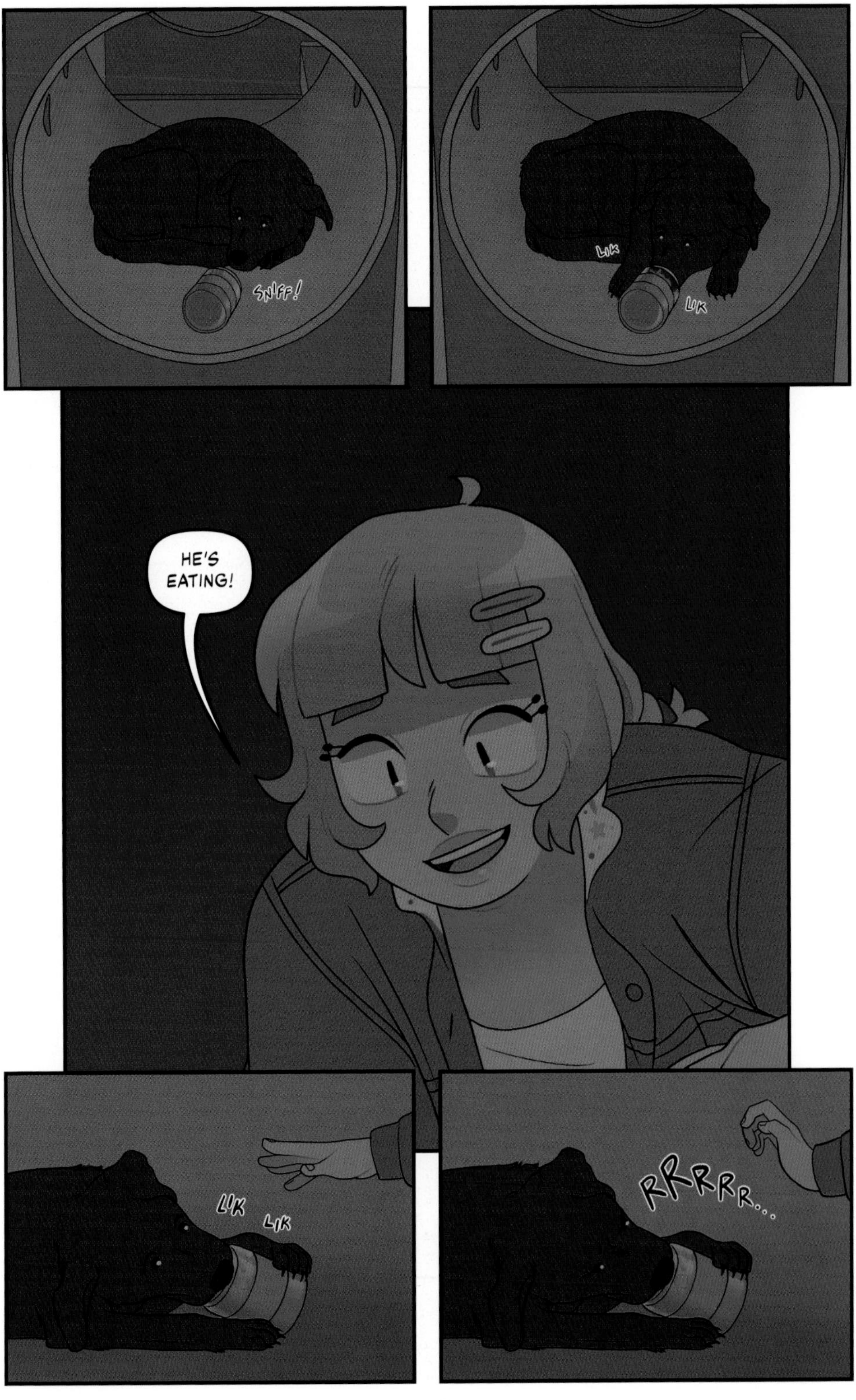
SNIFF!
LIK
LIK
HE'S EATING!
LIK
LIK
RRRRR...

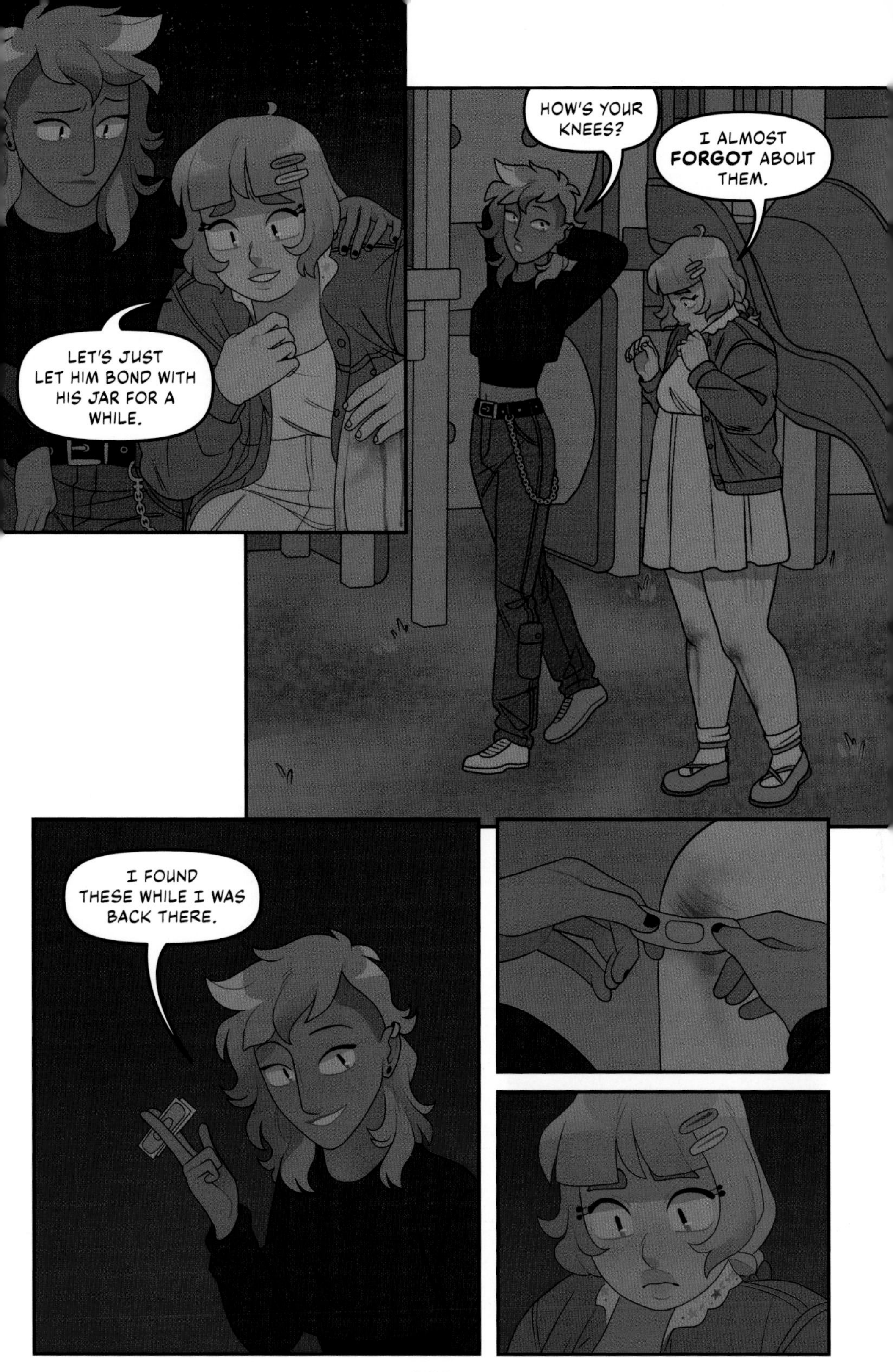
LET'S JUST LET HIM BOND WITH HIS JAR FOR A WHILE.
HOW'S YOUR KNEES?
I ALMOST **FORGOT** ABOUT THEM.
I FOUND THESE WHILE I WAS BACK THERE.

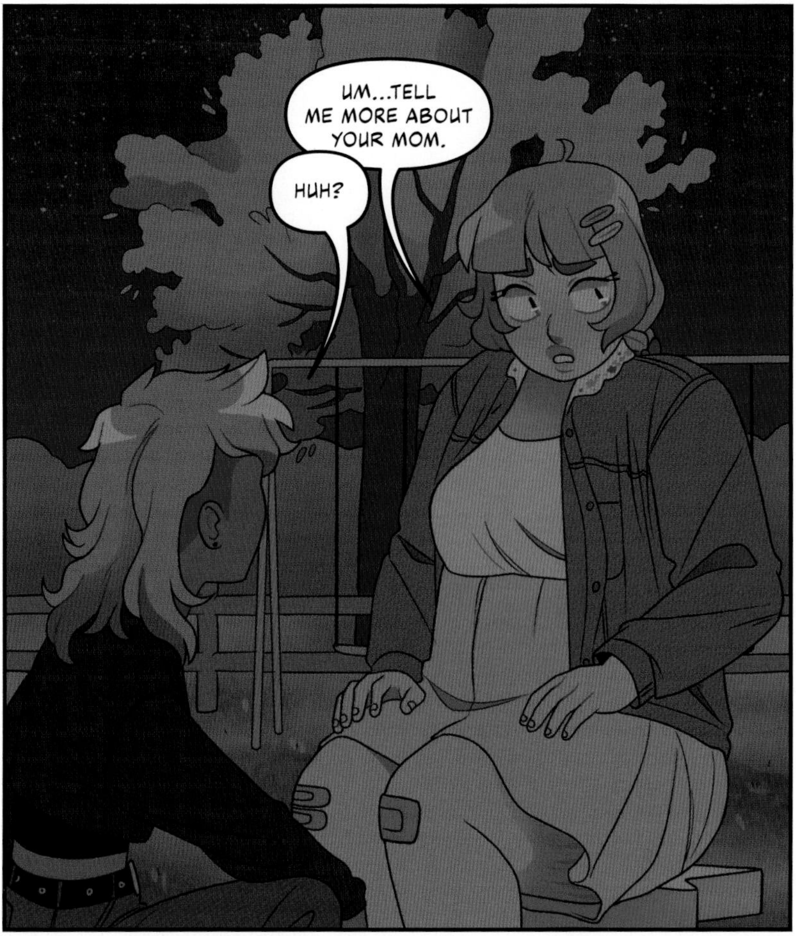
UM...TELL ME MORE ABOUT YOUR MOM.
HUH?

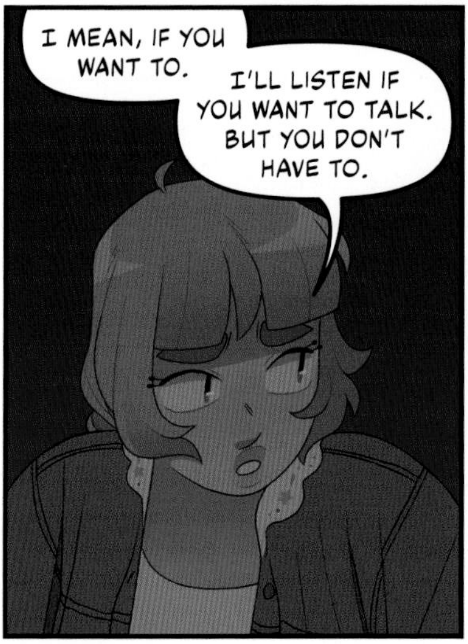
I MEAN, IF YOU WANT TO.
I'LL LISTEN IF YOU WANT TO TALK. BUT YOU DON'T HAVE TO.

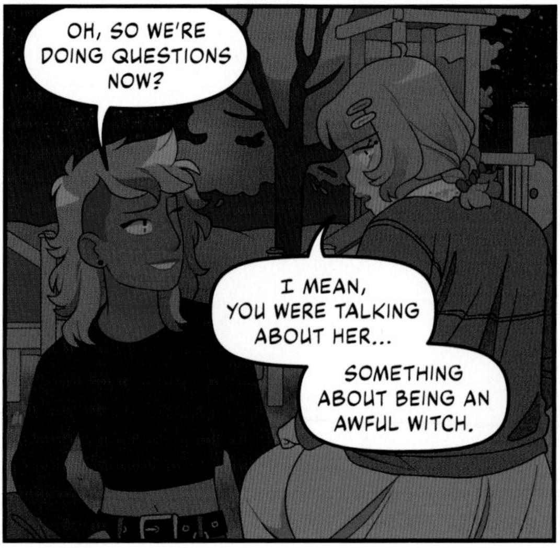
OH, SO WE'RE DOING QUESTIONS NOW?
I MEAN, YOU WERE TALKING ABOUT HER...
SOMETHING ABOUT BEING AN AWFUL WITCH.

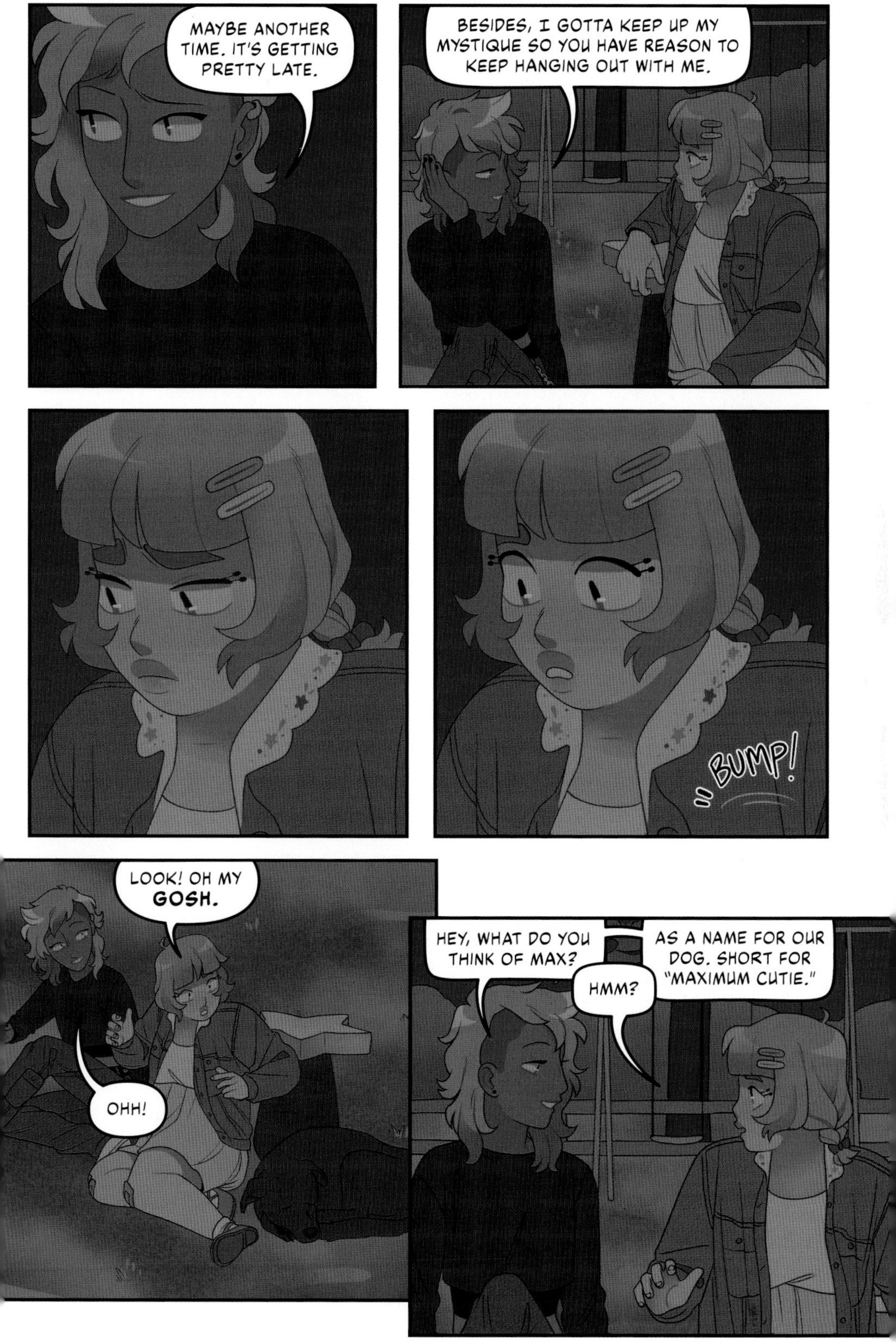
MAYBE ANOTHER TIME. IT'S GETTING PRETTY LATE.
BESIDES, I GOTTA KEEP UP MY MYSTIQUE SO YOU HAVE REASON TO KEEP HANGING OUT WITH ME.
BUMP!
LOOK! OH MY **GOSH.**
OHH!
HEY, WHAT DO YOU THINK OF MAX?
HMM?
AS A NAME FOR OUR DOG. SHORT FOR "MAXIMUM CUTIE."

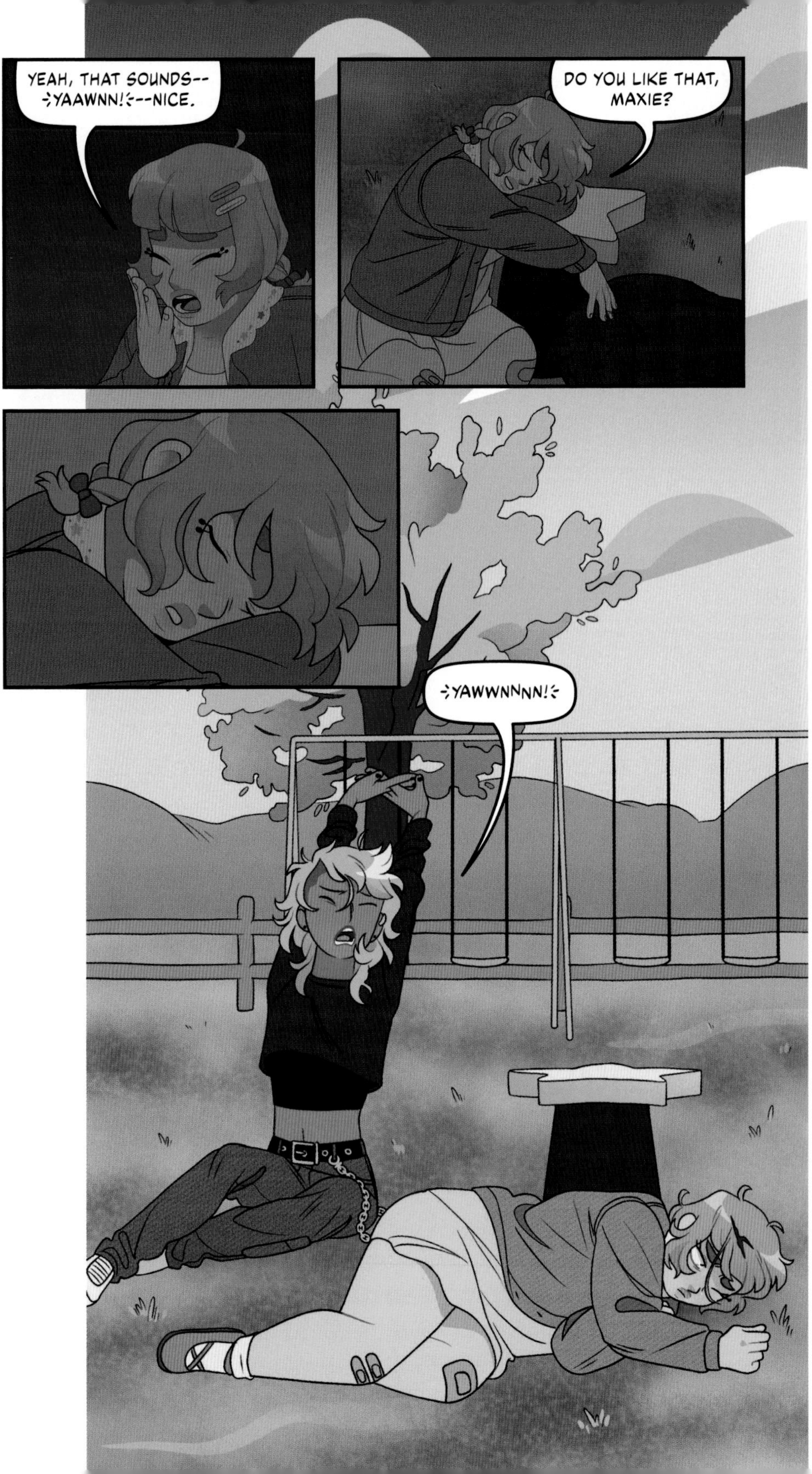
YEAH, THAT SOUNDS--
YAAWNN! --NICE.
DO YOU LIKE THAT, MAXIE?
YAWWNNNN!

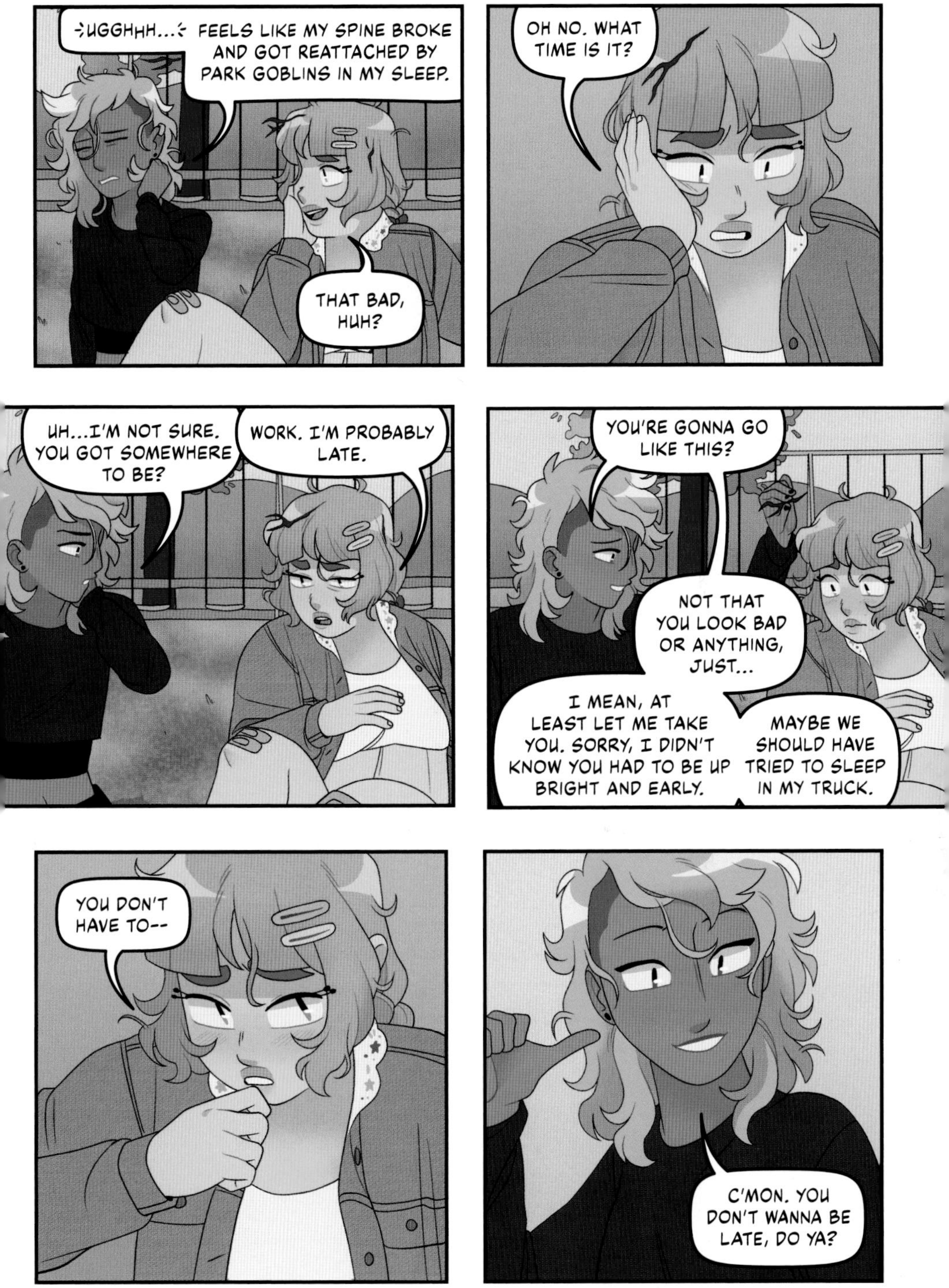

⁓UGGHHH...⁓ FEELS LIKE MY SPINE BROKE AND GOT REATTACHED BY PARK GOBLINS IN MY SLEEP.
THAT BAD, HUH?
OH NO. WHAT TIME IS IT?
UH...I'M NOT SURE. YOU GOT SOMEWHERE TO BE?
WORK. I'M PROBABLY LATE.
YOU'RE GONNA GO LIKE THIS?
NOT THAT YOU LOOK BAD OR ANYTHING, JUST...
MAYBE WE SHOULD HAVE TRIED TO SLEEP IN MY TRUCK.
I MEAN, AT LEAST LET ME TAKE YOU. SORRY, I DIDN'T KNOW YOU HAD TO BE UP BRIGHT AND EARLY.
YOU DON'T HAVE TO--
C'MON. YOU DON'T WANNA BE LATE, DO YA?

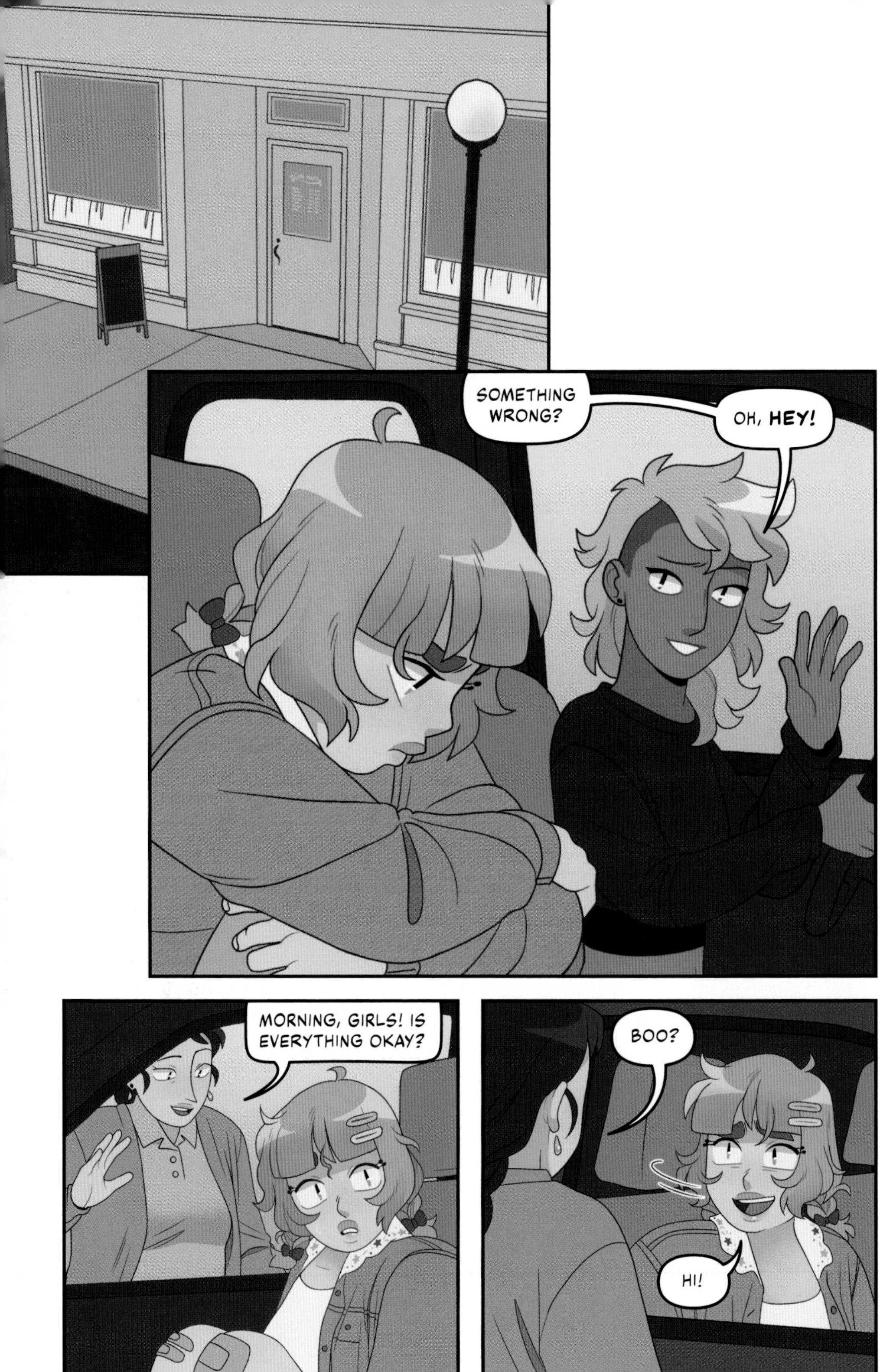
SOMETHING WRONG?
OH, HEY!
MORNING, GIRLS! IS EVERYTHING OKAY?
BOO?
HI!

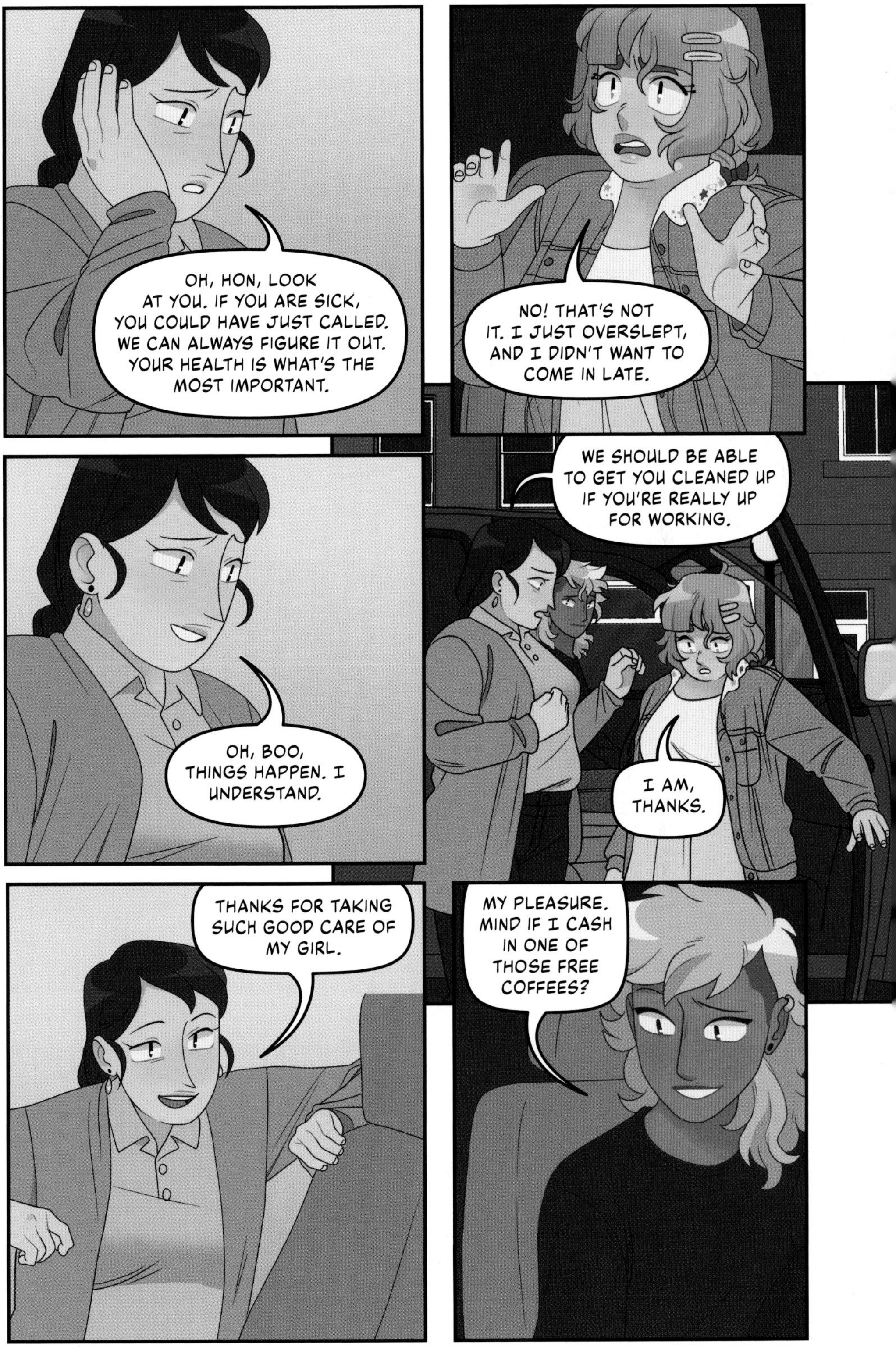
OH, HON, LOOK AT YOU. IF YOU ARE SICK, YOU COULD HAVE JUST CALLED. WE CAN ALWAYS FIGURE IT OUT. YOUR HEALTH IS WHAT'S THE MOST IMPORTANT.
NO! THAT'S NOT IT. I JUST OVERSLEPT, AND I DIDN'T WANT TO COME IN LATE.
OH, BOO, THINGS HAPPEN. I UNDERSTAND.
WE SHOULD BE ABLE TO GET YOU CLEANED UP IF YOU'RE REALLY UP FOR WORKING.
I AM, THANKS.
THANKS FOR TAKING SUCH GOOD CARE OF MY GIRL.
MY PLEASURE. MIND IF I CASH IN ONE OF THOSE FREE COFFEES?

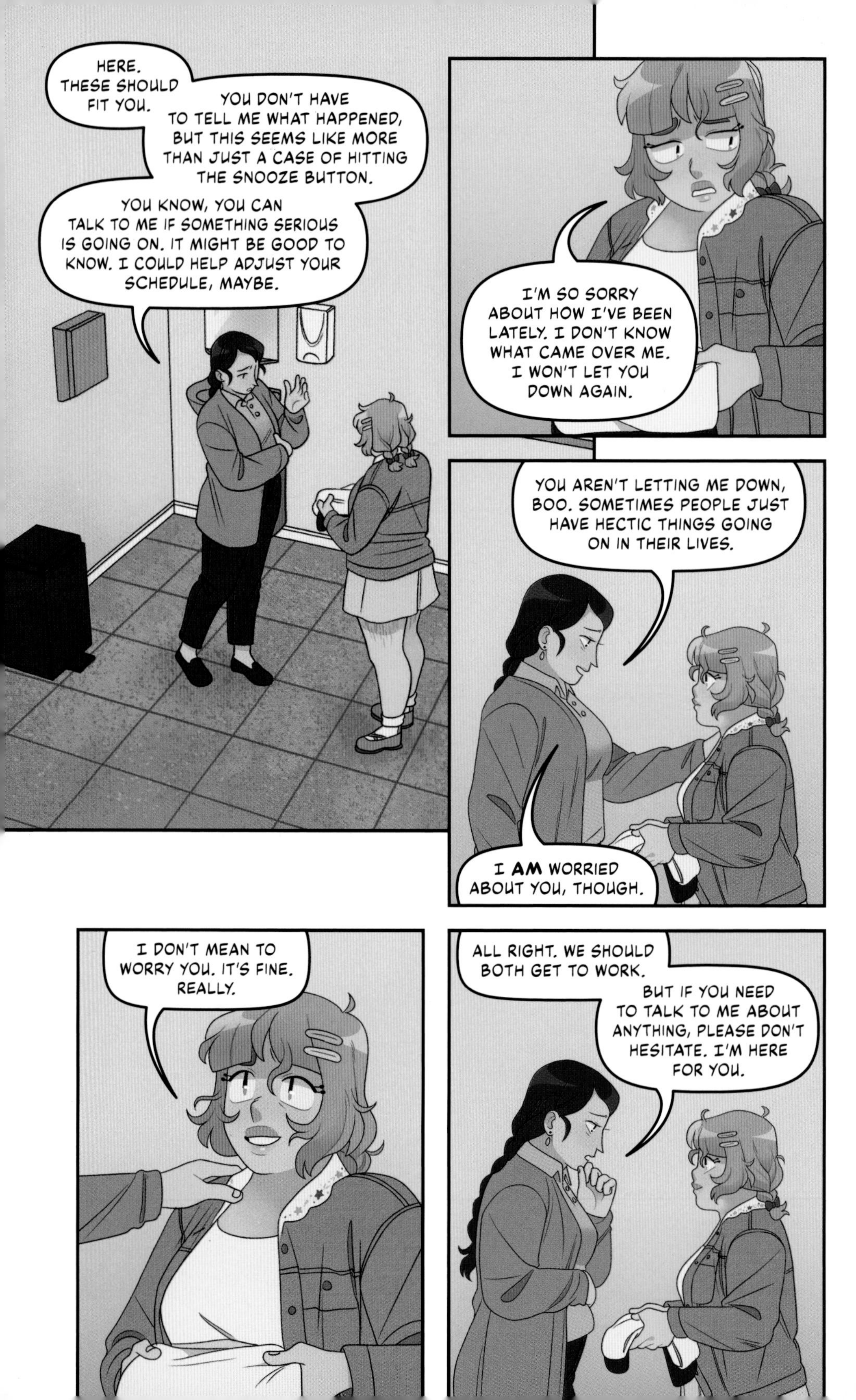
HERE. THESE SHOULD FIT YOU.
YOU DON'T HAVE TO TELL ME WHAT HAPPENED, BUT THIS SEEMS LIKE MORE THAN JUST A CASE OF HITTING THE SNOOZE BUTTON.
YOU KNOW, YOU CAN TALK TO ME IF SOMETHING SERIOUS IS GOING ON. IT MIGHT BE GOOD TO KNOW. I COULD HELP ADJUST YOUR SCHEDULE, MAYBE.
I'M SO SORRY ABOUT HOW I'VE BEEN LATELY. I DON'T KNOW WHAT CAME OVER ME. I WON'T LET YOU DOWN AGAIN.
YOU AREN'T LETTING ME DOWN, BOO. SOMETIMES PEOPLE JUST HAVE HECTIC THINGS GOING ON IN THEIR LIVES.
I **AM** WORRIED ABOUT YOU, THOUGH.
I DON'T MEAN TO WORRY YOU. IT'S FINE. REALLY.
ALL RIGHT. WE SHOULD BOTH GET TO WORK.
BUT IF YOU NEED TO TALK TO ME ABOUT ANYTHING, PLEASE DON'T HESITATE. I'M HERE FOR YOU.

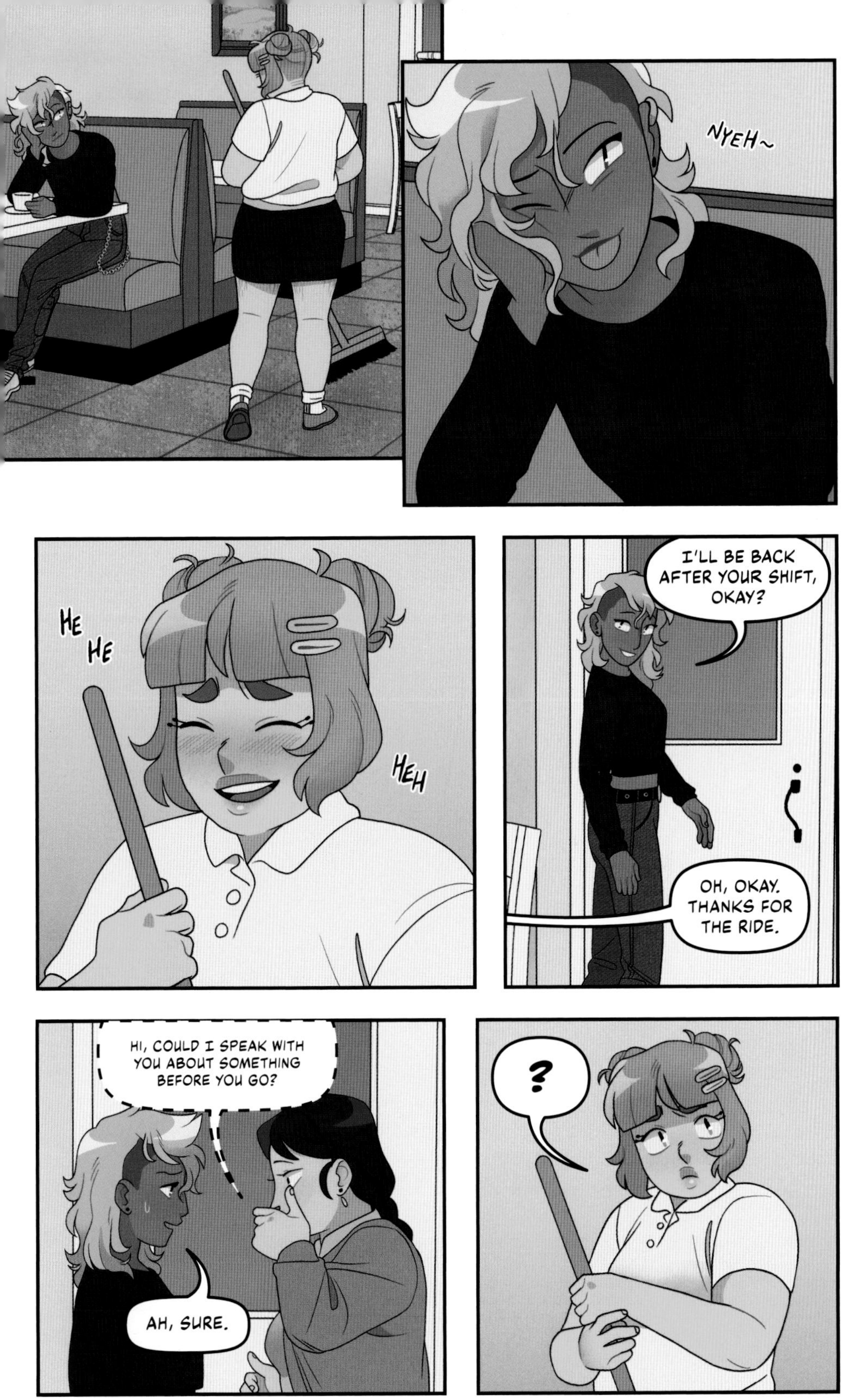
NYEH~
HE
HE
HEH
I'LL BE BACK AFTER YOUR SHIFT, OKAY?
OH, OKAY. THANKS FOR THE RIDE.
HI, COULD I SPEAK WITH YOU ABOUT SOMETHING BEFORE YOU GO?
AH, SURE.
?

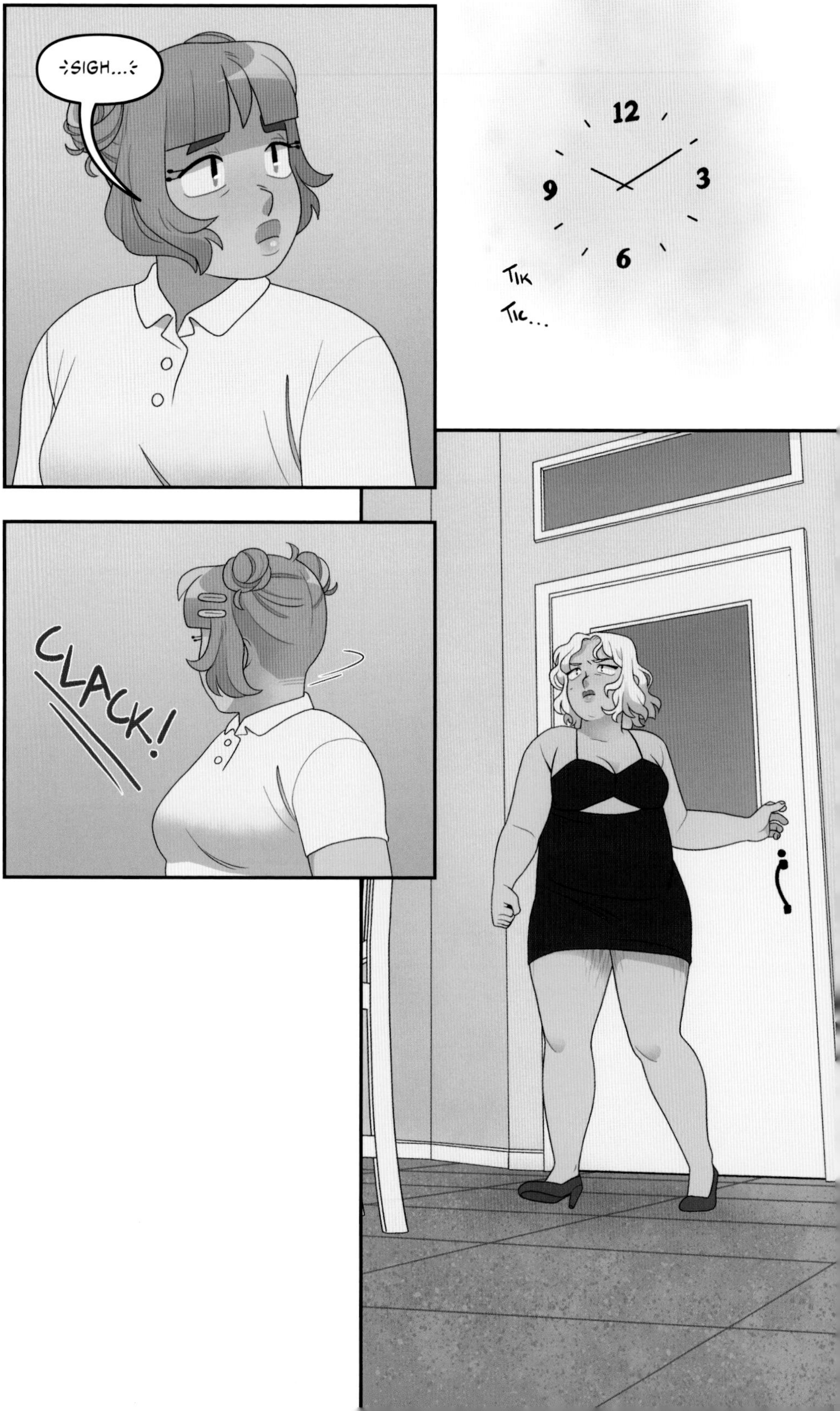
SIGH...
12
3
6
9
TIK
TIK...
CLACK!

GLOOMY

Angel Gloom, aka **GLOOMY**, has been making comics since they were ten, starting with a lovingly crafted Sailor Moon rip-off. Despite the soft magical girl influence in their work, their favorite genre is horror. Besides drawing, Gloomy loves to bake and garden (in theory, if they could only keep things alive), as well as collect merchandise from whatever is currently suiting their fancy, typically cutesy things like Ghibli or Sanrio. Opposite Sunny, they're as introverted as they come, yet consider themselves friendly anyway. They're also obsessed with bagels.

SUNNY

Sunny Gloom, aka **SUNNY** (they/them), is a neurodivergent, queer creator who has been writing ever since they were a teenager. Sunny is autistic with ADHD and likes to collect dolls, make reborn dolls, crochet, act, and sew. They love learning how to do things creatively. An avid tabletop gamer, Sunny is a big fan of Dungeons & Dragons and Magic the Gathering. Musical theater is their other love aside from writing and Gloomy. They're also an ENFP for people who like that sort of thing.

Special Preview of
MAGICAL BOY: VOLUME 1

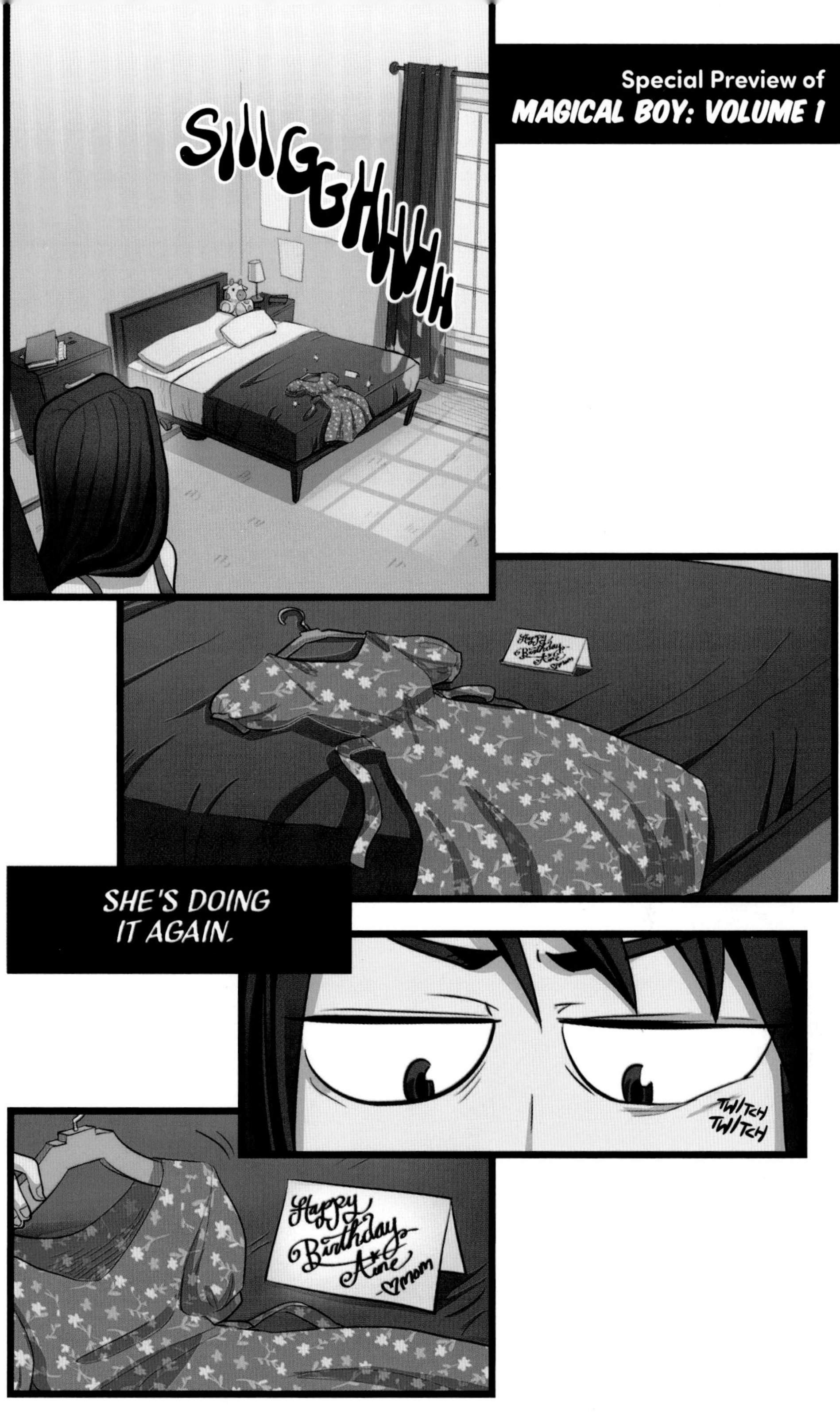
SIIIGGHHHH
Happy Birthday Aine -♥mom
SHE'S DOING IT AGAIN.
TWITCH TWITCH
Happy Birthday Aine -♥mom

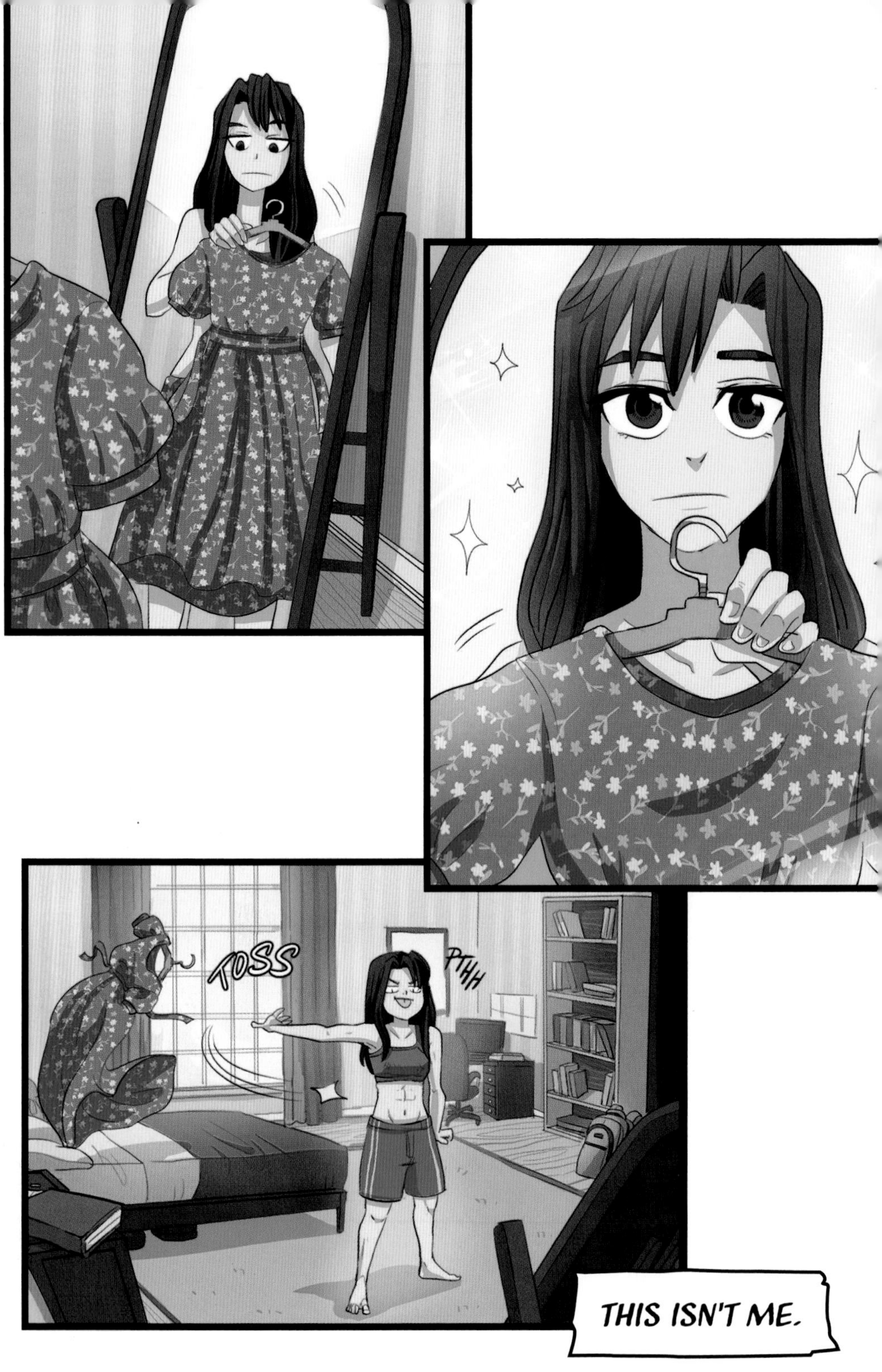
TOSS
PTHH
THIS ISN'T ME.

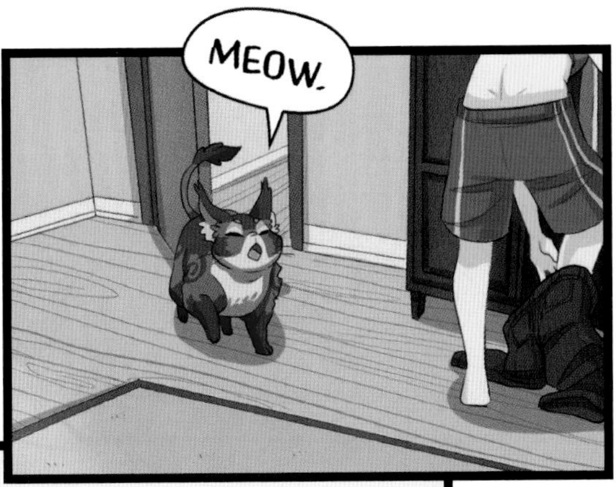
MEOW.

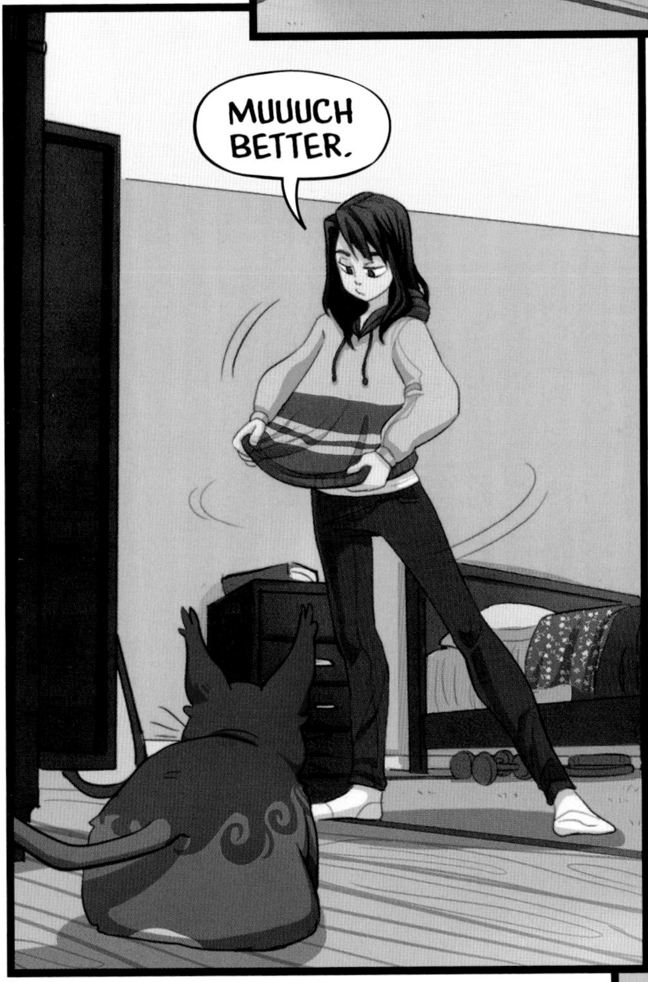
MUUUCH
BETTER.

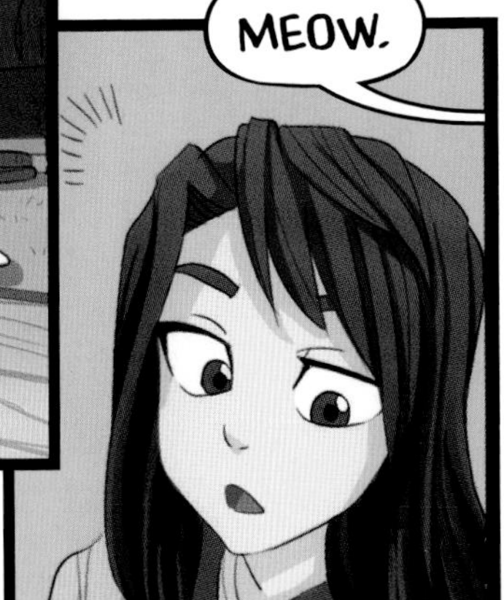
MEOW.

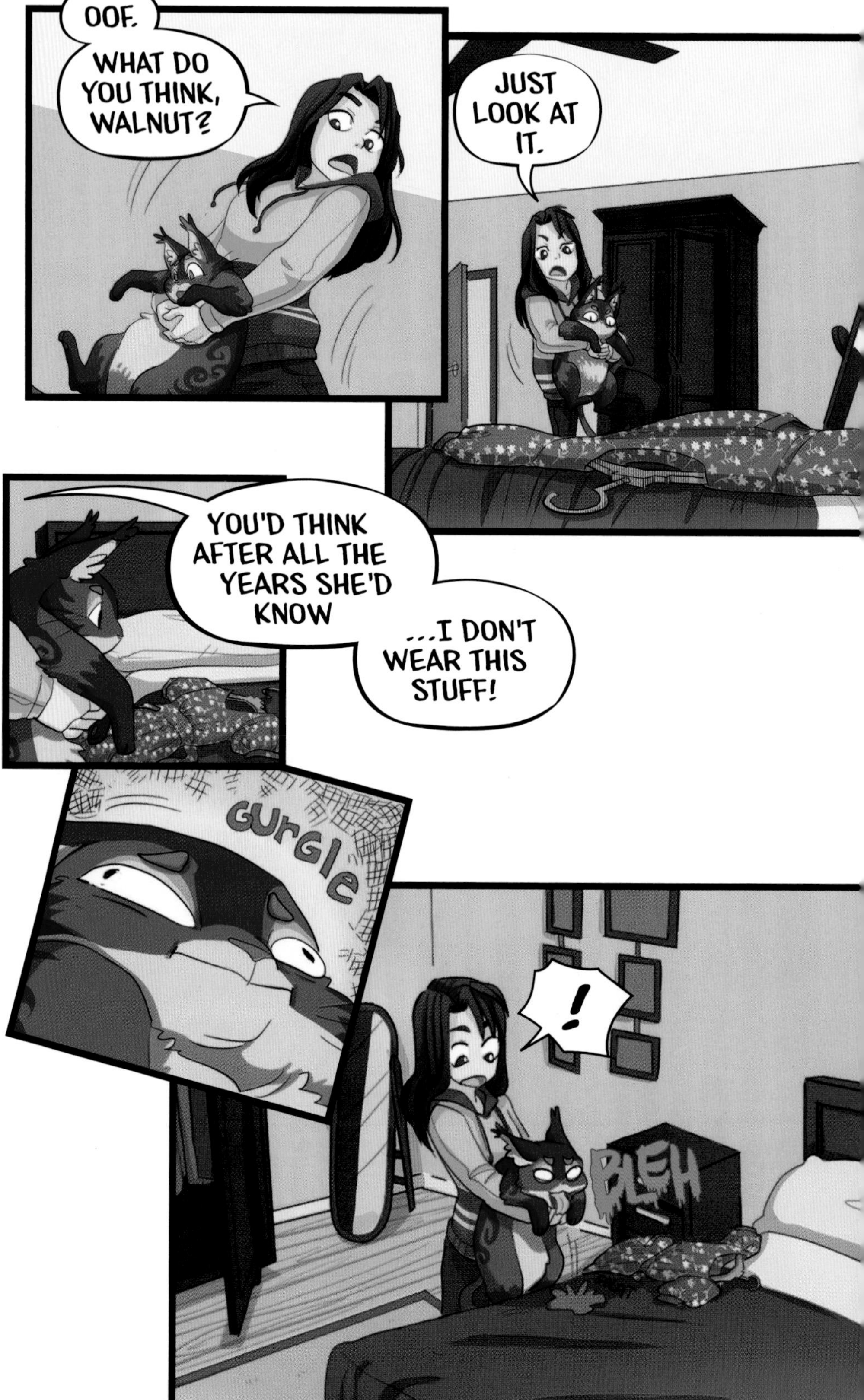
OOF.
WHAT DO YOU THINK, WALNUT?
JUST LOOK AT IT.
YOU'D THINK AFTER ALL THE YEARS SHE'D KNOW
...I DON'T WEAR THIS STUFF!
GURGLE
!
BLEH

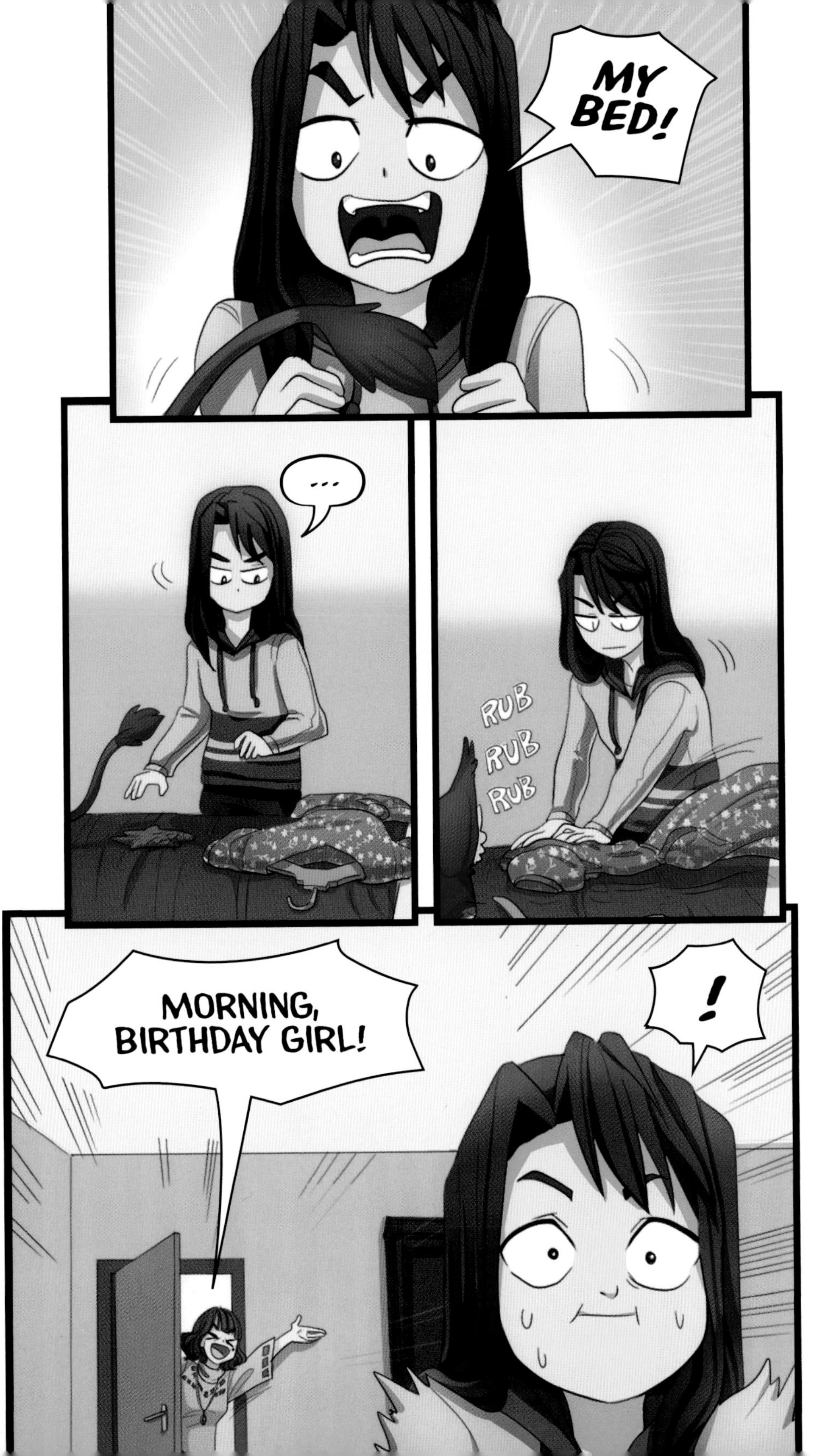
MY BED!
...
RUB
RUB
RUB
MORNING, BIRTHDAY GIRL!
!

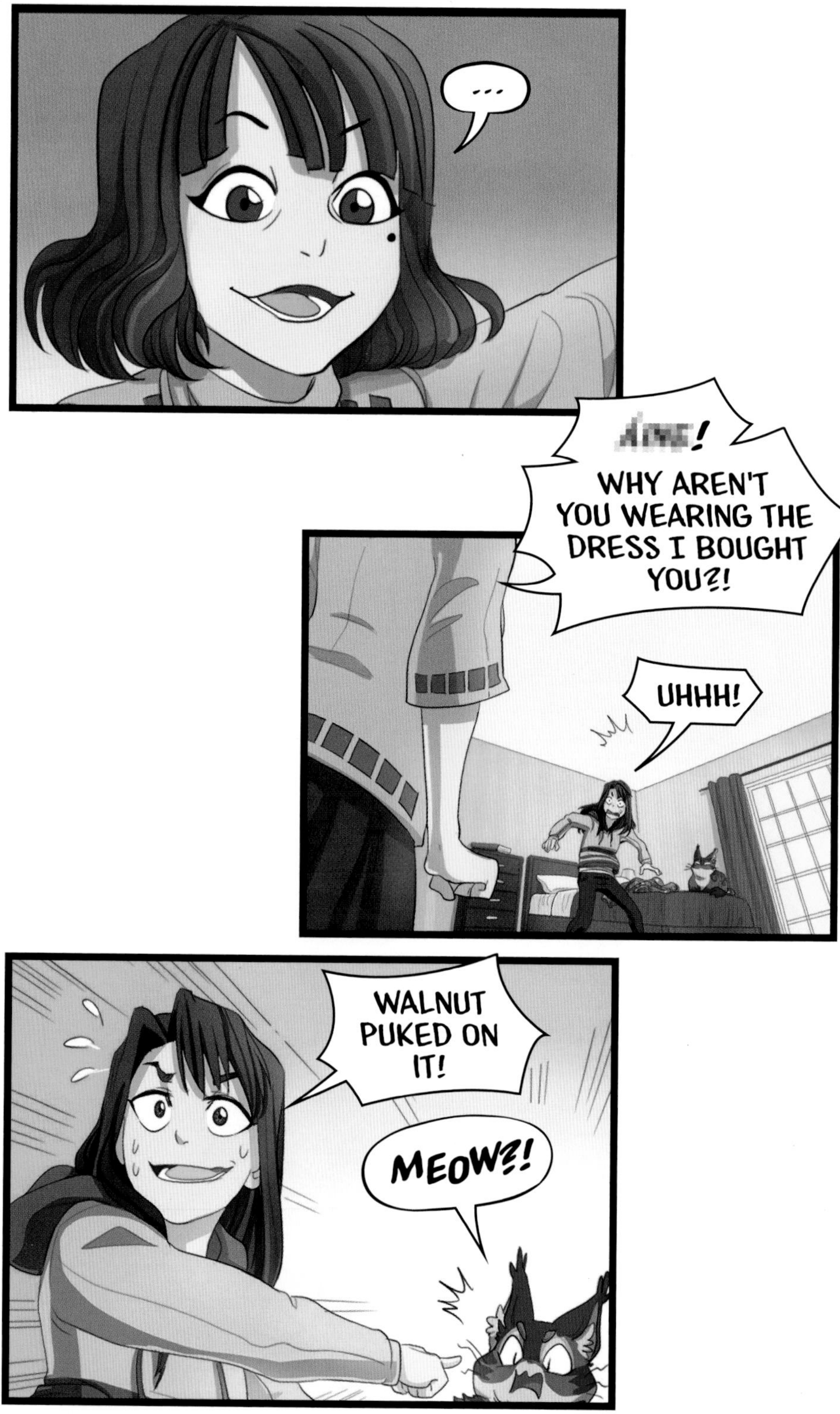
...
WHY AREN'T YOU WEARING THE DRESS I BOUGHT YOU?!
UHHH!
WALNUT PUKED ON IT!
MEOW?!

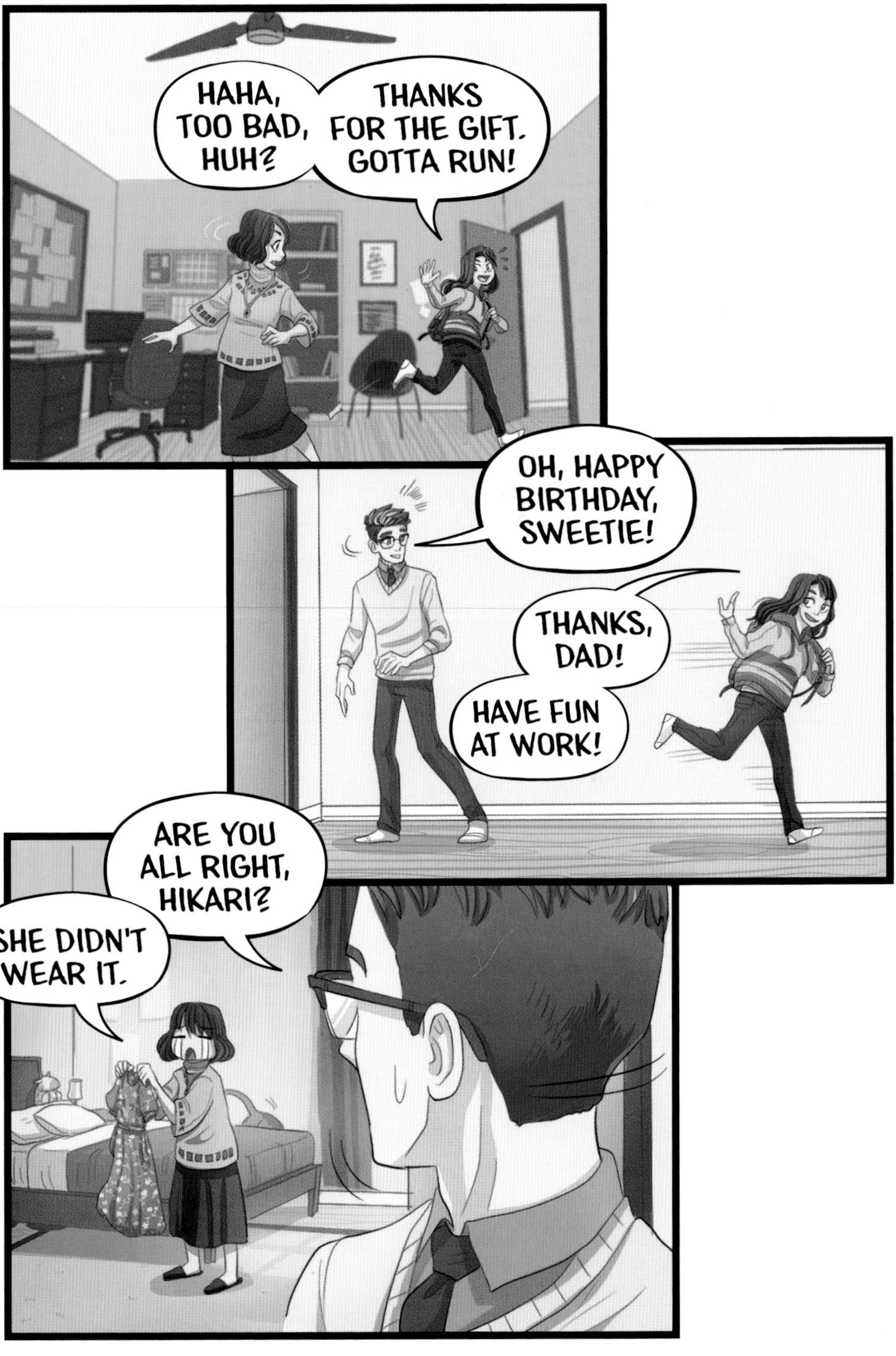
HAHA, TOO BAD, HUH?
THANKS FOR THE GIFT. GOTTA RUN!
OH, HAPPY BIRTHDAY, SWEETIE!
THANKS, DAD!
HAVE FUN AT WORK!
ARE YOU ALL RIGHT, HIKARI?
SHE DIDN'T WEAR IT.

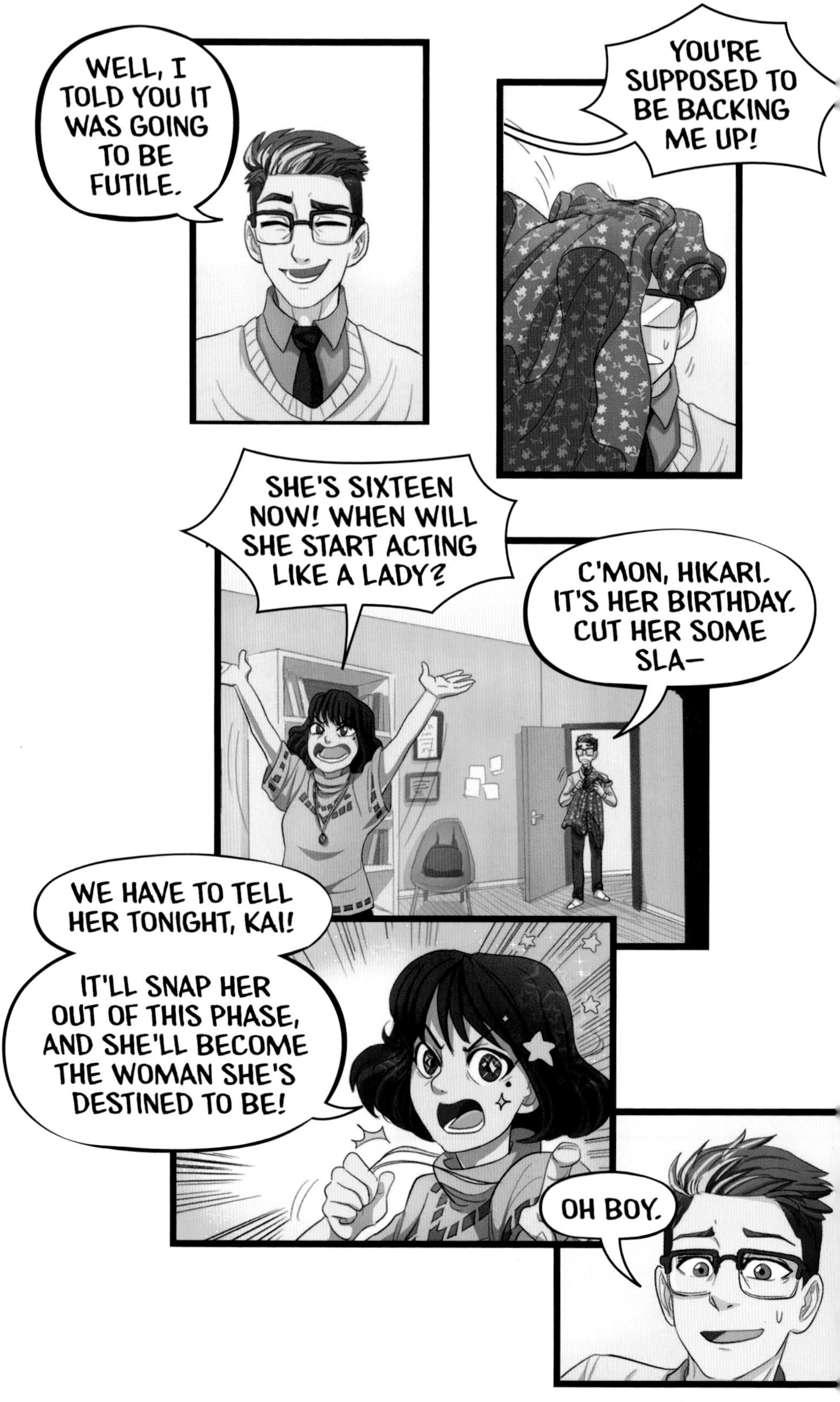
WELL, I TOLD YOU IT WAS GOING TO BE FUTILE.
YOU'RE SUPPOSED TO BE BACKING ME UP!
SHE'S SIXTEEN NOW! WHEN WILL SHE START ACTING LIKE A LADY?
C'MON, HIKARI. IT'S HER BIRTHDAY. CUT HER SOME SLA–
WE HAVE TO TELL HER TONIGHT, KAI!
IT'LL SNAP HER OUT OF THIS PHASE, AND SHE'LL BECOME THE WOMAN SHE'S DESTINED TO BE!
OH BOY.

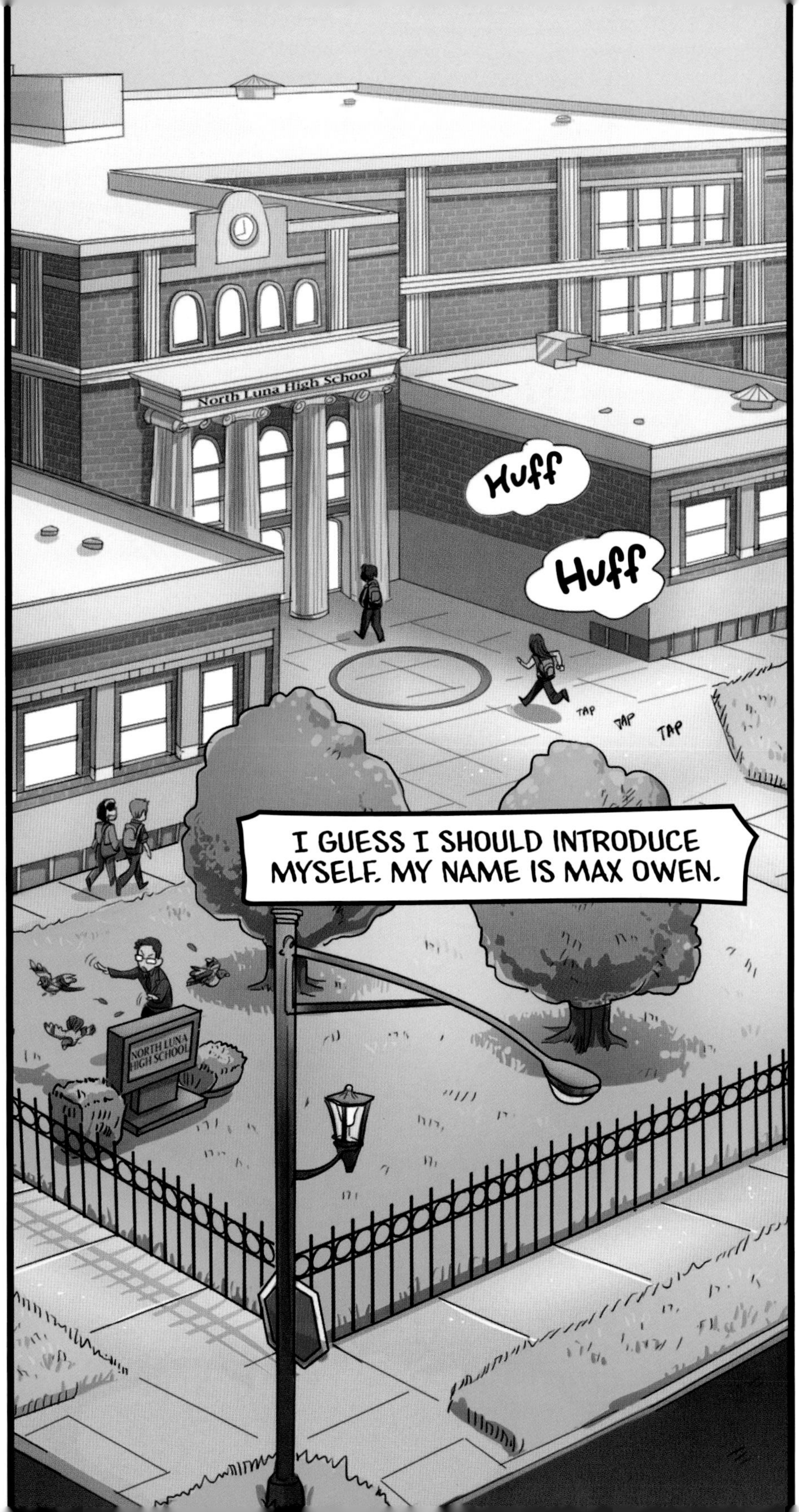
North Luna High School
Huff
Huff
TAP
TAP
TAP
I GUESS I SHOULD INTRODUCE MYSELF. MY NAME IS MAX OWEN.
NORTH LUNA HIGH SCHOOL

MAGICAL BOY: VOLUME 1!

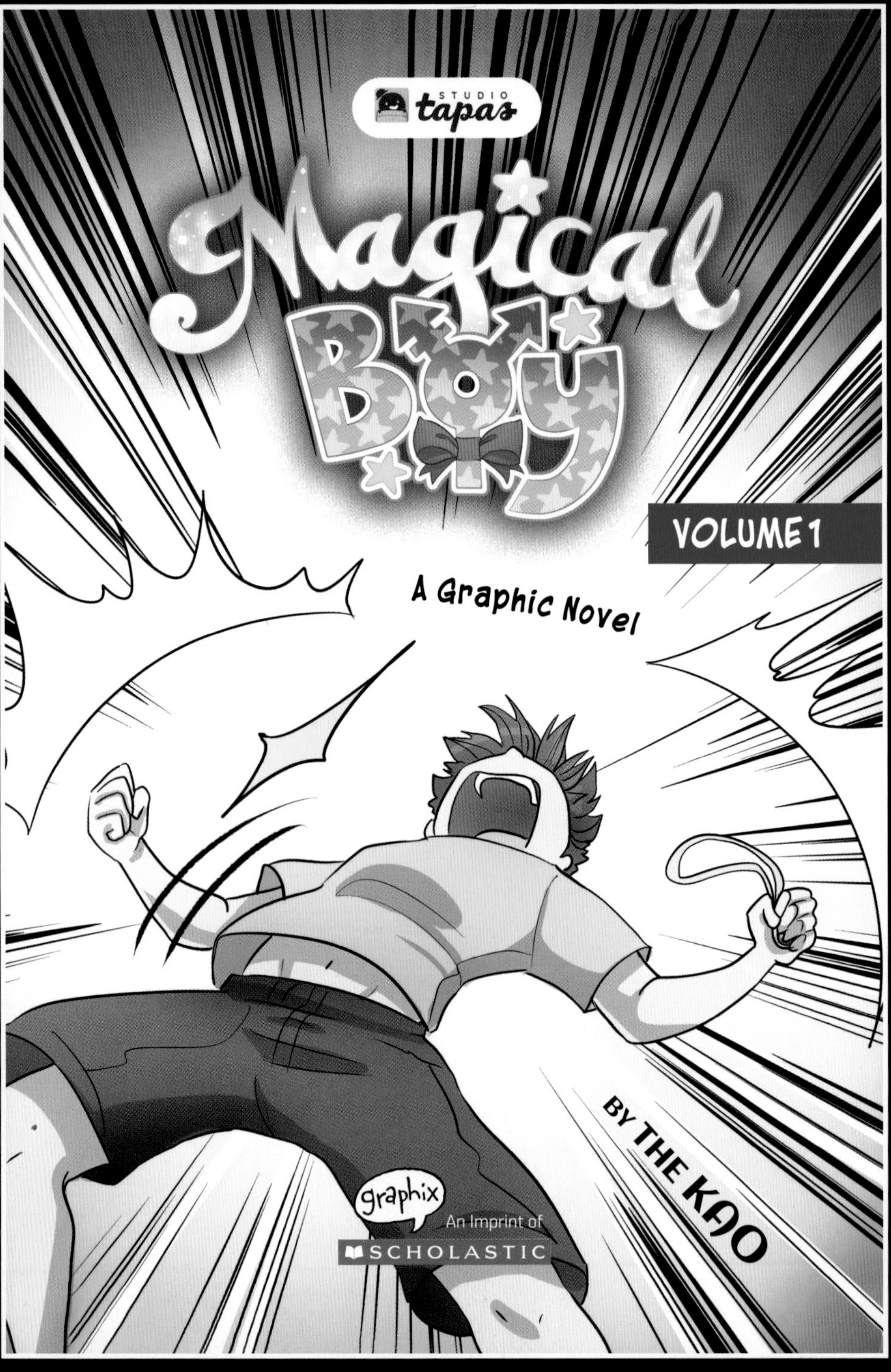
STUDIO tapas
Magical Boy
VOLUME 1
A Graphic Novel
BY THE KAO
graphix
An Imprint of
SCHOLASTIC